Arthur looked around th
Leon. He was surprised
looked like a well-fed ca.
was kept and he felt the hair rise on the nape of his neck. Behind Morgana, King Leodegrance was seated, his young daughter and her cousin beside him. The girls looked somewhat alike, Arthur thought, and then almost smiled. The cousin, Elaine of Carbonek, sat quietly, hands folded in her lap, auburn hair neatly braided, every bit the picture of a little lady. Gwenhwyfar wiggled on the bench, twisting and turning to see everyone who came in. Her braid looked like she might have tried to do it herself, locks of her red-gold hair sticking out everywhere.

He shook his head slightly. Elaine's future husband would have a docile wife. But Gwenhwyfar? Someday, that one would present a real challenge for some unsuspecting man.

Author's Note

For those readers not thoroughly familiar with the Arthurian legends, the great knight known as Lancelot du Lac was given the birth name of Galahad. A rite of passage at approximately age thirteen bestowed his grandfather's name, King Lancelot I, on him.

In future years, he will be coerced into marrying Elaine of Carbonek and she will bear him a son whose name will also be Galahad. It is this Galahad that achieves the quest of the Holy Grail.

In this book, the original Galahad will earn the name of 'Lancer' because his lance saves Arthur's life. Gwenhwyfar will eventually change that name to 'Lancelot.'

Prelude to Camelot

Cynthia Breeding

~ ~ ~

Highland Press Publishing
Florida

Prelude to Camelot

Copyright ©2009 Cynthia Breeding
Cover Copyright ©2009 Deborah MacGillivray

Printed and bound in the United States of America. All rights reserved. No part of this book may be reproduced or transmitted in any form or by any means, electronic or mechanical, including photocopying, recording, or by an information storage and retrieval system—except by a reviewer who may quote brief passages in a review to be printed in a magazine, newspaper, or on the Web—without permission in writing from the publisher.

For information, please contact
Highland Press Publishing,
PO Box 2292, High Springs, FL 32655.
www.highlandpress.org

All characters in this book have no existence outside the imagination of the author and have no relation whatsoever to anyone bearing the same name or names, save actual historical figures. They are not even distantly inspired by any individual known or unknown to the author, and all incidents are pure invention.

ISBN: 978-0-9818550-7-3

HIGHLAND PRESS PUBLISHING

Excalibur

PROLOGUE

Southern England
469 A.D.

"I tell you, Myrddin, I want that woman!" Uther slammed his wine cup down, sloshing the contents onto the remains of the evening meal and the table in the Great Hall at the fort of Ambresbyrig.

Carefully, Myrddin moved the sleeve of his druid's robe away from the spreading red stain. For a moment, he saw Gorlois lying in it, bloodied. He stood, his golden hawk eyes trained on the king. "Ygraine is married to your vassal, king of Kernow. Do you want to start a civil war there with the Saxons breathing down our necks?"

"Gorlois took leave of my festival without my permission! All because I smiled at her and she smiled back."

Myrddin lifted an eyebrow. "No doubt, he's heard of your reputation. You've never had any trouble getting any woman you want. Leave the man's wife alone."

Uther came around the table and faced Myrddin. "I've never wanted any woman like I do her."

Myrddin sighed, unfazed. "You've said that before if I remember. It's nearly Beltane. The moontide is up in you, that's all."

"Mayhap." Uther suddenly grinned. "All the better for her." Then he leaned closer. "Gorlois barricaded Ygraine in at Tintagel, but he went on to Terrabil. I've sent troops to bring him back to answer for his insult. While he's waiting for me here, I can be there."

Myrddin gestured to the wine stain, still spreading slowly. "There will be blood on your hands."

Uther frowned slightly. "Not necessarily. Most married women don't confess the pleasures of bed with other men to their husbands."

"Tintagel is nigh impregnable, that's why he felt it safe to leave her there." Myrddin ran a hand through his tawny, long hair. "How do you profess to get to her chambers? Just ask the seneschal for entrance?"

"You're the magician, Myrddin. Make the arrangements; I'll be back tomorrow morning." Uther swept his cloak over his shoulder and stomped out.

* * * *

Myrddin tossed and turned in his sleep that night, trying to sort things out. Suddenly, he realized he was not alone. He sat up in bed.

Cool, silver moonlight washed over the white samite of the maiden's dress. Her pale hair swayed gently as she came toward him. The scent of apple blossoms preceded her and something glowed golden in her hand. Myrddin squinted. Slowly, it formed itself into a silver chalice, rimmed in gold. *By the gods! 'Tis the Grail! And the maiden . . . she's real.*

"My name is Astrala, Myrddin." From somewhere, a cadence of low, soft music began, rising and falling softly like a small sigh. "It has been centuries since I've lent this cup back to the human world. *Certes*, you know its story?"

"It can bring understanding between enemies and peace to a nation." He was puzzled. "Are you going to lend it to Uther?"

"No," the Grail Maiden said gently. "The Grail serves only those who would serve. Uther is too selfish, but his son will be a great king."

Myrddin was more bewildered than ever. "He has no son."

She smiled. "Ygraine will bear him one."

"What? You want me to aid and abet Uther?" For a moment, Myrddin wondered if he were really having an illusion, after all. When she nodded, he stammered, "I don't work that kind of magic! What do you want me to do?"

"Faerie magic is what is needed, Myrddin. Call on the queen of Faerie; she's always interested in the ways of humans."

"Morgan le Fey?" Myrddin snorted. "She's flighty and unpredictable. I can only imagine all that could go wrong!"

Astrala leaned forward, a rosy light surrounding her. "But it won't. This child is destined to be. He will be a great king. You will raise him."

"Me?" Myrddin sputtered. "I know nothing about raising children."

She smiled as she began to fade. "You will. Call the faerie."

* * * *

Morgan le Fey twittered, floating a few inches off the ground in front of Myrddin in his tent the next morning. Her green gossamer gown matched her green slanted eyes. She tossed her long brown hair back.

"I can bring the glamour down so Uther will look like her husband and you as his squire, Ulfias." She giggled. "Can I watch? That would be fun!"

"No." Myrddin still felt it was a mistake to entangle the faeries. They made promises like lightening bugs and then forgot about them even faster. "'Tis bad enough that Uther can't satisfy his lust on some other woman instead of a queen. He doesn't need a spectator!"

Morgan pouted and set her feet on the ground. "Then . . . if I help you, what will you do for me?"

Myrddin looked at her warily. This was getting even worse. "What do you want?"

She tilted her head to the side, long hair covering part of her face. "I'd like to experience the mortal world."

"You already do, Morgan. You're here."

She sighed. "Yes, but human energy is so much denser that faerie. I can stay only a short time." She glanced up at him sideways. "Unless I'm attached to a mortal."

Uneasily, he asked, knowing the answer. "Who would that be?"

Morgan placed a light hand on his shoulder and ran her fingers down his arm. "I'd like you to be my host. I could learn all sorts of things from your kind of magic."

"I don't do magic," he started to say and then thought of something. "Won't your consort be angry if you choose to stay here?"

"Cernunnos?" She smiled slyly. "Probably."

"The Horned God of the Wild Hunt isn't someone I care to have for an enemy," Myrddin said.

"Leave him to me. And, unless a human has fey blood, no one will be able to see me." Suddenly, Morgan began to shimmer and drew together in a speck of light by Myrddin's shoulder. "See? Only you will know I'm here."

He sighed. The Grail Maiden's message must be obeyed. This child must be born. "All right. We have a pact. But I'm in charge."

"*Certes.*" Morgan stifled a giggle and tweaked his ear. "Call your king."

* * * *

Late that evening, Uther opened the door to Ygraine's chamber, still amazed at how easily the disguise had worked. He had almost thought the druid wouldn't help him. Myrddin had kept talking about the importance of a child that Uther would beget. Well, what was that to him? If Myrddin wanted to raise a babe, then so be it. If Ygraine were as good in bed as he thought, there would be more. He had already abandoned the idea of idea of letting her go back to Gorlois.

Startled, Ygraine dropped the brush as she turned from the dressing table. "My lord? Why have you returned?"

"I couldn't stay away. I kept remembering your smile . . ." He stopped abruptly, remembering he was Gorlois. He shed his clothes quickly. "Come to me, my wife."

Slowly, almost tentatively, she walked toward him. *Is that fear in her eyes? But I look like Gorlois. Why . . .?* He took her arm and pulled her into his embrace and felt her stiffen. *Is the illusion not working? By Mithras, I'll have Myrddin's hide.* He brushed her lips with his, once, twice, and then exerted more pressure. Uther nuzzled her neck and felt her quick uptake of breath. *This is more like it!* He returned to her mouth, circling it with his lips, with his tongue and felt her shudder.

He laid her down on the bed and slipped off her gown. Her breasts were large and soft as he cushioned them in his hands, but yet again, he felt her flinch. *Bel's Fires! What is she afraid of?* He flicked a thumb lightly over one nipple and felt it bud as he gently suckled the other.

Ygraine clutched his shoulders with talon sharp fingers. He winced and opened his eyes to find her staring at him, her blue eyes dilated nearly black. "What is it, woman?"

"You . . . you . . . aren't hurting me." Her voice was trembling.

"*Certes* not. I am trying to make love to you . . ." Uther's voice trailed off. "Is that what you want?"

"No! Oh, please, Gorlois, not again! I don't like the pain." She began to cry.

For a moment, Uther was stunned. As much as he was ruthless on the battlefield, he had never hurt a woman in his life. There was too much fun to be had in pleasuring them. *By all that's holy, if Gorlois has been hurting you, I'll kill him!* "Ygraine. Why are you crying? Look at me."

She looked into his eyes and her own got even bigger and Uther began to feel a subtle shifting in his body weight, the slight paunch that Gorlois had flattening itself into his own lean hard body. As Uther's hair fell forward, he realized it was returning to its normal brown color. His illusion was fading, overwhelmed by the emotion he felt.

"My lord king! You're not . . ."

Uther drew her close to him, caressing her back. "I'm sorry for the deception, but I had to have you. Ever since you smiled at me . . ."

"But how did you get in here? How did I not know?"

"My advisor, Myrddin. A little magic."

Ygraine frowned. "But magic is pagan. I am a Christian."

Uther leaned over and kissed her. "Would you rather I be Gorlois?"

"No." She gasped as he ran his hand down her ribs and belly and then up between her thighs. "You'll not hurt me?"

"Never." Uther lifted himself over her. "Let me pleasure you, my lady."

She clung to him, whimpering a little as he eased himself in and filled her. He moved slowly and rhythmically, nearly withdrawing and then languidly inserting himself again until she began to groan in earnest pleasure. He continued this exquisite torture until Ygraine writhed and bucked beneath him. Uther deepened the thrusts, causing her to wrap her legs around his thighs, pressing him closer. She shuddered and he growled low in his throat as the throbbing undulations began deep inside her and clasped his shaft tightly. He ground into her then, plunging like a wild stallion, feeling himself explode in the same instant that her body spasmed and the world shattered for her.

* * * *

Outside the door, Morgan gave Myrddin a huge smile and hugged herself happily. "I'm going to enjoy this."

Myrddin sighed, knowing what bloodshed lay ahead. He would have to find a home to foster the child, a Christian one, so the boy would be raised to know both the new religion and the druid ways. The foster parents must accept him, not knowing who he was. There was always the threat of assassination. The child, himself, wouldn't even know of his parentage until Myrddin felt it was time.

And, whether Uther knew it or not, his philandering days were over. He was getting more than he bargained for in Ygraine.

If the Grail Maiden were right, tonight's deed would sire a king Britain would always remember. Arthur!

CHAPTER ONE—ARTHUR: THE BEGINNING
480 A.D. – 485 A.D.

Ten-year-old Arthur crashed into the bread cart, scattering the still warm, freshly baked bannocks on the ground and bringing curses from the merchant. The noisy, clanging Market Square became still as sounds of the brawl brought out more of the gypsy boys.

Arthur moaned as he writhed on the ground, holding his groin where he'd been punched. The second kick to the small of his back made him snarl in fury and he rolled, catching his opponent behind the knees and knocking him down. His fist smashed into the other boy's face and he lay still.

From the corner of his eye, he could see his brother, Cai, struggling with two of the gypsy boys, even as a third started toward Arthur. *Why had Cai called them worse than Saxon dogs, anyway? We'll both be in trouble with Sir Ector when we get home!* Then he saw the knife. A dark-eyed man, his head covered with a dirty scarf, was edging toward Cai, the dagger by his side.

"Watch out!" Arthur shouted as he pushed himself to his feet and lunged at the man.

The man turned swiftly, the knife slashing through the air at Arthur.

An arm reached out from the midst of the crowd and seized the man's hand. He cried out in agony as his wrist was twisted and he dropped the knife.

Myrddin released the man as he stepped through the throng. "This is over. Take your wagons and be gone from here." He glared at the people surrounding them, his tawny mane of hair bristling like a lion's ruff. They dispersed quickly, leaving the two boys alone with the druid. He looked down at them. "What happened?"

Cai limped over. "One of them was trying to steal a meat pastie. I decided to stop him." When Myrddin said nothing, he added reluctantly, "Well, I may have called him a name, too."

Myrddin turned his golden hawk-eyed look on Arthur. "Why were you fighting?"

Arthur touched his split lip and licked the bitter iron taste of his blood. "I had to defend Cai. He's my brother."

"Aye. Thanks." Cai looked sheepish now. "I had no idea there would be so many. I could have taken the one." He grinned suddenly. "You know how I like a good fight."

Myrddin sighed. "How many times have I told both of you, it's better to use your heads than your fists? Fight only when you must."

"But . . ." Cai protested.

"But nothing." Myrddin drew himself up to his full height and Cai drew back. "You will put the carts and stalls back in order and you will pay for everything you've spoiled for the merchants. It doesn't make up for the loss of the food, which is a waste and an insult to the gods, but the gods will deal with you in their own way. We'll see what Sir Ector has to say."

* * * *

Ector's face went dark as he listened to their stories. His wife, Bronwen, clucked nervously as she wrapped Arthur's ribs and looked anxiously at her husband.

"Since you both managed to make fools of yourselves in the marketplace, you can take the place of the jesters at supper this evening and they can sit in your seats," Ector said in a graveled voice that brooked no nonsense.

Arthur's heart sank. He hated having to sing and act silly. And now, he'd have no time to study his astronomy lesson for Myrddin, either. And he would brook no excuses. He glanced sideways at his mentor, but Myrddin wouldn't look at him. He raked his hand through his light-brown hair.

"We were defending ourselves, Sir!" Cai said hotly, his face red. "The boy was trying to steal a meat pastie!"

Ector's head snapped up. "This is a Christian house, Cai. Do you not think the boy might have been hungry? The gypsies aren't well accepted, you know."

"He's still a thief!"

Arthur involuntarily caught his breath. His red-headed brother's temper was going to get them both into trouble again. *Be quiet, Cai!*

"And in your need to save that pastie, you managed to destroy food that would feed most of the villagers for a day or more." Ector glanced at Arthur and then back to his son. "Both of you can do without food for a full day. That will be your penance."

Myrddin tapped Arthur on the shoulder. "Karma, my boy. Did I not tell you? Never insult the gods."

* * * *

Over the next three years while the Saxon skirmishes continued, Myrddin oversaw the boys' lessons in Latin, history, math, science and astronomy. Cai developed a quick talent for math and accounting, but Arthur's interest lay in the ancient leaders.

He was rolling up the scrolls one day at the end of a lesson in early summer, when he asked Myrddin, "Why did Magnus Maximus forsake Britain and go to Rome?"

Myrddin placed the vellum inside its tube before answering. "Power is a fascinating thing, Arthur. You must have it and use it to rule, but if you learn to love it, it will be your downfall."

"I don't understand."

"Come sit, then." Myrddin patted the seat beside him on the bench in the small room Ector used as a library. "Maximus was originally sent here by Rome to secure Britain from the Picts. He was smart and took men from the south and established them in their own kingdoms just north of Hadrian's Wall. With their own land to protect, they fought well and held the Picts in place."

"And didn't the Britons honor him for that, giving him the name Macsen Wledig?" Arthur asked, narrowing his clear grey eyes in concentration.

"They did. And Maximus went on to secure the west with a buffer zone of Irish and then he married into a well-established Briton family in Gwent."

"Now I'm really confused!" Arthur stood up and began pacing. "If he married..."

"Yes, and that was the beginning of the problem." Myrddin swatted at his ear suddenly as Morgan le Fey tweaked it in bored protest, but Arthur didn't notice. "He was not only established as the *Comes* of Britain, he was politically connected as well. He decided to declare himself Emperor. He invaded both Spain and Gaul and held them with no apparent trouble."

Arthur turned to him. "How did he do that?"

"Ah!" Myrddin smiled. "A very important strategy; one you should remember. He took an old enemy from the north, a man named Conanus, and turned him into an ally by granting him rule of the part of Gaul called Armorica. This made Maximus doubly strong." Myrddin came to stand by Arthur. "And then his ambition grew. He invaded Rome itself and was slain by his childhood friend, Theodosuis."

"So you're saying a man can have too much ambition?"

"Mayhap. The business of an emperor—or a king—is to keep the people safe and make them prosperous, so they will stand by their leader in bad times. The real mettle of a king is if he is willing to serve his people and not his own ambition."

Arthur sat back down again. "Like King Uther?"

"Uther's passion is to clear Britain of Saxons."

Myrddin joined Arthur. "A hard task. The ones whom Vortigern brought in a generation ago are settled."

"Why do they keep coming, Myrddin? This is our country! Why don't they stay where they belong?"

Myrddin gazed into space for several minutes before answering. "Their coastal lands are being washed away. From the east, the Huns are closing in. Some of their relatives are here. Britain has rich, fertile land. They want it."

"But it's ours! I will defend Britain until I die!"

"Ah, yes." Myrddin smiled again. "Always, when two men want the same thing, there will be conflict." He stopped suddenly and stared at Arthur. "That applies to women as well."

"What women?" Arthur furrowed his brows. "Like Boudicca?"

Myrddin swatted at his ear again as the faerie tweaked it harder. "No, not a warrior queen, but a woman who will take your breath away and leave you vulnerable."

"Vulnerable? That won't happen to me!" Arthur exclaimed.

"Ah. Women can incite wars and cause kingdoms to fall. Remember Helen of Troy? Or Cleopatra?"

"Sort of." Arthur was still confused, but he shrugged. "Well, I intend to join Uther's army as soon as I am able. And I'll lead men. I won't let any woman bring me down. I'll be the best officer he's ever had!"

* * * *

"You've beaten me again!" Cai pulled off his helmet and thrust his sword inside the scabbard as he and Arthur walked from the bailey toward the Great Hall. "Ever since you had that talk with Myrddin last year about Maximus, you've not lost a match!"

"You're still better at the joust, though." Arthur flexed his right arm and felt the muscle harden.

Cai laughed. "Because I'm a year older than you and a lot heavier."

"Still," Arthur answered, "I'm four and ten. I need to build the strength so I will be ready for Uther's army."

They passed two of the serving girls hauling large pails of milk to the kitchen from the barns. The girls looked at them and giggled nervously.

Cai grinned. "Have you noticed the wenches seem to be noticing us lately?"

Arthur grinned back. "Ever since you stole that kiss last Beltane from the willing tavern girl, you've thought of nothing else. It's no wonder I beat you at swordplay!"

"Well, she did say I looked like a man." Cai puffed his chest out.

Arthur rolled his eyes and went over to the girls. "Let me help you with those."

They looked startled. "Oh, no, my lord," one of them said. "'Tis our job . . ."

"Are the buckets not heavy?" Arthur asked.

"Well, yes. But . . ."

"Then let me have them." Arthur took one in each hand, to the astonishment of the girls. He looked at Cai, who gaped at him. "I need to strengthen my muscles so I can beat that—man—over there." But the girls weren't looking at Cai; they stared mutely at Arthur as they followed him inside.

* * * *

The next day as they groomed the horses after riding practice, Cai said casually, "I think I've found the girl I want to bed."

Arthur came around the corner of the stall, brush still in hand. "That really is all that's on your mind!" He laughed. "Who is she?"

Cai's face was red. "Mary. The chandler's daughter."

Mary. A pretty little thing, with blonde hair and blue eyes. Shy and very protected by her father who worked for Sir Ector. Both of them would be furious. "Does she know about this?" Arthur asked.

Cai turned redder. "Not yet. But I did talk with her a little last night, after supper. I'm planning to talk to her again tonight. She likes to go sit in the garden."

"She's a lady, Cai."

"She's a servant's daughter. I'm the heir to Bonmaison. This is my home. I have every right."

"He's a merchant, Cai, not a servant. Anyway, it's how a girl acts that makes her a lady. I've never seen Mary flirt with anyone, let alone you!" Arthur saw the sting go home. "Look, I don't mean to insult you. If you must bed someone, then go to the village. The men say there are plenty of willing, experienced women there."

Cai looked at him for a long moment and then grinned suddenly. "That's a good idea, Arthur! Then I'll really know what to do!"

Arthur shook his head. "I don't think you've understood a word I've said." He went back to grooming his horse.

* * * *

A week later, Cai disappeared one afternoon and when he returned the next morning, he was sporting red swells on his neck and grinning like a buffoon. Not only did Arthur make him drop his sword during practice, but he actually unseated him during the jousting.

Cai stayed lying on his back, staring at the sky. Arthur leaned over him. "Are you all right?"

Cai laughed and sprang to his feet. "*Certes*! Never better. Little brother, you don't know what pleasures await you!" He did a little jig as he toddled back to his horse.

Arthur gathered the reins of his own mount, thinking. It wasn't that he hadn't noticed girls this past year. They did seem to be prettier than before. They were friendly when he talked to them, but he had no idea what was making Cai act so stupid. *Oh, well. Mayhap Cai will get it out of his system with whomever he'd found in the village.* He turned his horse in the lists to joust again, only Cai had disappeared.

More and more, Cai took to spending time in the village. Myrddin remarked on it one afternoon when Cai had been missing from lessons for several days.

"He's found a girl," Arthur said dejectedly, for he had been missing his brother. A gap had come between them that he wasn't able to bridge.

"Ah." Myrddin was quiet for some time, studying Arthur. "Don't be envious, Arthur. Soon enough, you'll understand what is driving Cai."

"I'm not sure I want to," Arthur answered. "It's making him act all goofy. He can't concentrate on weaponry or riding. He never has time to hunt or fish."

"In a way, you'd be better off not interested in women." Myrddin put hand to his head, closing his eyes. "I foresee a woman who will bring you much pain."

"Then I won't get involved," Arthur said practically. "I'll concentrate on being the best man in Uther's army."

Myrddin opened his eyes and put a hand on Arthur's shoulder. "Would that it be that easy. When the time comes, the attraction will be impossible to resist."

* * * *

A fortnight passed from that conversation, and Arthur had just returned from hunting. He put his horse up for the evening and was walking toward the Great Hall when he heard the muffled scream.

It came from behind the gardens. Quickly, he pulled his dagger and raced around the corner. At first, he saw nothing. Then, he heard sounds of a struggle in the corner where his foster mother grew her precious roses. He advanced quietly, listening to the deep grunts and another stifled scream. He burst through the bushes.

Cai lay on top of Mary, struggling to get her clothes off. Her bodice was already torn and he had one hand on her breast.

Arthur sheathed his dagger and pulled on Cai's collar, jerking him off and throwing him to the ground. Cai snarled and sprang for Arthur. Mary ran away, crying.

"What in Bel's Fires do you think you're doing, Little Brother?" Cai jabbed at Arthur, but missed.

Arthur circled. "That's a better question for you, Cai! We don't rape women here!" *What is wrong with Cai?* He hated fighting his brother.

"It wasn't that," Cai started to say when suddenly the area was lit with torchlight as his and Mary's fathers came running from the house.

The look on Sir Ector's face was something Arthur would never forget: pain, anger, embarrassment, and shame.

"Was she harmed?" he asked his son, cold fury in his voice.

Cai stood with his fists clenched, trying to stare down his father. Then he crumbled. "No. Arthur came."

Mary's father gave Arthur a grateful look, but Ector just nodded briefly. "Well," he finally said to Cai, "it seems you think you're a man. You'll leave for Uther's camp in the morning. I think you'll find you have a lot more to learn."

* * * *

Arthur was lonely the next year. After Cai's initial resentment at being sent away, he found he liked army life. He wrote Arthur frequently, informing him that Uther continued to hold the Saxons to their eastern lands and that he chafed at not being sent on a real mission. He had also made two friends named Gwalchmai from the Orkneys and Bedwyr of Cameliard. He had added, for emphasis, Arthur supposed, that although both friends were just four and ten, Gwalchmai already was a favorite with the ladies. Cai hoped Arthur would join them soon.

"But I want to fight the Saxons and keep Britain free!" Arthur told Myrddin after a particularly graphic letter. "Isn't that what soldiers are supposed to do? Does King Uther condone all this wenching?"

Myrddin raised an eyebrow. "Until he married Ygraine, Uther had more women than he could count. He's probably envious; Ygraine is a Christian queen and will allow no philandering."

Arthur thought he heard the sound of a woman giggling, but there wasn't anyone around. "Where do they find the women then?" He thought of Mary nearly being forced.

And he could swear the giggling of some unseen woman was louder now.

"Camp followers. Women who follow the men to cook for them and to be available in exchange for protection or sometimes money," Myrddin answered.

"Money?" Arthur was shocked. "We're supposed to pay?"

Myrddin swatted at his ear. "I think you're beginning to ask a lot of questions that need someone else to answer them. You're almost six and ten. Mayhap, 'tis time for you to go to Uther."

"Do you think I'm good enough?" Arthur asked in awe. "I've practiced and practiced . . . I don't want to disappoint the king."

Myrddin looked at him for several moments. "I doubt you'll do that. But I will take you to someone who can tell us if you're ready: the Lady of the Lake."

* * * *

Although it was early spring, Arthur pulled his cloak around him as they rode into unexpected fog. The day had been sunny minutes earlier.

Myrddin didn't seem to notice. He was peering through the mists apparently looking for something. "Ah, Barinthus," he said, "there you are!"

Arthur jumped in his saddle. A figure in a black-hooded robe loomed in front of them. "What . . . who are you?"

"Don't be alarmed," Myrddin said as he dismounted. He signaled with his hand and from out of the vapor, several small, dark-skinned people emerged. Myrddin handed over his horse's reins and motioned for Arthur to do the same. "They're hut dwellers," he said and pointed. "They'll take care of the horses while we cross over."

Arthur squinted. He could barely make out several small dwellings perched on stilts at the edge of a lake. Then he became aware of water gently lapping at some unseen shore. As his eyes became accustomed to the condensation, he saw the barge.

"Step on," Myrddin said.

"Why is there so much fog here?" Arthur asked as Barinthus poled silently away.

"It is the breath of the dragon that protects Britain," Myrddin answered. "Avallach stays hidden from the outside world by this bank. If the Lady chooses not to have you visit, you won't find the way."

Even as he spoke, they broke through to blue skies and sunshine. Ahead, the green Tor rose majestically. Across the tangy salt smell of the water wafted the sweet smell of apple blossoms. A young priestess waited for them on the shore.

As the barge scraped against the sand, she gestured for them to follow her.

"Her name is Ceridwen. She has taken a vow of silence," Myrddin said in response to Arthur's unasked question.

They were ushered into a waiting room with several comfortable-looking chairs, an ancient chest with runes carved into it and an ornate desk. Behind the desk was a beautifully woven tapestry of a white hart standing in the midst of a forest glade. From where Arthur stood, it seemed to be looking right at him, but when he moved to be seated, the eyes followed him. He was fascinated.

The entrance of two women broke his reverie. The older of the two had silvery hair and pale blue eyes; on her shoulder a raven perched. The younger woman was taller, with dark hair and eyes that were neither grey nor brown, but something close to a dark hazel. They wore simple gowns of white with blue tunics, but their bearing was regal.

Myrddin approached the older one and leaned over to kiss her cheek. "Lady Vivian. I have brought Arthur." He stepped back and bowed to the younger woman. "Niniane. It is good to see you again."

Vivian lifted a hand and Arthur found himself on his feet, standing in front of her. He knew he was being evaluated, but didn't know why. He straightened his shoulders and lifted his chin. This was the Lady of the Lake, the one that Myrddin said would know if he were ready. He'd not be found wanting.

She smiled in amusement. "He has his father's confidence."

Arthur's mouth dropped open in spite of his need to stay in control. "You . . . know who my father is?" Myrddin had always let him think he'd been discovered on the doorstep to the church near Bonmaison. The Lady lifted an eyebrow and Arthur wondered suddenly if he was supposed to remain silent in her presence.

Her voice was gentle, though, when she spoke. "Yes. And someday, you will, too. But that day is not yet. Do not ask about him. You have much to learn about yourself before you will know who you are."

She asked him questions then that seemed strange to him. They had naught to do with how well he rode a horse or handled a sword. The questions were about how he felt toward the Saxons, toward war, toward treating others, having respect and courtesy. He felt more like he was being groomed for the priesthood rather than soldiering. Finally, she leaned back in her chair and gestured toward Niniane. "This is my sister. She is high priestess of a lake in Brocéliande." Vivian looked at her. "What say you? Do you think him worthy?"

Niniane turned her odd-colored gaze on Arthur. "You have answered the questions well. I have only one piece of advice. Surround yourself with loyal friends, men who will stay with you through everything that you will face."

"Aye," Arthur replied. "I have my brother, Cai. He already has two close friends that will make me well come."

"You'll need a man who is your sworn companion first. Someone . . ." Her eyes glazed and when she spoke again, her voice sounded distant. "Someone who will save your life. You must find this person if you are to fulfill your destiny." Her eyes cleared, but the look she gave Arthur was puzzled.

CHAPTER TWO—ARTHUR: A SOLDIER'S WORLD
485 A.D. – 488 A.D.

Arthur and Myrddin arrived at Ambresbyrig as the men were breaking their fast. They dismounted and Arthur spotted Cai's red head immediately and started to wave, but Cai seemed strangely subdued. Arthur brought his hand down; mayhap, this wasn't proper behavior for the army. He felt himself blush. How could he be so stupid?

A man stepped out from a nearby tent. Arthur involuntarily caught his breath. The man was huge. Tall and broad-shouldered with arms as heavily muscled as a smith. He had a thick head of brown hair and clear grey eyes that penetrated and missed nothing. Even though he wore no torque or crown, Arthur knew this was the king. The Pendragon.

Uther strode over to them, nodded to Myrddin, and inspected Arthur. Arthur stared straight ahead, not daring to look at him and hoped he wasn't visibly trembling. It seemed a fortnight went by before Uther spoke.

"You want to be a soldier in my army? Ever killed anyone?"

"Yes, Sire . . . I mean, no, Sire."

"Well, which is it?"

Arthur took a deep breath and forced himself to meet that imperturbable stare. "I want nothing more than to serve in your army, Sire, but no, I have not killed anyone."

"Ummm." Uther moved around, looking him over again. "We'll see what stuff you're made of. Cadwy!"

One of his captains stepped forward. "I'm here, my lord."

"Take—Arthur, is it?—into your regiment. You've already got the other three cubs. Work him. Show no mercy." Uther turned and stomped off, yelling at his captains for not having the men in formation.

Arthur gulped. More than anything he wanted to ask Myrddin if the great Pendragon were always so harsh, but Myrddin had followed Uther. Arthur knew 'Uther' was a war name meaning 'terrible.' Somehow, it seemed fitting. He swallowed again and looked at the captain named Cadwy.

Cadwy watched him, too, but his blue eyes lacked the harshness of Uther's. In fact, a small smile played on his face. He was middle-aged, his hair just beginning to grey, and his belly showed no sign of a paunch.

"Come with me, Son. We'll get you a bunk for your belongings. And then, I think there's a red-headed young man who very much wants to see you."

* * * *

An exhausted Arthur flopped onto his bunk two nights later after supper. The day had been grueling. First there had been an hour of calisthenics, followed by a five mile run with full packs. *At least*, he thought gloomily, *Uther didn't have them carry picks and axes and shovels like the old Romans used to do to dig their trenches at night.* When they'd returned from that, there had been weaponry practice. He thought he'd done well with the sword until Cadwy stepped up and nearly dislodged it from his hand with a combined cut and blow. He'd nearly been too tired to hold the fourteen foot wooden lance for jousting, but he'd caught Cai watching him in amusement and summoned up his last ounce of strength. He knew every muscle would complain of movement tomorrow. Now all he wanted was some sleep.

"What are you doing lying down?" Cai burst into the barracks, followed by Bedwyr and Gwalchmai. "We're getting ready to go to the village; there's a tavern there with some pretty wenches." He poked Arthur.

Arthur struggled to sit up. Already, stiffness was setting in. He stared unbelievingly into his brother's face. "We have to be up at dawn."

Cai laughed and Gwalchmai joined in, but Bedwyr looked sympathetic. "You really will be better off if you keep moving for awhile."

It was the second time that day that Bedwyr had offered good advice. The first had been when Arthur started the run at a sprint. Bedwyr caught up with him and told him to slow down. Pacing was the important thing. Beneath his short chestnut-colored hair, his green eyes were serious now. Arthur groaned. He was probably right.

"Come on," Gwalchmai put a hand under his elbow and lifted him up. "We don't want to keep the ladies waiting!"

The only lady Arthur wanted to see at the moment was his mother, with a glass of warm milk in her hand. Not that he'd admit it. He looked at Gwalchmai: tall, fair-headed, good-looking. And smooth talking. He'd heard him flattering one of the serving girls into an extra portion of meat at supper.

"We won't be staying long?" Arthur asked.

Cai and Gwalchmai exchanged knowing looks. "We all leave whenever we want to," Cai answered.

"Usually with one of the wenches," Gwalchmai added, grinning.

Ah, good. Then I can come back in just a little while. Longingly, he looked at his bed before following them out the door.

* * * *

The tavern was warm and crowded. When they entered, a dark-haired, sloe-eyed woman with golden skin detached herself from the man she was talking to and came to Gwalchmai. She stood on tiptoe for his kiss and then saw Arthur.

"Who's this? Someone new?"

"My brother, Arthur," Cai said. "He just arrived today. Can you find someone to treat him real nice?"

The woman slanted a look at Cai and then smiled at Gwalchmai as she slipped from his embrace. She looked Arthur over as though he were standing inspection in front of Uther.

"Do you have any special needs?" she asked.

"What?"

Cai whispered in his ear. "Her name is Salome. She's the owner of this place. She wants to know what kind of girl you want."

Arthur felt himself turn scarlet. "What *kind*?"

The woman gave him another appraising look and then took his arm. "Come with me."

"Ah, no . . ." Arthur began and she smiled.

"He's shy!" She looked at Cai, then Gwalchmai and back to Arthur. "And so handsome, too!" She put her arms around his neck and before he could stop her, her mouth was on his, her tongue pressuring him to open his lips. His first impulse was to push away, yet as she began exploring his mouth, another feeling washed over him, sweeping the remnants of fatigue away. His skin felt pricked by a thousand needles and a throbbing began in his trews that spread flaming fever throughout his body.

He didn't resist when she took his hand again and led him to a back room, leaving his brother and friends staring after him in astonishment.

* * * *

She smiled as she bolted the door. An oil lamp lent a dim glimmer to the room which contained a plumped feather bed, a dresser with a wash basin and a small table and two chairs. Fresh rushes were spread on the floor.

Salome ran her fingers across his chest. "Are you really shy?"

Arthur made a growling sound and pulled her to him, his mouth urgent on hers, one hand finding a breast.

"Slow down!" She laughed as she pulled away slightly. "You young men are always in a hurry."

He pressed against her, his need creating an ache in him that he didn't know could happen. He fumbled with the bodice of her dress, and this time she took his hand and looked into his face.

He didn't misdoubt raw desire was probably written all over it, much as he tried to control his emotions. She widened her eyes suddenly.

"Is this the first time for you?"

He was grateful the room was dark so she wouldn't see his crimson face. Silently, he nodded.

She clapped her hands in delight. "That's wonderful! I can teach you then, to do everything the right way."

"Teach me?" Arthur wasn't sure whether to laugh or be angry. What was there to learn? Pretty much, he knew what he wanted to do and that was to have this woman's flesh against his, to be inside her, satisfying this throbbing erection that was near pain.

Salome looked amused. "Yes," she said. "Teach you. Like this."

She reached up and slid her fingers through his sun-bleached hair, letting her hands rest lightly on his shoulders. Slowly, she brushed his lips with hers, increasing the pressure slightly. She nibbled the upper lip, then the lower, and teased him with her tongue, probing his mouth, withdrawing when his ardor became too persistent. She let him taste her and then nipped his ear.

She pulled his tunic off and traced the muscles of his arms and shoulders. Her hand slid down his flat belly and undid the laces to his trews. She knelt to remove his boots and slipped the trews down. He groaned as her fingertips grazed the length of his phallus. Salome pressed up against his body as she slowly rose. She undid the laces to her bodice and let the top slip off her shoulders, exposing her breasts. "Now," she said, "you may touch me."

Arthur needed no further invitation. He scooped her up and laid her on the bed. He fought with himself not to ravish her as he wanted to do. She liked slow. He kissed her softly, teasing her as she had done, then he let his fingers glide down her throat to cup a breast. He paused, restraining himself again from taking her. He placed his mouth over her nipple and began to suckle.

Salome moaned and held his head to her breast and raked the nails of her other hand across his back. With a gasp, he lifted himself over her. Her hand guided him and then he felt the soft, wet, warmth he'd been seeking. With a groan, he thrust inside her. Her hips moved to meet him, her back arched to take him more fully. *No wonder Cai had become so addled-brained,* Arthur thought as he pummeled her, frenzied by her cries. Harder and deeper he drove into her, her hot tongue inside his mouth inflaming him farther. His body tensed and muscles strained as the blaze inside him ignited into a raging inferno. Salome's hot wet sheath clenched his rod, imprisoning him until her contractions subsided. He convulsed for one glorious moment and his world exploded.

Afterward, she held him in her arms. He felt sleepy and totally relaxed. She laughed when he told her. "You can come back anytime," she said.

* * * *

As the months wore on, Arthur adjusted to army life. He wondered from time to time who his father was. Myrddin would only say that when he was meant to know he would find out. The exercise and training made him muscular and by the end of the first year, he'd not only grown several inches, but become broad-shouldered as well. A fact that wasn't lost on the ladies.

After that first wonderful night, he understood how Cai had felt. But he also remembered how Cai had let his interest in women run his whole life. Arthur wanted to stay in control; his first goal was still being the best soldier in Uther's army. He learned quickly to detach his emotions from the act. He told no girl he loved her and although Salome always welcomed him, he didn't see the same woman twice in a row. What he did do, though, was learn how to please women. Word quickly got around that Arthur was a man who knew what to do. It aggravated Gwalchmai to no end and Arthur realized smugly that he liked the competition.

At the end of his second year in the army he was summoned to Uther's quarters.

Cadwy had told him, to "Wear your best uniform; it isn't often a young soldier is requested by Uther."

Arthur took a deep breath now as he stood in the outer hall, waiting. He was no longer afraid of the king. He had seen him lose his temper too many times and recover just as quickly to joke with the men. It had the strange effect of men showing respect for the Pendragon—they were professional soldiers—but not really liking him. Mayhap that's what he intended. But, Myrddin had always said to act the way you wanted to be treated. Well, mayhap Uther was getting ready to send him where the real fighting was . . . with the eastern Saxons. There had been raids lately and he'd been in training long enough.

He was ushered into Uther's private quarters. The king sat behind a massive desk. A fire burned low in the hearth to one side of the desk and two upright chairs were in front of it.

"Sit. I've received good reports on you from Cadwy." Uther shuffled some papers and held one up. "It seems you have developed a knack for persuasion."

Arthur furrowed his brow. "Sire?"

"There was an incident several months ago when you were out on maneuvers; your food wagon overturned in the river. You managed to get a local farmer's wife to cook dinner for all fifteen of the troops. And when Cadwy needed volunteers to rebuild the latrines, you got them for him. Not an easy thing to do, given the task." Uther put the paper down. "Also, I understand there was nearly a riot over some wench at the tavern last week and you kept two of my men from killing each other."

"All I did was ask them if they'd be willing to let the girl choose."

Uther leaned back in his chair. "What was the outcome?"

Arthur felt himself blush. "She chose me." Uther started to laugh and Arthur quickly added, "I mean, she knew me . . ."

"No doubt. From what I've heard, you've established quite a reputation."

"Sire?" Arthur couldn't believe the king actually knew about their nightly escapades.

Uther leaned across the desk and studied Arthur. "There isn't much I don't know about my troops. I make it my business. A good officer knows what's going on."

Officer? Am I here to be promoted? Arthur hardly dared to hope and then the next words stunned him.

"Some of the priests in the local churches don't want to pay their taxes. They feel they should be exempt. I need someone to persuade them to give me their due. I know you're young." He glanced at his notes. "Eight and ten? Still, I think you will make a good procurator."

Arthur stared at him. Procurator. Tax collector. One of the most despised positions in the army. People were reluctant to give their tithes, but when asked for even more . . . and now he was supposed to argue with men of God? He was aware that Uther was waiting for an answer. He took a deep breath. *This is a challenge. If I want to be an officer, I must prove myself.*

"When do I start, my lord?"

A smile broke out on the king's face. "Good boy. I'll have Ulfius draw up the list of churches that need to be visited. Take an escort of four or five men. You can leave tomorrow. And don't worry. This is not going to be your permanent position."

He breathed a sigh of relief and the king laughed again. "Every emotion shows on your face; if you ever think to lead men, you'll need to control that."

Arthur straightened his shoulders and lifted his chin. *Control. The king is right. Hold the emotions; think with my head.* "Thank you, Sire," he answered as the king dismissed him. "I'll remember that."

* * * *

Arthur chose to take Cai, Bedwyr, Gwalchmai and another young man, Gryflet, who had recently enlisted, to be his escort. Even though Cadwy had explained to them that his was a reserve regiment, Arthur's friends had been chafing at not being assigned to one of the commands that saw actual fighting on a regular basis.

When Cadwy saw his choices he shook his head. "Your friends are all untried, Arthur, as you are yourself. Even though most of these churches aren't close to the Saxons—or they'd see the need for protection and give their due—you need at least one seasoned soldier with you. I have just the man;

he's not an officer, but he's seen battle. I've fought beside him myself. His name is Gerient."

Gerient proved to be all that Cadwy said. He was only a few years older than Arthur, friendly and helpful. They had ten churches to visit and along the way, he'd point out signs of possible scouting activity: broken branches on bushes, dirt looser than the surrounding area, grass that had been trampled.

"Look for these things wherever you ride," he said. "We have no idea how far westward the Saxons send their scouts. We know there's been unrest near Lindum."

"Lindum?" Arthur asked with interest. "One of the churches is up there."

As they rode farther north, Arthur began to pick up the telltale signs even before Gerient would point them out.

Arthur was nervous at the first church they stopped at, but he decided to use a biblical passage from Matthew as his foundation. "Render unto Caesar the things which are Caesar's," he began. "Are you familiar with the story?"

The priest reddened and sputtered, but in the end, Arthur had his tithe. It wasn't until the ninth stop, the one near Lindum, that he faced absolute refusal.

They were standing inside the church. "The Romans are gone. Caesar no longer rules here. We barter more than we use coinage." The priest was young and plump and this was his first calling.

Arthur sighed. Over the last several weeks, he had learned that many of these priests talked out of both sides of their mouths. As well fed as this one was, there must be bounty. "Tell me," he responded in a voice that was soft and pleasant, "what do you require of your parishioners?"

"Only that they love and worship the one true God!" The priest looked highly insulted and then stuck his chin out as Gwalchmai grinned. "Do you travel with pagans who have no respect for the Lord?"

Arthur refused to be sidetracked. He kept his voice silky. "What do you require of your parishioners?"

The priest fumbled with his beads as Arthur's stare penetrated through him. "They . . . they give a tenth of their livelihood to Holy Church."

"Willingly?" Again, the mellow voice warred with the stern face.

"*Certes!*" the priest said.

Arthur knew he was lying. "Then why wouldn't you willingly give your tenth for the King's protection? Isn't there a parable here . . . the people give you a tithe; you represent God who saves their souls. I represent the king, who saves your lives."

"I don't . . . I don't have any coinage."

"That's fine." Arthur moved about the church, picking up candlesticks, a silk altar cloth, a pewter chalice for the Eucharist, and lastly, the silver crucifix from the wall.

The priest stood in shocked silence. Now he sputtered. "What do you think you're doing? These are sacred things!"

"Ah, yes," Arthur said affably, "and they should bring a good price. Worth the tithe, I think."

"No! No! You can't take them. They're mine . . ." The priest stopped.

"I thought they were the Lord's." Arthur smiled at the man as he started toward the door.

"No! Wait! I . . . I have coinage." The priest was near tears as he produced a small bag from behind the altar. "Here. Take this. Leave the Lord's things here."

Arthur set them down on the floor and took the bag. "For *certes*, this must be a miracle," he said benignly. "I shall look forward to another miracle next year."

The priest's eyes were huge in his face. "You won't have to do that, my lord. I'll pay the tithe."

* * * *

Cai and Gwalchmai hadn't stopped laughing until they were nearly a mile down the road from the church. Even Gerient grudgingly allowed a grin. Bedwyr slapped Arthur on the back.

"You handled that really well," he said as they stopped their horses at the River Glein to drink. "Most men would have lost their tempers and simply raided the place."

Arthur stretched. "All this diplomacy has made me feel like a strung bow; I'm going for a short walk."

Bedwyr nodded. "I'll watch your horse."

Arthur followed the river where it wound around a bend. It was peaceful here, the depth shallow enough for a ford, the water gurgling softly over the rocks. Trees lined both sides of the river and the gently rolling hills were green with the promise of spring. He walked further, letting his thoughts wander.

At first, he wasn't sure he saw anything. He squinted across the river. There it was again. The merest form of a shadow flitting behind the trees. Then another one. An arrow whizzed by his head as he dove to the ground and rolled. Crouching, he leapt for the cover of the trees.

He heard men splashing through the water and glanced back once to see ten or twelve Saxons. He sprinted toward the drinking hole, glad now that he'd done those runs every day.

"Saxons!" he gasped as he came upon his friends relaxing in the shade. "Just behind me!"

"Mount up," Garient shouted. "Lances ready!" But they had no time; the Saxons burst through the clearing, axes raised.

Arthur pulled his shield off his horse and drew his sword. He prayed he would remember his training and then he was in the middle of it, hacking and slicing, ducking an ax. He felt his sword hit a soft spot and drive in. For a moment the Saxon hung skewered on his sword and time stood still, while the dying man and Arthur looked at each other.

"Arthur! To me!" Gerient was fighting three men and Arthur's morbid fascination snapped. He pulled his sword and lunged, trying to get into the back-to-back position that was so strategic. In his peripheral vision, he saw his friends were holding their own.

The leader of the group was one of the men attacking Gerient. Arthur lunged and thrust and the blade went true. The Saxon grabbed the blade with both hands, and for a moment both of them grappled with it; then the Saxon's hands went slack and he sagged to the ground.

Seeing their leader downed, the remaining four were easily subdued. Gerient efficiently bound each of them and tethered them in a line. The leader, whom Arthur had wounded, was laid on a hastily improvised travois.

"Uther will be pleased to get these hostages," Gerient said. "We need to know what's brewing in Anglia." He turned to Arthur. "Good work. If you hadn't spotted them, we would have been ambushed."

Arthur nodded and walked to where the first man he'd killed lay. He knelt down beside the body. For that one moment, he had looked into the Saxon's eyes and seen the man there. Just an ordinary man, on a mission, doing his job. He looked at the entrails spilling out of the jagged tear, the blood already beginning to gel. Suddenly, he lurched and stumbled to the trees. In a moment, he was retching out his own guts.

He heard Gerient issue the orders to move out and was grateful no one would see his embarrassment. Soldiers weren't supposed to get sick for killing Saxons. They were the enemy. *A fine officer I'll make!*

When the hoofbeats had receded, he left the woods and mounted his horse. He looked one last time at the body of the man whose life he'd taken and wondered if one day they could live in peace.

* * * *

Just outside of Ambresbyrig, they parted ways.

"The King asked me to make one last stop at Amesbury Abbey," Arthur said to Gerient. "He has a package he wants delivered. You take the prisoners and go on ahead."

Gerient nodded. "Be prepared when you return. Uther will want to celebrate; I doubt any of you'll have to fret much longer. You're seasoned now; you'll be assigned to an active unit."

Arthur hesitated in answering.

Gerient laid a hand on his arm. "Do not torture yourself. You've nothing to be ashamed of. Many men react the way you did. It's human. War is war and it will harden you soon enough."

He rode on and Arthur took a deep breath. He thought no one had seen. He turned toward the abbey. At least, he could attend a Mass.

The abbess received him in the small waiting room just inside the front door of the priory. He handed her a bag of coins. "I've been weeks on the road collecting money from the churches, but King Uther said I was supposed to give these to you."

"Ah, yes." The abbess took the bag and set it aside. "His daughter resides with us. This is for her welfare." The lady's eyes looked troubled.

Arthur was surprised. He didn't know that Uther had a daughter. He'd heard stories about a baby that had been kidnapped and never found. A boy, he thought. "How old is the child?" he asked.

"She is not a child, my dear." Again, a worried expression crossed the abbess's face. "Morgana's twenty."

"Twenty? Then why isn't she married?"

She shrugged delicately. "Let's just say that her mother fears for her soul outside of a godly establishment." She changed the subject. "Would you like to join us in the chapel for Vespers before you leave?"

"Very much. I have some soul-cleansing to do." Arthur told her about the Saxons, glad he could share it with someone who wouldn't ridicule him.

The abbess patted his hand when he finished. "Never be ashamed of your humanity. The ability to feel for your fellow man will make you great. Now come."

The service was soothing. The chanting of the women's voices was sweet to his ears and easy on his heart. He was relaxing, letting himself be surrounded by the music when a scuffling noise sounded from across the aisle and looked over.

A petite woman was leaving the pew. She was dressed in a red gown that contrasted vividly with the sisters' habits. He couldn't see her face since her back was toward him and he thought idly that she must be Morgana. An odd smell clung to the air, like a scent of damp earth and rotted herbs. It faded as the woman walked away. The hair bristled on his neck as he turned back to the service.

CHAPTER THREE—MORGANA: CHILD OF DARKNESS
481 A.D. – 488 A.D.

Morgana perched on the stool next to the old crone's worktable and watched as the gnarly hands crushed the leaves in the mortar bowl with the pestle. She wasn't supposed to here in the forest at the witch's hut, but today was her three and tenth birthday and she should be able to do what she wanted! She tossed her raven-black hair back. There would be Christian hell to pay if Uther found out, but right now, Morgana didn't care. She hated Uther. He'd had her father killed, then he'd married her mother and sold her older sister, Margawse, to a king in the Orkneys. Her mother still cried about some baby that had been kidnapped when Morgana was but two. Morgana hoped the baby was dead. It was Uther's son and that made him her enemy.

The hag added a pinch of a foul-smelling root to her concoction and then carefully swept the contents into a small vial. She covered the mixture with wine dregs and sealed the container.

"Ah," she said as she placed the small jar on a shelf. "Now for your lessons, Morgana."

Morgana smiled. She loved learning about which herbs healed and which herbs were dangerous. And which might kill. Especially those.

"What cures stomach aches?" the old woman asked.

"Chamomile. Snakeroot. Goldenseal. Wormwood."

"Strains and muscle pains?"

"Lavender. Foxglove. Comfrey . . ." Morgana stopped. "I want to know about the others. The herbs that hold the real power."

The hag frowned. "You're young to learn about those."

Morgana stamped a foot. "Tell me which ones can hypnotize a person."

The woman closed her eyes. "Henbane. Belladonna. Woodruff."

"And the ones to keep a girl from getting pregnant?"

The crone opened her eyes quickly. "Why would you be wanting to know about those?"

"No reason." Morgana smiled again. "Mayhap one day they might be useful to me."

The old woman looked at her suspiciously. "I know you sneak out to watch the Black Rites that are held here in the glade, but you keep yourself pure, girl. Do you hear? The only reason I'm still alive is that King Uther has use of my herbals. If he found you out here, participating . . ."

"You worry too much." Morgana smoothed her gown across a thigh and liked the sensation of the silken feel. "I am three and ten. Lots of girls get married when they're only a year or two older than me."

"Married," the hag said. "They don't traipse through the woods at night watching grown men and women couple. If you got pregnant..."

Morgana looked at her, her nearly black eyes wide. "But that's why I'm asking to know which herbs to use. Besides," she wheedled, "wouldn't you feel better knowing I can protect myself?"

The witch sighed and Morgana knew she'd won. The old woman really was fond of her. *I suppose 'tis because everyone else is afraid to come here. I'm the only one who dares darken her door.* She never considered that the old lady might be lonely and, having found someone with a talent in herbals, was interested in passing on the healing arts. Morgana tossed her head. "So, which herbs keep me from getting with child?"

"Waldmeister. Mother's Wort. Brooklime. They can be steeped as teas."

"Will you show me how to mix them?"

"No. As long as you don't know, you'll be scared to take a chance."

Morgana looked at her out of the corner of her eye, but decided not to pursue the issue for now. Spells were another of her favorite things to practice and the witch didn't mind teaching her those. Although, she still hadn't learned anything strong enough to destroy Uther. Or his son if he ever surfaced again.

* * * *

Six months later, on Beltane eve, Morgana sat cross-legged in front of the brazier in her bedchamber. Carefully, she opened several small packets of herbs and sprinkled small pinches unto the glowing embers. They caught and blazed upward in shards of orange and yellow and blue. Morgana raised both hands and the flames leapt higher. She giggled and lowered her hands. The fire banked itself and she stared into it.

The scent of the herbs hung heavy in the air around her, cloistering her with heady intoxications. The crone had been teaching her to read the fire. She felt herself grow light-headed and drew inward, concentrating her conscience on finding Uther. If she could learn to hold the power long enough to watch him, mayhap she might be able to influence the action around him. How she wanted to find him in battle! She'd have to concentrate on an enemy's sword... She shook her head as a faint image of him emerged.

He was seated in the tent of his headquarters at the fort. A man in a flowing blue robe, with a mane of tawny hair, stood at his side. Morgana leaned toward the flames and the man suddenly looked up, his yellow eyes sharp as an eagle's. Morgana drew back and then remembered he couldn't see her. She strained to hear the conversation.

"Your son is doing well," Myrddin said. "At one and ten, he can already best his foster brother at swordplay."

Uther nodded. "A pity I won't be able to claim him when he enters the army."

"We've been through that. Until he's proven himself and men will accept his leadership, there's no need for anyone to know who he is. You just need to stay alive."

The scene faded and Morgana blinked. Uther wouldn't stay alive long if she learned the right curses. But the hag had refused to teach her those. *So, Morgana brooded, the bastard son exists*! Then another thought occurred to her. If Uther declared him heir, he would own Tintagel and Tintagel was hers! Her eyes narrowed. One way or another, she would find out who this boy was.

* * * *

Morgana opened the back door to the Great Hall stealthily, shoes in her hand, and stepped inside. She had intended to return from the forest Rites of Samhain well before dawn, but watching the sexual ritual had been so intense that she lost track of time. Luckily, she wasn't discovered. She just wished she were old enough to be initiated. Now if she could just get to her chamber before her mother was up and about.

Uther stepped into the back hall. Morgana's head snapped around. What was he doing here? Worst of all, her mother was standing behind him.

"Where have you been?" Ygraine demanded.

"For a walk, Mother. That's all." If only Uther weren't here! She knew she could convince her mother of the lie.

Uther stepped over to her and she shrank back, but he merely pulled a twig off her gown. "In the forest on Samhain." It was a statement and Morgana maintained her silence.

"Morgana." Ygraine led her to the small, private chamber off the hall and bade her sit down. "I've found some disturbing things in your room which is why I sent for Uther."

Sent for him! What right does my mother have to search my things? Morgana seethed inwardly; outwardly she struggled to remain calm. "I know not what you mean."

Uther picked several items up from the small table near the door. He threw them down in front of her. "Packages of herbs, even dangerous ones, wouldn't be so bad, but the list of enchantments, curses, and talismans is a problem. Especially when they're directed at me."

"My daughter! I fear the devil has taken hold of your soul." Ygraine placed her hands on Morgana's shoulders. "Why would you wish Uther dead? He's not harmed you in any way."

Morgana glared at her mother. "How can you say that? He killed my Da!"

Uther grimaced. "I didn't kill Gorlois. Had he come peacefully when my men went to get him, he might still be alive."

She frowned. "Would my mother still be married to him?"

The king arched an eyebrow. "Probably not, but it would have been your mother's choice."

Her mouth dropped open and she clamped it shut. "Mother? You would choose him over Da?"

Ygraine sighed. "There are many things you're too young to understand. My marriage to your father was planned to unite two coastal regions. There was no love and your father wasn't always kind to me."

"I'm not here to discuss why Ygraine married me," Uther said. "'Tis obvious you're dabbling in some black arts; I had that forest witch brought to me in chains." He looked Morgana over from head to toe. "Did you participate in last night's rituals?"

"What rituals?"

Uther looked irritated. "Do not lie. I know there is a group of Satan worshippers that still perform their blood sacrifices. I know you were there. Did you participate?"

Morgana knew from the steel ring of his voice that further argument would get her confined to her room or worse. "No. I did not."

Ygraine breathed a sigh of relief. "Thank the Lord. We're not too late to save you."

"Save me? From what?" *There'll be plenty of other times I can sneak out.*

"From yourself, my child." Ygraine took Morgana's hand. "'Tis time you do more than go to Mass. You needs learn the way of Light, not darkness. Uther will be taking you to the convent at Amesbury."

"A convent? Me?" Morgana stared at her mother and then laughed. Louder and higher and more shrill, until the hysteria bubbled over and she was sobbing uncontrollably.

* * * *

Morgana gave the broom a vicious sweep across the tiled entry of the abbey. Beltane. The night when the needfires would be lit and couples would dance through them to ensure fertility to the spring crops and young livestock. A night when women were free to couple with the man of their choice. This was the third Beltane she'd spent in these miserable confines. Even though Uther paid the sisters a good sum of gold each year, they still expected her to do manual work alongside of them! She'd had to do laundry and prepare meals, whitewash the walls, take out the soiled rushes, clean and polish endlessly. And for what? So she could sit in the chapel seven times a day, from Prime to Matins, while the offices were chanted? The new religion did not appeal to her—why would any man, let alone a god—allow himself to be killed? The only respite she had was when she was allowed to go into town with a sister as escort to sell the herbs she grew.

She was grateful for that. The town was always full of men. Soldiers who looked lustily after her, then turned quickly away at the sight of the accompanying sister. The smith worked with his shirt off most of the time, displaying a broad chest and massive arms. The tall, lank horse-trader always had a story to tell, although if the sister were near, the content was doctored considerably. There was the cooper, a good-looking man in his thirties, who always managed to let his fingers linger on her hands as she sold him herbs. She savored that touch for hours afterward.

Morgana made a malicious jab at a cobweb in the corner. She was of marriageable age, but Uther wasn't about to splurge on a dowry for her. Margawse had cost him well. She thought of her sister, not only married these past five and ten years, but with a son just sent to Uther. She sighed. The nuns loved the money Uther gave them and they valued her herb lore. She would never be able to leave this place.

But tonight would be different. While the needfires burned and the pagans celebrated, she was going to meet the cooper.

* * * *

"I cannot believe you defied me in this matter!" The Mother Abbess's voice, usually so soothing and controlled, rose on a shrill note.

Morgana slumped dejectedly in the chair in front of the desk where the abbess sat. She had been so close! Only one more corner and she would have gotten her greatest desire filled. Why did that wretched parishioner find her anyway?

"You are confined to your quarters for a week, with nothing more than bread and water." The sister studied Morgana. "We must cure you of your lust. The king entrusted you to us and we dare not fail him. In addition, as penance for the sin of concupiscence, you will prostrate yourself during each of the seven offices daily for a month."

"I did nothing wrong!" Morgana protested. *And I wish I had!*

"One of the four cardinal virtues is temperance," the abbess answered sternly. "If this continues, I will have to speak to King Uther about using the scourge."

Morgana stared at her, speechless.

"You may go," the abbess said.

As she stumbled to her room, tears stinging her eyes, she put another curse on Uther. She was only here because he didn't want any reminders of Gorlois when he visited Ygraine. Margawse was safely tucked away far to the north and she was stuck in this convent to rot. And his son—the one the druid said had lived—would one day be acknowledged as his heir.

Morgana slammed the door. She vowed she would have her revenge on Uther and on his bastard son.

* * * *

One summer morning, in her twentieth year, she looked up from her embroidery to see a young man standing in the entryway waiting to see the abbess. Seldom did men set foot inside the rectory and this one definitely was interesting. Tall, broad-shouldered, with light brown hair bleached blond in the sun, clear grey eyes, chiseled cheekbones, and a square jaw. She wondered who he was. After the Beltane mishap three years ago, she dare not ask for fear of getting more penance to do. *By the goddess, I'm tired of having raw knees!*

The abbess arrived and Morgana heard the man say he had delivery from Uther. Her shoulders slumped. Another of the king's minions. Still, when she saw him walking with the abbess to Vespers, she decided this was one time she wouldn't mind attending.

She donned a red dress, partly to attract his attention, but also to annoy the nuns who hated the sinful color. She chose the pew across from him, entering it from the other side so the sisters would not be suspicious. It allowed her to sit at an angle to observe him. He seemed troubled and she wondered what such a young man could have on his mind. She watched as he closed his eyes and rubbed his forehead. His hand was large and strong with sturdy fingers and she wondered what that hand would do pressed to her bare flesh. She gave a slight shudder as she imagined those fingers playing with her nipple.

Morgana took a deep breath and sent her strong sexual thoughts across the room to him. *Certes, now he will turn and look at me. No, he's still looking worried.* She inhaled again and drew in energy. She had been practicing mind-melding for two years and most of the time, if she concentrated hard enough, she could get a small glimpse of what people were thinking. It left her with a terrific headache afterwards, but this might be worth it.

One more breath and she managed to access his outer rays of energy. She nearly recoiled. Never had she felt such sorrow and desolation. There was some regret for a loss—no, a life—taken.

Morgana pulled back, leaving the air somewhat fetid with the residue of her exertion. How could a soldier feel guilt about a dead man? Life was survivorship. Only the most fit—or the most cunning—won. This man had obviously been the victor. So why not celebrate? She tried once more to get his attention, but he was riveted now to the music, his hands folded and his eyes closed.

Slowly, she got up and made her way from the pew. Again, she wondered who the man was. And all man, no doubt about that. She really wouldn't mind experimenting with some of the pagan rituals she'd observed. She sighed. She would probably never see him again.

CHAPTER FOUR—GWENHWYFAR: DAUGHTER OF DESTINY
488 A.D. – 490 A.D.

Young Gwenhwyfar regarded the unicorn solemnly. "Da says I can have a pony soon. Will you be my pony?"

The light blue eyes of the unicorn peeked back shyly from beneath the shadows of the forest. A breeze from the window caught the tapestry hanging behind the bed and made it flutter, giving the unicorn the appearance of speaking. And to Gwenhwyfar, he did. He was her unicorn. His name was Prince. "I'll come for you," he said.

Delighted, she clapped her hands, just as she heard the guard call that a rider approached. She ran to her upstairs window and looked down. She hugged herself and turned back to the unicorn.

"It's my brother, Bedwyr! Come to visit from King Uther's army!"

She skipped down the steps and out into the bright sunshine of the bailey. One of the wolfhounds sprang toward her, wagging his tail like a banner. She stopped to hug him, mindless of the hem of her shift trailing in the dust.

Bedwyr was about to dismount, but now trotted the horse toward her and held out his arm. Eagerly, she grabbed it and he swung her up behind him.

"Hold on tight," he said and kicked the big horse into a canter toward the gate. "We'll be back," he called and they were galloping down the road.

The wind tore at Gwenhwyfar's erstwhile braid, causing her auburn hair to streak behind her as the horse increased speed. She laid her head against her brother's back and screamed in sheer bliss. Da never let her ride this fast when she rode with him. It was magic! The horse was flying, the ground a blur below. She never wanted to stop!!!

Eventually, Bedwyr turned the horse and slowed it to a trot as they returned to the bailey. Leodegrance did not look pleased.

"The child's only four, Bedwyr! She could have been hurt!"

He brought his right leg over the horse's mane and slid down. Reaching for Gwenhwyfar, he tossed her in the air first, bringing another shriek of pleasure, before setting her on the ground. He looked at his father. "Not the way she held on." He laughed. "She's a natural rider."

"Please, Da! When can I have my own pony?" Gwenhwyfar's green eyes were huge in her flushed face. "That was the best ride I ever had!"

"I think you're a little young yet," Leodegrance began, but Bedwyr interrupted him.

"Doesn't Gwenhwyfar have a birthday coming soon, or did I come home for no reason?" Bedwyr winked at his little sister.

Her eyes widened. "I'll be five in two days."

Leodegrance sighed. "I'll see what stock is available." He looked at his son. "Thank God I did not spoil you like I do her."

Bedwyr grinned. "I can vouch for that; my backside burned many times." He stopped smiling. "But I didn't lose Mother when I was but two. Gwenhwyfar did. I want her to be happy."

His father nodded and looked down at Gwenhwyfar, but she wasn't paying much attention, too enthralled with petting Bedwyr's horse. She looked up suddenly.

"Are you crying, Da?" she asked, reaching for his hand.

"No, child." He wiped his cheek quickly and stroked her hair smooth. "No. You shall have your pony."

* * * *

The pony was pure white, with the clear glass eyes that looked blue in the early morning sunlight of the enclosed paddock. Gwenhwyfar stood in front of him, lifting his forelock and combing it with her fingers.

"You look like my unicorn," she said, "but where's your horn?"

"This isn't a unicorn, Gwenhwyfar," her father answered.

"But he said he'd come." She gave her father a puzzled look.

"Mayhap, he had to leave the horn in the land of Faerie." Bedwyr held out his hand. "Let me help you on."

Gwenhwyfar thrust her chin out. "I can do it myself."

He grinned and let go of the bridle. "Go ahead."

She hated being teased. Did her big brother not think she could do this? She took the reins and struggled to raise her foot to the stirrup and then felt unbalanced when she did. She reached for the pommel of the saddle, only to find a lot of space as the pony inched sideways. She hopped on the other foot.

"Lesson Number One, Gwenhwyfar," Bedwyr said as he stilled the pony. "Gather the reins tighter. You will learn to feel the horse's mouth. Then step in close, against him before you leg up. That way, if the horse moves, you move with him."

She knew her face was red, so she kept her head down. Then she felt his hand under her chin.

"Go ahead. Try."

This time she was more successful and wanted to shout out her happiness, but instinctively, she knew it would scare her pony.

"Ask him to walk," Bedwyr said. "Lift the reins and touch your heels to him."

She did and was proud of herself for knowing how to turn him. She had watched her father and his soldiers often enough. Mayhap, she could make Bedwyr proud of her! She kicked the pony's flanks hard and the startled animal leaped into a canter, turning sharply at the fence.

Gwenhwyfar landed in a heap on the ground. Bedwyr and Leodegrance rushed over. The wolfhound whimpered at the fence. "I told you she was too young," Leodegrance growled. "I'll take the pony back."

"No!" Gwenhwyfar sat up. "It wasn't his fault! I made him run." Leodegrance looked undecided and she looked at Bedwyr. "Please help me keep Prince!"

He looked serious. "A good horsewoman always gets right back on."

She scrambled to her feet before her father could say no. The pony stood with his head hanging down, not far away.

She went to him and hugged his neck. "Don't feel bad."

Prince turned his head and gently nuzzled her shoulder. The blue eye looked into her face. He lifted and twitched his lip and to Gwenhwyfar, it was a smile. "We'll be best friends," she whispered.

* * * *

"Tsk!" Gwenhwyfar's old nurse, Mirre, said as picked up the trews from the floor of the bedchamber and handed Gwenhwyfar a simple gown of blue linen. "If your mother were alive, she'd not be letting you dress like a little boy!"

Gwenhwyfar protested. "I hate wearing dresses. They get in the way when I want to run and now that I've got a pony . . ."

Mirre silenced her with a look. "Aye. Against your da's better judgment. Now if you want to please him, you'll dress like a little lady for supper while your brother is here."

Please her da. That stopped Gwenhwyfar every time. She wondered if Mirre did it on purpose. Since Bedwyr had left for the army at four and ten, she didn't have anyone to play with. She had attached herself to her father, following him around everywhere he went. More than anything else, she wanted to make him proud.

"And we'll re-comb and braid your hair," Mirre said.

Gwenhwyfar sighed as Mirre ran the brush through her tangled stresses. No matter how hard she tried, her hair was unruly and always came undone. Mirre would say it was because Gwenhwyfar insisted on being outdoors most of the time instead of learning to thread a needle and make a fine stitch like other girls did. She wrinkled her nose at the thought. Now that Prince had come she wouldn't have time.

She looked at the tapestry again. The unicorn was still there, but dimmer somehow, as if it were his shade. The shadow of the man standing in the thicket behind him seemed clearer. She'd always wondered who he was, but her mother had died before she could explain her weaving to Gwenhwyfar. She thought she could see antlers above the man's head and blinked. *No, that's silly. A man with antlers?*

"There," Mirre said and put the brush down. "Go on now. Your father and Bedwyr will be waiting."

They were talking about King Uther as Gwenhwyfar's slippers padded silently across the blue mosaic tile in the private dining quarters of the villa. She sat down next to her father and listened to the water splashing from the fountain in the atrium across the hall. She loved her home and never planned to leave it.

"And Da, you've got to meet my friends," Bedwyr said. "Gwalchmai and Gryflet, Cai and Cai's brother, Arthur. We had our first real fight with the Saxons just before I came here! If it hadn't have been for Arthur, we would have been ambushed!"

"Arthur?" Leodegrance furrowed his brows and then grinned. "Isn't he the young procurator that made a lot of the priests mad? It seems there was one at Lindum . . ."

"Yes!" Bedwyr nodded. "We all had a good laugh after that. Pompous ass."

Leodegrance frowned. "Those priests collect all that money because their flocks think the priest must pray for them; that they can't do it for themselves. Pelagius always claimed man had free will and could communicate directly with God. Those priests have fought long to deny that."

"Well, Arthur made them pay back their share," Bedwyr said with a grin. "I'll have to bring him along the next time I visit. You'll like him."

"How long can you stay?" Gwenhwyfar asked. "I miss you."

"I miss you, too, little sister, but I am a man now. The Saxons give us no peace. My whole regiment is about to move. I can't stay but another day."

She was disappointed. She had hoped they could go riding together now that she had Prince.

Seeing her face droop, he reached down under his chair. "I have something for you, Gwenhwyfar. I made it myself for your birthday."

She brightened immediately and ran around to his side of the table. "What is it?"

He held up an oak sword, cut all in one piece, the grip whittled small to fit her hand, the length short to accommodate her arm. He turned it and laid the blade across his arm, extending the hilt toward her.

She stood looking at it in awe. Then, slowly she reached for it. It was heavier than she thought and she almost dropped it.

Leodegrance stared at his son. "Are you determined to turn your sister into your brother? She's wild enough as it is."

"Not at all," Bedwyr answered and demonstrated to Gwenhwyfar how to hold the sword steady and get its balance. "Our grandmother was a warrior queen, was she not?"

"Yes, but that was two generations ago. Celtic women no longer fight."

Bedwyr raised an eyebrow. "Didn't our mother know how to use a sword?"

Leodegrance had the grace to blush. "Guenhumara was an unusual woman. But I would never have let her fight by my side in battle."

"Only because your Roman pride wouldn't let you. Still, Gwenhwyfar should know how to defend herself," Bedwyr answered. "With the Saxons trying to push westward, there may come a time she'll need to use it."

Gwenhwyfar slashed with the instrument. She thrust it at a startled servant coming in the door, who nearly dropped the wine jug.

Leodegrance admonished her and made her apologize, but secretly, he hid a smile. Gwenhwyfar caught it, though, and smiled too. *Da isn't mad at me; he's proud! I'll be the best sword lady anywhere! I will!*

* * * *

Gwenhwyfar practiced with her sword every afternoon in a corner of the bailey. Bedwyr had embedded a large agate into the edge of the hilt and Leodegrance showed her how the pommel helped to balance the weight of the sword. She learned the steps: how to advance, retreat and side step.

"But when am I going to be able to fight a person?" she asked plaintively one day several months later, when she had done dozens of thrusts and lunges at the straw dummy Leodegrance had erected.

Leodegrance smiled at her. "How about now? I'll be your first opponent."

Gwenhwyfar widened her eyes. "What if I hurt you?"

He laughed. "If you do that, I may have to send you to Uther's army, after all."

"Now remember what I've shown you about parrying. The idea for now is to avoid my blade. When you can do that, I'll teach you to attack."

Gwenhwyfar parried and retreated, then parried again. She soon tired of backing up. Determined, she pressed his blade and disengaged, met his parry and did a reposte.

Her father looked surprised and then a grin broke out on his face. "So," he said as he grounded his blade, "you have a warrior's spirit, just like your mother."

Gwenhwyfar knew there was no greater praise. *I'll practice until I'm as good as Bedwyr!* She didn't realize they had drawn a group of onlookers until she heard the applause. She raised her head determinedly.

Her father gathered her to him and spoke to his men. "Mark my words. Someday, this child will lead you!"

* * * *

When Gwenhwyfar turned six, Leodegrance took her to the county fair. She was delighted with all the new sights and sounds. And the smells! From freshly baked breads to succulent stews and meat pasties to the sweet scents of the custards and pies. The jugglers and jesters fascinated her.

"Why is the bear chained?" she asked as she watched the animal dance.

"It could be dangerous if it weren't tied," Leodegrance answered. Just then, the bear dropped to all fours and was quickly whipped. It grunted and slowly rose on its hind legs again.

"He shouldn't have been hit," Gwenhwyfar said. "I don't think the bear likes to dance. I think he should be free."

"Mayhap he gets better fed this way."

Gwenhwyfar remained doubtful as they moved away. "I still think he should free." Then she heard the wild screech of a cat nearby. Before her father could stop her, she slid her hand from his grasp and hurdled around a tent corner toward the sound.

A village boy of about seven or eight was holding a mother cat by her neck, over a cauldron of boiling soup. Her kittens lay nearby mewling and beside them, a girl younger than Gwenhwyfar was crying.

"I think I'll add yer cat ta me stew. It needs more meat." He laughed and lowered the cat slowly until its tail was in the fiery liquid. It howled again.

Gwenhwyfar charged at the boy, catching him from behind and bowling both of them over. The cat flew from his hands and landed on her feet.

They rolled through the dirt, the boy trying to throw her off. Enraged, she clawed at his face, leaving strings of red welts. The boy screamed and raised his fist.

Leodegrance caught it and lifted him into the air. He dangled there, kicking his feet helplessly. "Let me go! The girl drew first blood!"

"So she did," Leodegrance said as the magistrate came running to take charge. "It seems to me she had just cause."

"What was that about, Gwenhwyfar?" Leodegrance asked as the boy was led away.

But she had gone to the little girl. "Is your cat all right?"

The child dried her tears and nodded. "Just a singe is all."

"My da and I will help you carry the kittens. We will find a safe place," Gwenhwyfar said. "Don't you worry."

* * * *

An invitation to come to the abbey of Ynys Gutrin near the Tor arrived several weeks later. A resurgence of interest in the Pelagian theory had emerged and there was to be a debate.

Leodegrance laid the letter down beside his chair in their living quarters and looked at Gwenhwyfar. "I think, after the episode at the fair, that I had better take you with me. How do you feel about a week's ride south?"

Gwenhwyfar clapped her hands and bounced up. "When do we leave?"

Her father laughed. "The meeting is in a fortnight. We have a few days time."

For Gwenhwyfar, the time dragged. She brushed and curried Prince until his coat shone like silver and finally, the big day arrived.

They took the old Roman Watling Street to Eboracum and on to Lindum. Gwenhwyfar hadn't been farther south. The hills rolled more gently through the middle country and eventually became more pastureland than forest.

The last day, as they neared the abbey, fog rolled over the road. It lay heavy on the ground to their left.

"We stay to the right." Leodegrance pointed. "Ynys Gutrin lies that way."

Gwenhwyfar craned her neck to peer through the dense bank of mist. "What's over there?"

"Some say it's a dragon's lair and the fog is his breath." Her father smiled as Gwenhwyfar instinctively moved her pony closer. "Don't be scared. Actually, the Isle of Avallach lies in its middle of a lake. A group of pagan priestesses live there."

Gwenhwyfar widened her eyes. "Pagans? Like druids? Do they torture and kill people?" She remembered that Mirre was afraid of them.

"No, child. Not since the days before Caesar. In fact, I'm hoping one of the druids shows himself at this meeting. It's been a long time since I've seen Myrddin."

"Who's he?" They had reached the abbey now and dismounted as someone came out for their horses.

"He's King Uther's main advisor," Leodegrance answered, "and a magician, some say."

"Magic? Like the wandering minstrels perform?" Gwenhwyfar asked.

"No. His magic is much stronger. If the Christians wouldn't be so afraid of it . . ." He stopped as the abbott greeted them.

They were taken to the rectory and given lodging for the night. The next morning, after breaking their fast, Leodegrance made ready to attend the meeting.

"I want you to stay close to the abbey, Gwenhwyfar. No riding and don't walk far. I don't want you getting lost."

"Yes, Da."

She went out to talk to Prince. When she finished feeding and brushing him, she grew bored. The sound the sound of water gently lapping onto shore. *Part of the lake must be quite close. I think I'll have a look.*

Gwenhwyfar wandered down the winding path that led down toward the sound.

Tendrils of fog swirled around her feet. It reached upward, enveloping her as she moved forward. She waved her arm and giggled as it seemed to disappear and reappear in the mists.

Something bumped into her and she lost her footing on the slippery slope, but a hand caught and steadied her, holding her up. Startled, she turned to see a dark-haired boy of about ten. He held a wooden sword in his other hand.

"Where did you come from?" she asked as he released her arm.

For a moment longer, his smoke-colored eyes studied her. He shook his head. "It doesn't matter, really. I don't see many children around here. You probably should go back." He maneuvered his sword against an imaginary opponent.

"I'm six years old!" Gwenhwyfar tossed her head indignantly. "Da doesn't treat me like a child. I can handle a sword, too!"

He stopped suddenly and grinned at her, lopsidedly. "Show me." He turned the sword and extended the grip toward her.

She liked his smile. She took the sword and stepped back, about to thrust and lunge when a monk came hurrying up to them.

He shot a look at the boy and then turned to her. He had strange, penetrating golden eyes that made him look like a hawk. Gwenhwyfar tightened her hold on the sword and moved closer to the boy.

"Children shouldn't be playing this close to the water. It's deeper than it looks," the monk said. "It would be better if you joined your father in the abbey."

How unfair! Just when I've found a new friend, mayhap. Who is this man? She pointed to the boy. "First, I am going to show him I can use a sword."

She had no recollection of what the monk answered, only that he raised his hand and a force pushed her, even though he'd not touched her. She dropped the sword and ran.

When she reached the safety of the abbey door, she turned around. There was nothing but mist.

* * * *

The next three days were uneventful. Gwenhwyfar didn't see the boy again, neither did she see the strange monk. She was quiet on the way home.

"What's the matter?" Leodegrance finally asked as they neared Cameliard. "You have hardly spoken. Did you not have a good time?"

"Yes, Da. I am glad I went. I'm just tired." For some reason, Gwenhwyfar didn't want to talk about the man with those yellow eyes. She still felt that push that had come from him.

She wondered about the boy. *He seemed nice and had saved her from falling into the lake. Who was he?* Her lower lip slipped into a pout. *He would have been fun to play with.*

CHAPTER FIVE—GALAHAD: PRINCE OF BENOIC
489 A.D. – 490 A.D.

It was one of the few times his mother, Niniane, let him into her inner sanctum deep within the cave below the Black Lake of Brocéliande. Most of her rituals were with her priestesses only. She stood now, facing the altar, arms raised in supplication.

Galahad looked around as he always did when allowed in. Hundreds of candles glowed softly from scones in the walls. A white marble altar stone stood near the far wall. A painted mural on one wall showed a white hart standing majestically in a glade. Opposite it, inside a circle of stones, a druid stood in his white robes offering a spray of mistletoe. Behind the altar was a painting of the Goddess in her trinity: the Maiden, the Mother, and the Crone.

Niniane turned. "Come."

He rose and went to her. "Madame?"

"You are young, Galahad, only nine. Stand before the Goddess, so I will know if I am right in sending you to Myrddin."

He acquiesced, thinking that just this morning, he had been with his father, King Ban of Benoic. He and his brother, Ector, practiced swordplay and then they'd taken the horses out and raced each other home. He barely finished grooming his mare when one of the priestesses arrived for him.

He was used to living in two worlds. In the man's world, as he chose to think of it, he lived an isolated life. The fosterlings who were training to be soldiers avoided him, thinking it odd that he lived in a cave under a lake much of the time. But he and his brother, Ector, were friends and he had the horses. Ban first put him on a horse at the age of three and he found he had a natural seat and light hands, even at that young age. Essentials, Ban said, for a good horseman.

Now he was back in his mother's world. He was comfortable here, even though he was the only boy. When he was very young, all the priestesses played with him as though he were their special toy. Even now, as he was learning weaponry and how to fight at Ban's court, he enjoyed spending his evenings with the women. One of the younger priestesses, Gaia, was teaching him the game of chess and he was determined he would win. Soon.

"Galahad." His mother touched his shoulder, breaking his reverie. "The Goddess has answered me. You may go."

He hesitated. "What is the answer, Madame? Am I leaving?"

Niniane brushed the dark strands of hair off his forehead. "Your hair always falls like this." She took a deep breath. "Yes. You are going to Britain for Bardic training. Now all I have to do is convince your father."

* * * *

"I tell you, Niniane, he needs to live with me." Ban paced the glade near the entrance to her cave. "He is my heir; he needs to live in the world of men. Already, the other boys think he's fey and they avoid him."

"He is fey," Niniane replied mildly. "Any time a child is produced of the Great Rite, he or she will be part fey."

Galahad huddled miserably on the rock near them. He hadn't wanted to be a part of this conversation, but his father insisted he be present. He didn't feel fey, whatever that was. Mayhap he would have to ask Gaia.

"Taliesin was my grandfather, Ban. He always said one of his bloodline would be a bard greater than he. Mayhap even become a druid. Do you not think it worthy of your son?"

Ban hesitated and Galahad could almost hear him thinking. When his mother started directing questions like that, she always won.

"*Certes*. The Lord knows Uther listens to Myrddin before anyone else. But the training takes nigh to twenty years; he should be learning the duties of a king if he's to lead Benoic."

"Ector could rule Benoic," Niniane replied. "He is your wife's son. I was your consort for the Great Marriage. Galahad belongs to the Goddess."

Ban stopped pacing. "The boy was born to be a warrior. Do you have any idea of how strong he is with the sword? At his age? And the horses . . . I swear, he talks to them and they understand him. Don't let him waste those skills!"

Galahad watched his mother's eyes begin to glaze; she was about to have a Sighting. Even Ban grew quiet.

When she spoke again, her voice was hallow and distant. "Galahad's destiny lies in Britain, not Benoic. Whether as bard or warrior, I cannot say." Her eyes cleared and her voice resumed its normal softness. "He must go, Ban."

"Remember before Ambrosius and Uther returned to Britain we signed a treaty pledging military support?" Ban asked.

"We pledged support," Niniane answered. "Mayhap Galahad can give it another way. I had the strangest feeling when I met Myrddin's young ward, Arthur, that he would need Galahad one day."

"Arthur trains to be a soldier," Ban replied and then sighed. "All right. We'll send our son to Myrddin. Mayhap he will know the answer."

* * * *

Later that evening, as Gaia was putting away the chess pieces, Galahad asked the two questions that had been pressing his mind all day.

"What is the Great Rite? And why am I fey?"

She paused and then smiled. "So that's what's been bothering you tonight. You weren't playing very well." She put the board on a shelf and went to sit on the chaise. "Come sit by me, Galahad."

He went over and sank down beside her. "Is this a bad thing?"

"Not at all." She settled against the wall. "Our festivals all honor the Great Mother who brings the spring rains and gives us good harvest. When a King is crowned, he pledges his oath to Her by coupling with the high priestess. Symbolically, she becomes the earth, the receptor of his seed. If a child results, the people see that the Great Mother has accepted the king. It is a promise that they will live in abundance and prosperity."

Galahad thought about that. "But why does that make me fey?"

"Part-fey only. You're very human." Gaia smiled again. "You know who Cernunnos is?"

"The demi-god of the Wild Hunt and the forest," Galahad answered. "We have a painting of him with antlers on his head. He lives in the land of Faerie, I think."

She nodded. "During the Great Rite, your mother represented the Goddess. She called on Cernunnos to represent the god so there would be perfect balance of energy."

Galahad wrinkled his forehead. "I still don't understand."

"Cernunnos has the ability to spirit-meld, to enter into a human body for a short time. He was there. That is why you have fey blood."

"That makes me different?" Galahad thought about the boys at Ban's court.

"In a way," Gaia answered, "mayhap it's why you can talk to horses." She reached over and brushed his hair off his forehead in a familiar gesture. "Or it might be why none of us could resist you as a baby. Cernunnos presides at the fertility rites of Beltane. Your smile melts hearts. You may be fated to have women love you."

Galahad opened his mouth to ask another question, then thought better of it. He wasn't sure he wanted to know the answer.

* * * *

Galahad held onto the sides of the coracle and peered through the mist. He could see nothing. Standing behind him, Barinthus slowly poled the boat across the Lake. Then suddenly they broke through to blue skies. Ahead of them loomed the Tor; he could see the labyrinthine maze that meandered up the hill and the whitewashed buildings beside it. The smell of apple blossoms lingered on the air, overriding the salt marsh.

The blue-cloaked form of Myrddin waited on the shore. As the coracle scraped sand and Galahad stepped out, Myrddin threw his hood back. It was the first time Galahad had seen the druid and he was taken aback by that piercing golden-eyed look. He swallowed hard and remembered what his mother had told him to do.

He knelt on one knee and looked at the ground. "I am here to be tested to be deemed worthy of becoming a bard."

Myrddin touched his shoulder and a surge of energy passed through him. He looked up.

"Come then." Myrddin gestured and began to walk the shoreline away from the path that led up the hill. "That way leads to the priestesses' domain. Men are not allowed there except by invitation." He walked around a jut of the hill and Avallach passed from sight. Here there were only rocks and grass and a steep bank. "This way," Myrddin said, and slipped sideways through a narrow entrance in the rocks. "Well come to my cave of crystal."

Galahad stared. Torchlight reflected off of walls made of thousands of bits of crystal. The room seemed to dance in brilliant colors of yellow, red, green and blue. For a moment, he felt dizzy, and then his equilibrium adjusted. Myrddin watched him.

"'Tis beautiful."

Myrddin nodded. "One of your first lessons will be to compose a song about your reaction to this room. We will see if that is where your talent lies."

He motioned toward a man who had joined them. "Articus is our musician and poet. The memorization of the required tales will be done with him."

Articus was a young man, dressed in the robes of a bard. He gave Galahad a friendly smile and Galahad breathed a sigh of relief.

"You will also have lessons in weaponry as well," Myrddin continued. "Every man must be able to defend himself, even though bards are excused from war."

Galahad had mixed reactions to that and his face must have showed something, for the next question Myrddin asked was the one he had dreaded.

"Do you want to become a bard?"

He took a deep breath. He could only answer honestly. "I don't know. I like to read and learn." *Whatever I become, I'll be the best at it.* "But," he added, "I enjoy swordplay and when I ride my horse." He stopped. Already, he was missing the horses.

"Well,"—Myrddin studied him for some time—"we shall see. Niniane wants this for you, but your father would rather you be a warrior-king." Myrddin closed his eyes as though in pain and put a hand out to steady himself on a nearby chair.

Galahad started to speak, but Articus shook his head. They stood in silence watching Myrddin. He moaned quietly to himself.

When he opened his eyes again, he looked agitated, but he only said, "Your future may hold something far different from what either of them expects." He turned to leave. "One other thing. When you step outside, you will notice the fog bank has closed in and hovers near the shore. Do not attempt to pass through it."

* * * *

Over the next year, Galahad worked hard. He heard the word 'discipline' in every lesson from memorizing thirty stanzas of a tale for recitation to learning not only Latin, but the Old Tongue as well. Myrddin believed the physical body had to be in excellent shape to balance the energy of the mind, so there were also grueling workouts—running in the soft sand and again in knee deep water while carrying dead weight, rope climbing, archery and sword practice, and the practical work like chopping wood for the priestesses. Galahad didn't mind. Instead he pushed himself to do even more than Myrddin asked. He liked having a strong, hard body that responded quickly and lithely to whatever he demanded of it.

The only time he saw any of the priestesses was on the sixth night of the new moon. Myrddin would gather mistletoe from the sacred oaks that grew on the other side of the Tor and at sunset he would take Galahad and Articus with him to the top of the Tor where stood an ancient circle of stones. One or another of the priestesses would join them in ritual prayers and asking of blessings with the strength of the coming moon. The priestess always worked sky-clad and Galahad never failed to admire and respect the sheer beauty of female bodies, in all their different shapes and sizes.

One day in spring, he gathered a new song he had composed about the feats of Uther and went looking for Articus. He found him in the *pharmakeutkos* mixing herbs and steeping bark and twigs for tinctures.

"You're busy?" Galahad asked as he handed him the pestle from the counter. "I've got the new verses, but I can come back later."

"Yes, do that," Articus said, not looking up. "I got behind on these potions. They need to be delivered to the hut dwellers today."

Galahad went back to the sleeping quarters he shared with Articus and carefully stowed the vellum. He took his sword and went outside. Whenever he practiced alone he always imagined a man in front of him, someone he could thrust and lunge and pretend to feint with. He moved along, advancing, side-stepping, lunging forward, not realizing that the sky had turned damp and grey and that mist now formed around him.

Suddenly, he bumped into something and the air cleared. He stood on the bank of the Lake and a young, reddish-haired girl was beside him. With a frightened look in her huge green eyes, she started to slip into the water. He grabbed her arm and steadied her. *Who is she?*

She wanted to know where he had come from and since he wasn't sure how he had gotten through the fog bank, he told her she'd better go back. She tossed her head at that and he sensed she had spirit.

He brandished his sword and then stopped, surprised, when she told him she could handle one too. *She's little, but she's feisty. This is going to be fun.* He grinned lopsidedly. "Show me."

They were interrupted by Myrddin and Galahad didn't think he'd ever seen him so upset. *I know I'm not supposed to be here, but why is he trying to scare the girl?* He was surprised at her boldness in talking back to the druid. More and more, he found himself admiring her. Myrddin made a magical sign and she dropped the sword and ran. Galahad sighed. *Now I'll never find out who she is.*

* * * *

"What happened? Why were you there?" They were inside the cave and Myrddin raked his hand through his long, tawny hair in agitation.

Galahad trembled. How could he convince Myrddin he didn't know how he had gotten there? That he'd felt almost pulled along by some current? "I was practicing with my sword. I must have covered more ground than I thought..."

Myrddin sighed. "You were not supposed to have been able to get through. Once you're in bardic training, the mists bar you. Yet you went." He was quiet for some time. "I believe your destiny lies outside these boundaries. I'm sending you back to Benoic."

Galahad's heart sank. He had failed. *My mother will be so disappointed in me.* "Please," he pleaded, not even noticing the faerie twitching Myrddin's ear hard, "punish me any way you want. I deserve it for disobeying. But do not make me bring shame to my parents!"

The druid touched his shoulder. "You show courage, Galahad. What happened today should not have. Your parents will understand. I will see to that."

Galahad hung his head. He could face Ban; his father wanted him to be a warrior. *But my mother? Will she forgive me?*

* * * *

Niniane put the letter down beside her chair. She was silent for some time.

Galahad tried to study the tapestry on the wall behind her chair. The scene was a lake, much like their own; the various shades of blue reflected the depths and contrasted to the greens of the waves. A faerie woman formed out of the white wispy crests. In her hand she held a sword.

"Tell me about the girl," Niniane finally said.

Startled, Galahad looked at her. "She was six years old. Her father was participating in the debate at the abbey. I don't know who she was."

Niniane picked up the letter. "According to this, she is why you were sent back."

"What?" Galahad exclaimed. "I hardly spoke to her. How can that be important?"

She shook her head. "I know not. Myrddin thinks she is the reason you were drawn through the mists. All he says here is that you must be kept away from her or you could destroy some dream for the future of Britain."

"But I don't even know who she is! What dream?" In his mind he saw the first frightened look in those green eyes before he'd caught her. There was something about her . . . she had courage. But how can admiring someone ruin a dream?

Niniane looked at the letter again. "He doesn't say. He doesn't even give her name; better I guess, so you won't know. Myrddin always did speak in riddles."

* * * *

Galahad was glad to be back with the horses. He'd missed them most the year he was gone. "Did you miss me, Caireen, as much as I missed you?" he asked as he brushed his mare in her stall the first morning back. "We'll go for a real run as soon as I've finished." The mare bobbed her head and nickered gently.

"Still talking to horses?" Lovel, one of the fosterlings that was training at the court, sneered as he came to stand near the stall.

Galahad continued to brush the horse. Lovel was a bully and he had no wish to get into a fight his first day back. His father was one of Ban's most staunch allies, so he was tolerated.

"I'm talking to you."

Galahad turned. "Oh. Then, in answer to your question, yes, I'm brushing my horse." He turned back.

Lovel entered the stall and clamped a hand on Galahad's shoulder. "Don't be sarcastic with me."

Galahad looked at him. "Take your hand off me."

"Make me."

His left hand still held the brush. He spun, bringing his arm up, breaking the hold. Furious, Lovel raised his fist.

Caireen flattened her ears and her teeth closed on his arm. He yelped in pain and backed out of the stall, rubbing the bruise already forming.

Galahad smiled. "Sometimes it pays to talk to horses."

* * * *

He knew it wasn't over, though. Lovel would round up his bulky friends, Marok and Persant, and try to make life a living hell. Out of sight of Ban, of course. Marok and Persant were fosterlings from Britain. Brothers of one of King Uther's captains. They could be sent back if they caused trouble, but Galahad wasn't about to tell anyone. He'd handle his own problems.

Galahad and Ector were lining up in the lists the following afternoon, ready to practice jousting. Several of the younger maids, probably shirking their duties elsewhere, stood nearby watching and giggling. Galahad ignored them as he adjusted the lance.

Ban had short lances made that were less weighty so the boys could begin practice at a younger age. They were wearing only armored shoulder plates for that would be their target. Galahad had just mastered maneuvering the lance before he left and he was eager now to see how much he remembered. Ector kicked his horse to a canter from the far end of the lists.

"Let's go," Galahad told Caireen. She tossed her head and lifted into the rocking chair gait. He positioned the lance under his right arm, using the saddle's pommel for balance. As they closed, he lifted it and aimed it at an angle. It struck Ector's shoulder and set him back of his saddle, but not unhorsed. Galahad finished his canter and turned his horse. Lovel was waiting at the other end; his friends were standing on either side of Ector, holding the horse's bridle.

Galahad sighed. *Best to get this over with.* Lovel was almost three and ten, two years older and heavier than Galahad, but he was clumsy. *If his friends will just stay out of this* . . . He glanced at his younger brother and then shouted, "Between you and me Lovel. No one else."

Lovel raised his lance in response and grinned at the group of girls as the two took their positions. As they closed, Lovel lowered his lance and aimed for the mare's chest. The lance sliced her shoulder and she swayed to her right and then went to her knees.

Enraged, Galahad launched himself at Lovel and they both rolled off the far side of his horse. His fist made contact with Lovel's nose; he heard a crack before Morak and Persant were on him. He reached for the fallen lance and used it as a staff to fend off Morak. Peripherally, he saw Ector lying on the ground and then he wasn't aware of anything except making contact with whichever body was in front of him.

Dimly, he became aware of running footsteps and then someone grabbed him, pulling the lance out of his hands. He turned, fists raised, and lashed out.

King Ban ducked and caught his son. "Easy. 'Tis over."

Galahad struggled momentarily and then began to focus. All three boys lay on the ground, unconscious. His mare was standing, favoring her left leg and one of the grooms was already leading her away.

Ector stood gaping at him and Ban looked concerned. "What happened?" Galahad asked. "I remember Lovel striking Caireen . . ."

"Battle frenzy, my son," Ban answered. "You fight instinctively, without your senses."

"Is it because I'm fey?" Galahad asked hesitantly.

"No. Your grandfather had it. I didn't know if you would." Ban put a hand on his shoulder. "It gives you extra strength, but 'tis dangerous if you just rush in."

"Then I shall have to be more skilled than most men," Galahad said, "so the weapon will be an extension of me."

"That you will," his father answered and looked over at the three boys the medics were helping to sit up. "From the looks of things here, King Uther may be wanting to recruit you into his army in a few years."

Galahad nodded solemnly. "Then I will need to be ready. Right now, I'm going to see to my horse. She didn't deserve what happened today."

"She'll be all right," Ban said, "the wound didn't tear a muscle."

"Still, she'll be waiting for me." He walked over to where the boys were groggily standing. Morak stepped back and all three looked at him warily.

Myrddin had taught him to center his energy. He kept his voice low and pleasant as his eyes bore holes through the bullies. "If any of you ever hurt my horse again, I'll kill you."

He turned and walked away, unaware the girls had stopped giggling and were staring after him, infatuated looks on their faces.

CHAPTER SIX—NIMUE: CHILD OF LIGHT
486 A.D. – 489 A.D.

"Are you sure I am ready?" Nimue looked up her foster mother beseechingly from her seat on a tree stump in the clearing in front of the small forest hut.

Dyonas, known far and wide as the Lady of the Forest and cousin to Vivian of the Lake, smoothed the child's long, pale blonde hair. "You're ten years old. You were pledged to the Goddess at birth."

"I know. And more than anything else, I have always wanted to serve Her." A tree dryad slipped out of the trunk stump and curled herself in Nimue's lap. She stroked it gently and smiled. "It's just that I'm so comfortable here."

Dyonas nodded. "You were sent to me to learn the ways of nature. Now it is time for you to learn the ways of spirit. You must push yourself past what is comfortable."

Nimue sighed, knowing her foster mother was right. An air sylph, shaped like a butterfly, brushed a slight breeze gently at her face, tickling her. She looked up and the tiny faerie winked. *"Our sisters and brothers will be there with you,"* she said.

"Yes," Dyonas said. "The forest creatures live on the Isle of Avallach as well. Why wouldn't they?"

Nimue's smile trembled. "What if I fail? What if the Great Mother does not accept me?" Since she was seven years old, it had been her biggest fear.

"Nimue," Dyonas said gently, "have I not taught you 'As above, so below?' If your mind can conceive it, and your heart believes it, you will achieve what you want. You will not fail. Trust me, my daughter."

* * * *

An ancient-looking woman waited for her on the shores as the barge glided silently toward the small dock on the Isle. Nimue stepped from it and knelt at the crone's feet. "I wish to enter the sisterhood of the Great Mother."

The hand that lifted her was surprisingly strong. "I am Meg, the healer," the old woman said. "Come. We will go to the House of Maidens where you will be living."

The house stood on the slope of the hill. It consisted of twenty cell-like rooms and a large central meeting area. Meg led Nimue to one of the rooms. It held a padded cot, a dresser and wash basin, and a chest for clothes. There was a small table and chair. An oil lamp sat on the table and several sheets of vellum and an inkwell and quill lay beside it.

"You'll be studying your lessons at night to be prepared for the next day," Meg said, "and your days will be full."

"What am I to learn first? Divination? Scrying? Herbals?" Nimue asked as she sat down and fingered the soft paper. Dyonas had told her of all these things.

Meg laughed softly. "Right now you are a postulant, requesting acceptance by the Great Mother. You will spend several moons simply doing the work that needs to be done. Liming the walls, making soap, doing laundry, preparing meals. This is a way for you to decide if you want this simple way of life, if you have the temperament for it. You will be allowed to observe the Salutation to the day's end and then, the Drawing Down of the moon. Eventually, we will allow you to participate. Only then, when you have become a novice, will we begin your training in the Mysteries."

Nimue asked, "When will I be able to meet the Lady of the Lake?"

"My dear,"—the old hand that touched her face was very light—"your training will be done by senior priestesses, but you won't meet the Lady until your initiation, several years from now."

Nimue's face fell. She had been hoping to meet her foster mother's cousin and to establish a bond. To let the Lady know she was willing to devote her heart and soul to becoming a priestess. She felt the old woman watching her and looked up.

"Patience is the first virtue a priestess must have," Meg said. "There will be times when it is essential for you to hold yourself in trance for hours, to be utterly still and hear the silence. Let that be your first lesson."

* * * *

Nimue attended her first Esbat two months later. The full moon rose early that night, during the threshold time of dusk. She fell in line behind the other maidens and proceeded up the steep hill of the Tor to the standing stones. In silence, they walked deosil around the circle. The candle in the blue-glassed Pelen Tan each held in her hands left a shimmering residue of white light. One of the priestesses, wearing a silver band encrusted with a moonstone about her forehead, stepped inside the stones. She faced the moon's rising and lifted her left hand, calling the quarters softly: from the east, the gift of air, from the south, the warmth of fire, from the west, life-giving water and from the north, the nourishment of Mother Earth from whence the Goddess came.

When she finished, the maidens placed their Pelen Tans on the ground and removed the white shifts each had worn. Nimue shivered in as the night air brushed against her bare skin, but surprisingly, she didn't feel embarrassed to be nude among this group of women.

The priestesses picked up silver chalices from the altar stone inside the circle and gave one to each of the maidens. Filled with the reddish water from the Holy Well, Nimue was careful not to spill any as she turned east and lifted the cup. The cool radiance of the moon washed over her and she caught a moonbeam in the chalice's liquid. For a moment, she felt that light flash out and surround her. She heard the priestesses beginning to chant:

"Blessed Mother Goddess, your silvery light washes over us, filling us with vibrant life energy..."

The voices softly faded as an image appeared in the mirror stillness of the cup. *A child, with pale hair the color of moonlight and grey eyes as clear as a rock-fed spring gazed out at her. "Mother . . ." she said.*

A wind rose, ruffling the water and the image dissolved. Nimue shook her head to clear it and heard the last of the priestesses's chant.

"We thank thee for the strength of your light and we give back to you what is yours, to replenish the earth." Ritually, each maiden knelt and poured the water from her cup into the soil. They stayed on their knees until a priestess approached each of them and slipped a green shift over their heads.

"Arise, young novices." The officiating priestess smiled, the moonstone in her nian-lann reflecting a soft glow. "Now you are sisters upon the path."

* * * *

The last two years have passed so quickly, Nimue thought, as she bundled up against the cold of December and joined the other novices in the central room of their building. Only this last final lesson, on the meaning of a chalice the Christians called the Holy Grail remained before she would officially become an acolyte. And then, after learning to lead the rituals, she would be initiated, the blue crescent moon tattooed on her forehead and she would hold the rank of priestess.

She loved her life. Even though the daily routine required much discipline, Avallach seemed to float in a time beyond Time, protected by the mists that hovered off the shore. The druid, Myrddin, would bring them news of Saxon unrest and occasionally, he would request one of the priestesses to accompany him back to King Uther for a healing ritual, but mostly their world was one of quiet and contemplation. Each ritual learned only increased her ability to center energy. She was looking forward to this lesson on the Grail; she had been told it was a powerful experience.

Nimue looked with interest at the girl Ceridwen ushered in. It was hard to guess her age, for her face was young, but her blue eyes held a wisdom that belied her years. She was dressed in a simple gown of white with gold braid and her long blonde hair was held back with a white ribbon.

"I am Astrala," the maiden said. "I carry the Cup of Nourishment in a procession toward Enlightenment. The San Graal is one of the ancient treasures of Britain, brought to us when the Dagda successfully escaped from Arawen, god of the Otherworld. Just as the water that a cup holds replenishes the earth, the Graal fills the need of any who drinks from it." She paused and looked around the room. "It has its most potency when it is with the other ancient treasures: the *Lia Fail*, the stone of destiny that spins the Wheel of Fate for the earth, the sword of Nuada, forged with Otherworld fire, and the spear of Lugh, the Shining One, who lights our air. When these objects are together, there is perfect balance and harmony in the world."

Nimue raised her hand. "Don't the Christians claim this chalice as their own?"

Astrala nodded. "Yes. Centuries ago, it was lent to the son of a carpenter, a young druid named Jesu, who used it at his last supper before he was brutally crucified. The new religion calls the cup the Holy Grail because his friend, Joseph of Arimathea, caught the Sang Real, the Blood Royal, in this same cup when Jesu's side was pierced. But it is older than that. Far, far older. You shall see."

Suddenly, the room was filled with the scent of apple blossoms, sweet and fragrant as springtime. Gradually, Nimue became aware of ethereal music rising blithely on the air, resonating melodically from the walls, filling the room totally and then falling softly in a sigh.

Even as she watched, light surrounded Astrala. It began as a delicate shimmer, emanating from her aura. Its luminescence grew into golden brilliance. The maiden held her hands together and slowly, a cup formed between them. A silver chalice, etched with runes, rimmed in gold. It glowed with a blazing luminosity that was blinding.

The music increased in intensity, yet remained somehow muted, and Nimue became a part of it. The light was reaching for her and warmth spread through her body, filling her with complete love and contentment. Never had she felt such peace. *It's coming from the Grail . . .*

And then the light began to withdraw, pulling itself back into the Grail and the image of Astrala faded until she became translucent. "The cup will be placed in the world again when the right person seeks it," she said, her voice a whisper on the wind, fading into silence.

The room was cold, the music gone, and only the crisp smell of coming snow hung in the air.

* * * *

The winter had been long and Nimue welcomed the warmth of the sun this late April day. Through the trees she had followed the small creek that tumbled down the Tor toward the holy well. She was seeking the tender shoots of brooklime that could be used for so many things from poultice for itching and burns to a tincture for expelling a dead fetus. Her basket was filled now with the stalks and paired, bright blue flowers.

Nimue set the basket on a large flat rock that jutted into the water, forming a bend in the stream and sat down beside it. She leaned over and let her hand trail in the water. A naiad rose to the surface, laughing, and sprayed her with droplets. The faerie dove gracefully under only to reemerge again.

As Nimue played with her, she wondered why more people didn't see the faeries. Even here on Avallach, most of the priestesses doubted the creatures existed. Yet they were everywhere! In the air, in the water, on every plant and tree. And the one that perched on Myrddin's shoulder when he came to visit . . . she was always tweaking his ear when she disagreed with him or ofttimes just to annoy him. No one ever seemed to see her; they just thought the druid had a peculiar habit of swatting his ear.

Nimue heard a twig break and looked up. She caught her breath. A beautiful white hart stood across the stream, antlered head raised majestically, looking at her with large limpid eyes. He didn't seem to be afraid of her.

"Well come, noble creature," she whispered. "Is it a drink you want?"

The hart stepped forward and lowered his head to drink. Nimue sat as though she were a part of the rock. White harts were messengers from the Otheworld. Seeing one meant something significant was going to happen, a big change mayhap.

He finished drinking and raised his head. To Nimue, it seemed the animal nodded once before he leaped gracefully into the forest and was gone.

It grew late; reluctantly she rose and walked back to her quarters. She took the basket to the room off the kitchen where the herbals were kept. A novice was there, preparing poultices, so Nimue left the brooklime on the table. She would have to hurry to get washed in time for the evening meal.

She took a short cut across the lawn and, as she rounded the corner of the Lady's private quarters, a young man accompanying Myrddin literally ran into her, sending her sprawling to the ground, breathless.

He knelt beside her and strong hands turned her, helping her to sit. "Are you all right?" he asked worriedly. "I'm terribly sorry. I wasn't looking where I was going."

She found herself looking into crystalline grey eyes, as clear as a northern spring.

"Yes . . . I'm fine." Suddenly she was aware he was still holding her and that his hands were spreading a strange warmth through her. Hurriedly, she tried to scramble to her feet.

He lifted her easily. She was surprised to feel that her legs were shaky. And why was Myrddin's faerie laughing? *Well, I must look a sight with grass stains and dirt all over my front.* She blushed in embarrassment.

Myrddin asked, "You're sure you are all right, Nimue? Arthur's not usually this clumsy."

She nodded and he looked relieved.

Arthur gave her a boyish smile. "Am I forgiven?"

She grew warm again under his gaze and wondered why. "*Certes,*" she said, "but I must go now . . ."

"We must, too," Myrddin added and tugged on Arthur's arm. "Uther will be waiting."

Nimue watched as they walked away. Whoever Arthur was, power radiated from him. That and something else, but she didn't know what.

* * * *

A fortnight later, on Beltane, Nimue was escorted from the House of Maidens to be prepared for her initiation that evening.

Two of the novices had bathed her, sprinkling the water with rare frankincense oil. They washed her hair in lavender water and braided it tightly, so that when it was loosened for the ritual that night it would hold little waves like the swells of the sea.

Then she was led to Meg. The woad had been prepared and the healer was carefully holding a tiny needle in a flame. Nimue lay down on the table that had been prepared. She had been told the tattoo would hurt, but that she must not cry out.

"Do you want some wine with a drop of henbane?" Meg asked before she began.

With all her heart, Nimue wanted to say yes. But she shook her head. A priestess must be able to bear pain. When she had to make a choice of vows to take, she had chosen chastity. The image of the blonde child calling her mother had bothered her, but conserving sexual energy and converting it to spiritual energy would give her stronger Sight. She would never feel the pain of childbirth, so accepting the pain of the needle was her atonement.

"All right then. Center yourself and think of the Great Mother. The crescent moon on your forehead will forever be her symbol of accepting you."

Nimue bit her lip as the needle pricked her skin, then again and again. She breathed deeply and willed herself to go into trance. Light flowed toward her, slowly enveloping her, a cocoon of protection, blanketing the pain. She relaxed and thought she heard the words: "Well come, child, to My service."

* * * *

The priestesses, led by the Lady this evening, proceeded single file to the top of the Tor. The full moon had risen and far below them, across the Lake, the needfires of Beltane were burning. Once this ritual was completed, many of the priestesses would be leaving to officiate at them.

The Lady stood in the middle of the circle of stones. Meg walked forward with Nimue.

"This is our newest daughter?" the Lady asked.

"This is she, Lady," Meg responded formally.

For the first time in four years, Nimue was able to look straight at Lady. She had, of course, seen her in rituals, but hadn't been allowed to speak to her. Now she was terrified. The Lady's voice was full of power. *The Goddess speaks through her.*

The Lady placed a nian-lann with three moonstones on Nimue's head, just above the moon crescent. "Come. Do not be afraid, Nimue. You have been Chosen."

Nimue stepped up to the Lady and the other priestesses formed a circle around them. She hoped she could keep from trembling on this most important night of her life.

Vivian removed Nimue's cloak, leaving her skyclad. "Feel the moon's silver rays wash over you. Draw it down, become one with Her."

A soft chanting had begun and the sweet smell of myrrh incense wafted toward her. She raised her arms in supplication. "Mother Goddess, your light cleanses me, filling me with your spirit. Let me come to you, my Mother. I draw down the moon." Nimue relaxed, going deeper into trance.

There was a battle. Men were shouting; metal clashed on metal. Dust churned everywhere as the great war-horses thudded against each other. A man emerged from the melée. He was tall and broad of shoulder, his hair bleached by the sun. Around his neck, he wore a golden torque. A king. His sword flashed flames of fire.

Another man rose through the clouds of dirt: a black-haired man who bore a startling resemblance to the first. They circled each other warily.

A third man, dark-haired and dark-eyed, battled his way toward them. He rode his horse as though it were an extension of him, slashing right and left as he fought his way through. "Lancelot!" someone called, but he didn't hear, so intent he was on reaching the king.

The king and the other warrior were struggling in earnest now, both of them wounded. He turned and Nimue saw his clear grey eyes.

She screamed, breaking the vision. The Lady was beside her, wrapping her in her cloak, holding her while she trembled.

"You have the Sight, child. I knew you would. Tell me what you saw."

"A king. He fell wounded . . . he looked liked . . ."

"Wounded? Not dead?" The Lady gripped her shoulders.

Nimue shook her head. "Who is he?"

Vivian released her. "His name is Arthur. He is our hope for keeping darkness from overtaking this land."

Arthur? Nimue remembered the power that she'd felt in the young man. Her image had been of him fully mature. At once, she knew he would be their future king. He already had that presence. She wondered if he knew.

And, somehow, she would be there to guide him.

CHAPTER SEVEN—THE CAPTAIN
489 A.D. – 491 A.D.

"Well?" Uther asked when Myrddin and Arthur returned from a trip to the Lake. "Does the Lady agree with you?"

Myrddin nodded. "She scryed and saw the same thing I did. The Dux Britannairum is amassing Scots and Picts at Eboracum."

Uther slammed his fist down on his desk and paced in the map room where they were seated. "Damnation! That man has been a thorn in my side for years. He sits between our Lothian allies and us and he's friendly with the Anglian Saxons. Now he's nourishing the northern barbarians as well?"

"There's more," Arthur said. "I talked to Cadwy before coming here. It seems those Saxons the Dux is so friendly with have a new leader. A man named Colgrin. He commands not only Anglia, but Linnuis to the east as well. That's at least twenty thousand men."

Uther stopped to stare at Arthur. "Then we won't sit here and wait. I'm mobilizing Cadwy's regiment. You will march to Eboracum and chase those barbarians back to the Wall." He signaled for Ulfius. "Notify Cadwy."

When his squire had gone, Uther sat back down and rubbed his hands together.

"You shouldn't have any trouble. They won't be expecting us to march that far north without provocation." He looked at Myrddin. "I'll take the Lady's word and yours."

"'Tis too bad we can't take one of the priestesses with us," Arthur said.

Myrddin raised an eyebrow. "Any one in particular, Arthur?"

Arthur felt himself blush. "Well, she was pretty." *And so tiny and, delicately built! She had been light as a butterfly in my arms.*

Uther looked at him quizzically. "You fancy a priestess?"

"He does not!" Myrddin leaned forward. The faerie tweaked his ear hard and he swatted at her. "Arthur, Vivian told me Nimue has chosen vows of chastity. You will always respect and honor the women of the Isle."

Arthur met Myrddin's glare. "I have no intention of disrespecting her. There are enough willing women close by."

"True enough." Uther sighed a little. "I miss those days; Ygraine is not about to let me loose."

Arthur was surprised. The women he bedded sometimes mentioned that Uther had a reputation for taking any woman he wanted, willing or not. It was one of the things, they said, that they liked about Arthur; he never pressured them. *Why would I?* "But you're the king."

Uther laughed. "Ah, yes. If you should marry the woman you desire, you'll soon find how strong that delicate thread is that binds."

"I doubt I'll ever marry," Arthur replied. "I don't have time to spend humoring some clinging, dependent woman. I'm a soldier first." He felt a sudden, sharp pain on his ear, but when he reached up, there was nothing there.

"You are young. Wait until you meet some spirited woman who stands up to you." Uther grinned. "Like Ygraine."

They were interrupted by Cadwy's arrival. "You wanted to see me?"

"Yes," Uther answered and gestured him to sit. "It's time to see what these young cubs you've trained are capable of. Take your entire cohort of five hundred cavalry and ten centuries of infantry as well. And find Pellinore; you'll have need of his Welsh archers." He turned back to Arthur. "Because of your success as my procurator, I'm making you a lieutenant. You'll answer to Cadwy as your captain."

Arthur swelled with pride. *This is what I've wanted!* Then he realized all three men were watching him. Myrddin always told him pride was useless; producing what was what counted. Doing the job. He struggled to control his emotions, but he still couldn't help grinning. "Thank you, my lord. I will do my best."

* * * *

Arthur always enjoyed talking with King Pellinore, for he was a born storyteller. He insisted a strange beast inhabited the forest near his fort and his goal, when he returned, was to hunt it down. Myrddin sniffed indignantly when he heard it. Pellinore had arrived from Dinas Emrys several months ago as part of Uther's build up of troops, and although he was at an age where many men were retired, he insisted on staying with his men. He also brought his oldest son, Lamorak, with him.

Pellinore had just finished another description of the beast he was questing after at the campsite one evening when an outrider rode in on a nearly spent horse.

"Colgrin has joined with the Dux," he panted.

"How many troops?" Cadwy asked.

The scout accepted a tankard of ale. "Several hundred, I'd say."

"Do you want to send for reinforcements?" Arthur asked.

Cadwy shook his head. "We've a thousand infantry. We should be able to handle this."

The next morning they approached the river Dubglas, within sight of the walled city of Eboracum. Cadwy had ridden to the back to form the cavalry into right and left flanks. Suddenly, ahead of them, Colgrin's men emerged from the woods, axes raised, their berserkers driving them on. With their light hair, they looked like the swells of a yellow sea as they surged forward.

Arthur spun his horse around. Cadwy was too far back to command the infantry. He turned to Gwalchmai, Gryflet and Bedwyr. "Help the centurions define their maniples. Phalanx position, *hastati* at the fore. Make sure they carry two spears." He turned to search for Gerient, but the man was already at his side. "Work with the archers. Mayhap we can stop them first." Gerient nodded and was gone.

In amazement, Arthur watched the unquestioned discipline as the troops formed squares and the shield walls went up. The first two lines had their spears thrust out. The outside units thrust sideways, the inner troops held theirs straight up, making each maniple of twenty men look like an advancing porcupine. The archers had lined either side of the road and the sky soon rained black arrows.

The Saxons halted. Arthur held his breath. *Their round shields, half the size of the oblong Roman ones Uther's army still uses aren't any match for our speared units advancing on them. Throwing their axes will do little harm against the solid shield wall. Their only other weapon is the seaxe. A long knife, yes, but nothing to compare to our long swords if we close with them.*

"Thank God the devils don't fight on horseback." Cadwy was beside him. "All we have to do now is herd them back." He gestured with his hand and Arthur realized the cavalry was doing just that, although a great deal more menacingly. The foremost riders had their lances in position and were beginning the canter.

The Saxons broke and ran toward the town. The gates swung open, even as volley after volley of arrows rained at Cadwy's men from the battlements. The cavalry stopped outside of arrow range. They had managed to run down the Saxons who were in the back of the line.

Myrddin thumped Arthur on the back. "Well done. We didn't have a single casualty. Can't say that often."

Arthur felt a wisp of something brush his cheek, but when he touched his face, there was nothing there. He thought he heard a soft sigh. *Odd.* He looked at the closed gates. "Still, we have a job to do."

Cadwy rode up and heard him. He nodded. "Now you'll get a real taste of why the Romans were so powerful. We'll lay siege to the city the way they used to do."

Over the next week the cavalry surrounded the city and waited for the heavy siege engines to catch up to them. Some of the infantry went in search of rocks and others were instructed to begin building the earth mound toward the wall that would allow the tower engine with its battering ram to strike at the upper levels where the wall was weaker. Archers covered them as they worked. When the two big catapults called onagers finally lumbered into camp, several piles of large rocks at the ready.

They hurled these toward the battlements, keeping the Dux's men busy while more men worked on the mound, ever closer to the wall. When darkness fell, they withdrew to their camp dragging their wounded and dead with them.

Arthur dreaded taking the body count daily. Death was a fact of war and he gritted his teeth, determined they'd be ready to storm the wall and break the siege.

The next morning brought bad news. Another scout arrived as they were breaking their fast. Colgrin's brother, Baldulf, was marching west toward them, bringing reinforcements.

"At least five hundred," he said.

Cadwy looked like he wanted to swear. He turned to Arthur. "Take half of the cavalry. About ten miles from here the road cuts through some fields. There's enough tree cover for you to wait until his troops are out in the open. They'll be in marching formation and won't have time to regroup."

"You're putting me in charge? As senior officer?" He looked at Myrddin, seated across from him, but the druid only smiled and tapped his rowan staff to the floor.

Cadwy grinned. "Uther said to find out what you young cubs are made of. Do you want me to send one of the other captains with you?"

Arthur didn't hesitate. "No, Sir! I've waited for this for nearly four years. I won't let you down."

* * * *

Arthur chewed on his fingernail as he anxiously waited within the shade of the forest late that afternoon. They had arrived well in advance of any Saxons and it was the waiting that was making him nervous. He glanced over at his friends. Bedwyr was calm, as always, conversing quietly with Gryflet. Gwalchmai looked like a small boy on his way to a county fair and Cai's face was set in stern lines. He was ready for a fight.

He wished Myrddin were beside him, but the druid had told him if he were to become any kind of officer, he must not depend on him. As always, Myrddin was right.

"There!" Gerient pointed. "Dust."

Arthur squinted. He could just make out the front line coming over the horizon. For a moment, he questioned himself. *Is this the best place? Would I have been smarter to look for the road's passage through the trees? We could have ambushed them from both sides and behind . . .* He took a deep breath. *Cadwy recommended this spot. And cavalry would have a hard time within the confines of a narrow road. Better that two hundred fifty horsemen charge five hundred walking men in the open.*

Harnesses began to jingle. "Wait!" he said quietly. "Remember, the closer they get, the less time they'll have to be ready. Wait until you can see the color of their eyes!"

Cai hissed and balled a fist. "That close? Are you sure?"

Arthur looked at him. "Yes. And keep the horses quiet!"

Every nerve fiber he had stood on edge. The Saxons were getting bigger. He gripped his spear. They had left the heavy lances at the camp, knowing the charge would have to be fast and there would be no time to maneuver the lance into place.

The steady clomping of booted feet sounded like thunder. Closer they came. Closer . . . "Get ready!" Arthur whispered and the command went down the ranks like a rustle in tall grass. He lifted his arm. *Wait. Just another minute . . .* He dropped his arm and two hundred and fifty horses sprang from the forest as one unit.

There was nowhere for the Saxons to go. Their front lines went down to the thrown spears and they tripped over their dead comrades trying to reach the forest. The horses blocked them, using their teeth and hooves as they had been taught to do. Only a few managed to escape. The wings of the cavalry line swung closed, encircling the survivors.

Arthur looked for the leader, Baldulf. He found his standard, lying on the ground, but no signs of the man. He sighed. The man would have made a good trophy of his first successful command. He signaled for their wounded to be lifted on horses and the prisoners tied in a rope chain. Slowly they began the march back to Eboracum.

* * * *

Another surprise waited for him when he arrived. Myrddin and Cadwy were pacing in front of the command tent. Word had come from Uther.

"The German, Cheldric, has landed six hundred ships near Durovernum. At this time of the year! Near Samhain! Twenty thousand men." Cadwy shook his head unbelievingly. "That's Aesc's, land."

"Is that Saxon amassing numbers, too?" Arthur asked.

"That's what it looks like," Cadwy answered. "Uther's orders are to abandon the siege and meet him in Londinium."

Arthur narrowed his eyes in concentration. "That would be a strategic spot. We're closer there if the Dux should try to move south, than we are at Ambresbyrig. And from Londinium we can watch Anglia and the southeast as well."

Myrddin nodded. "Correct. I can see you remembered your lessons, Arthur. Uther will be pleased."

* * * *

Uther set up headquarters in the old Roman walled part of town. A wooden drawbridge with a three-story gatehouse served as security.

They were seated in the lavish guest quarters of the Bishop of Londinium's rectory. Arthur had just started his account of halting Baldulf when the bishop interrupted them.

He was in a state of excited agitation. "What is it that cannot wait?" Uther asked.

The bishop drew himself to his full height. "You forget, Sire, that you are my guest."

Uther raised an eyebrow. "And have you forgotten that I am your high king?"

But the bishop wasn't about to be cowed. "Our newly appointed bishop in Caerleon has had a vision, my lord! One that is of utmost importance to the Church."

Uther looked annoyed and Arthur almost smiled. The king didn't have much use for the pomposity of the church.

"Dubricius? He's young. Did he dream of saving the world?" Uther asked.

The bishop appeared offended. "I thought, since he is the bishop for the area that Ambresbyrig is in, you would want to know."

"Go on, then. We have things to discuss."

The bishop glanced from Uther to Arthur and then a little skeptically at Myrddin, who fixed him with a yellow-eyed glare.

"Dubricius didn't have a dream, Sire. It was a vision. He was leaving church on the night before Samhain, when suddenly he heard music and didn't know where it was coming from and then a light began to glimmer . . ."

Arthur heard Uther groan under his breath and almost did the same. The bishop tended to be long-winded.

"There was a procession," the bishop said. "A man led it with a spear that dripped blood and a girl followed him, carrying a platter to catch it. Then came two boys with candlesticks. Dubricius said those candles made the whole church bright as day."

"Are you sure the good bishop didn't have too much wine? Get to the point."

"I am." The bishop sniffed and his eyes held the glaze of rapture. "The last person in the procession was a maiden, dressed in white and gold and light radiated from her. She was almost transparent because of the luminosity. And then a cup formed . . . a silver chalice, etched in runes, rimmed in gold. The cup itself glowed with a blinding light." He paused and looked at them again. "It was the cup Jesu used at his Last Supper! We call it the Holy Grail."

"Did he keep it?" Arthur asked.

The bishop shook his head. "No. Just as suddenly as the whole procession appeared, it disappeared, leaving only darkness. But I thought you would want to know."

With barely concealed politeness, Uther dismissed him. He turned back to Arthur. "As I was about to say, I've sent to Armorica for reinforcements. I grew up with Kings Hoel, Ban, and Bors. Now that their enemy, King Euric, is dead, the major threat to their lands is gone. Hoel will be here in early spring; if we need more men, Ban and Bors will come later." He paused and looked at Arthur. "What do you think the Dux's next objective will be?"

Arthur was surprised and pleased to be asked. *He wants my opinion!*

He furrowed his brows. "The Dux wants to conquer the south. To do that, he will have to take Lindum."

Uther exchanged a glance with Myrddin. "Why?"

"It sits at the crossroads of the Fosse Way and Ermine Street," Arthur replied. "The Pennine Mountains and the forests of Eboracum divert most north and south bound traffic in eastern Britain to those roads. From there he could control Anglia and Linnuis and still hold the north."

"Very good. As much as the petty kings grumble and complain, they've all seen the need for a united Britain. Only the Dux Britanniarum still claims title to the old Roman province." Uther glanced at Myrddin again and then back to Arthur. "Cadwy tells me you did well at your first command."

Arthur had been hoping the king would have received word. "Yes, Sire. We stopped the Saxons. I brought the surviving hostages back."

Uther nodded. "Baldulf got away?"

Arthur's face fell. He wasn't proud of that. He needed to be the best at whatever he did. He should have been able to capture the leader. "Yes, Sire."

"Don't look so upset. You'll have another chance to fight him." Uther leaned across the table toward him. "Your face still shows your emotions. When you lead your men, they must never see your doubt or feel your fear."

"My men?"

"Your men. I'm giving you command of your own company. Captain of one hundred men."

Arthur stared at him, speechless. Uther laughed and rose to leave. "On the other hand, sometimes an expression is worth a lot of words."

* * * *

The Dux, with Colgrin and Baldulf, laid siege to Lindum shortly after Imbolc, although February was a cold month. Hoel arrived in March, bringing a full cohort of cavalry and a thousand infantry. He also brought his fosterling, a twelve-year-old boy named Accolon.

"He squires for me," Hoel explained when Arthur asked where he wanted him placed.

Uther's army moved to harry the Dux. As they rode north, Arthur observed Accolon. The boy was tall for his age, with black hair and blue eyes, and he was strong. He had little trouble handling his foster-father's fourteen-foot wooden lance.

"He's good with that," Arthur told Hoel one evening as they prepared camp and were watching the boy make a practice run at a shield hanging from a tree.

Hoel nodded. "Our Breton boys start practicing with the lance when they're six or seven years old."

Arthur was surprised. *I couldn't even hold one until I was eight!* "How does he have the strength?"

Hoel saw his look of disbelief and laughed. "They practice with shorter lances made of lighter wood. 'Twas Ban's idea. He thought his son, Galahad, was spending too much time with his mother, Niniane, and her ladies, so he wanted to be sure the boy grew up to be a man."

Niniane. Where have I heard that name? Then it came to him. *The Isle. Seven years ago.* "Is this Galahad's mother a priestess?"

"Yes. Galahad was a product of the Great Marriage. Are you familiar with that?"

Arthur nodded. Myrddin had explained it to him once. Ambrosius had used it when he was king and removed Vortigern from power. Uther hadn't taken part; it was why, Myrddin said, the petty kings still fought among themselves. The next king would have to perform the ritual to ensure Britain's peace and prosperity. *Well, I'm not worried about that.*

"How old is Galahad?"

"Almost two and ten."

"Close to Accolon," Arthur said. "Is he as strong?"

Hoel raised an eyebrow. "He can THROW the lance, overhand."

Arthur looked at him incredulously. "That is nearly impossible."

Hoel shrugged. "He's competitive, hates to lose."

Like me. "I should like to see that lance throw," Arthur said. "Mayhap I'll meet Galahad some day."

* * * *

When they arrived at Lindum, most of the fighting had already been done. Uther met them in front of his tent with a grin on his dirt-smeared face.

"Colgrin and Baldulf left under cover of darkness last night with what was left of their army. We have killed nearly half. Damnation, if I'd thought they were going to run, I'd have chased them myself."

Hoel laughed. "You'll get the opportunity. What's left that must be done here?"

"The Dux," Uther replied and stopped smiling. "Tomorrow, with your men and Arthur's, we'll rout the bastard and send him packing."

Arthur's men worked alongside Hoel's the next day. The Armorican was an experienced warrior and master strategist. More than once, his fighting technique impressed Arthur. *If all Armoricans were trained like this . . .* Arthur decided he could definitely learn more and stuck to Hoel as they met the sally coming out the gates.

It was late in the day when the white flag waved over the battlement. Arthur was the first to see it. "He's surrendering!" he yelled at Uther. "Lindum is ours!"

* * * *

They returned jubilant to Ambresbyrig. The Dux had signed a treaty allowing him to keep his fort, but forfeit a great portion of his land. He would be licking his wounds for quite a while.

Hoel settled his men in Londinium. With twenty thousand new Germanic troops, a semi-permanent fortification was needed closer to the east. All was quiet that summer into the fall.

They were breaking their fast one crisp, cool morning, when Pellinore received good news. His brother, King Pelles of Carbonek, along with King Uriens of Rheged and King Leodegrance of Cameliard, had been successful in turning back the Picts from an early spring raid along Hadrian's Wall. Pelles was about to hold a large feast and wanted the high king's attendance.

Uther nodded when Pellinore read the note to him. "It might be a good opportunity. The past two years, we've had so much fighting in the south. With Hoel stationed in Londinium for now to watch the new Germans, this will give me a chance to make sure I still have the northern king's alliances. And," he added as he patted the small paunch he'd developed, "Pelles always has a fine spread."

He was right. Arthur sat back in his chair at Pelles' banquet, held his stomach and groaned. He had been a glutton. There had been roast boar and mutton and venison stew, quail in pomegranate sauce, pasties, oatcakes and honey and several kinds of cheese. But it was the seafood, for Pelles loved to fish, that had done Arthur in. Broiled trout and pike and lobster soaked in butter. He moaned again and closed his eyes.

"Do you care for a pudding or pie?" a young girl asked.

Slowly, he opened an eye. A pretty child was standing there, her auburn hair neatly braided; her blue linen gown matched her eyes and was smooth and unstained. She couldn't have been more than five or six.

"Who are you?" he asked.

She smiled, showing a dimple. "My name is Elaine. I am a princess. Pelles is my father."

Arthur returned the smile, but the thought of more food made him a little sick. "No thank you, Elaine."

"Princess Elaine," she said.

Arthur raised an eyebrow. Even Uther didn't generally go by his title. "I beg pardon, my lady."

She frowned and looked him. "You have soiled your shirt. There are stains on it."

He looked down. *Certes*! All the men had stains on their shirts. It came from eating. Then he noticed she had none. How could a mere child be so neat? He smiled at her. "Don't princesses eat?"

She didn't smile back. "*Certes*, I eat. I'm just careful and don't dribble. My nurse, Briesen, says a lady can never be too clean."

Prissy little thing. An older and very attractive serving girl caught his eye and then he was interrupted by a commotion across the hall where Pelles was now on his feet, shouting at Balin. *Balin. He and his twin Balan were forever getting into trouble and trying to pick fights. He was glad those two weren't in his company of men. What had Balin done now? Pelles was obviously insulted.*

He excused himself from Elaine who looked like she was about ready to launch into a lecture on proper eating habits, and drifted closer to Pelles' table, near Myrddin.

"How dare you say I don't have the Grail?" Pelles' face was red.

"Show it to us then," Balin answered. "You claim it can give a man any food he desires, just like Jesu did with the loaves and fishes. I say, prove it."

"Isn't this banquet proof enough?" Pelles responded angrily.

Arthur looked at Myrddin and whispered, "Are we talking about the same cup the bishop mentioned?"

Myrddin nodded, eyes semi-closed as he did when he was in half-trance. "It would appear so. There is an old legend that a cup was one of Britain's thirteen treasures, brought here by The Dagda."

"Did it have magic powers like the bishop said?"

"No doubt," Myrddin answered. "Supposedly, the cup was guarded by the lineage of a centuries old dynasty linked to Joseph of Arimathea."

"So there is a Christian connection?"

Myrddin opened his eyes. "The Christians have claimed it. The Romans decided to change Jesu's message."

A table was overturned and suddenly the hall became still. Pelles had asked for a sword and challenged Balin. In response, Balin had thrown the table down even as his own sword was brought.

Uther stood. "Enough! I'll confine you to the gaol, Balin. Pelles is our host."

Pelles glanced toward the king. "If it pleases you, I would like to finish this. No one calls me a liar."

Uther studied him and then nodded. "This is your home. As you will."

A space was cleared and the two men circled. Balin was much younger and more agile, but Pelles was a seasoned warrior and much more levelheaded than the hot-tempered Balin. They engaged and pressed, lunged and thrust, feinted and parried and Balin finally delivered a blow that found not Pelles, for he had side-stepped, but the oak table. The blade went in and stuck. Frantically, Balin tried to pull it out. It broke.

He looked over to Pelles, who stood waiting for him. "I will not yield!" He sprinted toward the door.

Pelles pursued him. At the doorway to the hall, spears were hanging in neat rows, having been left there when the soldiers entered the dining hall. Balin grabbed one and turned, jabbing fiercely.

Pelles had no time to stop. The spear cut through his upper thigh, barely missing his groin, and lodged there, quivering. Balin gave him one horrified look and ran into the courtyard. Minutes later, his horse was heard, pounding out the gate.

Myrddin was the first to reach Pelles. Uther called for the army medics and Elaine's mother, who was quite pregnant, hovered anxiously behind them as he was carried to the infirmary.

Arthur followed Myrddin. If anyone could stop the man's pain, it would be the druid. How many times in childhood had Myrddin not said strange words that he didn't understand over a cut or scrape and the pain had gone?

But Myrddin was looking worried. He held the king's hand while the medics worked to remove the spear and chanted, but something wasn't going right.

It was only when they returned home the next day that Myrddin brought his white mule alongside Arthur and finally spoke.

"The wound won't heal."

"You mean, for a long time? Or that he'll walk with a limp?" Arthur asked.

The druid shook his head. "If Pelles was the guardian of the British treasure, he did it ill service by foolishness of fighting with Balin."

"But it was his right," Arthur answered. "Even Uther said so."

"Pride is a deadly sin, Arthur, in any religion. And that is what Pelles is guilty of." He sighed. "Look around you. This land is green and fertile. Pelles has always been successful enough in the fishing he loves to do to supply our armies." He swept his hand across the expanse. "Soon this will be a wasteland. And the Fisher King will fish no more."

CHAPTER EIGHT—FATE OF BELTANE
491 A.D.

Morgana walked sedately beside the sister as they distributed their herbs, but her eyes were watchful. Uther's army had returned, victorious from a battle at Lindum and the men would be lusty. Beltane was just a day away. This year, she was going to slip away. Ever since last Beltane, she had done nothing but act pious. She had quit complaining about the chores she was given. She attended chapel faithfully and confessed to small sins she cared nothing about, but accepted her penance with humility. The abbess had praised God and declared that Morgana had seen the Light. Morgana had snickered at that. To her, life was survival of the fittest . . . or most cunning. No one would suspect if she became ill suddenly after the evening meal and couldn't attend Compline. No one would be waiting for her to try and sneak away.

I'm near four and twenty, far too old to be a virgin still. Why is that demon Uther still alive and paying the sisters to imprison me? She sighed, knowing the answer. The sum he paid them was nothing to what a dowry would cost for a proper marriage and she was, by blood, a princess. But tomorrow night would be different. She would be a woman.

She smiled a little as she gave the cooper the supply of herbs he regularly ordered. His blue eyes twinkled at her as he held her hand for as long as he dared with the sister standing in attendance. Morgana felt his thumb circling her palm and her smile widened. She had some other herbs—hellebore, woodruff, vervain—that would go well into a stew and have some very pleasing after effects. In the year of her 'conversion' she had devised the idea of visiting and tending to the sick in town. The abbess was pleased with that as well. *By their Christos,'tis easy to fool the lot of them!* Now, in the cooper's supply, a note nestled, asking him to send word that he was ill and needed tending. She hoped her feigned humbleness this past year would work.

* * * *

Morgana slipped like a shadow along the wall of the abbey. It was past Compline and the needfires of Beltane were dying, but Uther's men would still be rowdy in the village.

She walked quickly to spot near the road about halfway between the village and the fort. It was a secluded thicket of bracken and hawthorn near a copse of beech trees. In her black hooded cloak, she was invisible until she chose to show herself. She shivered, either from anticipation or from the fact that she was wearing only a thin shift under the cloak.

She let several groups of drunken men stagger by. It was nearly midnight by the time a single man made his way up the road. As he got closer, he appeared to be about her age, tall and broad shouldered. *This is the one.* She stepped out onto the road.

The man stopped abruptly. "Who are you?" he asked.

Morgana smiled. "Follow me," she said and backed away toward the thicket.

She removed her cloak and faced him, knowing that in the slanted moonlight, he would be able to see her large breasts through the thin material.

He needed no other invitation, stripping his clothes off quickly. She inhaled sharply as he walked toward her naked. She had chosen well. He was solidly-muscled, his belly flat, and the appendage that protruded stiffly from him fascinated her. She had no idea a man would be so big.

She reached out to touch him and found herself suddenly on the ground, his hands feverishly pushing the smock over her face, pinioning her arms among the folds. *I cannot touch him!* She struggled for a moment to free her arms and then gasped as he pushed her breasts together, running his tongue from the tip of one to the other. *This is what I have been waiting for! Sheer ecstasy. I was made for this.* He put a hand between her thighs and spread them. She welcomed his weight as he rolled on top of her and felt that hard shaft probing. Then she screamed.

He clamped a hand over her mouth as burning pain seared through her. It seemed as though a knife had pierced her, tearing at her insides. With each thrust, the raw skin was mangled further. She felt ripped apart. The man plunged inside her forcefully one more time and then lay still.

"You were a virgin." He sounded surprised, but Morgana was too sore to answer.

Suddenly she heard the sounds of men coming up the road. By their laughter, she could tell they were drunk. *Sweet Mary! What if he called them over? Men shared women on Beltane. She couldn't take any more of this. They would kill her.*

"Arthur! Arthur! Where are you?" one of them called.

The man quickly pulled on his clothes. "Those are my men." He slipped his boots on and turned to her. "I didn't mean to hurt you. I thought you were . . . that you wanted . . ." He stopped. "Stay here and be quiet until I can get them moving." He leaned over and gave her a soft kiss. "I'm sorry." And then he was gone.

She stayed in the thicket, hugging her knees to her chest, until all was quiet. The pain had diminished and she recalled now, the pleasure she had felt when he suckled her breasts and the sensualness of his kiss. Somehow, in her mind, it blended. The pain dissolved into pleasure.

His men had called him Arthur. She would have to find out who he was.

* * * *

A fortnight later, a note arrived from town. The abbess found Morgana tending the herbal garden.

"It seems the cooper has fallen ill. He's requested some medicinal herbs be brought."

Morgana hid a smile and stood. "I'll put some snakeroot and figwort in a stew. That should help him."

The abbess nodded. "I'm going to have to trust you to go by yourself. All the sisters have chores this afternoon."

Morgana was the picture of innocence. "Yes, Mother. I will be sure to leave the door open at his place so nothing amiss happens."

The abbess excused her and Morgana could hardly restrain herself from leaping into the air. The memory of pain had passed and she longed to be taken again. The cooper wasn't as powerfully built as Arthur had been, but he was a man.

She found him sitting in a comfortable chair in front of a small brazier, a blanket over his knees. She set the bowl of stew on the table and went to him.

When he saw she was alone, he grinned widely and shoved the blanket aside.

"I didn't know if I were going to have to be sick or not," he said and pulled her into his embrace. His lips were hard and crushing and she pressed her breasts against his chest, already aching with need. Laughing, he pulled her toward the bedchamber.

"Wait," she said. "Have the stew first."

"I'm hungry only for you," he answered and leaned over to bite her neck.

It hurt a little, but before she could wince, the spot tingled pleasurable. She smiled. "This is a special stew. You will like the effects."

His eyes gleamed and he sat down and began to eat.

"Do you know a soldier named Arthur?" she asked while he was eating.

"Who doesn't?" he answered, barely looking up from the stew. "He's Uther's protégé. The youngest captain in the whole army."

A captain! From the brief glimpse she'd gotten of his face before they stepped into the darkened thicket, he was a good-looking one as well. She wondered if she could arrange somehow to see him again. She sighed. She was lucky to have been able to come here without an escort. How would she ever be able to get into the fort or find him? He probably had all the women he wanted. Then the cooper's next words affirmed her thoughts.

"The word is that he never beds the same woman more than once in a moon. There are too many of them waiting." He laughed. "Has he caught your eye?"

Morgana felt herself blush. "No. I don't know him."

The cooper leaned over the table toward her. "Don't bother with him. While he likes his sport, he's all soldier. I've never seen anyone more determined to lead his men and win battles." He leaned back and pushed the bowl away. "I think you'll find I know how to satisfy a woman and I'll be available whenever you are." An odd expression crossed his face as the stew began to work its magic. He reached out and took Morgana's hand. "And with you, my little witch, able to concoct . . ."

There was a knock on the door and he groaned. A moment later, one of the sisters walked in.

Morgana's heart fell to her stomach. *All my work! The effects are starting. I wanted to get into his bed and in just a few moments, I would have.* She clenched her fists below the table. *I thought all the sisters were supposed to be busy today!*

"There you are!" the sister said brightly and came toward them. "Mother was getting worried that you were gone so long." She turned to the cooper. "Are you feeling better?"

"You can see his eyes are glazed," Morgana said irritably for she knew now if she touched him that he would be in a frenzy. The old hag from back home had schooled her well in the aphrodisiac's use, for it was a profitable herb to sell. "He obviously has a fever. I'll stay a little while longer."

"Oh, no," the sister answered. "You'll be late for choir practice. Since we learned this year that you can sing, Mother insists you be there."

Morgana groaned. *So close. So very, very close.*

* * * *

When her courses didn't come with the next moontide, Morgana wasn't concerned. She had skipped them before, but when she began vomiting in the mornings, she knew something was wrong. She tried to hide the sickness by not eating in the mornings.

The abbess called her into her private office and closed the door one afternoon several weeks later and gestured for her to sit. The abbess paced and Morgana watched her uneasily.

She stopped in front of her. "Are you with child?"

Morgana felt the blood drain from her face. *Certes. How stupid have I been? I never even thought that one time—a first time—could do that. Why didn't I chew the motherswort?* Hysteria rose inside of her. *Of all people, I should have known better!* She took a deep breath. "I think I am."

The abbess's face grew hard. "How did that happen?"

Suddenly, Morgana was tired of the charade she'd been playing. *Let these holy sisters go to their Christian hell. I have a right to use my body.* She raised her head and looked into the abbess's face. "At Beltane."

The woman was livid. "Beltane? You took part in a pagan festival while you reside in a house of the Lord?"

If only you knew the Rites I've witnessed. And how I wanted to participate in them like I never have your endless hours of praying and chanting. Time for the truth. Sort of anyhow. "Yes. And not just one man. Lots of them. I lost count." She actually enjoyed watching the abbess bend over and grasp the edge of the desk. *Is she going to faint? Too bad it isn't true!*

The lady held onto the desk and helped herself around it to sink into the chair. "I have failed in my mission to God," she said, her voice nearly a whisper. "I vowed I would keep your soul clean. And I promised Uther and Ygraine that you would come to no harm."

Uther. Morgana wondered what he would do.

* * * *

He came thundering into the rectory the next morning, his hobbled boots making fast, clacking noises on the tile. Morgana waited for him in the same chair.

"By Mithras," he swore, "what in Bel's Fires did you think you were doing on Beltane?"

She looked at him evenly, trying to keep the hate out of her voice. "Claiming my womanhood. What were you doing on Beltane?"

Uther raised his hand to slap her, but the anguished twittering of the abbess stayed him. Morgana raised an eyebrow. "You hit women now, my lord king?" She felt a slight tingle of excitement that he might.

"Don't tempt me beyond my endurance, Morgana. He turned and paced, raking a hand through his hair. Finally, he took a deep breath and turned to her. "Who is the father? One of my soldiers?"

Briefly, the thought of telling him it was Arthur flitted through her mind. What would Uther do? Make him marry her? That thought was appealing, but she realized instantly, not plausible. Arthur would simply deny he'd ever bedded her. In fact, he probably wouldn't even recognize her; it had been that dark. For some reason she didn't understand, she wanted to keep that secret to herself. Better for now just to try to keep tabs on him.

She shrugged. "I don't know. There were several."

Uther banged a fist on the desk and began pacing again. "You were whoring? Like a common wench?"

Morgana lifted her head. "You have no right to call me a whore! Look what you did to my mother!"

Uther stopped in mid-step. "Ygraine. This will devastate her. Have you ever cared for anyone but yourself?"

Morgana refused to answer. *No one has ever cared for me. If my mother cared, she wouldn't have sent me here.*

Uther sat down across from her. "I'll have to arrange for a proper marriage and quickly, so people will believe the child to be early born. Someone who would be willing to take soiled goods, along with a large dowry, and my insured protection of his lands." He ran his hand through his hair again. "A king who is not married, whose lands are threatened . . ." He narrowed his eyes in concentration and then suddenly nodded. "Uriens! He's widowed and the Picts live on the doorstep of Rheged. Promising to have the King's army at his back should convince him to accept you."

Morgana stared at him. "He's old!"

"That's not your concern, Morgana. It would be a good match."

"He has a son my age," Morgana answered. "Let me marry him."

"Why would I ruin Owain's chances for a happy marriage?" Uther asked sarcastically. "I'll send a messenger immediately." As he turned to leave he added, "Uriens will probably enjoy having a young wife to bed."

* * * *

Uriens was not only willing, he positively beamed when he came for her. "I've thought of getting remarried," he told her. "To marry Ygraine's daughter is an honor for me."

She looked at him. He had lost most of his hair and he was portly, but he had treated her with nothing but respect in the two days he had been here. She wondered if Uther had told him she was pregnant. It would be like Uther to think that after bedding her on their wedding night, Uriens could be led to believe it was his child. She contemplated the advantages of that. Hatred of Uther got the upper hand. She would not help him deceive anyone.

"You know I'm with child?" she asked directly.

His kind eyes didn't waver as he patted her hand. "Uther told me. In Rheged, we are still pagan enough to think a Beltane child a blessing. I will accept him."

And so they were married. Uriens bedded her, even though he didn't have the stamina that Arthur had. It wasn't an unpleasant experience, but it lacked the excitement of her Beltane night. Uriens had fallen asleep immediately afterward. All the better, she thought. I won't have to talk to him much.

When they arrived at his fort in Rheged a week later, his son, Owain, came out to the bailey to meet them. With him was another man: a soldier, an officer by his uniform. The stranger was tall and massive; his face had a hardness to it that made him seem both dangerous and alluring. His hair was thick and almost blond, yet his eyes were a deep brown. The man looked over Morgana appreciatively and she smiled.

"Owain! Bertilak!" Uriens said jovially, "I want you to meet my new wife, Morgana."

Owain gave her a stiff nod. "I hope you're not expecting me to call you Mother."

Morgana forced a laugh, realizing that Owain didn't like her. She supposed she couldn't blame him. "For *certes*, not!"

Bertilak bowed and kissed her hand. She tightened her hold slightly and when he straightened, he had an amused expression on his face. "I'm sure it will be a pleasure to get to know you."

Morgana held his gaze. "I'm looking forward to learning a lot of new things."

He raised an eyebrow slightly and then turned to Uriens. "The Picts have been marauding again. Owain and I were planning on a show of power along the border."

Uriens nodded. "I'll ride with you. It never hurts for them to see the king is alive and well." He turned to Morgana. "I'm sorry to have to leave you so soon after getting married, but I won't be gone for long. Two weeks, mayhap."

Morgana didn't care how long he'd be gone. She suddenly realized that even though she was married, she was freer than she'd ever been. No more convent, no sisters, no constantly attending services. Uriens treated her well; if the bedding wasn't exciting, at least she was no longer in a state of constant frustration.

She looked at Bertilak again and found him watching her covertly. She wondered if, here in the semi-pagan north, women still had the privilege of thigh freedom. Even if they didn't, it would be interesting to find out what he would do with her in bed. He had the look of a man used to getting what he wanted. She began to tingle, thinking of the possibilities.

* * * *

She didn't have long to wait. When the army returned, Uriens was taken ill. He was coughing and hacking and his lungs weren't clear.

"Too much wind and rain exposure," Owain said as they settled Uriens comfortably in his bed upstairs. "Even in the summer, it's cold."

Morgana busied herself with preparing herbal teas and took to sleeping in a guestroom downstairs. "So I won't bother you and you'll get good night's rest," she told Uriens. She put a drop of henbane in his wine at night to help him sleep.

Bertilak watched her dose the wine one night as he came to Uriens room to report on the daily business. Uriens was soon asleep and Bertilak followed Morgana out into the hall.

"It occurs to me that the medicine will assure a solid rest," he said ironically as they walked down the steps and stopped in front of her chamber. "What are your plans for the rest of the evening?"

Morgana tilted her head and gave him a sideways glance. "I wouldn't mind some company."

He opened the door with a grin. "After you."

She had barely driven the bolt when he carried her to the bed. His mouth was harsh on hers, his tongue probing deeply as he deftly undid the laces of her gown. Morgana pulled frantically on his tunic and ran her hands across his bare shoulders.

He traced a trail to her breast and suckled. She arched her back toward him. "Harder," she whispered.

He complied, increasing the pressure until she moaned. Her breasts were more sensitive now that she was four months pregnant and the sensation of pleasure and pain at the same time was exquisite, just as it had been that first time with Arthur.

Bertilak braced himself on his elbows and looked down at her. "Are you sure I'm not hurting you?"

Morgana pulled his head down and bit his lip and then raked his chest with her nails, causing him to wince. "I like it like that."

He looked at her a moment and then grinned. "My kind of a woman," he said as moved on top of her and forcefully rammed himself inside. He rode her until they were both drenched in sweat and almost too exhausted for that final explosion. Then, they lay panting in each other's arms.

Morgana was bruised and sore and felt wonderful. Bertilak would make a fine lover. She smiled, thinking of all the times ahead.

CHAPTER NINE—THE LADY FROM GWENT
491 A.D.

Uther crushed the note in his hands and threw it to the floor. His captains remained silent around the table in the map room.

"I thought when the Dux surrendered and Colgrin retreated, we would have peace for some time. I was obviously wrong."

Cadwy shrugged. "Who knew a contingency of the Saxons from Linnius would try to reclaim their lands? How many have settled? Five hundred? Six?"

"Probably." Uther sighed. "We'll have to rout them. Burn their fields, slaughter their herds, level their homes."

"Must the destruction be so total?" Arthur asked, thinking of the waste of food and cattle. It was so close to harvest.

Uther gave him a penetrating look. "They had the chance to retreat and keep peace. Now I set an example. A king cannot be thought soft. Ever." He paused. "You will lead the expedition, Arthur. Leave no stone unturned."

Arthur felt himself pale, even as the rest of the captains looked at Uther. Beside him, Cadwy stirred.

"Uther. Let me go with him. I've lead these kinds of raids before."

"No." Uther still watched Arthur. "I expect all of my captains to be capable of following my orders."

Arthur understood that the gauntlet had been thrown. He would have to supervise this carnage or forget about his career. He lifted his head then and looked Uther in the eye. He took a deep breath. "No stone unturned. Yes, Sir."

* * * *

Arthur paused, sweat mixing with the dirt on his face as he watched the fields burning. By Mithras, he was tired of smelling smoke.

In the past four weeks they had pushed north, past Lindum, harrying the Saxons who had resettled. He'd not been surprised to see some of Colgrin's forces helping defend the Linnius' factor. His men had savagely attacked those fighting under Colgrin's banner with the order to take no prisoners. It worked effectively and the Anglians fled over the Wash back to Anglia, leaving the Linnius Saxons to fight their own war.

Arthur pushed on. The first weeks saw heavy fighting as the Saxons tried to defend themselves and their families. Even their women fought fiercely, to the delight of some of Arthur's men.

He turned away in disgust when one of them told him it made the raping even more fun. He didn't believe in using women, even though they were the expected spoils of war. Then one day he came upon a young girl—probably a virgin from the blood between her thighs—nearly unconscious. Four soldiers, with their trews down, surrounded her. Three were bloodied; the fourth was about to assault her. Arthur pulled his sword, to the astonishment of the men. "This is done," he said. The girl whimpered and crawled away. It was then that he ordered his lieutenants, Bedwyr, Gwalchmai, Cai, Garient, and Gryflet, to control their companies. Any man found gang-raping would be flogged and demoted.

Now, he surveyed the damage done. Another village gone. Crops destroyed. Men and women killed. He wondered if they could ever live in peace. *There must be a way,* he thought as he made his way to the campsite for the night. *There must.*

* * * *

The Saxons made their last stand on the banks of the Humber River.

"Why don't they just cross it?" Bedwyr asked, standing beside Arthur as the infantry fell into formation. "Diera lies on the other side. Saxon territory."

"We'd just follow them," Cai answered, a gleam in his eye. "Why stop now?"

Arthur gave him a stern look. "I've no intention of bringing the whole Saxon nation down on us." He looked out toward simple barricades the Saxons had erected. These were mainly farmers; few soldiers were left to fight. He could see the faces of women and children peeking out from behind some of them. He knew his cavalry would ride them down like dried leaves in the wind.

"Do you want me to give the signal to charge?" Gryflet asked as he rode up.

Arthur mounted his horse. "No. I'm going to offer them their lives." He reached for the parley flag and rode toward the barricade, leaving his officers to stare at him.

He stopped midway and raised the flag. A soldier stepped forward.

"Your people are free to cross the river without bloodshed," Arthur said. "There's a ford not far from here."

The Saxon stared at him. "Is this a trick? Why now?"

"Because I have done what I was ordered to do," Arthur answered. "I've cleared Linnius. You are free to join your people on one condition: Do not return or there will be no mercy."

The Saxon considered him. Slowly, he touched his forehead and dipped his head. "We will go."

Arthur nodded, wheeling his horse. He lifted the reins and trotted back to his line.

"What is your name?" the Saxon called. "I will tell my people not all Britons are barbarians."

Barbarians? For the first time in weeks, Arthur smiled. *So that's how they see us. Just like we see them.* He turned in his saddle and shouted, "The name is Arthur."

* * * *

Uther was well pleased with the rout and when Arthur suggested a permanent base be established at Lindum to ensure no further insurgency, he agreed immediately.

"That will keep the Saxons from trying to divide Britain the way the Dux tried," Uther said as they finished debriefing in the council room. "Once again, I need to show the vassal kings the need to stay united. Mayhap a tournament would be the best way to go about it. It's still not too late this fall to host one."

"And it would be a way for all the kings to meet your youngest captain," Myrddin added and then looked at Arthur. "You never know which part of our country you'll be fighting in: Picts in the north, Saxons to the east and south, Scotti from Eire."

"Eire," Uther said. "There's been unrest in the west. Mayhap, I'll issue a special invitation for Cauritus of Gwent to attend. His fortress at Caer Leon has been a stronghold since Maximus first used it. I must be sure we are allied."

In the midst of the bustle of preparation, a stranger appeared at the gates of the fort—a Saracen from beyond the Holy Land. Although he dressed in western clothes, the sword he carried was a wicked-looking scimitar. He had brought with him horses for sale.

"My name is Palomides," he said when he was introduced to Uther. "Word of your cavalry has spread even to Mecca. Our horses are the swiftest in the world, born to run through soft sand. Can you imagine what they are capable of on a flat road?"

The Saracen's hair shimmered blue in the bright sunshine as Arthur accompanied them out to the bailey. Twenty mares, colts, fillies and foals awaited them. Their large, limpid eyes were set in slightly dished faces and their small ears stayed pricked. The necks arched naturally and even their tails seemed to flow. Arthur walked around the small herd and then stopped.

Slightly apart from the rest, a three-year-old colt stood watching him. The coat was dappled grey, the mane and tail white. Even at his age, his chest rippled with heavy muscles and his conformation was superb. He had the most intelligent eyes Arthur had ever seen in an animal.

"I must have you," Arthur said as he slowly approached the horse.

"I see you have found Valiant." Palomides's white teeth flashed in his golden face as he followed Arthur. "He is the best stock I have."

"I can see that," Arthur answered appreciatively. "What is his asking price?"

"He will make a fine sire for many mares," Palomides said.

"Yes, *certes*," Arthur replied with a trace of annoyance in his voice. No doubt the price would be triple what he would pay. "How much?"

"He is free if you'll help me," Palomides said.

Arthur looked at him in surprise. To give such a piece of horseflesh away, the man must be in a lot of trouble. Were the horses stolen? Had he murdered a vassal king?

"Don't look so alarmed," the Saracen said. "I simply want to stay and be King Uther's Master of Horse. If you could convince him of that, Valiant is yours."

Arthur studied him. "Why do you want to live here?"

"My older brother, Safere, will inherit my father's lands. As second son, I must find a business to support me. My life is horses. King Uther's use of cavalry is well known."

"If you've heard about our cavalry, you know our horses are the heavy destriers meant to carry a man in full armor." Arthur turned his attention to the mares. "These horses would be good for light cavalry, though, when we want to make speed."

Palomides nodded. "And the Saxon fight on foot; what would you need full armor for in most cases?"

"It seems you know a lot about us," Arthur said as he brushed the grey's satiny coat with his hand.

"I wouldn't have come with this offer if I hadn't learned all I could about your king," Palomides said simply. "King Clovis has asked for these horses already."

"The Merovingian?" Arthur asked and narrowed his eyes. "Is the king of Gaul thinking to expand his territory?"

"He is ambitious and since the queen has Christianized him, he's been talking of a cleansing crusade against pagans." The Saracen grinned. "Since I am one, I would choose not to work with him."

"Interesting," Arthur answered. "I think Uther is going to be very impressed with you."

* * * *

The tournament drew nearly all of the vassal kings. Leodegrance came and brought his seven-year-old daughter, Gwenhwyfar, with him. She tagged along behind Bedwyr and when he was busy, she could be found in the stables. Often far too close to the big warhorses for anyone's comfort. She ran her nurse ragged. Arthur just shook his head and gave orders that the new horses be guarded. It would be just like a child to think a foal was a pony and get kicked.

Uriens arrived a day before the tournament was to begin with his pregnant, young wife. Arthur looked her over with interest. Raven hair, nearly as blue as the Saracen's and eyes that glittered almost as darkly in her alabaster face. When she caught him looking, her red lips curved into a smile and she tilted her head, eyelashes sweeping her cheek before she met and held his gaze. Her boldness startled him. Not that he wasn't used to inviting looks from women, but this one was pregnant! And married to a king. Then he noticed the soldier beside her, almost blond with an aggressive look. Arthur knew that look. It meant 'stay away.' Well, he wasn't planning on getting close. Strange though, that she would have a lover, for he was sure that's who the man was.

Uther approached them and said, "Hello, Morgana. Life seems to be treating you well."

Morgana. Uther's stepdaughter. Myrddin had told him the woman had been at a convent and there was some scandal about her getting pregnant while there. He looked at her again and pitied the poor sisters who had, no doubt, tried to get her to see the Light. He had the feeling this woman never would.

When Cauritus of Gwent arrived, Uther took Arthur with him as the carriage rolled into the bailey. "This is one of our most potent allies in the west," he said. "I want you to make a good first impression."

The man who stepped out was tall, of middle age with dark hair that showed a lot of silver. He was dressed in formal Roman military attire and gave the Roman salute as king to king.

"Well come," Uther said and introduced Arthur. "You've arrived just in time. The kings are meeting to draw lots for tomorrow's events."

"And would you have some of that fine red wine at the table?" Cauritus laughed. "And an escort for my daughter?" He turned and held up his hand toward the carriage.

The girl put her small hand in her father's and stepped down daintily. She looked young, mayhap five and ten or so.

Arthur stared. She was beautiful. Her complexion was the color of rich cream, her cheeks blushed with a touch of pale rose, her full lips only a shade darker. Fair, flaxen hair framed delicate cheekbones. She had the most cobalt blue eyes he'd ever seen. And she's no doubt a virgin, he told himself sternly and quelled the ache that had begun in his loins.

"My daughter, Leonora," Cauritus said.

Uther bowed toward the girl and belatedly, feeling doltish, Arthur did too. When he looked up, a hint of amusement flickered in her eyes and then was gone. She smiled prettily.

"I'm sure your captain can be trusted to escort my daughter?" Cauritus asked Uther.

The look Uther gave Arthur brooked no breach. "I'm sure he can."

Arthur wasn't at all sure. He looked down at the girl and offered his arm. "Shall we go in?"

She accepted, her touch as light as the fluttering of silk, yet her hand sent searing flames of desire coursing through him.

* * * *

Leonora was certainly enjoying herself, Arthur thought as he watched her dancing with Gwalchmai that evening after supper. She flitted from one partner to the next, like a butterfly lighting, never to stay too long in one place. Her face was flushed from the exertion, which made her even more appealing. She looked up at Gwalchmai, laughing at something he'd said.

Arthur rose and made his way through the dancers. He tapped Gwalchmai on the shoulder. "I believe the next dance is mine."

His friend scowled, but Leonora was already turning to him. He placed an arm around her waist and swept her around.

"I thought you'd never ask, Arthur," she said, a smile playing on her mouth.

He looked down at those inviting lips. *Does she know the impact she has on men?* And then answered his own question. *Certes. Most women do.*

"I hadn't noticed you in need of a partner," he answered as he maneuvered her away from the approaching Cai.

She stuck her lower lip out in a pout. "I expected you to be the first to ask."

Arthur brought her closer and felt her tighten her hold on his shoulder. "I'm not much of a dancer."

She ran her fingers through the hair curling at the nape of his neck. "But I love to dance."

Bel's Fires! What is she doing? The thought appeared briefly that mayhap she wasn't a virgin, but she was the picture of wide-eyed innocence as she watched him. And he was sure her father kept her properly chaperoned.

She moved a little and he felt the soft brush of the curve of her breast before she stepped back.

"'Tis warm in here. Could we go for a walk?" she asked.

Involuntarily, Arthur looked around to see where her father was. Still at the high table; Uther was plying him with wine. He looked down at Leonora. So beautiful. Mayhap a stolen kiss wouldn't be so bad. Just one.

He led her outside. The fort didn't have much in the way of creature comforts. No walled gardens or niches where lovers might hide. Not that he'd ever worried before. If he brought a woman to the fort, he'd always taken her to his tent. But he could hardly do that now.

"Would you like to go up on the battlements? The view is nice from there."

She smiled and accepted his hand as he helped her up the stairs. Arthur leaned sideways against an embrasure, looking at her. In the moonlight, her hair shone silver and her eyes looked dark.

Leonora inhaled the night air. "It's so quiet up here, away from the crowds."

Arthur reached for her and she came willingly into his arms and lifted her face. He brushed her lips lightly and then with a little more pressure. She responded quickly and when his tongue gently probed her mouth, he met no resistance. He crushed her to him then and she clung tightly, arms wrapped around his neck.

Eventually, he stepped back and removed her arms from him. "I think," he said shakily, "I had better take you back."

She sighed. "Can we do this again tomorrow night?"

Arthur grinned. "*Certes.* I had no idea you were such a good kisser."

She gave him an oblique look, but said nothing more as they made their way down the stairs.

* * * *

Arthur tossed in his bunk, unable to sleep. For three nights, they had walked the battlements, holding hands and taking pleasure in their kisses. He got as far as opening her bodice to touch a breast and the pent up desire in him was nearly unbearable. Even the serving wench he'd tumbled and paid well hadn't brought him the satisfaction he wanted. The tournament would be over tomorrow and Leonora would be going home.

He threw the covers back, suddenly overcome with heat, although it was November. He had discarded his bedclothes long ago. Then he heard a rustling at the front of his tent. In an instant, he was on his feet, his sword drawn.

Leonora lifted the flap. For a moment, Arthur just stood there and stared. Then he pulled her through the doorway and looked quickly outside. *Had anyone seen her?* He turned back, aware that he was naked and already erect.

"I had to come," she said. "Just once, before I leave . . ."

She didn't have an opportunity to say more. His mouth was on hers as he lifted her and placed her on the bed. His hands, usually so deft with lovemaking, fumbled with the laces of her bodice. He restrained himself from tearing the garment from her and then, at last, her breasts were bare. Arthur groaned and suckled on a nipple, his hand teasing the other until her moans matched his.

He let his hand drift slowly down her ribs and across her belly, seeking the spot between her thighs that was sure to delight. He played with her, inserting a finger to find her already wet and pliant.

When her thrashing and mewling reached a level where he thought the pain of his entry would be minimal, he lifted himself over her, keeping his weight on his elbows, and probed gently.

Leonora grabbed his shoulders and pulled him down, wrapping her legs around him and arching her back to take him more fully. He gave himself over to his lust then, ramming his thrusts home, feeling her meet them. And then he felt that wonderful, undulating contraction that rippled along his manhood. He gave one great final effort and the world exploded for him as well.

It was only later, after several repeated episodes, that he realized she had been no virgin.

CHAPTER TEN—HONOR BOUND
491 A.D. – 492 A.D.

Ygraine visited Ambresbyrig several times a year, although she preferred that Uther come to Tintagel. This year she arrived just before Yule. Uther summoned Arthur to his tent. As Arthur stepped inside, he wondered what the pretense would be this time.

For Uther used all kinds of excuses for Arthur to spend time with them. For Ygraine's part, she always seemed happy to see him and he didn't know why. Myrddin finally told him to stop thinking about it; mayhap the king and queen had their reasons.

Arthur wasn't prepared for this one, however.

Uther handed him a cup of wine. "I want you to escort Ygraine to Rheged; Morgana is about to give birth and her mother wants to be there."

He was glad he was sitting. That would be a fortnight trip if they took a litter. And it would be cold. He wondered why Uther didn't escort his wife himself. All was quiet at this time of year.

As if in answer to his unspoken question, Ygraine leaned forward. "Uther would go, but Morgana has no love of him. A woman's first child is always hard; his presence would just upset her." She looked at her husband and back to Arthur. "And it is of utmost importance that we leave as soon as we can."

When they arrived in Rheged, Uriens greeted them warmly and Morgana's eyes widened as she saw her mother's escort. As huge as her belly was, she insisted on hugging Arthur, thanking him over and over for bringing her mother.

Arthur had an uneasy feeling about that hug. She clung to him longer than necessary and actually rubbed those full breasts against his chest. He quickly stepped back, lest he offend Uriens. Morgana's eyes were full of sly laughter, although her mouth was still. He remembered the look she had given him at the tournament. Why did he always feel like a cornered mouse just within reach of a cat's claws when he was near her?

They were there only three days before Morgana went into labor. Ygraine and the midwife bustled about, ordering the servants to prepare swaddling and clean linen strips. Ygraine ordered tea, but Morgana said she'd already given the cook a recipe for something that would ease the pain.

Even so, as Arthur sat with Uriens and Owain in front of the hearth in the living quarters, they could hear Morgana cursing all men that had ever been born from her bedchamber across the hall. It seemed she knew more choice words than most sailors, Arthur thought ironically. When the curses turned to snarls in a language he didn't understand, he looked at Uriens.

Uriens shrugged unhappily. "The Old Tongue. When she was a child, Uther found her dappling in the black arts. It was why she was sent to the convent."

The words chilled Arthur, even though he had just taken a sip of mulled wine. Something about Morgana was definitely strange; his skin prickled when he found her watching him as she had done since he arrived.

A blood-curdling scream assailed them and sent another shudder through him. *Did all women have such a time of it?* Arthur had never given it much thought. The serving wenches at the fort commonly got pregnant and seemed no worse for it.

Ygraine came out of the birthing room. "You can go in now, Uriens."

He rose, beaming as happily, Arthur thought, as if it were his own child. Arthur respected him for that. *If I were married, I don't think I could ever accept another man's child.*

Morgana stayed in her chambers for several days following the birth and Ygraine spent much of her time with her. Arthur found it both interesting and suspicious that Bertilak managed to find some excuse to visit the new mother each day and he filed the information for future use. Mostly, Arthur spent his days riding with Uriens along the border, making sure there was no tension mounting among the northern Saxons.

"When Vortigern first sent Octa and his warriors north to curb the Picts, we accepted them," Uriens said with a rueful smile. "What else could we do? But you know Saxons; if they can get an acre, they want a hide."

Arthur was still thinking about this when they returned home. They had missed the noon day meal and he went to the kitchens to see if he could convince the young cook to scrounge something warm for him.

The kitchens were empty, except for Morgana. She sat beside a table, a cup of herbal tea beside her, nursing the baby. Arthur stopped abruptly and turned away.

"Do not go," she said as she stood and walked toward him. She made no effort to cover herself. "Are you hungry?"

"It's all right. I can get something later."

Morgana removed the child from her breast. Arthur tried to avert his eyes from the bulging fullness and the swollen, dark red nipple. She smiled as she pulled her blouse together with one hand.

"Here, hold him. I have to tie my laces." She raised an eyebrow as he stood there mutely staring at her. "Or would you rather lace my bodice for me? I wouldn't mind."

Arthur felt himself color and held out his arms. She placed the child in them and gave him a strange look.

He looked down at the child. It had its eyes closed and was sucking contentedly on its thumb. The hair was as black as his mother's. He wondered what color the eyes were or who the father had been.

"His name is Medraut," she said.

* * * *

On the way back south, Arthur had to stop and seek shelter several times from near blizzard conditions. By the time they delivered Ygraine to Tintagel, Arthur was tempted to continue on to Lyonesse. The warm current of the sea kept things almost balmy there at a time when most of Britain lay under a blanket of snow. The thought was tempting, but he had been gone nearly two moons; Uther would be wanting to plan for spring campaigns.

When he arrived back at Ambresbyrig, Uther sent for him. As soon as he was seated in front of the big desk, he knew something was wrong.

"You don't want to hear about how the trip went, do you?" he asked.

"If Ygraine is content, than so am I." Uther leaned forward, his arms on the desk. "Did you learn anything about childbirth?"

Arthur furrowed his brow. "Why would I need to know anything about that?"

Uther gave him a long, thoughtful look. "Because you're about to become a father."

"What?" Arthur laughed. "Don't tell me one of the serving wenches is trying to claim I fathered her child. I always give them the motherswort and hop to chew after."

"The mother is no serving wench."

"Well, then, who?" Arthur asked and when he received only a stare he inhaled sharply. "Leonora?"

Uther nodded. "You'll need to pick a wedding date. And soon."

You're jesting. I enjoyed Leonora, but to marry her? "I don't think I'm the marrying kind," he said. "I'm a soldier."

A dark cloud passed over Uther's face and Arthur began to feel his first misgivings. "You might have thought of that sooner. Of all the women at your beck and call, why couldn't you leave Cauritus' daughter alone? He worships that child and you've deflowered her. His words, not mine."

Arthur straightened. "She wasn't a virgin, Uther."

The king raised an eyebrow. "Ah. Well, in her father's eyes, she was. I can't afford to lose him as an ally because you couldn't keep your trews laced. Pick a date and I'll send word."

Arthur felt the blood drain from his face. He had never thought about getting married. He enjoyed women—a variety of women—and never thought about limiting himself to just one. Uther was still watching him and Uther was serious. *By Mithras, this was a fine mess to walk into . . .*

"Look," Uther said finally, "she's a pretty thing. You were hot enough for her when she was here. Think of the nights you can have together."

That's true. Arthur brightened a little, remembering how eager she had been to please him. *But a baby? I'm not ready to be a father.* He felt panic begin to bubble to the surface. He forced it back with his will, determined to stay rational. He must always stay in control of his emotions.

He remembered how awkward he felt holding Medraut. And then he thought that Medraut would never know his real father. And Arthur had never known his own either. *Every child should know his parents.* He gulped and took a long shaky breath. He would do his duty. He was honor bound. "Send the message. Tell her I will be in Gwent within the week."

* * * *

Bedwyr rode silently beside him, with Gwalchmai on the other side. They had brought twenty men with them to serve as an escort.

Uther decided to take advantage of the event and host a big celebration at Caer Leon. The Romans called it Isca Silurum and it was a major stronghold, housing the great Legion II Augusta. The fort's hypocausts for heating the floor still worked, as did the baths. It was large enough to hold a wedding of this magnitude.

In truth, Arthur thought, the king is more elated over this than I am. He'll have a firm ally now. He suddenly felt like a pawn in a game of chess.

"It won't be so bad, Arthur," Bedwyr said after some miles of silence.

"Bah!" Gwalchmai answered. "Women know how babies come. They don't expect you to marry them for a little fun that was had!"

"This one does," Arthur answered. "I don't know what I was thinking not to have given her the motherswort."

"If I remember," Bedwyr said with a smile, "you were smitten. You weren't thinking with the head that's on your shoulders. Mayhap, love will grow."

"I hope so," Arthur replied, "for limiting myself to one woman for the rest of my life is a big price to pay."

Gwalchmai stared at him. "Why would you do that? The woman's your wife, not your keeper."

Arthur smiled wanly. "She's a Christian. The vows I take will say I forsake all others. I cannot break an oath."

"Damnation!" Gwalchmai answered. "The Orkneys follow the pagan ways; we are free to choose. I can't imagine settling on only one woman."

Arthur didn't answer; he only spurred his horse to a full gallop.

* * * *

Arthur looked around the huge, crowded stone church at Caer Leon. He was surprised that Morgana had made the trip. She looked like a well-fed cat who knew where the heavy cream was kept and he felt the hair rise on the nape of his neck. Behind Morgana, King Leodegrance was seated, his young daughter and her cousin beside him. The girls looked somewhat alike, Arthur thought, and then almost smiled. The cousin, Elaine of Carbonek, sat quietly, hands folded in her lap, auburn hair neatly braided, every bit the picture of a little lady. Gwenhwyfar wiggled on the bench, twisting and turning to see everyone who came in. Her braid looked like she might have tried to do it herself, locks of her red-gold hair sticking out everywhere.

He shook his head slightly. Elaine's future husband would have a docile wife. But Gwehwyfar? Someday, that one would present a real challenge for some unsuspecting man.

Myrddin stood at the back of the church. Arthur was pleased that he had come. The druid believed God was meant to be worshipped in natural settings, not man-made buildings, and he had a tenuous relationship with the Christians, at best. Arthur had gone to him when he first learned about Leonora's pregnancy, hoping for some reprieve, and Myrddin had gone into trance. When he regained focus, all he said was to treat her well.

As if I wouldn't. He looked at Leonora now, standing beside him. She was pale and subdued and he hoped she wouldn't be sick again. When he'd first arrived in Gwent, she'd looked pleased to see him, but then promptly excused herself to be ill. In the two weeks it had taken to plan this rushed wedding, she had been moody, smiling brightly one moment, looking depressed the next. Even Gwalchmai, who could charm a stubborn mule into thinking it was a prize stallion, gave up on trying to make her feel good. Arthur had seen the look of pity he had given him.

The priest started the vows. As he recited his, he thought with longing for the pagan ways of the north that might have left him some freedom. Leonora glanced at him briefly as she repeated her vows in a barely audible voice. Arthur wondered, not for the first time, if she really wanted to get married any more than he did. Mayhap, this was only her father's doing. He sighed. They would have to make the best of it. And there was tonight. They would, at least, enjoy the bedding.

The priest pronounced them man and wife. Arthur turned with his bride to face the congregation. He was a married man.

* * * *

The first thing Leonora did when they were finally alone on their wedding night was cry. Bewildered, Arthur held her, trying to soothe her, but she only sobbed louder.

"Shhh!" he whispered, "the maids in the outer room will think I'm hurting you."

"I don't care," she wailed. "I'm going to get fat and be ugly. No one is going to look at me anymore!"

"You have me now," Arthur said, "it doesn't matter if anyone looks at you. Actually, they'd better not. You're my wife."

She stopped sobbing and stared at him. "So you do think I'm fat. Already!" She went back to crying.

Arthur raked a hand through his hair. This wasn't exactly how he pictured his wedding night. He wasn't used to dealing with tears. "All women grow large with a baby. It'll go away once the child is born."

Her weeping continued, softer now. "I don't want to be pregnant!"

Arthur placed his hand under her chin and forced her head up. "Then why," he said in frustration, "didn't you do something about it? Don't you have a wise woman in Caerleon? She could have given you herbs."

She pushed his hand away. "My father was afraid I'd try. He's practically had me under guard since we found out. He wants this grandchild, not me."

A pity he didn't have you under guard the night you came to me. "Is it my child that you don't want? Is there someone else? You were no virgin."

Fire blazed in her eyes. "Do not think to condemn me because I enjoy being bedded. There was only one time and it was an experiment. I liked it."

"Then," Arthur said softly as he reached to undo the laces of her bedgown, "let me give you that pleasure."

She slapped his hand away and then just as quickly grabbed it and pressed it to her breast. Her arms went around his neck and she clung, still sniffling. "Promise me you won't leave me. Please. I need you to make me feel beautiful."

As he murmured the words and eased her down on the bed with him, he had a strange foreboding that the next months would not go well.

* * * *

They moved into a building that housed several married officers and their wives. As Leonora's belly grew larger, her temper became shorter.

"You don't love me," she snarled at Arthur one day when he was busy working with Uther and didn't pay enough attention to her.

Another day, he was laughing at a joke one of the serving wenches told him as she was preparing the sideboard. Leonora walked in and she slapped the girl and told her to leave her husband alone. Then she'd run off crying again.

Arthur made what amends he could to the girl later and resolved to avoid any woman in his wife's presence. Leonora's tears were getting more difficult to handle. During the first months, he'd been able to squelch them by making love to her, always dutifully telling her the words she wanted to hear. Now that she was really large, she no longer believed him.

"How can you find me attractive?" she sobbed one night in bed. "No one else does either. I haven't been flirted with since I got here!"

He tried to hold back his anger. *She is my wife. Why should anyone flirt with her?* "Is my lovemaking so unexciting that you need someone else to flirt with you?"

He reached for his clothes.

She pulled on his arm. "No! Please, don't go. I need you. Don't leave me!"

He looked at her. *If this continues much longer, I'll go mad. One minute she can't stand me, the next, she doesn't want me out of her sight.*

As if sensing his indecision, she tugged on him again and then wrapped her arms around his waist. "Come back to bed, Arthur. Let me hold you." And slowly, she kissed him, again and again, until he lay back and began to respond.

* * * *

Uther finally took pity on him about a month before Leonora's time. He called Arthur into his office and gestured for him to sit.

"I hear all is not well in your marriage," he said bluntly.

Arthur felt too drained to even be embarrassed that Uther would know. The public arguments were common knowledge. "It's the constant crying I can't handle."

"Ygraine says some women get moody like that when they're with child."

Arthur sighed. "I'll put up with it. What can I do for you? Why am I here?"

Uther grinned. "I thought I'd give you a reprieve. How would you like to go on a peace negotiation mission for me?"

Arthur brightened. *Go? Be gone from here? Have silence at night?* Then he frowned. *Leonora would beg and cry and plead with him not to leave.* "I don't think my wife will want me leaving with her time so close."

Uther frowned. "I think that little lady has run you just about ragged enough. She is not in charge of this fort. I am. And I am giving my captain an order. Is that clear?"

A smile formed on Arthur's face. "Clear, Sir."

"Good. The Saxon, Aelle, has inhabited the southern coast area around the Weald for nearly ten years. Several weeks ago, he led an uprising against the garrison stationed near Mearcredesburna."

"He wanted the land all the way to the River Arun?" Arthur asked. "I take it the garrison defeated him?"

"Not exactly," Uther answered. "He laid siege and has asked to treaty."

Arthur lifted an eyebrow in surprise. "A Saxon that would rather talk than fight? What do you want me to do?"

Uther picked up the note from his desk. "He's asked to settle some of his people near the river." He held up a hand to forestall Arthur's question. "In return, he will ally with us against Aesc in the east."

"He's fought Aesc before to hold that coastline," Arthur said. "He sees this as advantageous for himself as well, then. Your army behind his."

"You're the one who thinks peace can be had, Arthur. Do you want to give it a try?"

Arthur grinned. "I think dealing with a Saxon right now, instead of Leonora, will be child's play. I'll leave tomorrow."

* * * *

Arthur found Aelle to be surprisingly hospitable. He offered Aelle half of what he wanted and then dickered with him, trying to drag the talks out for as long as he dared. The Saxon seemed to be enjoying the bartering as well, for when it came time for Arthur to leave, he had a wagonload of mead to take with him.

Now Ambresbyrig was in sight. Arthur took a deep breath. Two weeks gone had strengthened his reserve. Leonora should be delivered soon and then, hopefully, they could work things out.

He arrived to find things in turmoil. Myrddin met him in the bailey, a serious look on his face.

"What is it?" Arthur asked.

"Leonora," the druid answered. "When you left, she threw herself into such a fit that I asked Uther to let me contact Vivian."

"The Lady of the Lake? Here? Because of my wife?" Arthur asked incredulously. *When is this going to stop?*

"She sent Nimue," Myrddin answered. "And your wife is in heavy labor. They're in the infirmary."

Instead of the cursing and screaming he had heard with Morgana's birthing, there was only an unnatural stillness inside the infirmary when Arthur entered.

'Where is she?" Arthur asked the medic.

He pointed toward the rear, where a section had been curtained off. "A midwife and the priestess are with her. I doubt they'll let you in."

"We'll see about that," Arthur answered and stomped to the makeshift private room. He pulled back the curtain and stepped in.

"No!" The midwife stopped him. "Men aren't allowed at birthings."

He ignored her and went to the bed. Leonora's eyes were closed and face was chalk white, her skin glistening with sweat. She lay naked and looked wan and fragile except for her huge belly. *How could she have gotten so much bigger?*

Nimue had her back to him and was wiping Leonora's face with a cloth dipped in rosewater. A spray of mistletoe lay over her heart and a poultice of some sort lay on her stomach.

The midwife protested when Nimue said, "Let him stay." The older lady grumbled to herself, but stopped tugging at his sleeve.

"What's this?" Arthur asked, pointing to the poultice. "She is all right, isn't she?"

Nimue straightened and looked at him. He had forgotten how clear her eyes were, like the blue-green sea of Lyonesse.

"She's been fighting the labor for three days now. She has not much strength left," Nimue answered. "The poultice is broom and goldenseal, meant to help deliver the babe." She looked back at Leonora. "If it still lives."

"You think the babe is dead?"

"There has been no movement for the past day. The midwife has not discerned any widening of the canal," Nimue said as she picked up a cup with thick white liquid. "I was about to have her drink the brooklime; it will expel the child if it does not live."

"Is there nothing else that can be done?" Arthur took his wife's limp hand in his and was rewarded with just the ghost of smile and then she groaned as if the effort had pained her.

"The babe must come out or she will die," Nimue said simply. She studied Arthur and then put down the cup. "We can try one more thing. I can send your energy to her."

He looked into her eyes. "Do it."

Nimue took his hand in one of hers and Leonora's in the other. She closed her eyes and began to chant in what Arthur recognized as the Old Tongue. Suddenly, he felt a bolt jar him, nearly pushing him backward and then he felt the pain. Hot, searing pain through his abdomen. His chest felt tight and he couldn't breathe as though a leaden ball pressed him down. He fought for air, for light—he couldn't see—then the pain roared through him, nearly breaking his back.

He clutched the side of the bed, breathing heavily while the world refocused around him. *What had happened?* Then he felt Nimue's cool hand on his face. Strength flowed from her to him and he straightened.

"She needed your energy," Nimue said. "The babe came."

Arthur turned toward the midwife with a smile, but stopped at the sight of her face. "It's dead?"

She nodded. "'Twas a boy."

A son. She wanted to name him Amir. Arthur took a deep breath and turned back to Leonora. She appeared worse than she had before. He looked to Nimue, but she was chanting again, one hand on the mistletoe, the other on Leonora's forehead.

Arthur bent over his wife. "Can you hear me?"

For just a second, her eyelids fluttered and she slowly opened them. "Arthur."

He took her hand. "It is going to be all right. 'Tis over. Now you can get well."

She smiled and gave his hand a feeble squeeze. "I don't think so," she said and closed her eyes for the last time.

* * * *

"I was a rotten husband." Arthur put both hands to his head, knocking over his wine cup and pouring the contents unto the table in his quarters. "Now I've killed her."

Myrddin righted the wine cup. "You didn't kill her, Arthur. 'Tis always a risk in childbirth."

"But if I hadn't gone to see Aelle . . ." Arthur moaned, remembering how he had delayed returning so he wouldn't have to deal with Leonora. "If I had stayed home . . ."

"She was an unbalanced woman," Myrddin said, "and she was driving you to join her. None of us needed any special wisdom to see that."

"I didn't love her," Arthur said miserably. "She deserved more."

"You stood by her." Myrddin answered. "We don't choose whom to love, neither can we force it where it doesn't exist." He took a flask from his cloak and poured a small amount into Arthur's empty cup. "Here. Drink this. Nimue left it for you."

"What is it?" Arthur said.

"A mixture of felonwort, woodrowel and fly agaric. It will help you see to the depths of your sorrow and understand."

"No, thanks. I just plan to get drunk."

"Drink will only dull your senses. Tomorrow you'll feel just as guilty." Myrddin pushed the cup to him. "Uther needs you to lead your men, not wallow in self-pity. This will help you grieve and be done. Drink."

Dutifully, Arthur took a swallow and nearly gagged. "I hope the meals Nimue prepares taste better than this." He took a deep breath and drank the whole thing down.

"Now lie back," Myrddin said. "In a moment, you'll be in another place. I'll stay by your side."

Arthur looked woozily at him. Myrddin was appearing in waves, rippling toward him and fading away. Colors began to swirl in front of his eyes, making him dizzy.

Suddenly, a woman materialized from behind Myrddin's shoulder. She had long brown hair and slanted green eyes. Yet . . . she wasn't really there. It was as though she were transparent. He blinked and tried to focus to no avail.

"It's all right," Morgan le Fey soothed him. "Take my hand. We're going on a journey."

He reached for her hand and then he was floating. *How can I float?* The earth rushed by below him, slashes of green and brown. They were headed to where the sun was setting over a turquoise sea. The sun's bands of scarlet and tangerine light scathed him, yet he felt no pain, just an irresistible pulling toward the western horizon.

Then it was dark. They were falling, deeper and deeper, into a vortex that spun them wildly and Arthur suddenly knew this was the Tunnel of Death. A speck of light emerged and Arthur felt its warmth. *I must get to the light.*

"Don't worry," the faerie murmured beside him. "This is not your time."

They tumbled from the tunnel to land on soft grass. Only the grass was blue and the sky green with an odd purple sun shedding light. "Where are we?" he asked.

Morgan le Fey smiled. "The Otherworld. Come, Janus will be waiting."

"Who?"

"The Keeper of the entry. He sees both the past and the future. I think he will give you peace." She tugged at his hand and they slowly approached a stack of boulders. Some were pure white and others ebony. They rounded the pile and stopped.

The two-faced god, Janus, stood at the entrance to what looked to be a cave. "So," he said, "you have brought him. Rhiannon escorted Leonora some time ago."

"The druid, Myrddin, wishes for him to see," the faerie queen said.

Janus nodded and the landscape vanished.

Leonora was sitting on a damask chaise, in a room of crystal. Light reflected from the walls and caused her beautiful face to glow. Several young men willingly danced attendance on her. Arthur heard the tinkle of her laughter. It was the same sound she had made the first night she had come to his tent. *She's happy.*

"Yes." Janus answered his thought. "Here, in the Otherworld, she will have what she wants. No mortal could have ever satisfied her needs."

Arthur looked at him questioningly even as he began to fade away.

"Come," the faerie said. "We must get back."

He felt the same pull as before, but in reverse and then, for no reason he could explain, he felt nothing. There was no form to him or to the world. He was free.

* * * *

Arthur opened his eyes, but didn't move, waiting for the objects in the tent to stop moving and weaving.

"How are you feeling?" Myrddin asked.

Arthur struggled to sit up and two Myrddins began to merge into one. "Like I had too much wine," he finally said when the nausea had stopped. He looked at Myrddin. "Did I really visit the Otherworld? There was a woman—a faerie—who came to me . . ."

"I cannot say," Myrddin answered, "only that you went where you needed to go to be free of the guilt that's overshadowed you these past months."

"I would never have been able to make her happy," Arthur said. "She's happy where she is now." He looked up at Myrddin seriously. "If I ever marry again, I swear I don't want to make a woman pregnant and put her through that."

"Ah, Arthur." Myrddin shook his head. "Be careful what you wish for."

CHAPTER ELEVEN—AN IVITATION
494 A.D. -495 A.D.

Galahad was glad his cousins, Bors and Lionel, had come to live with them. *It'll even the odds. Four of us against that lout, Lovel, and his cronies.* His kin arrived yesterday, a day after Beltane; Bors was a year older than himself and Lionel, a year younger.

Four years had passed since the day he'd knocked the bullies all unconscious, but they had neither forgotten nor forgiven, although they gave him a wary berth when he lost his temper. Sword practice sometimes became too serious and Ban had called all of them on it several times, but he refused to send them away. "You'll have to learn to live with men like that, Son," he'd said, "and I refuse to show favoritism. You won't get any when you're on the battlefield."

Neither did he expect any. At four and ten, his biceps already bulged and his pectorals were flat and hard. His body had to be a finely tuned instrument to compensate for the battle frenzy he couldn't always control.

Now, Galahad took his cousins into the armory, a large stone building near the stables. Along one wall pikes and spears were stacked, according to size, and lances comprised a corner. Shields were hung carefully on the opposite wall and swords hung by the scabbards along a third. An assortment of spiked balls called morning stars, battle axes, hatchets and maces rested on shelves on the fourth wall, along with boxes of daggers and knives.

Galahad went to the sword wall and took two down. "Here." He gave a sword to each of his cousins. "Try these. Those bullies I told you about will issue a challenge soon. They'll want to see how good you are, but we'll practice first." He led them outside to the practice area beyond the smithy.

It didn't take long before a group of soldiers gathered. Galahad was used to the audience, for many of them practiced with him long hours and they were always ready with comments. In the beginning, when he'd returned from Britain, there was far more criticism than praise for his skills, but over the past year, the tables had turned.

He circled Bors now, watching his cousin's footwork, although his eyes were centered on Bor's face. He lunged and thrust, only to have Bors parry and repost. *He's good.*

Galahad cut low and the return parry turned into a press from which he disengaged, retreated and then feinted to the right. Bors followed course and moved left; Galahad quickly double-feinted to the left and his sword tapped Bors exposed side. A point earned. The double-feint was a trick Ban had taught him and nearly all of the time, it was impossible for the opponent to anticipate. A cheer went up from the group, but Galahad didn't glance over. Bors did, though, and received another tap.

"Enough, cousin!" Bors grounded his point. "I think I need more practice. You need to teach me that double-feint."

Galahad nodded and they shook hands and turned to leave the area, arms around each other's shoulders.

A small group of serving girls had gathered near the end of the field and looked admiringly at Galahad. Some smiled openly and one bold one even waved and winked.

"You seem to have a following," Bors said with a grin. "Any favorites?"

Galahad felt himself color. The group had just started following him around this year, whenever they could duck away from their chores. Although he was unfailingly polite when one of them spoke to him, he tried not to encourage their behavior. Ban had been quite plain with both Ector and him. They were to leave the wenches alone. He would have liked to talk with them for he missed the priestesses. *Sometimes I'd rather talk about something other than fighting and war.* He had begun dreaming lately of a red-haired girl who rode toward him on a horse, laughing, only she never got close enough for him to see her face. Somehow, though, he felt he knew her.

"No favorites," he replied, "for any of us. My father's orders."

"That's too bad," Bors said wistfully. "Where do you find your pleasure then?"

Galahad was sure he must be scarlet. *Has Bors bedded a girl? I'm nearly five and ten and never been kissed.*

When he said nothing, Bors grunted. "So that's how it is. Mayhap, cousin, I'll have something to teach you, too."

* * * *

At supper, several months later, Ban announced he'd had a letter from Hoel. "Colgrin and his brother have retreated to Anglia, at least for now, licking their wounds. Some of the Linnius group tried to reclaim the land north of Lindum, but a young captain named Arthur drove them back. It seems he's making quite a name for himself."

"Arthur?" Galahad asked. "When I was with Myrddin, he mentioned that name."

Ban picked up the letter again and scanned it. "From what Hoel says, he's the youngest captain in the army and hasn't lost a battle. His lieutenants are young, too, but well disciplined; the full cohort of five hundred has only lost eleven men. Amazing."

"Then that's who I want to fight with," Galahad announced. "Do you think we'll be called soon?"

Ban shook his head. "Not this year. The fighting season is nearly finished and peace has reigned. One Saxon, Aelle, even pledged to be an ally. Hoel says Uther sent Arthur to accomplish it. And he did. I think this young man is destined for great things."

* * * *

"Check," Galahad said as he moved his bishop to align diagonally with the opposing king. His queen was in a defensive position for the only move he could see Gaia could make.

Gaia studied the board. They were in the outer room of Niniane's cave. It was near Yule and Galahad had been able to get an afternoon away. He needed the company of the women who had raised him. It looked this time like he might win. Finally.

She moved a bishop to counter his, but it was a sacrifice. He swooped it up. "Check mate."

She smiled. "Congratulations."

He grinned and gave her a big hug. "You even lose well. I'm going to miss you when we go to Britain."

"When are you going to Britain?" Niniane had entered the room and stood watching him with a slight frown.

"Madame." Galahad stood and went to her. "Don't worry. Father says they have no need of us this year. But," he added, "I know who I want to fight for when we do go. His name is Arthur. You remember. Myrddin once said I would be of help to him someday."

"Myrddin. The note he sent about the dream for Britain . . ." Niniane's gaze turned inward. "Arthur," she said in that distant, hallow voice that meant she was in trance. "He is the Dream. Your destiny is linked with his, yet you may destroy it." She broke from her trance suddenly and looked at Galahad. "You must take care, my son."

For a moment he swelled with pride that he would one day he'd be fighting with Arthur. Then he frowned. "How could I destroy him, Madame? You know my sense of loyalty, once given, would not be forsworn."

"It is a woman that will come between you, I suspect," Niniane answered.

A woman?" Galahad felt himself color and remembered his conversation with Bors months ago. Nothing had come of it for Ban kept a close watch. "I can assure you, I would never stand in the way of any—woman—that Captain Arthur may want."

"Her future is linked to both of you, I think," Niniane said softly. "And if it is the will of the Goddess, there may be naught that you can do."

"Why would the Great Mother put me in such a situation?"

Niniane smiled at him. "Surely I have taught you better than that? We each have our lessons that we must learn. Mayhap yours is to resist temptation. Well, what will come, will come." She changed the subject. "I have something I've been holding for you. I think the time is right for you to receive it."

He waited, puzzled, as the priestesses who lived with his mother began filing into the room. They formed a circle around him and he felt the warmth of their love. His mother left the room and then returned with a package wrapped in silk. She unwrapped it, revealing a soft leather pocket that held an athame. He took it from its scabbard and admired the sharpness of the double-edged knife. Then he noticed the runes that had been engraved on its ebony handle. "'Tis beautiful . . . and unusual."

His mother nodded. "It is made from a stone that fell from the sky before even the druids came to these isles. Its name is Secace. There is a sword that was forged from the same stone. My sister, Vivian, has it. But it will be worn only by the king who can unite all Britain."

"Unite all Britain? In my lifetime?" Galahad asked wonderingly.

Niniane smiled. "I would not have given you the athame if its mate would not be of service in your lifetime."

The priestesses filed past him, one by one, giving him their blessings, but it was Gaia who ruffled his hair.

He gave her his lopsided smile.

* * * *

They finished the jousting practice one early spring afternoon when the sun had nearly melted the snow and Galahad practiced throwing his lance as he rode past the quintain with its round ring. He rode back to where the group of boys stood watching him and dismounted.

"Why do you waste time on that?" Marok wanted to know. "In battle, we throw pikes, not these heavy lances."

Lionel gave him a disgusted look. The fosterlings had an uneasy truce with Galahad's cousins. "It can do a lot more damage and it strengthens his sword arm."

"You're probably only trying to show off for those wenches over there," Lovel jerked his head in the directions where the serving girls gathered. "Have you tried tumbling any of them yet?"

Galahad set his lance in its side pocket and appraised Lovel. There were times he had to control his desire to knock the boy out again. "No," he said in a clear voice. "Those girls deserve respect just like a lady would."

Lovel laughed, his two friends joining him. He wiped tears from his eyes and when he could finally speak, he said, "They're servants. Meant to be used as their master—or his guests—sees fit. Do you think they'd be out here if they didn't want our attention?"

"Besides," Persant added, "girls like that expected to be handled. They like it rough."

Galahad looked over to where the girls stood, giggling. He'd heard Lovel and his friend brag on what they did when they went into the village tavern. Somehow, he couldn't see these girls, who usually acted silly when they were around him, liking anything like what Lovel bragged that he had done. Now, seeing him watching them, the boldest one, Ena, waved. He glanced quickly away.

"I know," Lovel said as he tried to withhold his laughter, "let's show you what I mean. Come on." He turned and started walking toward the girls, his friends tagging along behind him.

"No! Wait!" Galahad called and then gave his brother a worried glance. Reluctantly, they followed the fosterlings.

By the time Galahad had reached them, each of the three boys was kissing a girl, their hands roving over the female bodies predatorily. "Stop!" Galahad said.

For an answer, Lovel shoved Ena toward him. "Go ahead," he told her, "let him know what you want."

"This isn't . . ." Galahad began and then she had her arms around his neck and her lips were on his. Momentarily, he felt dizzy. Her lips were soft and pliant under his and he could feel the curves of her body as she pressed herself against him. An ache began in his loins and spread throughout his body. His legs suddenly felt weak and his breath was fast and shallow. Then he heard struggling and one of the girls screamed.

He pushed himself away from Ena and saw that Lovel had taken a girl to the ground and was wrestling with her, trying to open the front of her dress. Marok and Pesant let go of their girls and reached down to help him. Marok caught the girl's flailing fists and held them.

"Don't!" she cried. "I only wanted a kiss."

Galahad yanked Lovel off the girl and pounded his face with his fist. Blood spurted from his nose and the next blow split his lip. Lovel snarled in fury, and struck back at Galahad, but he hardly felt the blow to his shoulder. He punched again, this time below the rib cage and Lovel went to the ground, moaning in pain.

Galahad took a deep breath and rubbed his fist. The knuckles were raw. He saw that his brother and cousins were holding back Marok and Pesant.

"Do either of you care to join Lovel?" he asked, the blood lust still strong.

They shook their heads mutely and Galahad turned to the girl. She was surrounded by her friends and crying. His breathing slowed and he walked toward her.

"Are you all right?" She looked up at him and he saw the bruise already forming on the side of her face. His fingers touched her cheek gently. "Nothing seems to be broken." He looked back to where Lovel was being helped up by his friends and then back to the girl. "I'll walk you to the infirmary and we'll get some salve for you."

Ena narrowed her eyes and glared at him as he led the girl away, but for the life of him, he didn't know why.

* * * *

He tossed and turned that night, unable to sleep, thinking about his reaction to Ena's kiss. Toward dawn, he fell into fitful slumber.

He was astride a black stallion, not his beloved Caireen.

The riderless sorrel stallion came pounding up the road to the fort where he was staying. He shouted for someone to catch the colt and put spurs to his own mount.

She must have gone for a ride by herself and been thrown. I should have stayed with her instead of preparing for this tourney.

His horse pounded the cobblestone road that led away from the fort toward the forest.

He heard her scream as he neared a bend and heard two horses galloping away.

She lay in a heap, trying to hold the torn shreds of her shirt together. He slid off his horse and gathered her in his arms, noting the bruises on her face and breasts before she buried her face in his neck and sobbed uncontrollably.

"You're safe now. They're gone. It's all over," he murmured as he stroked the long, glossy copper hair. "I'm here. I won't let anyone hurt you again."

Without lifting her head, she pulled his down to her breast. "Please," she said, "make me feel clean again. I feel so used."

For a moment, he didn't understand her meaning. Her hand guided his head and he began to suckle a nipple gently . . .

Galahad awoke in a sweat. By the gods' sweet light, what had he been doing? It had felt so real, but he'd been a grown man. Was THAT what it felt like to touch a woman . . . ? And who was the woman with that glorious hair? He knew he'd never met her. *Mayhap, the dream is just a reaction to yesterday's events.* Yet, in his soul, he knew that wasn't true. Whoever she was, he wanted her totally, heart and soul.

* * * *

In anticipation of possibly being called to Britain, Ban hosted a tourney a few weeks later. "To get my men in peak performing condition," he said.

Galahad was excited. It was his first real tournament against adult men. After the incident with Lovel, Ban finally sent the fosterlings home in disgrace and Galahad took to competing with the hardened soldiers. He wouldn't be six and ten until late July, but Ban told him he was ready. He couched his lance now as he looked down the lists at his opponent. The man outweighed him by two stone.

The flag dropped and Caireen lifted into the rocking horse canter. As they closed, he pressed her flanks with his thighs and brought the lance into better position. She reached out and drummed a steady cadence on the packed earth. The impact on the other shield shattered his lance and his opponent's hit made his arm numb. He shook it vigorously as a squire handed him another lance and he rode toward the opposite end of the list.

He turned and they charged again. This time he was ready for the way the man shifted his weight and threw it behind his lance. Galahad did the same and was rewarded with pushing the man unto the crupper of his horse. Only because the war-horse was trained to stop immediately when his rider left the saddle, did the man manage to hang on. The crowd laughed and they took position for a third attempt.

Galahad rubbed his shoulder. The second hit hadn't been as strong, but it landed in the same place. He adjusted the pad as much as he could and urged Caireen forward. This time, his lance hit square on the shield and he raised himself in the saddle, feeling the connection remain intact. Caireen slowed and leaned into the rail. Galahad was able to literally shove the man from his horse, using the heavy lance almost as a staff.

The crowd cheered and Galahad grinned, holding the lance in victory. He reached down and rubbed the Caireen's neck. "Well done," he said and she nickered softly in reply.

When he finished rubbing the mare down later, he pulled an apple out of his pocket that he had wheedled the plump, young cook into giving him. Apples were a rare, highly prized delicacy to be savored slowly. Galahad took his dagger and cut the apple into slices.

"Here," he said as he fed the first one to his horse. "You deserve this. You made me win today." She accepted the morsel with the dignity of a queen and looked questioningly at him.

He laughed. "You won't beg, will you?" He laid another piece on his palm for her.

"Well, 'tis yours. All of it."

"Do you always treat your horse so well?" Ena stood near the door of the stall, watching him.

He looked up and then went back to doling out slices. "Why wouldn't I? Someday, she may save my life in battle." He stroked the silky coat. "She's my best friend."

Ena stepped inside, her eyes on his long, strong fingers that were so gently stroking the horse. She sighed audibly.

"What is it?" Galahad asked as he gave the last slice of apple to Caireen.

"Your hand," she said, stepping closer. "I wonder what it would feel like if you touched me like that."

Galahad inhaled sharply. *I should tell her to leave.* "Why are you here?"

She laughed and brought his hands around her waist and put her arms around his neck. "I think you know," she said as she tilted her head for his kiss. "I want to finish what we started that day."

He hesitated but a second and then his lips were on hers, pressing her mouth open, his tongue demanding entrance. She willingly complied, pressing her breasts against him and he wrapped his arms tighter around her, caressing her back, feeling the curve of her hips. He felt himself harden and heat pulsed through him, obliterating anything else from his mind. There was only this moment with a girl who was soft and pliant and willing . . .

"Galahad!" his brother, Ector, said and for a moment, he didn't focus as he tore himself away from the deepening kiss. "Father is on his way here to congratulate you personally! He'll not approve of this!"

It took most of his willpower, for Ena continued to cling to him and nibble on his neck, but he managed to remove himself. "You'd better go," he said, "and quickly or you'll find yourself working in the village."

With a petulant pout and one last wet kiss she raised her skirts and ran out the back door of the stables.

None too soon. Ban came striding in the double front doors a moment later. "Well done," he said as he neared.

Galahad hoped his breathing had slowed enough that he appeared normal, for his heart was still beating fast and he had a throbbing in his trews that needed some kind of attention. "Thank you, Sire."

Ban gave him a strange look, glanced around, and then looked back. "Well," he said, "there's other news. A messenger arrived this afternoon. From Uther. Apparently, Colgrin has had sufficient time to lick his wounds and has rebuilt his army. We're requested to go to Britain."

The sexual energy that had built up in Galahad transformed itself into anticipation.

Finally! He'd be able to meet Arthur. Over this past year, rumors had trickled in about Arthur fighting in the Caledonian Wood, routing Saxons that were established there since the time of Hengist and Horsa. More and more, Galahad had developed an intense desire to meet his young warlord who was so successful. All the training Galahad had would be put to the test and he was determined he wouldn't come up lacking.

"There's something else," Ban said and Galahad came out of his thoughts and looked at him. His father had that strange expression on his face again and Galahad wondered guiltily if he knew Ena had been there.

"Your mother also sent a message. "She wants you to spend the last ten days before we leave with her."

"How did she know we were going?" Galahad asked. "The messenger just came today."

Ban shrugged. "I long ago stopped asking how your mother's intuition works. She has the Sight. You should know that better than I. She only said there was something important that you must do before you left."

Galahad wondered what could be so important that it would take ten days. With his mother, it was hard to tell. But it would be great to see the priestesses again.

"Well, whatever it is, it can't be more important than going to Britain."

Ban raised an eyebrow. "If this is what I think it is, you may change your mind about that."

CHAPTER TWELVE—WARRIOR CHILD
495 A.D.

The messenger arrived as Gwenhwyfar and her father had finished the mid-day meal. Leodegrance's face grew grave as he read the letter from Pelles.

"What is it, Da?" she asked.

"Your aunt has died in childbirth and the babe, too. Pelles is asking that your cousin, Elaine, come and live with us. Since his leg wound never healed, he's in constant pain and doesn't feel he can take care of her properly, now that she's getting older."

"She's nine, two years younger than me." Gwenhwyfar considered. "It might be fun to have someone my own age to be with."

Leodegrance studied his daughter. "It hasn't been easy for you, has it, not having any girls to play with?"

"I'm fine, Da. I've learned Latin and to read and do my numbers. The tutor taught me to play chess. Bedwyr showed me how to use the sword and a bow and the head groom has taught me a lot about horses..."

Leodegrance laughed. "That's because you practically live in the stable. I hardly see you except at meals."

"I like talking to Prince. He's my best friend."

"And soon, you'll have outgrown him," Leodegrance answered.

Not yet! She knew her legs were dangling now when she rode, but Prince was a large pony. They'd have more time. "He'll always be my best friend," she said.

"Well," Leodegrance answered, "I think it's time you have a human friend as well. I'll tell my brother Elaine is well come here."

* * * *

A month later, in July, Gwenhwyfar watched from the steps as Elaine stepped daintily from the carriage that bore her and Briesen and looked up at the villa. She hadn't seen her cousin since they'd attended Arthur's wedding and Elaine had been only five.

Elaine was dressed in a traveling jacket and matching skirt that weren't wrinkled at all, although she was now smoothing the skirt. Her hair was neatly plaited around her head and her shoes shone.

Gwenhwyfar wiped a smudge of dirt from her nose and tried to tidy her hair. She probably should have followed Mirre's advice and worn a dress. *Well, if we're going to be friends, Elaine will have to see me as I am.* She walked down the path to greet them.

"Well come, Elaine, to our home." She turned to the nurse. "And you also."

The woman looked over Gwenhwyfar's linen shirt and trews and sniffed. "My name is Briesen. Does your father allow you to dress like that?"

For a moment, Gwenhwyfar bristled. *How dare this stranger criticize my da?* Then she remembered that Mirre always said Celtic hospitality must be shown. She said evenly, "Yes. And Elaine will probably want to dress like this too, once she learns how to ride."

Elaine gave her a wide-eyed stare. "Oh, no. Horses are smelly beasts. I prefer to stay clean."

The young wolfhound, Glena, nudged her wet nose against Elaine's hand and wagged her tail in greeting. Elaine pulled away in fright, holding her hand out as though it had been contaminated.

Gwenhwyfar took Glena's collar and tugged gently. "She won't hurt you."

Elaine sniffed. "Just keep that brute away from me."

Gwenhwyfar became aware now of the scent of roses coming from Elaine. *How can anyone smell like that in the middle of the day?* Her da made her bathe daily in the warm Roman baths that still worked, but by lunch, she generally had dirt on her breeches and straw in her hair.

"My pony doesn't smell bad. I wash him every week," Gwenhwyfar answered. "Wait until you meet him. You'll see."

"I have no desire to go inside a barn," Elaine replied and picked up her skirt carefully to keep if from the dirt. "Could we go inside? It's frightfully warm out here and Briesen says I must stay out of the sun to keep my skin soft and white."

Gwenhwyfar felt herself redden. *My manners again!* "Certes. Follow me."

She showed Briesen her room and then took Elaine to hers. "You'll have your own chamber, but I wanted to show you my unicorn." She pointed to the tapestry. "Isn't he beautiful?"

Elaine studied the hanging. "It's all right, I guess." She looked around the room. "Don't you have any dolls?"

Dolls? Why would I have dolls? There's too much to do outside! "No," Gwenhwyfar admitted. "I've never played with them."

Elaine gave her an unbelieving look and then glanced around the room again. "And where is your loom? Don't you weave?"

Inwardly, Gwenhwyfar groaned. She hated weaving, and embroidery, too. So far, it didn't seem like she and Elaine had anything in common. "I don't have time for that. I have weaponry practice every day and Da is showing me how to do the accounts."

Elaine looked shocked. "But those are jobs for men!"

Gwenhwyfar shrugged. "Someday, I am going to run Cameliard. Da tells me I must learn how."

"Not me," Elaine answered and giggled. "I'm going to marry the best-looking, strongest man in Uther's army! And he'll treat me like a queen. I'm already a princess you know."

"So am I," Gwenhwyfar said, "but I'm never going to get married. I never want to leave Cameliard." She looked at Elaine. Aside from the fact that they both had the same color of hair, for their mothers had been twins, they had little in common. She had a sinking feeling her cousin was going to take getting used to.

* * * *

Bedwyr arrived unexpectedly shortly after Lugnasad when the August heat was upon them. He brought Arthur with him, as well as Cai, Gwalchmai, and Gryflet.

Gwenhwyfar flew down the steps to meet him as they rode through the gate. He picked her up and swung her around and set her down. "You're getting too tall for me to do that much longer," he said.

"Never!" she laughed. "We didn't know you were coming! How long can you stay? Wait until you see how I've improved my swordplay! Can we go riding? Prince has learned some new tricks . . ."

"Do you always ask so many questions?"

She stopped in mid-sentence and looked up. Arthur. His clear grey eyes were laughing at her. *I don't like being laughed at.* "Why does it matter to you?" she asked flippantly.

"Another question." He dismounted. "Your brother told me his baby sister was a whirlwind."

She lifted her chin. "I'm not a baby! I'm eleven."

"My apologies. I should have realized you were a lady." His discerning gaze took in her trews and the stains on her shirt and then her hair, half of which had escaped her braid. He grinned.

She felt herself blush and furiously tried to stop. So this was the Arthur Bedwyr so admired. She glared at him and someone else laughed.

She glanced at the other man, but he was looking at Arthur.

"It seems this is one . . . lady . . . you haven't impressed!" Gwalchmai swung down from his saddle. He bowed toward her. "I'm happy to meet you, Gwenhwyfar."

She looked into his eyes, wondering if they were all going to tease her, but she saw nothing in his bland expression to indicate that. *At least one of Bedwyr's friends is nice.*

"Let's go in," Bedwyr said and wrapped his arm around Gwenhwyfar's shoulders.

She remembered her manners then and invited all of them to come inside.

Once they were seated in the Great Hall, Bedwyr explained the situation to Leodegrance. "We cannot stay but the night. We're on our way to Rheged. Uriens says there's trouble with the Saxons and Octa has been spotted across the Wall."

"So close?" Gwenhwyfar asked before her father could.

Bedwyr nodded. "Octa's not Hengist's son for nothing. When he stayed north and held the Picts at bay, all was well. Now Uriens thinks he may have other plans."

She frowned. "If King Uriens needs help, why doesn't he come to Cameliard? We're neighbors. We could muster troops much faster than King Uther could."

"For a girl, you seem to understand strategy." Arthur looked amused. "Mayhap Uther would let you into the army."

Gwenhwyfar glared at him again. He had a way of setting her temper aflame and it didn't help that his friends all seemed to think him funny. She didn't.

She deliberately turned to her brother. "Is King Uther going to send troops?"

Arthur leaned forward. "I'm the one that's in charge of deciding." He didn't try to hide his grin this time. "What do you think I should do?"

I will not let him goad me. Again, she wondered how Bedwyr could nearly worship this man. Arthur was arrogant. She met his gaze. He raised an eyebrow. *I will not be intimidated.*

"I think," she said, "that you are going to do exactly what you want to do. You've probably never valued anything a woman has said or done."

She didn't understand why all the men laughed at that, and Arthur's grin widened. He straightened. "You're wrong about that, Gwenhwyfar. But we'll let it go. For now."

* * * *

"Watch me now, Elaine." Gwenhwyfar notched her bow, sighted the eye in the target, took aim, pulled, and released. The arrow arched in the sky and made a graceful descent and struck just right of the center. "Damn." She quickly made the sign of the cross. Leodegrance was quite strict about her not cursing.

Elaine looked bored. "Why should I watch this? I have no interest in becoming an archer. I'd much rather talk about how good-looking that Captain Arthur is."

Gwenhwyfar sighed. Elaine had been so quiet at that dinner several nights ago that Gwenhwyfar had almost forgotten she was at the table. But she had talked of nothing else since then.

"He's way too old for you," she answered. "He must be at least twenty-five."

"Well, Gwalchmai is younger, I think, and he spent some time talking with me."

Elaine looked hopeful. "Do you think he likes me?"

Gwenhwyfar laughed. "You're nine. They're grown men. We're both children to them."

Elaine remained unruffled. "I want to get married as soon as I'm old enough. It doesn't hurt to look and dream."

Gwenhwyfar rolled her eyes and turned back to the target. This time the arrow flew true. She sighed with contentment. She would be able defend herself and Cameliard. Let Elaine flirt with the village boys and have her dreams. Gwenhwyfar certainly didn't understand them. She doubted there was a man alive who would ever be able to make her fall in love.

* * * *

As the autumn months turned chill, Leodegrance asked Gwenhwyfar one day if she would like to join the hunting party. "We have to provision for the winter," he said, "and you've never been on a hunt. This will be a good experience for you."

They set out on a crisp morning. Frost lay on the ground, but the sky was a brilliant azure. In the distance, clouds were building. The leaves were still on the trees in their flush of scarlet, orange, and gold. Geese flying south honked overhead as they set out. Gwenhwyfar filled her lungs with the clean air and thought about how right everything was in her world.

They rode several miles into the nearby forest before the hounds took up the scent. They left the road for the deer path and at first, Gwenhwyfar saw nothing except thickets of gorse. Then suddenly, the hart broke through the brush into the clearing. He bolted for the trees on the far side, but not before a bevy of arrows rained through the air. Gwenhwyfar saw him lurch to the side before he leapt into the shadows.

"Spread out," the head huntsman shouted. He looked up at the scudding clouds moving in from the west. "I know he's hit. He'll be close by. Mayhap we can get home before it rains."

Gwenhwyfar took the path to right. It led in a twisted way through tall pine and bramble. She made her way around a small pile of rocks and stopped. She was in a small glade and there, before her, stood the stag.

He was magnificent, his antlered head holding eight points. He did not seem to be particularly frightened of her. She stayed in her saddle, wondering what she should do. Mostly, she wanted to shoo the animal away and give him his freedom.

He turned soft, luminous eyes toward her and only then did she see the arrow lodged in his neck on his other side. Blood flowed down his beautiful, tawny coat. She inhaled sharply as he sank to his front knees.

She was beside him in an instant, not caring that her father always warned her that wounded animals were dangerous. She must try to get that arrow out. This creature was too noble to die.

The hart seemed to understand. He looked at her with pain and acceptance in his eyes and Gwenhwyfar knew she would never forget that look nor the animal's hurt. She could feel it inside of her. Sobbing now, not noticing that the sky had turned overcast, she reached for the arrow and yanked. It came out and the buck bleated weakly before it rolled over onto the grass, its eyes glazed.

The storm broke, great sheets of rain drenching Gwenhwyfar and washing the blood off of the deer. She looked up as the huntsmen came riding into the clearing and she knew, without any doubt, that she would never hunt again.

* * * *

The next morning, Gwenhwyfar had the cook pack her a lunch and she took Prince for a solitary ride. She had to be alone with her thoughts. She went through the forest in the opposite direction from yesterday's excursion and came to a small stream, flowing through tumbled rocks. Trees lined the opposite side, but where she was, only a hawthorn grew. She found a place in the sun, near a patch of primroses, where she could prop her back against one of the stones.

She realized there was a need to hunt. Her father's people needed to be fed. She had just never envisioned the reality of the kill, or the beauty of the animal who gave up its life. *I need to understand.*

Gwenhwyfar closed her eyes and lifted her face toward the sun; the warmth felt good, almost like a healing. From somewhere, she heard a meadowlark calling its mate, its bubbling, flutelike notes rising at the end. She heard the response and grew drowsy. She inhaled the sweet scent of the primroses wafting on the air. *It would be so good to sleep just a little . . . to forget yesterday.*

Her unicorn was there, the one from the tapestry. He stepped out from the shadows of his thicket, his satin coat the color of moonlight. The unicorn's great blue eyes were sympathetic as he folded himself neatly to the ground and laid his head, with the horn of pearl, in Gwenhwyfar's lap.

"*Be at peace,*" he said.

It seemed so natural for her to stroke his silky mane, as she lay dozing in the sun.

She wasn't particularly surprised when the man who wore the antlers and always remained sheathed in the shadow of the tapestry stepped forward.

He was ageless. His eyes were a clear hazel, a blend of brown and green, and his curly hair dusky amber, nearly matching the bronze of his skin. He was powerfully built, but he moved with catlike grace. On his head was perched a magnificent rack of antlers.

A hand reached out to touch her and gently stroke her shoulder. Gwenhwyfar's lethargy grew deeper. It was so comfortable here . . .

"I am Cernunnos," he said, "the demi-god of the Wild Hunt and of all forest creatures. Know that none of my creatures dies in vain."

"I didn't think you were real," Gwenhwyfar mumbled groggily.

He smiled. "Hawthorn and primroses are always portals for Faerie. Take my hand and I'll show you."

Something compelled her to move toward him. His eyes held her spellbound. Mesmerized, she reached for his hand.

The unicorn neighed shrilly and lunged to his feet. He pushed at Cernunnos with his horn.

A look of anger flashed across the demi-god's face and then he sighed. "You are right, I suppose. She is too young for me to take yet." He looked past the unicorn and into the future. "But I see this girl in the Land of Faerie." He looked back at the unicorn and gestured. "Do what you came to do."

The unicorn gently nudged Gwenhwyfar toward the water. He lowered his head and dipped his horn into the stream. "Drink," he said, "and you will understand why my brother gave his life yesterday."

Cernunnos leaned close and whispered, "When you awake, you won't remember me. But one day, we will meet again."

Gwenhwyfar opened her eyes to find herself kneeling by the water, Prince by her side. His muzzle prodded her shoulder and for a moment, she could have sworn she felt the horn of a unicorn instead.

CHAPTER THIRTEEN—THE RESCUE
495 A.D.

Arthur, his lieutenants, and Myrddin met in Uriens' Great Hall shortly after their visit to Cameliard. Uriens' news wasn't good.

"The Saxons haranguing the Wall may have been a decoy, or more likely, scouts that were spotted," Uriens said. "Their real intention is to move north from the settlement at Dumfries. Their target is Alclud."

"That fort is our defense against Picts. So the Saxons seek the whole of the north to Antoine's Wall," Arthur answered and looked at Gwalchmai. "Your father owns land in Lothian, does he not?"

Gwalchmai nodded. "I'm sure he'll be ready to fight."

Uriens smiled. "Lot's already on his way. Things have been way too quiet for him these past several years."

"We'll have need of Pellinore's archers, too," Arthur said as he took notes. "I'll send for Cadwy's troops and Hoel's, in addition to my cohort. That'll give me nearly a thousand cavalry. Adding your men and Lot's, we should have three to four thousand infantry. Enough to lay waste to these Northern Saxons once and for all."

"Octa has the shrewdness old Hengist had," Myrddin warned. "And you know what happened at the Cloister Massacre."

Arthur narrowed his eyes. "I doubt any of us will make the mistake to sit down unarmed again. But I don't plan to treaty with them. They are too far north for us to keep a watch on unless we spread our troops thin. I mean to clear the whole area."

"A wise choice," Uriens said. "All of the troops should arrive in the next week or two. Until then, please consider yourselves my guests, although I'm sorry to say that Morgana is away; Ygraine asked her to bring Medraut for a visit. He's three now."

For some reason, Arthur felt relieved. When she was around, he always felt he might just be the rabbit caught in a badger's hole. "I'm sure my officers will appreciate your hospitality," Arthur said, "but I had better stay with our men who are camped. For morale and to stop the brawls I know will happen if I'm not there."

Bedwyr glanced at Cai. "We'll go, too; the men are under our direct command."

Gwalchmai tore his gaze away from the voluptuous young woman pouring his wine and sighed. "Ach. I'll come, too."

Arthur grinned. "Did you miss that village we passed through? You won't go lonely for long." The girl gave him a dour look and he winked at her. "He'll be back."

* * * *

Arthur's horse threw a shoe on the way back to camp and he stopped off at the smith in the village. When Arthur introduced himself, the smithy's eyes widened. "Sure, now, 'tis a pleasure to be meetin' you," he said. "Your name's known in these parts."

A tall, attractive black-haired girl came to stand beside the smith. "Da," she said, but her eyes were on Arthur, "supper's going to get cold."

Arthur recognized the look and gave the girl a smile. "I wouldn't want your father waiting on his supper. Go ahead and eat," he told the smith. "I'll wait."

"That would be rude of us." The girl's hazel eyes held just a hint of mischief. "Please join us. I'm Miara." She held out her hand.

"Arthur." He held her gaze as he bent over her hand. He brushed his lips lightly over the top, but a finger caressed her palm unseen. It had the desired effect. He heard her sharp intake of breath and then the return pressure of a squeeze. He straightened. "I'd be honored."

"Go on ahead," the smith said. "I'll be along in a minute."

She led the way to the attached rooms behind the smithy. "It's simple fare," she said as she motioned Arthur to sit. "Just a stew and some freshly baked bread."

Another girl turned from the cauldron she was stirring and Arthur caught his breath. She was even prettier than Miara, but in a different way. Her hair was dark, but her eyes were blue. Where Miara was tall and slender, this girl was petite and pleasantly curvaceous. She gave Arthur a straightforward look.

"My sister, Minerva," Miara said as she leaned over and set a steaming bowl in front of him. He had a glimpse of the tops of her breasts and he let his hand graze hers as he took the bowl from her before looking back to Minerva.

"A pleasure to meet you," he said and gave her a boyish smile.

She studied him. "You're here with the troops, aren't you? There's bound to be trouble with so many men in town. There always is."

Arthur blinked. *She certainly is candid.* "You should have no reason to fear my men if you stay near your home."

"I don't fear them," she said, "it just gets annoying not having them understand what the word 'no' means."

Arthur nearly choked on a swallow and Miara giggled. "She's just really picky."

Minerva glared at her before she turned back to the cauldron and Arthur took the opportunity to stroke Miara's arm. "And you?" he asked.

She ducked her head and her dark hair swung over her face. She tilted her head and looked at him sideways. "I find you quite satisfying."

Arthur grinned and started to lean forward for a kiss when a shadow darkened the doorway. Miara stepped away from him as her father entered and took a seat.

As they ate, Arthur told the smith some of their general plans to rout the Saxons.

The man grunted. "Aye. It shoulda' been done long ago. The yellow-haired devils have no place on Briton soil."

Arthur was surprised to hear the vehemence in the man's voice. He could have sworn the smith was Scotti, from the accent. But then, some of them had been here so long, they didn't remember their roots in Eire.

"Ye say ye will be goin' all the way to Alclud?" the smith asked.

"Mayhap," Arthur answered. "Depending on where we catch up to them."

"Might it be that you'd be needin' a farrier along the way?" he said. "I can hardly make a living here since the fella across the way set up his smithy."

Arthur appraised him. They normally traveled with their own, but if he used this man, he wouldn't have to send to Ambresbyrig. He stole a look at Miara to find her trying to suppress a smile. Minerva had a look of distress on her face.

"We will," Arthur said slowly, "but what will you do with your daughters?"

The man sighed. "Minerva I don't have to worry about." He gave Miara a stern look. "But this one I need to keep an eye on. I'd like to take them with me, if you can guarantee they won't be molested. They aren't camp followers."

"*Certes*, they aren't." For a moment Arthur felt himself entering the dizzying world of near madness. *How can I guarantee that when it is I who wants her?*

"Da," Miara said, "mayhap if you let me cook for Arthur, he'll keep me under his personal protection. No man would defy his captain."

What a quick thinker she is. Then he frowned. *I have no wish to deceive this man if he'll be working for me.*

"I have no objections to that," the smith said, "if you'll offer that protection to Minerva, too. She can cook and launder and sew . . ."

Arthur held up a hand. "There's no need for either of them to be my servants, although I'll welcome a good meal now and then." He looked directly at the smith. "I can put them under my protection, but I can't guarantee that I, myself, won't be tempted. Your daughters are beautiful. All I can swear is that I'll never make one of them pregnant."

"You don't have to worry about me," Minerva said. "I choose my own partners."

Arthur stared at her and then slid a glance to her father. *Does he know his daughters aren't virgins?*

The man shrugged. "Northern customs are different from yours. I don't approve of it, but they're both old enough to know their minds. I just don't want them to become camp followers. Can you promise me that?"

"Yes," Arthur answered, "that I can promise."

* * * *

Within the week, the armies marched. Lot, for some reason, hadn't joined them and Arthur was hesitant to wait. It was September and winter came early in the north.

They passed through the Saxon settlement of Dumfries with little trouble, for the fighting men had gone north to lay siege to Alclud and their women traveled with them. What was left in the town were the too old and too young who would hamper their time. Arthur corralled these without much bloodshed and left a half-company of guards. "We'll send them back when we rout their soldiers," he said.

Now, they approached the area known as Caledonia Wood where the Roman road narrowed and made it difficult to maneuver the horses. Ever aware of an ambush, the infantry marched first, the cavalry following them and Pellinore's archers bringing up the flank.

"Do you hear the beat of their drums?" Cai asked as he brought his horse alongside Arthur's. "They can't be more than a mile in front of us!"

"With all that noise, I hope they can't hear us," Arthur replied. "I'd rather be out of these woods before we fight."

"Aye," Cai said, then stopped. The drums were no longer beating.

"Damnation," Arthur said. "They know we're here. Once we round that bend, be prepared." Silently, he signaled to his officers to prepare the men.

The infantry dropped into phalanx position and the cavalry spread out as much as it could. There would be no room to do a full charge; they would have to depend on the sheer size and bulk of the horses to mow the Saxons down and that meant close combat.

The first flurry of arrows fell harmlessly on the raised shields. Pellinore's archers ran alongside and returned fire before falling back.

The Saxons stood firm, blocking the road. The cavalry spread out, ready to press forward after the initial clash of the foot soldiers. *I'd much rather have broken their lines, crushed them, and then given the fighting to the infantry, but this is the road we had to use.* Arthur raised his hand to signal and then whirled his horse at the sound of hoofbeats coming from behind.

The infantry engaged and dust clouds filled the air. The stamping and rearing of the horses only added to the fray, making vision difficult. Dimly, Arthur could see Pellinore's archers run for the trees under cover of the arrows they fired. Pellinore pulled his sword and was charging the front line. *Fool! You'll get killed!* "Sound the signal; turn half the cavalry to me," Arthur commanded the young centurion who rode beside him. "I don't know who those men are, but Pellinore needs back-up and quickly." He didn't wait for the order to be carried out, but galloped to the rear, Bedwyr and Gwalchmai right behind him.

"Wait!" Gwalchmai bellowed. "Archers, hold your fire!" He turned to Arthur. "Those are Orkney men!"

For a moment Arthur stared at him. He raised his hand to stop the charge, but not every horseman stopped; filled with battle frenzy some rode on. Arthur swore and took a quick look at the Saxon front. The infantry was holding and the cavalry that had remained were pressing through. He turned back to the melee in front of him.

"Where's Lot's banner?" he asked Gwalchmai.

"He wouldn't have raised it until he was ready to fight," Gwalchmai answered. "Arthur, we've got to stop this!" He didn't wait for an answer, but kicked his horse forward.

Arthur followed. "Sound the retreat," he yelled as the centurion reappeared at his side. He reached under his hauberk and tore a piece of his tunic. *Thank God it's white.* He waved it furiously above his head. "Truce! Truce!"

Slowly, the din died down. Men on both sides seemed confused and then looks of horror came on Arthur's men, realizing they had fought an ally. *There will be hell to pay tonight. Flogging will only be the start.* Arthur rode forward grimly. *Lot's a hotheaded man and only bids marginal allegiance to Uther. Now I'll have to pacify him. Damnation!*

He saw where the standard was being unfurled and then he heard Gwalchmai's keening cry. Only an Orkney man could make that cry sound so totally wild and feral. With even more misgiving, Arthur nudged his horse on.

Lot lay on the ground with Gwalchmai huddled over him. Beside them, Pellinore leaned heavily on his bloodied sword. Tears streamed down his face.

Arthur swung down and felt for Lot's pulse, but knew from the color of his face that the man was dead. He put a hand on Gwalchmai's heaving shoulders and looked up at Pellinore. "What happened?"

Pellinore shook his head. "My men reacted instinctively. Lot's men returned fire. I didn't see a standard and thought they might have been Saxons, disguised in spoils-of-war armor."

"Didn't anyone try to tell you who he was?" Arthur raked a hand through his hair. "By the Christos, Pellinore!"

"He didn't tell me who he was and he probably didn't know who I was either." Pellinore dropped to his knees beside Gwalchmai. "Forgive me. It was an accident. Your father was defending himself and then I . . . I had to defend myself . . ."

Gwalchmai looked up, his eyes red-rimmed. "In time, mayhap I can learn to forgive. Not now. I demand blood payment." He turned to Arthur. "It is my right."

Arthur nodded. "How do you wish the payment to be made?"

Gwalchmai was quiet for some minutes. Finally, he said, "I have lost my father. Let Pellinore lose his son."

Arthur heard Pellinore's sharp intake of breath. "Lamorak is a strong soldier, Gwalchmai. One of the best. Would you have him killed?"

"It is my right to seek revenge!"

"Yes," Arthur answered patiently, "but there is another way. Hear me out. Your mother, Margawse, has also been left without support. If I were to send Lamorak north, to pledge fealty to her, to be her champion until you or one of your younger brothers is of age to take over, would that suffice? He would not be allowed to leave her lands, or Pellinore to visit."

Gwalchmai wiped at his eyes and then gave a mighty sigh. "Aye. Lamorak has been a friend; I shouldn't take his life. Send him, Arthur. If my mother accepts the terms, it's okay with me."

Arthur patted his shoulder. "You can escort your father's body and talk to your mother yourself. If she accepts the hostage, you can bring your brother, Gaheris, back. We can use him to replace Lamorak." Arthur looked up to see Bedwyr approach. He took in the situation and hesitated.

"What is it?" Arthur asked.

Bedwyr dismounted. "The Saxons have disappeared into the woods. When they saw our horses moving forward, they broke and ran. The infantry started to follow, but I called them back, not sure what was going on here."

Arthur nodded wearily and helped Gwalchmai to stand. "I'll decide what to do tonight. Right now, let's give Gwalchmai's father the respect he deserves."

* * * *

It was Myrddin who had the idea to barricade the Saxons in the woods.

"What?" Arthur said unbelievingly that night at the campfire. "You want me to cut down trees and build a stockade around the forest?"

Myrddin eyed him calmly. "Yes. At the end of a day's march, the Romans would dig ditches and form earthworks topped by a palisade of pointed poles that would encompass thirty to one hundred acres. This forest isn't much bigger. Surely your men can build a fence?"

Arthur hated it when Myrddin needled him like that. Even when he was Myrddin's student, the ruse had always worked. *Tell me I can't do something and I will!* And he could have sworn he heard a woman laughing somewhere, but there wasn't anyone around.

Myrddin scratched his ear, a crooked grin on his face.

"All right. Let me think about it. Can I let you know in the morning?" Arthur yawned and stood up. "I'm going to call it a night."

He walked to his tent, thinking. It might work. And it would avoid more bloodshed. He lifted the flap and went inside, removed his tunic and splashed water from the basin on the nightstand over his face and chest. He kicked off his boots and removed his trews and fell onto the cot, exhausted.

A warm body pressed against his, and a soft hand caressed his face. "I thought you might need me tonight," Miara said.

He rolled over and took her into his arms. "More than you'll ever know," he whispered and then there was silence between them, save for her soft moans and his harsh grunts as he sought solace from the abomination of war and killing.

* * * *

The ruse worked. Using the horses for hauling and every pair of arms available, including the non-combats, it took Arthur's men a day to build the stockade and three more days before the Saxons finally felt the pangs of hunger hard enough to surrender.

"I'm sending them all back to their homeland," Arthur told Myrddin. "I'll have the army march them to the sea and set them afloat there. We'll send a company to escort the refugees at Dumfries. If they aren't allowed to take anything but what they're wearing, we shouldn't require too many ships."

Myrddin raised an eyebrow. "Do you have a fleet waiting on the east coast?"

Arthur grinned. "No. I thought we'd build one. Or, better, have the Saxons build their own, under our supervision."

Myrddin looked at the compound of several hundred men. "I haven't spotted Octa. He had to have led them."

Arthur stopped smiling. "I asked to have him brought to me. You think it's possible he's still hiding in the woods? We've scoured them pretty thoroughly."

"Some may have slipped through. Octa has survived this long because he uses his wits. His men would be willing to protect him at all costs, for they know he'll try to rebuild. They may have dug a hole that we overlooked."

Arthur leapt to his feet. "Then he must be found and stopped." He called to Bedwyr. "Collect about a dozen men for one more search party." He turned back to Myrddin. "But Octa's mine when I find him. He won't be going home."

* * * *

They searched the woods without any luck. As they emerged on the opposite side, Arthur said, "There are several homesteads near here. Let's split up and ride to them. Ask the farmers if they've seen any Saxons pass this way."

He and Bedwyr headed north over rolling hills and through pastures that would be lush with green grass come spring. In the distance rose Blackcraig Hill, standing tall like a sentinel on duty. As they came around a curve, two homesteads lay ahead, within half a mile of each of each other.

"You take that one." Arthur pointed to his left.

"Shouldn't we stick together?" Bedwyr asked.

Arthur scanned the horizon. There was little movement save for some sheep grazing nearby. "I don't see any smoke rising anywhere. It's doubtful they've come this way," Arthur answered. "It'll save time to split. We'll almost be within yelling distance."

He set his horse in a canter toward the holding on the right.

As he approached the small grove of trees that hid the actual hut from his sight, he heard the first scrapping sounds of a struggle and then he heard a scream. He burst through the trees.

A raiding party of Saxons—five of them—his mind made a mental count, even as he drew his sword and bore down on them. The farmer lay dead, his throat slashed. His wife lay beside him, skirts hiked above her waist, a knife protruding from her chest. A girl—still nearly a child—lay where she had been tossed near a clump of bracken, bruise marks around her neck and blood between her thighs. A second girl, already stripped of her clothes, was struggling with two of the men.

Arthur slashed through the shoulder of the first man to come at him. He yanked his sword back and slashed again, the blade slicing through the man's neck. He swung his war-horse around and the horse lashed out with his hind hoofs, catching the second Saxon in the stomach, even as he was raising his ax. Arthur wheeled and met the third man head on. The horse's barred teeth bit deep into an arm, even as Arthur brought the sword down on top of the man's head, splitting it open. His sword broke.

Arthur jumped from the horse and pulled one of the Saxons off of the girl. He landed a punch square in the man's face, smashing the nose inward and upward for instant death. The last man reluctantly let go of the girl, who scampered away, and lunged at Arthur, a dagger in his hand.

Struggling, they rolled over in the dirt, Arthur desperately avoiding the blade inches from his face. With a massive effort, he managed to bring his elbow up and crack the man's cheekbone. It gave him just enough leverage to twist the Saxon's wrist and drive the dagger home.

He lay panting for a split second before he became aware that another Saxon had stepped from the house. *By Mithras! How many more are there? I should have heeded Bedwyr!* Quickly, he pulled the dead Saxon's sword from its scabbard and leapt up.

Octa leaned against the doorway, a half-smile on his face. "You're quite a fighter."

Still gasping, Arthur warily looked around. "Where did you come from?"

The big Saxon jerked a thumb over his shoulder. "I had a little unfinished business in there; the girl wasn't cooperative and it took a longer than I expected."

Arthur stared at him. "You didn't come to the aid of your men?"

For a moment, a flicker of remorse flitted across his face and then disappeared. He shrugged. "There were five of them and only one of you. I didn't see the need." He straightened abruptly and drew his sword at the same time. "I guess it's up to me now to seek vengeance."

Thank God he talked and gave me time to recover. Arthur adjusted his hold on the grip, testing the balance of the broadsword. It was heavier than the longsword he was used to, and the tip was rounded, not pointed. He would have to chop with it rather than thrust. Luckily, Octa wore only a leather cuirass and no helmet.

They circled. Arthur cut low, but Octa parried easily and returned the blow. Arthur sidestepped and lunged, slashing sideways with the sword. It cut through the cuirass and drew first blood. Octa swore and thrust back. The swords engaged, each man pressing against the other's blade, feeling out the strength of the opponent's arm.

In a sudden movement, Arthur disengaged and brought the huge sword under Octa's and lunged, praying he had enough strength left to drive the blade into the Saxon's groin, for there was no armor there to protect it. His raping of the girl inside the hut had given Arthur that advantage.

Arthur threw all of his weight behind the thrust and felt it rip through cloth and then skin and bone. Octa looked slightly surprised and then he slumped to the ground, the sword still embedded in his genitals.

A fitting way for you to die. Arthur took a deep breath and looked around at the carnage. The Saxons were all dead and he had put an end to Octa. Rarely did he feel good after killing, but this time, justice had been served.

The girl huddled next to her dead sister, trying to cover her nakedness with her arms. Arthur went to his horse and pulled his cloak from the bedroll. He walked over to the girl and draped the cloak around her shoulders. Gently, he helped her stand and felt her quiver at his touch.

"It is over. You're safe now," he said.

She pulled the cloak tightly around herself and looked up at him, her velvet brown eyes still wide with fear.

Arthur smiled. "You have nothing to be afraid of. I won't harm you." She just stared at him mutely. "Do you have relatives I can take you to?"

She shook her head and looked down at her sister. Slowly, she walked over to where her parents lay and then to the house. She glanced inside and shuddered, but didn't go farther than the doorway. Arthur wondered if she would start crying. As much as he hated tears, he knew she would feel better if she did.

He walked toward her and saw the look of apprehension leap into her eyes. He stopped a few feet away. "I promise I won't hurt you."

Hoofbeats sounded along the road and Bedwyr came into sight. He pulled the horse to a stop and slid from the saddle. "What in God's name happened here?" he asked as he strode toward them.

The girl flung herself into Arthur's arms, clinging desperately to him. He wrapped his arms around her protectively. "Stay where you are, Bedwyr. She's frightened out of her wits." He stroked her long, dark hair somewhat awkwardly, for he wasn't used to nurturing. "Shhh. You're all right. He's a friend."

Bedwyr turned and examined the Saxons. Slowly, he swung his head around. "You got Octa? Good work!"

Hesitantly, the girl turned her head from Arthur's shoulder to look at Bedwyr. For the first time, she seemed to take in the dead Saxons. Arthur felt some of the tension leave her body and he gently disengaged himself. "We'll bury your family and then I'll take you with me. Why don't you find some clothes and pack the things you'd like to bring along?"

She nodded slowly and went inside.

"Bel's Fires," Bedwyr said when she'd gone. "Did they rape her too?"

"I don't think so," Arthur answered and explained what had happened.

"What are you going to do with her?" Bedwyr asked.

"I have no idea," Arthur replied. "I can't leave her here. Mayhap, she can live with Miara and Minerva."

"Have you taken leave of your senses, Arthur? Your woman is hardly going to welcome competition."

"What competition? The last thing that girl needs is to be bedded. Minerva will accept her." Arthur took a deep breath and hoped he sounded more confident than he felt. "I'll handle Miara."

* * * *

Miara stood beside Myrddin as Arthur and his men rode into camp. She narrowed her eyes dangerously as she saw the girl pressed close against his back, her arms wrapped tightly around him.

Myrddin looked from her to Arthur and shook his head. His faerie giggled. Arthur swung his leg over the stallion's withers and slid down. He lifted the girl from behind the saddle and set her on the ground.

"It's not what either one of you thinks," he said as he looked from Myrddin to Miara.

Miara folded her arms across her chest. Arthur sighed and then was glad to see Minerva approach. He explained the situation to them and Minerva nodded and turned to the girl. "You'll be safe with us. What's your name?"

"Brigid," Arthur answered. "'Tis the only word I've been able to get her to say."

Myrddin raised an eyebrow and then cocked his head, as though listening to something. "Yes," he said softly.

"Who are you talking to?" Miara asked.

Arthur smiled. He had long ago become accustomed to this eccentric habit as well as Myrddin swatting at his ear. It wasn't the only odd thing Myrddin did.

"Myself," Myrddin answered. "Arthur, I think Brigid needs more help than even I can give. She'll find healing on the Isle. Send a messenger to the Lady. By the time we reach Ambresbyrig, she can have someone waiting."

Brigid looked up at Arthur and he smiled reassuringly. "Avallach is a place of women. You could be no safer anywhere else."

She considered and then nodded. Minerva gently took her hand and led her away.

* * * *

Nimue arrived the day after they returned to the fort. When Arthur led Brigid into Myrddin's quarters where Nimue waited, he was struck again by her ethereal beauty and those limpid turquoise eyes. He felt a bulge in his trews that he promptly squelched. Or tried to. *Why am I so drawn to her?*

She gave him a brief smile and turned her attention to Brigid. Her small hands slowly skimmed the air around Brigid's head and then the rest of her body. A slight frown creased Nimue's forehead and she sighed.

"Much damage has been done inside; she cannot grieve." She touched Brigid's forehead and chanted softly. "If anyone can build your trust again, it is the Lady of the Lake. Go, now, and get your things."

When Brigid had gone, Nimue turned to Arthur. "She will be well come to live out her life with us, if need be."

Arthur was startled. "Surely, she'll get well and want to marry someday. Isn't that what all women want?"

Nimue raised an eyebrow. "It is not the life that I have chosen."

Arthur felt himself color. "Forgive me. I did not stop to think."

She favored him with a smile. "Brigid seems to trust you, but I don't think there's a man alive she'll ever allow to bed her. I saw what happened in her mind."

Brigid returned and Arthur walked them outside to the awaiting carriage. As he watched them leave, he hoped that somewhere there was a man who could make Brigid forget.

CHAPTER FOURTEEN—THE POWER OF NINE
496 A.D.

Galahad dismounted near the shore of the Lake and approached the glen hesitantly. Two years had passed since he visited his mother's secret caves, deep within the heart of Brocéliande. Now he was getting ready to leave for Britain. His hand touched the knotted knob on the stout oak tree. Within seconds, the wind singers stirred from the leaves and carried the message to the Lady that her son had returned.

He proceeded to the stone pilings and slipped through a notch not seen by those without fey blood. Once inside, the pathway opened to reveal the glistening crystals reflecting the shafts of light through the crevices above. Quickly, he descended the stone steps that led far below the surface of the lake. The large cavern at the stairs' base was filled with richly brocaded stuffed chairs and polished tables. Hundreds of scented, beeswax candles sat in the wall's niches. He turned at the sound of her step.

"You sent for me, Madame?"

He knew how he must look to her. The past two years spent in weaponry training with King Ban had developed his shoulder and arm muscles. His thighs were already hard from years of riding. He'd also grown several inches. He was no longer a boy.

Niniane reached up to brush back the unruly strands of dark hair on his forehead. "Yes. You'll be leaving to join for Britain in ten days. I asked Ban to let me have you until then."

"I am glad for the opportunity to see you, Madame." Galahad chose his words carefully. "But why ten days? My father is selecting men for his units and we are polishing our skills."

Niniane smiled. "You still have need of one more skill, my son."

"What? I'm accomplished at swordplay and lance throwing. I can pull a bow; horses have never been a problem."

His mother shook her head. "I was speaking of something else. Have you lain with a girl?"

Galahad felt himself blush and looked away. "No."

"I thought not. The moontides will soon rise for you, and I will have my son learn the skill of pleasuring a woman."

His chin jutted out. "Madame, surely, I will know what to do!"

She laughed. "Ah, yes. Instinctively, men know how to satisfy themselves. I was speaking of satisfying the woman. Those can be two quite different things." She laid her hand on his arm. "Our women enjoy thigh freedom; they have the right to choose their partners. When one chooses you, she is a gift to be savored and appreciated. In the next several days, you will learn to do that."

His eyes widened as he looked at her; Ban kept the young soldiers restricted and in particular, himself. "You want me to couple with a girl?"

"Not yet. I have selected seven of the best courtesans in all of Armorica and one from Britain that is especially skilled. You will spend a day with each of them, learning what pleases the particular lady . . . how individually distinctive she is."

Galahad's smoke-colored eyes turned darker. He swallowed hard. "Adult women? Eight of them? Who have lain with many experienced men?" His voice rose. "I will be made the laughing stock of Benoic!"

Niniane smiled. "I can assure you that quite the opposite will happen. Besides, I have another reason to train you well."

He looked at her questioningly.

"I have a maiden here, sent to me from Vivian."

"From Britain?" Galahad broke his silence. "Why?"

"Her family was murdered by Saxons. She was forced to watch her mother and sister be raped and slaughtered. The brutes had already stripped her naked when the young warlord, Arthur, rescued her. He sent her to the Lake, but the girl went half-mad at the thought of staying on the same soil with the barbarians, so Vivian sent her to me to heal."

He nodded uncertainly. "It is what happens in war, Madame. Why is this girl so important? Does she have a royal bloodline?"

"No." Niniane's voice was sharp. "She is merely a farmer's daughter, but you will treat her as though she were a queen. Every woman deserves that."

"Treat her? I don't know her!" Galahad protested.

"You will." The Lady's voice was soft but full of authority. "She has been with me four moons, and still she will not speak. She skittles away from any man who gets near. I do not want her to be frightened of a man's touch for the rest of her life."

"But what do you want me to do?" Galahad's voice trailed off as realization dawned. "Surely not . . ."

"Yes," his mother answered. "You are young, close to her own age. I want you to help her get over her fear. Show her the pleasure of the act, once you learn it."

With an effort, he kept his voice even. "Madame, you expect too much from me."

She studied him for a moment, her soft hazel eyes glowing. "Nine is a scared number and she will be your ninth. You have fey blood, Galahad. You will be ready."

* * * *

Her name was Brigid. Galahad met her the next morning. She sat in the glen with his mother, the sunlight catching the chestnut reds in her dark hair. Even though he stopped several feet away, he could see the frightened look in her soft brown eyes. *Like a wounded deer*. She moved closer to Niniane and for a moment, relief flooded him. He would never get close enough to even touch her in ten days.

His mother spoke. "Brigid. My son, Galahad. I thought you might enjoy the company of someone near your age. He will not harm you."

Galahad smiled at her, the lopsided smile that would endear him to another woman one day. Brigid simply stared at him.

"Come, both of you. Let us walk a ways." Niniane linked an arm to each, keeping herself in the middle. "Tell us what Uther has planned for the men from Benoic, Son."

As they walked, Galahad took care to talk only of the battles already won and how the Saxons would be overthrown. "My father says there is a young captain, Arthur, who is making quite a name for himself."

Brigid looked up at the mention of Arthur's name. For a moment, Galahad thought she might smile, but then she looked away. He sighed. *How can my mother expect . . .?* He continued to talk about the preparations being made and when he took his leave, he spoke directly to Brigid.

"My mother told me what happened. When I meet Arthur, I will tell him you are alive and well. Would you like that?"

She didn't answer, but the fear was gone from her eyes as she held his gaze.

* * * *

He felt like a dolt. The woman curled up in the chair beside him was beautiful. Her long, straight hair was the color of cornsilk and her green eyes slanted upward slightly. When she smiled at him, she displayed small, even white teeth and dimples on each side. Overall, she gave the appearance of a well-fed and contented cat. He could almost hear a self-satisfied purr.

She trailed long, slender fingers of her well-tended hand slowly down his cheek.

"You are alluring, Galahad," she said easily, leaning closer to him. "Do you enjoy my touch?"

He struggled to breathe normally. "Yes . . . 'tis . . . quite nice."

Her eyes smiled at him as she undid the ties of his shirt and let her hand rest against the bare skin of his chest. "Have you kissed a girl?"

"*Certes*!" He tried to sound nonchalant, remembering Ena.

She moved closer, her hand caressing him now. "Kiss me, then."

Flooded with emotions, he closed his eyes and brushed his lips against hers. He started to draw back when he felt her arms go around his neck and then came the soft pressure of her lips on his. She parted her lips slightly, kissing first his upper lip and then drawing in his lower one.

He groaned when her tongue probed his and wrapped his arms around her, his desire kindled like dry tinder to a flame. When his hand reached for her breast, she caught it and sat back.

"That comes much later, Galahad." Her voice rebuked him gently and he felt himself blush. She brushed his hair back. "But I will look forward to it."

He forced himself to look at her. "What do you want me to do?"

She laughed. "Oh, you'll do, my dear. You're a natural toucher." She tilted her head and glanced at him sideways. "Am I to be your first?"

He thought about lying, but she would know he was untried. He took a deep breath. "Yes."

She took his face between her hands and kissed him slowly and deeply. "Then," she said quietly as she slipped off his shirt, "I will have to take my time, teaching you all the pleasures of your own body."

He touched her hand lightly. "I am supposed to be learning how to please you."

"You already are, because you care." She undid his trews and he moaned when she touched him. "Now, lie back and let me make this special for you."

* * * *

The mare stood quietly as Galahad brushed her shining, chestnut coat. It was almost the same color as Brigid's hair, he reflected, and knew she had come to stand behind him.

He turned, smiling, and held out the comb. "Would you like to do Caireen's mane?"

Shyly, she came forward and took it from him and turned to the horse. Galahad stayed where he was, close enough to smell the jasmine scent of her hair. This was the morning of the sixth day; only two days ago she had actually spoken her first words.

He had been grooming the horse, talking to it in soft, crooning tones when he became aware of her watching him. He deliberately ignored her and eventually, she stepped closer.

"You are gentle with the horse," she said.

Now, he watched her as she carefully pulled the comb through the long, silky hair. The mare nickered contentedly.

"She likes you," Galahad observed. "Normally, she only allows me to do that."

Brigid didn't turn, but he could tell she was smiling by the way she dipped her head. Slowly, he brought his hand up and softly stroked her hair, lifting it and letting it fall on her shoulders. She stopped combing and he heard her quick intake of breath, but she didn't flinch.

"I will not hurt you," he breathed in her ear as he reached around and covered the hand that held the comb with his. "Let's finish this together."

* * * *

On the eighth day, the last courtesan arrived. Galahad wasn't sure he was glad this was the last one or not. He felt he'd aged ten years in the past week. The ladies had been incredible; he had no idea, even in his wildest, adolescent imaginings, that there could be so many places to touch or different positions in which to achieve pleasure. And it wasn't just his pleasure; the ladies were generous in sharing the secret desires of females and he found himself wanting to fulfill them. He was even becoming confident that, mayhap, he could convince Brigid the act was enjoyable.

He wasn't prepared, then, for a different kind of courtesan when the final one arrived. She was a tiny thing, with raven black hair and soft slanted eyes. Her golden skin belied her foreign birth from a land beyond Byzantium, as did her softly accented voice. Her hands worked magic on him, like a thousand butterflies lighting gently on his arms and legs and torso and then leaving again, but she hadn't kissed him or tried to arouse him past where he was. Now, she sat up and reached for her bag and took out two long strips of silk and a cluster of ostrich feathers.

Galahad stared at the items and raised an eyebrow. She smiled and let the silk glide across his bare chest. "Do you like the texture against your skin?"

"Ummm."

"Or this?"

The ostrich feathers tickled his belly and he reached for her. "I'd rather have you," Galahad murmured.

"Not until you can bear my touch no longer." She reached up and tied the silk around his eyes and then pushed him back onto the pillows. "Stay there and do not move."

She massaged his shoulders and chest, her fingers lightly tracing his flat nipples. He lurched toward her, but she pushed him back again.

"I said not to move. Be patient and enjoy the sensations."

Galahad felt the heat radiating from himself, or maybe it was from her. All he wanted at the moment was to rid himself of the blindfold and grab her, but he forced himself to stay still.

Her hands became demons that tormented him, but in exquisitely delightful ways. Each time, when he thought he could stand her touch no longer, she would become slow and easy, or move on, only to return when his writhing slowed. The feathers he could hardly bear. When her mouth covered him, he began to think he would go mad with desire. His body was soaked in sweat as he strove to accept the teasing touch that tickled and tormented. He felt himself getting lightheaded and then, blessedly, she straddled him and guided him inside her warm dampness. He bucked wildly two . . . three times and then the world exploded into a dizzying away of shimmering light points. He lay panting.

* * * *

Niniane sat down beside him the next morning, as he was breaking his fast. "What do you think of the new skills you have acquired, Son?"

Galahad smiled. "I doubt even Uther, himself, has had the variety of experiences that have been mine. I thank you."

"Did you enjoy last night?"

He looked at her warily. "It was . . . different."

She nodded. "You were with someone who would not harm you. I wanted you to know the feeling of being helpless so you might temper the bloodlust that is a part of war. I pray you never rape."

"You have my word, Madame. I will never force a woman to have me."

Looking relieved, Niniane stood. "Good. Now, I want you to spend the day with Brigid. You leave tomorrow."

Galahad stood also. "I know you want her to lose her fear of men, but I will not do anything she does not want me to do."

"The ladies have shown you how to honor a woman and how to please her." Niniane gestured. "I have lunch and a wineskin packed. There is a meadow not far from here that she likes to go to. Let the Goddess work Her will."

* * * *

Galahad lifted Brigid down from the mare. She stepped away quickly from his arms. His mother had designed a divided skirt that allowed her to ride astride and she busied herself smoothing the simple lines of the garment.

He sighed inwardly as he took the bedroll from behind his saddle and spread it on the ground. He placed the food and wineskin in the middle, sat down and looked around.

The meadow really was a pleasant spot, the new grass brightly green, the first of the spring flowers standing yellow and blue in the field. Not far away, a brook bubbled its way through the forest; the sounds of the water splashing and birds singing were relaxing. For a moment, he almost forgot he would be leaving the next day to go to war.

Brigid sat across from him and divided the lunch. She handed him a trencher.

He took a bite of cheese, "Do you come here often?"

Brigid shook her head. "The Lady doesn't want me out alone and everyone is busy most days."

"A good idea, especially after what happened." He stopped and bit his lip.

She looked up, her brown eyes like liquid pools. "It's all right. The night dreams no longer bother me." She hesitated and then looked away. "I know why we're here . . . what you're supposed to do."

Galahad reached over and took her hand. "Look at me, Brigid."

Slowly, she did, the expression on her face apprehensive.

He looked intently into her eyes, his own becoming smoke-colored. "I will not do anything you don't want me to do, regardless of what my mother said. She's not here."

Relief flooded her face and he fought the urge to pack everything up and go back. His mother wouldn't be pleased and Brigid would still be frightened. He shook his head. *Slow. Go slow.*

"Could I have some wine, please?"

Her hand shook as she poured two cups. He reached for his as she moved to give it to him and their hands bumped, spilling the red wine on his white shirt. She sat back, embarrassed. "I am so sorry!"

"Do not worry about it." Galahad sprang to his feet, pulling the shirt off. "There's water close by, I can soak the stain out in a few minutes. I'll be back." Turning, he strode toward the trees, then stopped. "You better come with me."

She followed him a short distance to the brook. He took off his boots and hunched in the shallow water, rubbing the shirt. He stood up and wrung out the shirt and then wiggled his toes.

"This feels really good. Take your shoes off and join me!"

Brigid held her skirts carefully as she stepped in and promptly slipped on a rock. Galahad caught her easily, an arm around her waist.

"Are you all right?"

She nodded and looked down. Just then, a school of small silvery fish swam over her toes, rippling the waters. Forgetting Galahad, she squealed in delight.

Galahad smiled and took her hand; they followed the stream for a distance, trying to find the elusive fish. Finally, they returned to the lunch site, where the horses grazed contentedly.

He put his shirt out to dry in the sun and lay back on the blanket. Puffy balls of cotton filled the deep blue sky. He pointed to a cloud. "Look at that one. Can you see the shape of a dog? There are the feet . . . and the head . . ."

Brigid craned her neck from where she was sitting. "The face is too pointed. I think it's a fox . . . or maybe a cat!" She gave a soft giggle and pointed to another one. "And there's a rabbit . . . see the long ears?" She stopped and rubbed her neck.

"Here. Lie back." Galahad pulled her down gently beside him and tucked an arm under her neck. "This should be more comfortable."

Her body was stiff beside him, but he ignored it. "Pick out another cloud and tell me what you see."

They spent some time doing that and he found she was very imaginative, literally drawing pictures on the backdrop of the sky. As they talked, she gradually relaxed until she naturally nestled her head unto his shoulder.

"You're really very pretty," Galahad said as he reached to brush some strands of hair from her face. His hand traced the curve of her cheek and his thumb grazed her chin. He leaned over and kissed her forehead and lay back again. "Tell me what you see in that huge cloud that is building up over there."

"Rain, I think," she said practically and he laughed, his fingers gently stroking her neck and shoulder.

"Don't you see a hill fort?" he asked.

She looked harder. "Mayhap."

"It may be where we're going," Galahad answered. He continued caressing her face and throat. "Tell me about Arthur."

Brigid turned toward him and he moved her arm across his waist. For an instant, he thought she would pull back, but she didn't.

"Arthur is the most wonderful man I've ever met!" she said seriously and then colored. "Oh, I don't mean . . ."

He turned on his side and pulled her closer, kissing the tip of her nose. "'Tis all right. He saved you. I would expect you to think him near perfect."

"No. Well, yes. 'Tis how he acts." She looked at him in earnest. "When he found me I wasn't wearing any clothes, but he didn't ogle me or try to take advantage after the Saxons were dead. He simply wrapped me in his cloak, lifted me on his horse and rode for the king. He kept telling me everything would be all right."

Galahad trailed his hand along her waist and hip. "Are you in love with him?" he asked softly.

She smiled weakly. "It wouldn't matter if I were. Many of the daughters of wealthy men have set their caps for him."

"Really? Those stories I haven't heard; only that he is a fierce fighter."

"He is. There were six Saxons that day." Suddenly, she buried her face against his chest.

Galahad put both arms around her and held her. "I'm sorry to have brought it up," he whispered and began a series of small kisses on her cheek and ear and throat. Her shaking subsided and she turned her face toward him. Gently, he kissed her lips. And again, increasing the pressure a little.

Slowly, she brought her arms up around his neck and returned his kisses. He let his hand drift lightly across her breasts, over the fabric of the shirt and felt her tense again.

"Do you want me to stop?" His voice tickled her ear.

She stared into his eyes. "I saw what . . . they made me watch . . . they hurt . . ."

Galahad brought her hand to his mouth and kissed the palm. "What those men did was brutal. Inhuman. No sane man would treat women like that."

Brigid hesitated a moment longer and then pressed his hand to her breast and closed her eyes.

He took his time in undressing her, letting his hands explore the exposed skin. Only when she finally began to smile and squirm under his touch did he begin to tease a nipple with his tongue.

She gasped and her eyes flew open. "Galahad!"

He moved to the other one, taking it carefully in his mouth and suckling. She gasped again and he softly pushed her breasts together, flicking his tongue from one nipple to the other, quickening his pace and pressure. A soft mewling escaped her lips.

"I had no idea this could feel so good." Her hands clutched his shoulders.

Galahad grinned. "Then, tell me how you like this." He slipped down, his mouth working across her stomach and then lower while his hands caressed her inner thighs.

She groaned in earnest when his tongue lapped at the wetness that was forming. He began to play a delightful game with his fingers, inserting and retracting them, until her body was moving in the ancient rhythm.

Silently and fervently, Galahad thanked the courtesan who had shown him how to prepare a virgin by the slow stretching. *Dear Goddess, let there be no pain for her.* He worked his way upward along her body and this time, she did not hesitate when his mouth covered hers and his tongue explored her mouth.

He lifted himself over her and prodded her legs apart, probed gently with his thighs. Slowly, he inserted himself into that tight, wet sheath, a little bit at a time. When he filled her, he waited, letting her adjust to the sensation. She inhaled sharply with his first hard thrust, but then wrapped her legs and arms around him, clinging to him as they lost themselves in the pleasures for which their bodies were made.

* * * *

King Ban looked at him sharply when Galahad returned to his training grounds in Benoic the next day.

Galahad edged into position and tried to pay attention to what was being said to him, but he could feel his self-satisfied smirk threatening to turn into a grin.

"Obviously, the ladies your mother selected were successful," Ban said wryly. "Remember this: Uther's men are known for their exploits with women and you won't find any of them wearing the silly expression that is on your face."

"Yes, Sire." Galahad managed to straighten his mouth.

"You'll need to concentrate on fighting if you want to be in Arthur's unit; he's as lustful as any of them, but he won't tolerate a man who can't keep his heads separated."

"Arthur?" Galahad was suddenly serious. "Am I to be attached to him?"

Ban nodded. "Yes. Arthur commands a cohort of light cavalry. I told Uther you were a natural with horses."

Galahad thought briefly of what Brigid said about all the women who wanted Arthur. It made him even more interesting, now that Galahad, himself, had been enlightened to the pleasures of the opposite sex. "It will be an honor to serve with him."

"That it will, Son. Don't disappoint me." Ban started to leave and then turned and winked. "But you do feel like you invented the act, don't you?"

CHAPTER FIFTEEN—LANCER
496 A.D.

The Armorican ships docked at Clausentum a week later and the soldiers proceeded to Ambresbyrig.

"Do you think we'll get to meet Arthur tonight?" Galahad eagerly asked his cousins, Bors and Lionel. Both of them had hardly been able to contain their excitement on learning they would be placed with Arthur, also.

"I hope so!" Lionel answered, a squeak in his voice that he immediately tried to control.

"Uncle Ban told us Arthur would probably still be north." Bors gave his brother a superior look. "Don't you ever listen?"

"Don't argue." Galahad pointed ahead. "Look!"

A group of perhaps twenty men were galloping toward them, the banner carrying the

red dragon unfurled and flying in the wind. King Ban halted his men and waited for the escort to approach.

Uther pulled his stallion to a rearing halt only feet from Ban's horse. For all of its training, it barred its teeth at the other, ears flattened. Ban gave a sharp tug on the bridle and the horse stilled.

The Pendragon seemed not to notice. "Ban!" He slapped him jovially on the shoulder. "Well met! Your men are just in time. Since Octa has been killed in Caledonia, his young, hot-blooded son, Aesc, will be straining the borders to prove himself. We may be fighting him before we rout Colgrin and Baldulf. Well, we'll talk later," his sharp eyes looked over the boys behind Ban. "Are these your sons?"

Galahad forced himself to sit tall in his saddle. King Uther radiated sheer force and power; this was a man who would have use only for the brave and courageous.

His father introduced them. "Son and nephews for Arthur's cavalry."

"Ah, yes! Recruits for the light cavalry. We have a new breed of horses the Saracen in his unit brought from Mecca. Beautiful animals. When Arthur returns, he'll explain what he has in mind."

"Arthur's not . . ." Lionel blurted and was silenced by a horrified look from his brother. Galahad clenched his jaw. *No one interrupted a warrior king.*

An amused expression passed over the king's face. He turned to Ban. "The young ones are always eager to meet Arthur." He looked at Lionel and the boy blushed. "You'll have your chance in a few days."

As they made their way through the gate, the boys all noticed the serving girls standing on the steps of the Great Hall. They giggled and some of the bolder ones winked. One called out, "You, sir, in the middle . . . my name's Eren!"

Bors looked across Galahad to his brother and grinned. "Our cousin's already had an offer, just like at home!" He glanced at Galahad. "She's a comely lass. Do you think you'll know what to do?"

He didn't answer, but there was a smile on his face as he stared straight ahead.

* * * *

Galahad was practicing swordplay with one of Uther's men when the gong sounded on the battlement. "Arthur returns!" the guard shouted and Galahad fought the urge to turn and run to the gate. He concentrated on his opponent, ready to lunge, when the man grinned at him.

"Go on. You'll want to see your new commander, I expect."

Galahad threw him a grateful look and sheathed his sword. Quickly, he joined the others who lined the road.

The standard bearer furled the silver banner with the huge black bear on it. Behind him rode a group of four men, one red-headed, another fair, the third with chestnut hair and the fourth . . .

For Galahad, there was no mistaking Arthur. The muscular, broad-shouldered man rode easy in the saddle, but his eyes were penetrating even from where Galahad stood. He carried himself with both authority and dignity and when he pulled up his horse, his men halted at attention.

Uther waited for him in the bailey. Arthur dismounted and presented himself to the king formally. "We've scouted all the way to Camulodunum. Colgrin is definitely building forces again."

"Well done, Arthur." Uther gave him a soldier's embrace.

A shout went up from his men and Galahad felt his heart swell. He straightened his shoulders and stood a little straighter as did Lionel and Bors. He watched as Arthur dismissed his troops.

Uther spoke again. "Ban's brought his men, a full cohort to add to our own."

"Good. We can use another five hundred men; I already have the Anglia campaign planned." Arthur turned to Ban. "How are your brother, Bors, and your wife, Queen Elain?"

"Never better," Ban replied with a smile. "And I've brought three eager recruits for your cavalry . . . my son and two nephews." He gestured to where Galahad was waiting, near the stables. "Come here, boys, and meet your captain."

Boys! Did he have to call us that? Galahad held his head up, forcing himself to meet Arthur's clear, direct grey gaze.

Arthur offered his hand. He had a powerful grip and Galahad was glad now he had spent those countless days in not only handling, but also throwing the lance. Out of the corner of his eye, he saw Lionel wince and even Bors flexed his hand behind his back.

"For *certes*, I can tell you two are brothers." Arthur smiled at Bors and Lionel and then turned to Galahad. "And you must be the Lady Niniane's son, am I correct?"

Galahad was surprised. It was no secret in Benoic that he was a product of the Great Rite, but he didn't think the story would have reached this far.

Arthur saw his consternation and placed a hand on his shoulder. "You have her eyes. I saw her once, when Myrddin and I visited the Lady of the Lake. They both made quite an impression on a young boy."

Myrddin. The arch-druid. He looked around speculatively. "Is he here?"

Arthur's eyebrow lifted, "Myrddin? At the moment, he is at the Lake. Do you know him?"

"I've met him." Galahad willed himself not to look away.

"I see." The grey eyes studied him and it seemed Arthur sighed a little. He changed the subject. "Well, I suggest all of you get a good night's sleep; tomorrow, I'll see how well you handle horses."

* * * *

Several weeks later, Arthur finally let Galahad ride the black stallion from Mecca called Pryderi.

"His name means 'trouble,'" Arthur said as he led him out. "I've yet to find a man who can stay on him. But, I've never seen a man who sits a horse as well as you; mayhap, you can convince this brute he has a job to do besides producing foals, pleasant as that may be."

For a moment, Galahad glowed with pride. In the weeks he'd been here, he'd heard the stories about this horse. Anyone who could manage him would have a place beside Arthur in battle. His captain was offering him a challenge and it didn't just have to do with the horse.

He stepped up to the black. It could have been the horse from the dream of several years ago, the one with the mysterious woman with the copper hair. He'd never been able to get the woman or the horse out of his mind. The horse's small ears were pricked forward and the large, luminous brown eyes watched him steadily. The horse stood still, neither shying nor stamping, its neck set gracefully in a curve, head tucked in. Galahad wasn't deceived. He'd watched the animal act like a well-trained palfrey until someone settled on his back.

"Do you mind if I spend some time with him before I ride him?" he asked.

Arthur handed the reins over. "Suit yourself. Stay in the paddock; I'll have a devil of a time catching him if he gets loose."

Galahad nodded, but already his mind was communicating with the horse. They stood silently, looking at each other, then Galahad slowly began stroking him, running his hand down the deep chest unto the forelegs, watching for the telltale ears to go back. Pryderi snorted once, but remained quiet.

"You are beautiful, you know," Galahad said. "If we could be comrades, I would treat you as well as I treat any woman." He grinned and whispered in the horse's ear, "I've been shown how to treat them well, too."

Pryderi nickered and snuffed at his tunic and Galahad rubbed his forelock. "I don't have anything for you right now, boy." His hand moved to the girth and the dented cinch buckle that pinched the horse's skin. "Maybe it's the saddle you don't like." He loosened the strap and studied the buckle. "I think I can come up with something that won't pinch." He made his decision.

Quickly, he removed the saddle and blanket. Pryderi turned his head toward him. "I'm going to try you bareback," Galahad told him. "I hope you don't make a fool of me." He gathered the reins and a patch of mane and vaulted up.

Pryderi flung his head up, ears laid back. "None of that." Galahad rubbed the horse's neck gently, but kept the reins in check. "Let's start with a walk." Lightly, he tapped the horse's flank and to his own surprise, the stallion moved forward. He asked for a turn and the horse complied. Delighted, he tapped again for the trot.

He was so engrossed in working with the horse that he didn't realize a small crowd had gathered, a safe distance from the paddock fence. Arthur stood in front of all of them, watching the fluid movement of horse and rider.

"Well done!" he called, when Galahad finally brought the horse to halt and slid down. He and Bedwyr came to the rail and Galahad joined them there.

"I've never seen anyone ride that well," Arthur commented. "The horse understands you."

Bedwyr nodded. "The only other person I know who can whisper to horses like that is my sister, Gwenhwyfar."

"That hot-tempered child that followed you everywhere while we were there?" Arthur asked. "I would think she'd make the horses nervous."

"No. She's stubborn, but she loves horses. She's different around them."

Galahad stroked Pryderi's soft muzzle. "I can understand that," he said off-handedly.

* * * *

"I'm ready to move the two cohorts to Camulodunum." Arthur laid a map of Anglia flat on the table in the large council room. "From there, we can move straight across to the sea, taking what's in our path."

Galahad watched as Uther studied the map. Even though he wasn't quite seven and ten, ever since he had ridden Pryderi, Arthur had taken to mentoring him. He was excited to be a part of the planning.

"Only three roads lead into the area," Uther said. "One crosses over the marsh of the Fens, another through forest. Too risky for an ambush. The third road is the Icknield Way, through open country, best for the cavalry."

Arthur frowned. "What makes you think they won't know we're coming?"

"It's early in the season. The Saxons will be busy planting their crops. I don't intend for you to linger at Camulodunum. Ride swiftly through to the coast. The infantry can follow and clean up the remains."

Galahad looked at Arthur's lieutenants, Bedwyr, Gwalchmai, and Cai. He knew they would back him; they waited now on Uther and Ban.

Slowly, Ban nodded. "We came here for this; best to get it done."

Uther folded the map and handed it back to Arthur. "May Mithras protect you."

Arthur turned to Ban. "I'm assigning Bors to Bedwyr and Lionel to Gwalchmai. They'll keep them safe. I'd like Galahad to ride with me. He'll be mounted on that black menace; I don't want either of them killed in their first battle."

Galahad stared at him, unable to believe his good luck. He glanced over at his father who gave an imperceptible nod. Galahad straightened his shoulders. He would fight and fight well. For himself, for Benoic and for Arthur.

* * * *

The invasion took nearly two months, but they successfully plowed a path through the heart of Anglia. Tomorrow, they would rout Colgrin and Baldulf from their castellum at Guinnion. The fort was positioned on the edge of the sea; Arthur hoped to lay siege to it.

Since Galahad rode beside Arthur, he was included in Arthur's evening meals beside the campfire. Galahad was grateful to learn so much of war strategies; that the men respected Arthur was obvious. Arthur treated him as an equal, even asking for his opinion at times. Could there be a better man to fight beside? *I'll be loyal always.*

The daughters of the smith that traveled with them approached. Gwalchmai and Bedwyr grinned; Cai scowled as they approached. "Those girls shouldn't be out; they aren't camp followers."

"Hello, Miara." Arthur took the hand of the taller, raven-haired girl and pulled her down beside him. She nestled against him with familiarity and he gave her a kiss. "Why is your sister here?"

Miara giggled. Arthur looked back to the younger girl who still stood. She stared at Galahad, her pupils dilated so much that her blue eyes looked dark, her lips parted slightly. He turned his gaze to Galahad, as did Bedwyr and Gwalchmai.

Galahad returned her look, and then slowly, he gave her his lopsided grin.

"I see," Arthur said softly. "Galahad, meet Minerva. It's not often she honors us with her presence."

"Minerva. Jupiter's daughter, Goddess of wisdom." Galahad held out his hand and she took it, sinking gracefully beside him.

"She's not so wise to be out here," Cai growled. "Her father will kill you."

Arthur raised an eyebrow. "The boy's old enough to know what he wants." He turned to Miara. "Still, it would be better to seek some privacy. Why don't you take your sister to my tent? We'll be along shortly."

After the girls had gone, Bedwyr said, "Cai's right, Arthur. The smith was none too pleased to find out about you, but you're a captain. Galahad is a different story."

Arthur shrugged. "I've never hurt Miara and I make sure she doesn't get with child. Her father has accepted that. I don't see why it should be any different with Galahad." He turned to him. "But if you'd rather not take the risk, there are plenty of camp followers about."

"I'd think it riskier to get involved with one of them," Galahad answered evenly.

Arthur gave him a speculative look. "Aye. They carry diseases. I expect you will treat her well?"

"I gave an oath to my mother that I would never hurt a woman."

"Your mother?" Cai laughed. "You've discussed your needs with your mother?"

"His mother," Arthur said sharply, "is the sister to our Lady of the Lake."

Cai stopped laughing and stared at Galahad. "Then you have fey blood?"

Galahad turned dark eyes on him. "Mayhap. But the courtesans my mother chose for my training were real enough."

"Courtesans." Arthur shook his head and smiled. "I suspect your reputation will be well established, then, after tonight. I'd best make sure Miara stays with me." He gestured. "Shall we visit the ladies?"

* * * *

Arthur's troops approached Castellum Guinnion before dawn. He spoke to his lieutenants as the troops formed. "Remember, these Saxons have been here long enough to fight on horseback. We'll try to draw them out by appearing to be disorganized." He went over the plans again. "Part of Ban's cohort will wait farther down the road in the forest, ready to close the flanks, the others will join with us when we take our stand. Any questions?"

The men shook their heads and went to ready their troops. Arthur turned in his saddle and faced Galahad. "Have you a clear head this morning?"

"For *certes*." Galahad was puzzled. "I had nothing to drink last night."

"Sometimes a man is still drunk from bedding a woman." Arthur glanced at him. "From the sounds of it, she had a good time."

Galahad grinned. "I tried."

"And this morning, you had better do more than try to focus on war," Arthur answered sharply. "Once we engage, I can't be worried you're thinking of a woman instead of a Saxon."

His face went still as he answered the challenge. "I won't forget."

"Good. I want you to stay to my right and a little behind. That way, my sword will be the first to slash. Let's ride."

They barely had time to position their lances. Colgrin's men sallied as soon as the first turma of thirty cavalry was spotted. Saxons poured out from the near forest as well. The ground was soon dotted with downed men, many still fighting on foot.

"Do you see either Colgrin or Baldulf?" Arthur shouted.

Galahad strained to see the Saxon banners that would indicate the leaders. There were none. "They must like to hide among their men!" he shouted back.

"Look for the biggest horse then. Colgrin is a massive man."

They were fighting nearly a half-mile from the fort, near the trees, when Galahad spotted the huge destrier. "There!" he shouted. "He's heading back to the gates!" The Saxon army was retreating back to the shelter of the palisades.

"Follow me!" Arthur put his heels to his stallion. His grey was much faster than the heavier horse and he closed easily. Colgrin looked back once and spurred his horse on.

Galahad pulled his lance from its pocket. Although it wasn't a conventional way to fight, if he could get close enough to throw it, he could unseat the Saxon. His side vision caught movement suddenly from the trees. A Saxon warrior stepped out, his axe raised, aimed at Arthur's head.

Galahad saw the axe lift through the air and his lance flew straight and true. The axe deflected as he heard a whistling past his ear. Something bit deep into his back and then the world went black.

* * * *

When he awoke, he saw the room through a red glaze. The pain searing through his shoulder was almost unbearable. He nearly slipped back into a coma, but something strong was held close to his nose and his eyes opened again.

He became aware of his father standing at the foot of the bed and a man with the golden eyes of a hawk handed him a cup. He stared. Myrddin.

Arthur put an arm behind him and propped him to a sitting position. "Drink. It will help the pain."

He took a sip. Liquid fire seared his throat and he sputtered.

"All of it," Myrddin commanded. Arthur held the cup for him.

"What happened?" Galahad asked, when he could finally speak.

"You saved my life," Arthur said simply. "That axe would have split my head in two if it hadn't been for your lance."

"I don't remember throwing it," Galahad replied and turned to Myrddin. "Why are you here?"

Myrddin gave him a strange look. "You've fulfilled a vision I had once, long ago, of a warrior saving Arthur. I have been here several days."

"Days?" Galahad looked from him to Arthur. "How badly am I hurt?"

"We weren't sure you'd pull through." Arthur gave him a relieved smile. "Apparently, there was another Saxon ax meant for me. It found you instead."

"If you hadn't still been leaning over your horse's neck from the throw, it would have found your head, not your shoulder," his father said gravely. "I could not have returned to Niniane with that news."

Myrddin swatted at the air beside his ear and took a breath that sounded close to a sigh. "He will live, Ban. Arthur will have need of him in the future."

"Be that as it may," Arthur said and stood and looked at down at Galahad, "you have my geis . . ."

Myrddin's eyes flashed yellow heat. "A geis is a powerful thing, Arthur."

His cool, grey eyes met Myrddin's. "That is why I am giving it. I will protect Galahad for as long as I live. My geis. My oath."

Galahad grasped his hand. "I will always fight by your side."

"I think we had better let him rest," Ban said. Arthur nodded and they moved toward the door, leaving Myrddin with him.

"Oh, one other thing." Arthur turned in the doorway. "You have acquired a new name. The stories are spreading like wildfire about your lance finding that ax. Someone started calling you The Lancer and the name has stuck." He grinned affably. "No doubt, it will probably be Lancer the Legend soon."

CHAPTER SIXTEEN—SEER AND HEALER
496 A.D.

Nimue stood on top of the Tor, inside the sun ring of stones. She and the other priestesses faced east, arms raised in supplication and waited for the sun to rise. They chanted the litany to greet the day as the round red ball rose from the horizon of the distant sea. The breeze was stiff this May morning and brought the strong smell of salt. Nimue filled her lungs with it and felt the subtle shift of a new energy nudge at her. Something was going to happen.

The priestesses finished their ritual and Nimue wound her way through the Maze and across the grasses to walk down the Processional Way to the sacred pool. The flagstones, worn smooth by many pairs of feet over the years, felt warm under her bare soles. When she reached the pool, she knelt at the altar stone and retrieved a tinderbox from behind it. She placed a pinch of incense on the rock and struck the flint, giving thanks to Bel for the fire it ignited.

She closed her eyes in meditation and was surprised when an image of Brigid rose before her. The girl had been sent to Armorica six months before and word had recently come from Niniane that her son had broken the barrier that held Brigid an emotional prisoner. All would be well. *Why then, Great Mother, has this image come to me?*

When she opened her eyes, a white hart stood across from the pool, waiting for her. Nimue inhaled deeply; whenever he appeared to her, it indicated change or a major life lesson. "So you've come."

The stag dipped his head, his magnificent rack of antlers glowing softly silver. *The man whose son is destined for a great feat needs your services. Go now. Myrddin awaits.* The image of Astrala shimmered in the air behind the buck. She reached out her hands and for a brief moment Nimue thought she saw the Grail glowing incandescently in them. The hart leapt gracefully into the hedge of hawthorn and disappeared.

Nimue hurried back up the hill to the bundle of whitewashed buildings that housed the priestesses. As she approached the Lady's quarters, Myrddin's white mule stood patiently outside.

"I was going to send someone for you," Vivian said as she entered and then smiled. "But I should have known there was no need."

Nimue made her obeisance and turned to Myrddin. Even his faerie, who usually was into some form of mischief, looked serious. "What is wrong with Galahad?"

If he were surprised that she knew, he gave no indication. "He was wounded at Gurnion, saving Arthur's life. I thought I had brought him through, but the wound has festered again. Yours are the healer's hands, Nimue, not mine."

She nodded. "I'll gather some herbs from our supply and we'll be on our way."

Minutes later, Barinthus was poling them across the lake. "A horse awaits you, my lady," he said as they scraped ashore.

Nimue thanked him and quickly mounted. As she and Myrddin rode, she said, "The white hart appeared to me, just before you came. Galahad has some special mission to fulfill, I think."

Myrddin gave her a long and thoughtful look. "All I can tell you is that Arthur is destined for great things and Galahad—the men call him Lancer now—is going to help him achieve that." A far-away look crossed Myrddin's face and he was silent for some moments. Finally, he said softly, "But what a price they will both have to pay."

* * * *

Despite Lancer's wound, when Nimue arrived she found the rest of the fort to be in the midst of a victory celebration. She sidestepped a drunken soldier who staggered into her path and avoided a second one, who was involved in kissing one of the serving girls. Another soldier tried to ease the blouse off the shoulder of another girl and she protested, albeit with a giggle.

"We've never been able to advance all the way through Anglia to the shore at Gurnion," Uther explained as he led them through the Great Hall, seemingly oblivious to the near fornication taking place in the remote corners. "It will be some time before Colgrin can rebuild his forces, not to mention their fields and holdings."

Nimue didn't see any reason to celebrate destroying what the Great Mother had given the land: fertile fields, rich harvest, and livestock. Men desecrated the earth and while they were rebuilding their forces to prepare for even more bloodshed, it would be the women who worked to replenish their holdings. Nimue sighed. There was no end to war. *May you forgive us and bless us, Mother.*

Arthur burst through the crowds, laughing, an arm around a pretty, raven-haired girl. When he saw Nimue he straightened, his arm at his side. The girl looked at him reprovingly, but he didn't notice. Instead, he gave her bottom a playful slap. "I'll see you later, Miara," Nimue heard him say.

He came to stand beside Uther, his level grey eyes serious now. Nimue looked at Uther and then back to Arthur. *They have the same eyes . . . the same look. Odd that I haven't noticed that before.* It gave her a disconcerted feeling or perhaps it was Arthur's physical presence, close enough that she could feel his body's heat.

"Thank you for coming," he told Nimue. "Lancer is in need of you. He has my geis," Arthur continued as he accompanied Nimue and Myrddin to the back hall where Lancer had been given a room.

Nimue raised an eyebrow. "Your geis? It is a powerful commitment. Galahad—Lancer—must be very special to you."

Arthur nodded. "I can't really explain it. He saved my life and for that, I owe him. But there's something else. Ever since he arrived, he's felt like a brother to me, even more so than Cai! We're both competitive and we both want to be best . . . you'd think we would hate each other. But we don't. We think alike in many ways. I'd put his loyalty beside my lieutenants any day."

Beside her, Myrddin frowned and she remembered what he said about a price to be paid. She wondered again what it meant.

* * * *

Lancer tossed feverishly in the bed, his chest and arms glistening with sweat, the sheets damp beneath him. A dark-haired girl with blue eyes blotted his face with a wet cloth.

Nimue moved quickly to the small table beside the bed and took out her herbs. "I'll need hot water," she said.

The girl nodded. "I'm Minerva. I'll get it."

"I'll go with you," Arthur said.

Nimue approached the bed and laid a hand on Lancer's forehead. She closed her eyes and concentrated, sending rays of cool white light into him, feeling the heat radiating outward. He began to still under her touch and her mind melded with his.

You're safe now. Nimue thought the words and then, in startled surprise, realized they were coming from him. *He's kneeling beside a woman on the ground. Now he draws her to him, holding her, caressing her copper-colored hair . . . she's been hurt . . . she pulls his head down . . .* She heard him groan and opened her eyes, breaking away from the dream.

Lancer watched her. She knew then that he had fey blood. His eyes were the most unusual color she had ever seen, neither brown nor grey, more like the color of peat smoke. *Fey . . . he is to be Arthur's protector . . . that's why there is such a kinship.* She felt Morgan le Fey hovering near her.

"He is a handsome one, isn't he?" The faerie giggled and reached a transparent hand to touch the dark strands of hair that fell forward. "It's too bad he can't see me like you can."

"Get back here," Myrddin hissed as Minerva returned with the boiling water. Morgan looked at him belligerently and then heaved a long sigh, whisking herself back to the speck of energy on his shoulder.

"Ouch!" he said and rubbed his ear.

Nimue moved quickly and mixed marigold and black willow with the water, adding enough slippery elm to form a paste. She came back to the bed. "Can you turn over by yourself?"

"I'll help him," Minerva said quickly.

She's in love with him, but he's not with her. Nimue applied the poultice to the red jagged wound on his shoulder and wrapped it with a clean strip. "Have you any moldy bread?" she asked Minerva.

"I'm sure we do. Why?"

"The mold will help draw out the infection faster. You'll need to alternate the poultice and the bread every few hours."

Minerva helped Lancer roll over on his back; he winced as his wound touched the pillow, but he gave her a lop-sided smile. "Thanks," he said.

Happiness beamed across her face. *He is not for you.* Nimue thought again of the dream she had shared with him. Whoever the auburn-haired woman was, he belonged to her, heart and soul. Nimue felt the threads that bound them together from past lives. In the present, though, that was yet to come. She wondered if she should warn Minerva not to be taken by that infectious smile; it was a trait all men with fey blood shared. They were beguiling. And she knew it would not matter what she said.

"Priestess." Lancer turned his dark-eyed look on her. "Your hands are indeed magic. I felt the fever leave me." He looked puzzled for a moment. "There was something else... I was somewhere else... I just can't remember."

She smiled. "My name is Nimue. Sleep now. I'll check on you later."

* * * *

She pushed through the throngs of people still crowded into the Great Hall. The revelry had reached a new pitch. Now that the meal was over, the serving girls had taken leave to join the soldiers, many of them nearly as drunk as the men. Several of them were in various states of undress, seemingly not caring who watched.

Nimue shook her head. She had taken vows of chastity; even had she not, the union of a man and woman should be sacred. It was, after all, symbolic of the Earth Mother receiving the fertile seed of the god to ensure prosperity.

The god. In ancient times, when festivals such as Lupercalia or Beltane became debacles, such as this, Cernunnos could be counted on to be present. Nimue concentrated on her sacral chakra and sent out orange energy. He was here.

She saw him then, standing in translucent form in a far corner, wearing a tight-fitting tunic of forest green over his broad chest. His trews were of brown leather, and his thigh muscles bulged under them when he moved. His antlered head turned slowly toward her and gave her an inviting smile, one that most mortal women would not be able to resist. Then his attention riveted on the door through which she had just come.

Morgan le Fey floated through the air, transparent, her filmy green gossamer gown swirling around her as she made her way to her consort. They embraced, his open mouth on hers, his hands pressing her buttocks, crushing her against him. They began to undulate in familiar rhythm and a wave of frenetic light vibrated from their source. Nimue was surprised no one else could see it. She could feel the heat even from where she stood.

"Have you seen Morgan?" Myrddin asked furiously as he stomped toward Nimue. "One moment she was here and then she was not. I don't even want to think of the havoc she can cause..."

"There." Nimue pointed toward the far wall. "She's mating with Cernunnos."

"What?" Myrddin spun around and stared. "By the gods, with them there, do you know how many babies will result from this day?" He looked frantically around the room. "Where's Arthur?"

Nimue searched the room and found him straddling a bench at one of the trestle tables. Miara faced him, her legs over his thighs. Arthur kissed her, his hands roaming her back, hers in his hair. Even as she watched, Arthur deepened the kiss and pulled her against him. Momentarily, Nimue felt a twinge of longing which she deliberately pushed aside. She had chosen her path.

"We must stop him," Myrddin said. "That woman is not to be the mother of his child. Blend your energy with mine, Nimue. Quickly."

But Nimue stared, dumbfounded, not sure of what she had seen. She blinked and unfocused her vision. Yes, there it was. The image again. It formed in the ether above Arthur's head. The same green-eyed, auburn-haired woman from Lancer's dream. *Why is she here? She is to be Lancer's.*

She looked up at Myrddin and knew, from his horrified expression, that he had seen it, too.

"Who is she?" she whispered. "I saw her in Lancer's fever dream."

Myrddin inhaled sharply. "Her name is Gwenhwyfar."

"What is she doing in Arthur's aura?" Nimue asked. "I felt she belonged to Lancer."

"She does. She always has," Myrddin answered softly, his eyes still on Arthur. "And unless I can keep Arthur away from her, she will destroy all I have sought to build and all Arthur will accomplish."

Nimue turned troubled eyes on him, for Gwenhwyfar's apparition began to glow ethereally. "There is great strength in her. Arthur may need her help one day."

"Never." Myrddin gathered his prana and sent a blaze of light to Arthur who suddenly looked up, breaking his hold with Miara. Gwenhwyfar disappeared. Myrddin breathed a sigh of relief and turned back to Nimue. "Her help might very well result in bringing down the greatest fellowship this land has yet to know."

Nimue closed her eyes and concentrated. Parts of visions swirled through her mind. *Gwenhwyfar in a white samite gown, in a church, marrying Arthur. Lancer befriending her atop a battlement, an unbidden brief kiss startling them both. Lancer's leaving, Gwenhwyfar trying to make her marriage work. Much later, Lancer's return . . . and then something threatened Gwenhwyfar's life.*

I am there, too.

Arthur and Lancer helped Gwenhwyfar to a cot in a small room and sat down on either side of her. She slipped an arm around each of them.

"Hold me," she said, "both of you. I need to feel your strength." As they complied, she drew their free arms around her, topping them with her own. "God help me, but I love you both."

Above her head, Arthur and Lancer exchanged looks. Lancer's eyes turned darker and he lifted his chin. Arthur held his gaze, his grey eyes sad.

And then it was night. A servant came for Lancer. Gwenhwyfar had asked to meet him secretly. He struggled with his emotions and then threw caution to the wind. He met who he thought was Gwenhwyfar, but was her cousin, Elaine.

I am there, too. I am the one who finds them.

Elaine's screams bring a crowd, including Arthur and Gwenhwyfar. The sense of betrayal hangs like a shroud over the three of them. Arthur pulls Gwenhwyfar away.

"He's never cared for your cousin. Obviously, he thought he was meeting you."

Arthur's voice was flat, devoid of emotion.

"I knew nothing of it!" Gwenhwyfar was furious.

"Mayhap. Tell me," Arthur said, "if he had made the arrangements for this tryst, would you have gone?"

She stared at him and then looked away. "I cannot say that I would not have."

Disgusted, Arthur stomped away.

I am there. It is I who devises the plan . . .

Nimue opened her eyes and reached out a hand for support.

* * * *

"What is it?" Myrddin asked. "What did your Sight bring you?"

"Gwenhwyfar will play a part in both their destinies, Myrddin. Not even you can stop the Wheel of Fate. We don't choose whom we love. All we can do is choose how we behave. Many lifetimes have gone into the making of this eternal triangle. How it will conclude I cannot say."

CHAPTER SEVENTEEN—COMRADES
496 A.D. – 497 A.D.

As Arthur went to visit Lancer the next morning, he couldn't shake a feeling of uneasiness that haunted him since yesterday's festival. It had turned into a licentious, near orgy. Had Myrddin not stopped him—or was it Nimue? She should never have been in that room—he would have taken Miara then and there. He preferred privacy with the act, and yet . . . it was almost a compulsion, as though something had driven him. The air had been permeated with sexual tension. *And who was that woman with the wild, copper hair that came into my mind? I know I've never seen her before.*

He poked his head inside Lancer's door to find him awake. "You look like you're feeling better."

Lancer nodded. "That priestess has magic in her hands."

Arthur pictured Nimue's small, delicate hands and could almost feel them sliding across his chest, encircling his neck…He pushed the thought away abruptly. She was sworn to chastity. Arthur managed a smile as he came to the bed. "And it doesn't hurt to have Minerva ready to meet your every need, either!"

"I'm afraid my needs have not been great lately."

"Ah, well, that will soon change now that you're healing," Arthur said. "Did you know two of the serving wenches got into a cat fight yesterday over whom was going to bring you lunch?"

"It wouldn't have done either of them any good. I was too weak to eat, let alone anything else!" Lancer grinned feebly. "Besides, I doubt that Minerva would let me anywhere near them."

"Why tie yourself down to one woman? I don't, fond as I am of Miara." Arthur raised an eyebrow. "You aren't in love with her, are you?"

Lancer shook his head. "No. But, as you said, she's more than willing to meet any—need—I may have. Why make her mad?"

"She may read more into your relationship than you intend," Arthur answered. "Women do that quickly."

"I've never told her I love her. If she asks, I won't lie," Lancer replied. 'The least I can do is not humiliate her by bedding some wench."

Arthur smiled. "I think being raised by all those priestesses has made you too caring. It's much safer not to tie yourself down."

The door flying open interrupted him. Minerva came running in, crying.

"What is it?" Lancer asked, struggling to sit up.

She threw herself on the bed and wrapped her arms around his neck. He winced at the pain from his shoulder, but put his good arm around her. "Tell me what's wrong."

Minerva looked up tearfully. "We're leaving. The smith at our old home was killed. Da got the message this morning. The village wants him back."

"I'm sorry to hear that. I shall miss you." He reached up and stroked her hair. "But don't you have friends and family still there?"

She stared at him. "Yes, but . . . but I don't want to leave you! I love you!"

Arthur almost laughed at the irony of the conversation they just had, but the stricken look on Lancer's face stopped him. *By Mithras, he really doesn't realize the effect he has on women!* Arthur knew he'd miss Miara, too, but it wouldn't take Miara long to find another man. They would probably have several really lusty couplings before she left.

"I'm sorry. I didn't realize . . ." Lancer started to say.

"How could you not?" Minerva grabbed his hand and held tightly to it. "I know I'm a few years older than you, but we could get married. I could stay here then . . ."

"Do not do this," Lancer pleaded. "Save your self-respect. I cannot marry you."

"Why not?" Her lower lip trembled and a tear slipped down her cheek.

Here it comes. In a moment, she'll be wailing, Arthur thought. *That should put Lancer on the defensive and make short work of this.* But Lancer surprised him. He raised his hand and brushed the tear away and then held her.

"Shhh. I will never marry unless I love the woman with all my heart and soul. It would be unfair to her—to you—to do otherwise. I like you, I'll miss you, and I'll remember you." He lifted her gently away from him and looked into her eyes. "But I don't love you."

The look on her face changed to anger. She slapped him suddenly and ran from the room.

"I tried to warn you," Arthur said as Lancer rubbed his cheek. "Now you're going to have a bruise for your efforts."

"I hurt her. I did not mean to do that." He took his hand away from his stinging, red cheek. "You're right. I should have listened to you before. I think I'll keep my distance from women."

"No," Arthur said, "do the opposite. No woman twice in a row. When I have one, so will you. We can make it a friendly competition."

Lancer stared at him and then a slow grin appeared. "You know I can't turn down competition. All right then. No holds barred."

The uneasiness settled on Arthur again. Somehow, he felt like he had loosed a panther and holding unto its tail wasn't a wise thing to do.

* * * *

The smith left two days later and Minerva refused to say good-bye. Lancer didn't pursue her, telling Arthur it was better for it to be a clean break. "Let her blame me for being a lout; it'll make her feel better," he said.

Nimue stayed at the fort and, with her ministrations, Lancer was up and about within a week, but after she left, it took a good two months to recover. One evening, after supper, Arthur approached him.

"Come with me," he said, "I have someone you need to meet."

"A woman?" Lancer asked.

Arthur nodded. "You did say if I were going to bed one . . ."

Lancer grinned. "You're going to hold me to that?"

"Absolutely. A little friendly rivalry never hurts. Come on."

They made their way into the village, to the brothel Arthur had visited eleven years ago. Salome remained a good friend and Arthur thought she was just the person to give Lancer some relief.

She saw them as soon as they entered and her eyes widened at Lancer, then her face took on a mischievous expression as she walked toward them. She gave Arthur a long kiss and then looked at Lancer.

"Galahad. A pleasure to see you again."

Arthur stared, first at her and then at Lancer. Lancer himself was nearly gaping at the woman.

"You two know each other?" Arthur asked.

Salome smiled and ran a slender hand down the side of Lancer's face. "We've met. And how is your mother, Galahad?"

His mother? How would she know Lancer's mother? A sense of near giddiness rolled through Arthur. She must have been one of the courtesans!

"She is fine," Lancer stammered.

"And you?" She moved closer, until she almost brushed against him. Almost. Not quite. "I'd like to find out what you've learned in the past year. You were quite an apt pupil."

Lancer suddenly grinned.

Salome arched a delicate brow and Arthur wondered suddenly if she meant the bondage she seemed so fond of. She had tried to introduce himself to it once, but he had declined. His need to stay in control was too strong.

She traced a pattern across Lancer's chest and down his arms. "Such powerful muscles."

He gave her his slow, lopsided smile.

Salome made a sound that sounded distinctly like a contented cat's purr. As they walked toward her room, Arthur thought about the untamed panther again. It was more appropriate than he knew.

* * * *

All was quiet as the crisp fall air turned into the cold bit of winter. Arthur concentrated on preparing Valiant as a warhorse.

"I think he's ready to prove himself in battle," Arthur said to Lancer one early spring day as he brought Valiant down from a thrashing rear. "You've been using Pryderi for several months."

Lancer nodded and vaulted the paddock fence. "Valiant's seven; old enough to be sensible in battle." He reached up to pat the velvety nose and received a small nicker. "Pyrderi's a year younger, but he's a born fighter."

Arthur laughed. "Only you could appreciate that in him. I'll only breed him to the calmest mares, like your Caireen."

"Smoke signals!" the guard yelled from the battlements, interrupting them.

Arthur handed the reins over to the stableboy and bounded up the steps followed by Lancer. Uther came running from his tent. Arthur shaded his eyes with his hand. To the west of Ambresbyrig were a series of hill forts, the closest one being Cadwy's and the most distant on the other side of the Isle. Fires were kept ready to signal any type of invasion.

"The Scotti?" he asked Uther.

"Probably. Vortigern has a grandson, Pascent, who's tried to stir trouble in Demetia for years."

Arthur frowned. "But those Scotti have been at peace since before you returned from Armorica. What reason would they have to rebel now?"

"They wouldn't. That's what worries me," Uther replied. "Pascent may have recruited warriors from Eire." He turned to leave. "Mobilize your troops, Arthur. There'll be a messenger soon. We need to be ready to leave as soon as we know what we're fighting."

The messenger arrived late in the afternoon, his horse nearly blown. He gratefully took the cup of wine Arthur handed him as he sank into one of the chairs in Uther's tent.

"Scotti," he confirmed. "Almost a hundred ships landed and joined forces with Pascent. They're led by a man called Mannion the Boar. The first King Cauritis heard of them was when they rampaged through Gower."

Uther banged his fist on the table. "They managed to move an army of that size nearly fifty miles inland before one of Cauritis' scouts reported it?"

The man reddened. "I'm a relay rider from Cadwy's garrison. I didn't think to ask . . ."

"Never mind," Uther said. "Is Cauritis moving against them or does he wait for us?"

"His man said they were going to try and stop them at the River Llwchwr."

"If the Scotti managed to bring five thousand men in those ships and combine forces with Pascent, Cauritis will be far out numbered," Arthur said. "And even if we march at dawn, we don't have enough ships to cross the channel. We'll have to go north nearly to Glevum where we can ford the Severn."

"You think he'd be better to hold in Caer Leon until we get there?" Uther asked.

"He'd lose fewer men, waiting." Arthur had gotten to know his former father-in-law fairly well and he shook his head. "But he can't afford to let the Scotti—or Pascent—conquer the coastline."

Uther nodded. "Send to King Marc of Cornwall for re-enforcements as well. He has as much to lose as any of us if the Scotti get control of our seas. We'll leave Hoel in Lindum to hold off any Saxon thoughts of moving westward while we're engaged."

It only took Arthur's cohort of light cavalry two days to reach Glevum, but the infantry lagged several days behind. By the time Arthur reached Caer Leon, Cauritis had been forced to retreat and the next coastal city, Glevissig, had been plundered.

"Mannion's ships lie off shore," Cauritis told Arthur the evening of his arrival. "Not only do they bring him supplies, but he has an escape route as well."

Arthur frowned. "Marc should be sailing north, rather than riding, so we'll see if we can get them to run when his ships appear on the horizon. Meanwhile, while we're waiting for the full force of infantry, I can put the light cavalry to use. We can harry Pescant's lands, do hit-and-run assaults, ambush foraging parties, burn villages. It will make Pascent turn back, for the time at least."

His plan worked for Persant, but didn't keep Mannion from advancing toward Gwent. By the time Uther arrived with the infantry, Mannion was only ten miles away from the stronghold of Caer Leon.

"We can withstand a siege," Cauritis said, "the summer harvest is in, but it gives Mannion time to establish ports that will have to be taken back."

Uther looked grim. "I've no intention of waiting for him. The men rest tonight. Tomorrow, when the Scottis waken, they'll find themselves looking eye-to-eye with the fighting force of Britain."

* * * *

Arthur pressed his right thigh into Valiant's flank, turning him, and slashed at the oncoming Scotti with his sword. A fountain of blood gushed out from the man's stomach. Arthur yanked his sword and plunged back into the melee around him. *They're brave fighters. Not afraid to run on to a mounted horseman. Foolish, though.* Arthur looked around briefly and caught sight of Lancer. He almost smiled before he met another onslaught. *I don't have to worry about him.* At first, Arthur had tried to keep Lancer close, but soon realized that when the fighting frenzy came upon him, which it often did in battle, he needed a wide berth. *He's only seven and ten; in a year or two he'll surpass any of my lieutenants, even Bedwyr.* For a moment, the battle swayed away from Arthur and he had time to catch his breath. *Funny, that. Bedwyr's style of fighting is totally opposite of Lancer's. He always fights with a cool, calm head. He's as collected in battle as though he were practicing for a tournament.* He thought suddenly of Bedwyr's feisty little sister they visited two years ago. With her hot temper, she'd probably fight like Lancer. *Strange. Why am I thinking of her in the middle of a battle?*

Then he had no more time for thinking. Horsemen from Pascent were approaching. "To me!" Arthur cried and his men fought their way back to regroup.

"Hold the line!"

The clash of metal as shields and swords met was deafening and the impact of horse upon horse a silent, harsh thud in contrast. One blow nearly unseated him, but Valiant bit the other stallion's neck, causing it to wheel suddenly, and dislodge its own rider. Arthur's arm tired. *Will we ever have peace and not have to fight?* He took a renewed breath and heard the horn sound retreat sound for Pascent's men. He saw the surprise on his opponent's face.

"Follow the call and I'll spare your life," he said and then watched in amazement as the men turned around. He called a halt to his own troops not to pursue.

"What in Bel's Fires is going on?" he asked Bedwyr as he and Lancer approached. "I've never seen a retreat when they were still holding their own!"

Lancer pointed. "Look out to sea."

Arthur turned in the saddle. Sails loomed over the horizon, growing larger until the hulls of the King Marc's ships were clearly visible. Mannion wouldn't want to be caught between land and sea forces. His men were fleeing to their boats and Pascent hadn't the numbers to hold off Uther's army.

Arthur dismounted and wiped his bloody blade on the grass. "It's over," he said, "for now."

* * * *

"Bloody hell," King Marc said at the feast in Caer Leon's Great Hall that night. He put his hand over his portly stomach as he belched. "We didn't even get to fight the bastards. I've never seen sails hoisted so fast before."

"Aye, and they had fair winds," his son, Custennin, said wryly.

Beside him, his cousin, Tristan, shrugged and pushed his black hair away from his face. "They turned tail and we shed no blood. I may have to write a song about it."

"You and your harp. You'd spend all your time with it if you could."

"That's not true," Tristan answered reproachfully, but there was a hint of mischief in his green eyes. "If I didn't have to fight, I'd split my time equally between music and willing women."

Custennin looked heavenward and sighed. "Both are useless pursuits."

Arthur raised an eyebrow. "Useless?"

Custennin turned his hard, brown-eyed gaze on Arthur. "Women have their place. Every man has needs. But they talk too much and about nothing interesting."

"What do you consider interesting?" Lancer's voice was low, but Arthur saw his eyes darken in defense mode. *Dear Lord, we don't need a fight at the table.*

"Tell me," Arthur interrupted, "what had your battle plans been for today if Mannion had faced you?"

Custennin broke into a smile. "I'll show you the strategy we mapped out, if we can be excused."

Arthur nodded and as they stood to leave, Tristan exchanged a glance with Lancer and shook his head.

Lancer grinned. "I think I know where we can find some willing women."

* * * *

As Marc's men boarded their ships the next morning, Arthur thought the king almost looked jealous of the contented, nearly-a-smirk grin Tristan wore. *Whoever Lancer procured for him certainly made him happy.* Then he noticed Lancer was grinning like a fool, too. *Too bad I couldn't join them.*

Marc watched as Tristan went aboard and then turned back to Arthur. "Ah, to be young again."

"Cauritis would have arranged for a woman for you," Arthur said.

"He offered," Marc answered, "but my randy days are behind me. I wouldn't mind getting married again, though. Mayhap a pretty, young thing."

Arthur gave a slight shudder, thinking of Leonora. "Sometimes beauty has a big price. One I doubt I want to pay again."

Marc nodded. "Aye. Well, 'tis a thought. Too bad we missed a good fight though. Keeps a man young."

"I'm sure there will be others," Arthur answered dryly. "Uther will expect you to protect the western coast."

"That we will do."

Arthur watched as the ships slowly grew smaller until the horizon was clear once again. Then he turned and called to his men. It was time to go home.

* * * *

They followed the estuary southward, keeping pace with the infantry, and were near the mouth of the River Brue when the shout went up.

"Smoke!" the outrider called.

Arthur looked up. The fire atop the Knoll fort had been lit. *Sea raiders again? Mannion?* The cavalry spurred their horses forward.

Minutes later, the beach lay just beyond a bend in the road. Arthur halted his men and dismounted. He kept to the brush along the banks of the river until he had a good view. Mannion's ships lay anchored just off shore, but his men hadn't yet come ashore. Lancer and Bedwyr came up behind him.

"He's double-backed," Arthur said in amazement. "He must have hove-to just past our line of vision and waited for Marc to leave."

"Only this time, he isn't interested in Gwent," Bedwyr said with a grimace. "He can easily take Cadwy's with the garrison gone."

"Over half of Ambresbyrig is with us," Lancer added. "No doubt he was expecting we would rest up before returning."

"We do have the element of surprise," Arthur answered. "Let's use it."

"Look!" Lancer said as they turned to go back to the horses.

Arthur followed his outstretched arm. Marc's ships were closing in, effectively shutting off Mannion's means of escape. He grinned. "The old sea wolf is clever. Marc must have anticipated a trick. He really wanted to fight."

"I can't blame him," Lancer said. "Tristan told me that Marc's had to pay tribute to the Eire king for years. Taking Mannion would be sweet revenge."

Arthur studied him. "Well, then, we'll let him have first honors. We'll wait in position to finish them off."

It was strange, Arthur thought, as he sat his horse, his line of cavalry behind him. Watching a battle instead of fighting it.

Once Marc's ships were spotted, Mannion's men frantically weighed anchor, the oarsmen trying to turn the great boats about without the keels grinding the bottom. There was no time to raise sails as Marc's ships closed, the bronzed-tipped ramming beams slithering just below the waterline. If the beam hit broadside, the damage would be devastating.

Arthur watched as the first boats collided with a resounding clash of wood splintering. Another vessel clipped the oars off the port side of a second boat bringing it to a grinding, screeching halt, dead in the water. A corvus, the long boarding platform that swung from the bow of Marc's boat, dropped unto the deck of Mannion's, a large spiked grapple securing it.

A sailor from one of the Eire boats threw a burning torch onto a ship of Marc's. The fire began to spread, catching the hemp lines of the sheets.

"I think Marc could use a little help," Arthur said and signaled for his archers to fall into place. "Let's keep the Scotti busy while they put out that fire."

Infuriated, the Scotti turned to fend off the land soldiers. Then, suddenly, a halyard was raised, carrying a white flag.

"Mannion's dead!" Marc shouted. "Surrender yourselves!"

Instead of doing so, the sailors on the crippled ships either leapt to safety on the Scotti ships now making a desperate run for the open sea, or they splashed overboard and tried to make for shore.

Arthur closed his eyes for a mere second. What fools. Had they stayed on board the ship they would have been taken as hostages. Now, he had no choice. He looked to his archers. "Pick them off," he said wearily. "We take no prisoners."

CHAPTER EIGHTEEN—THE ALLIANCE
497 A.D.

"I think," Myrddin said to Arthur as Uther and the rest of the men gathered in the council room behind the Great Hall, "we need to look to keep our southern ports safe as well as the western ones."

They had returned from Demetia less than a fortnight ago. A few days after they got back, Hoel sent a message that some of Aesc's Saxons tried to pirate a ship from Gaul.

"Marc has a good fleet of ships," Arthur said, "but we can't expect him to watch for Scottis in the west and Saxons in the southeast."

"What about Aelle?" Lancer asked. "He's a sworn ally."

"And he'll remain one as long as we stay stronger than him," Uther answered. "To ask him to protect Portus Adurni and Clausentum would be allowing him to expand his lands westward. Too risky."

Myrddin nodded. "Didn't Cauritis mention a distant relative of his that had been dispossessed of his lands by Pescant? He'd taken to trading on the high seas. Cerdic, I think the name was."

"Cerdic?" Arthur tried to remember what Cauritis had said. Pescant claimed bloodright to the land, citing Cerdic as half-barbarian. They were both grandsons of Vortigern, but Cerdic's grandmother was the Saxon concubine, Rowena. "The man's half-Saxon and, if I remember, he also married a Saxon woman."

Uther raised an eyebrow and looked at Myrddin. Myrddin shrugged. "That means he understands the culture and can speak the language. A boon for us. But he's half-Briton, too, and must want some land. Let him have the swamp around the ports; it will be an incentive to him to patrol our waters."

Slowly, Uther nodded. "Arthur, send a messenger to Cauritis. Have him locate Cerdic and send him here. We'll talk, but I'm not making any promises."

* * * *

Cerdic arrived just after the August festival of Lugnasad. He was a massive man, taller than either Uther or Arthur by half a head, broad-shouldered and heavily muscled. His blond hair was long and his blue eyes blazed with an intensity Arthur usually saw only on the battlefield. *He's not much older than I am, but he's hardened.*

"Please sit." Uther indicated one of the chairs in front of his desk. "Wine?" He looked Cerdic over. "Mayhap, mead would be your preference?"

"It would." Cerdic did not look away. "I understand you want a seasoned sea captain to protect your ports?"

Arthur handed him the mead and took the seat beside him. *Certes, he's blunt. Mayhap, that is a good thing though.* He listened as Uther and Cerdic bartered for terms and conditions. Cerdic didn't appear intimidated, although he gave Uther the respect due a king.

"I have one ship with crew. I'll need four more," Cerdic said.

"Your crew . . . are they Saxon?" Uther asked.

"They are." Cerdic leaned forward. "Be aware that not all Saxons come from the same place. Having yellow hair doesn't mean we're brothers." He leaned back. "I'll have to hire mercenaries—foederati—that are experienced seamen."

"How do I know they can they be trusted?"

"You don't. I will. Mercenaries work for money. I'll discipline them. They'll be my men and my problem."

"And you? Besides being paid, where does your loyalty lie?" Uther was equally blunt, his eyes boring into Cerdic's.

Cerdic didn't blink. "I want the land."

* * * *

Uther decided to host a huge tournament that fall to celebrate the alliance. After that, he told Arthur, he would be sending Arthur's cohort to Cadwy's fort to permanently take charge of the garrison.

"It's much closer to the western sea. You can put a stop to any Scotti invaders quickly from there with your light cavalry," he said. "I'm making you commander of your own post."

Commander. There really wasn't a rank higher, unless Uther wanted to designate someone as second-in-command to him. *And my own post! Well over a thousand men, plus servants and workers! I'll have to convince Cai to be my seneschal. No one is more efficient at keeping accounts than he.* Then Arthur thought of something else and frowned. "Won't Cadwy mind? It is his home."

Uther laughed. "Your face still shows your emotions. But no, Cadwy won't mind. After his wife died, he said there were too many memories there. That's why he requested to be assigned here. Now go. There are preparations to make before all the vassal kings descend on us."

* * * *

Marc was in good spirits when he arrived and wasted no time in joining the older men in the tent that served as a daytime tavern.

"What's he so happy about?" Arthur asked Tristan as he and Lancer walked with him back to the hall.

"After he returned the hostages he had taken, he asked a boon of the Eire king. He wanted to be relieved of the tribute he'd been paying. King Anquish agreed if he won a trial by combat."

"Who's going to champion him?" Arthur asked.

"I am," Tristan answered.

"You?" Lancer grinned. "I thought you said you were a lover, not a fighter."

The corner of Tristan's mouth quirked up. "Sometimes I've had to fight my way out of a lover's situation. Haven't you?"

"A time or two." Lancer squinted as another party arrived. "Who's that?"

Arthur turned. A carriage stopped just inside the gates and Morgana stepped out. She wore her inky hair piled on top of her head, with long tendrils hanging down. Her crimson gown clung to her body, revealing every curve. She raised her arms over her head and stretched slowly and sensuously. Like a cat, Arthur thought as she directed her slant-eyed look at him. *As though she knew where I was standing.* She looked away and then back and smiled, waving her hand slightly.

"Whoever she is, she seems to know you." Lancer said with a laugh.

"That's Morgana, Ygraine's daughter," Arthur answered. "There's something about her though. She always makes my hair bristle."

"Mayhap bedding her would make your hair lie down," Tristan quipped. "For *certes*, she was inviting you."

"No thanks," Arthur said as he turned away. "Come on, we have work to do."

* * * *

The tournament was a success. Hoel brought Accolon, who was eight and ten now and quite a handsome young man with his black hair and blue eyes. He entered the hand-to-hand combat and drew Cai as his opponent.

Ouch, Arthur thought as he watched them step into the ring. *Cai is a seasoned fighter and he loves the sport.* But even as he watched, his jaw dropped in amazement, for Accolon was getting the upper hand and eventually, he won. Arthur made a mental note to avoid Cai for the rest of the day.

Arthur's eyes scanned the stands as he waited for his number to be called for swordsmanship. Cerdic was seated in the place of honor to the right of Uther. It was hard to tell if he was enjoying himself or not. He rarely smiled. Morgana sat next to Uriens, her hands folded in her lap, but her eyes were fastened on young Accolon. *Like a predator.* Briefly, he wondered where Bertilak was.

Horsemanship was next. Palomides had a natural seat and his horse performed well, but Lancer and Pryderi moved as a unit. Arthur had never seen a man ride who was so much an extension of his horse. And the black devil behaved as docilely as a lady's palfrey when Lancer rode him.

As the day wore on, Arthur realized how nearly evenly matched Lancer and Tristan were. Tristan took a first in archery, but Lancer won the ribbon in spears. He, himself, had just managed to claim the prize in swordsmanship, but he suspected it was because Lancer had twisted his wrist in the lance throwing, which he won. Arthur retained the lead, just barely. Now they were lining up for the joust.

Bedwyr rode first, unseating Gwalchmai on the second run. Then Gryflet and Gaheris competed. Arthur took his turn with a fairly new recruit. *Too easy.* He watched as Tristan and Lancer met.

The first run broke both lances. They were replaced and on the second run, blows glanced off shields. On the third try, Tristan made a direct hit and Arthur saw Lancer take the impact on his shoulder. *He'll be sore tonight.* Finally, on the sixth attempt, Lancer got the lance under Tristan's arm and lifted him from the saddle. The tournament was over.

* * * *

Morgana managed to seat herself beside Arthur at the banquet that evening. "My husband is dining at the head table with Uther and that Saxon.

Do you mind if I join you?" Her hand stroked his shoulder lightly and she didn't wait for an answer.

Lancer and Accolon were seated directly across from him and he saw the flicker of amusement on Lancer's face before he turned to talk to Accolon.

Arthur looked around to see if there was another lady available to keep Morgana company for the meal. He didn't think Uriens would approve of Morgana sitting alone with all these men, either.

Ygraine was entertaining Cerdic's pretty wife, Olga. Beside her sat a flaxen-haired boy of about seven. *Cynric, I think they called him.* Olga looked too young to be the boy's mother. Then Arthur remembered Cerdic had been married before. Arthur wished he could send Morgana over there, but Ygraine's duty was to play hostess to Cerdic's wife.

"How's your son?" he asked Morgana politely.

Morgana raised a delicate eyebrow and her lips twitched as though she knew some private joke. "Medraut? He's five now and doing quite well. I had a wooden sword made for him." She moved closer, the side of her breast brushing his sleeve. "He'll be a fine soldier some day. One you would be proud of."

Arthur moved his arm. "*Certes*," he answered half-heartedly. "Good soldiers are always welcome in the army."

Morgana gave him a reproachful look and sighed softly. She turned her attention to Accolon. "You're quite accomplished in swordplay, as I saw this afternoon." She lowered her eyelashes and tilted her head before she looked back at him, the tip of her tongue at the corner of her mouth. "Mayhap you would consider being my son's instructor?" She reached across the table and laid her hand on top of his. "My own champion has been removed and my son could benefit from your help." She let her fingers graze his wrist.

So Bertilak has been sent away. Uriens probably got tired of your brazen flirting. Arthur looked at Accolon, hoping he would see through her.

But Accolon was gaping at her, mesmerized. "It would be an honor, my lady," he finally stammered.

"Don't you think your husband and Hoel might have something to say about this?" Arthur asked.

Morgana glanced at him sideways. "Don't worry. I think I know what to do." She turned back to Accolon. "You're going to like living with me."

* * * *

"Whew!" Lancer shook his head, laughing, when they finally finished dinner and left the table. "That woman would make a she-wolf with cubs seem like a friendly pup."

"Aye," Arthur answered as they entered the council room for the meeting Uther called after the meal. Several of Uther's captains were there along with Cerdic, looking at maps and drawings of new ships. Arthur was surprised to see Cerdic's young wife sitting nearby. Women rarely attended council meetings, but mayhap Saxon women did.

Cerdic explained his strategy for patrols and manpower. "I've hired two men to be subordinate under me. Beide is a Saxon; Maegla is Briton. The mercenary crews are mixed."

Uther nodded and Arthur thought he looked pleased at how things were turning out. Mayhap they were one step closer to having peace.

Cerdic rolled up the maps and tucked them into their tubes. Then he gestured for his wife and looked at Uther. "The Saxons have a custom. When an alliance such as this is reached, we seal the agreement by sharing that which is most important to us. I offer you Olga for the night."

Talking ceased. Scraping chairs halted; those who were half standing, sat back down again. Uther stared at Cerdic and Arthur could see the warring emotions play across Uther's face. Olga was tall and slim, but with ample breasts. Her long, golden hair rippled like silk and her blue eyes were bright as she looked at Uther. Any man would want her.

Cerdic spoke quietly into the silence. "It is an honor I'm bestowing and an insult if not taken."

Uther cleared his throat. "Indeed, the honor would be mine. Your wife is beautiful. But my wife is Christian and it is against her belief for me to lie with another woman, much as I would like to."

Cerdic looked puzzled. "Your woman controls you? Iam not asking for an exchange. Your acceptance of my offer verifies that your word will not be broken."

Uther began to look desperate and Arthur found himself wondering if they were going to have to cover for him tonight. He wondered what excuse Ygraine would believe. *None, probably.*

"Might someone else not do? A proxy?" Uther asked. "A man worthy of your wife, *certes*. He could be of her own choosing."

Cerdic turned to Olga and they exchanged a fast conversation in their guttural tongue. "If she chooses," Cerdic said to Uther, "the man must not refuse her."

Uther smiled, relief on his face. "There isn't a man in this entire room who would do that."

Cerdic said something else to her and she looked shocked, then slowly nodded. She looked around the room and then turned and came toward where Arthur was standing with Lancer. *Ah. Lancer. I should have known. Women are always drawn to him.*

Olga stopped in front of Lancer and held out her hand. He gave her his lopsided smile and bent low over her hand. "My pleasure, my lady."

At least he'll treat her well, Arthur thought as he started to turn away. Then he felt her take his hand. Startled, he looked down.

"You, too," she said. "You tied for first place at the tournament today. My husband says if the king won't honor me, that I request his two best men do."

Lancer straightened, his smoky eyes dark as he looked at Arthur. "Well," he said softly, "this will be new."

* * * *

They entered the guest bedchamber and Arthur threw the bolt. He leaned against the door. *By Mithras, this is awkward.*

Olga swallowed hard, stepped over to Lancer and tentatively tugged on his tunic. He caught her hand. "You're beautiful."

And she was. Her breasts were firm and high, her waist willowy, her belly flat. She had long slender legs that would easily fit around a man's thighs, holding him firmly in place. Arthur took a sharp breath. Cerdic must be out of his mind to allow any man access to her.

Lancer turned her palm over and kissed it. "What is your wish, my lady?"

She looked at him and then at Arthur. "I am to do whatever you ask." Her voice trembled and then she lifted her chin. "But I don't like pain, if you will spare me that, my lord."

For a moment, Lancer looked nonplussed. Then he brushed her cheek gently with his fingertips. "Put that fear to rest." He glanced at Arthur and then back to her. "Neither of us will do anything you don't want."

Arthur moved over to the window. "We don't have to do anything at all. Cerdic will never have to know if we left this as is."

Her eyes grew wide. "You are displeased with me?" She sank down on the bed and covered her face with her hands and began to weep. "Cerdic will be angry with me."

Dear God. Don't let her cry. The girl was so young—hardly more than a child—and obviously frightened; the best thing would be to let her go. *But if Cerdic sees any of us this soon . . . will he take his wrath out on her?* Some men beat their wives.

Lancer sat down beside Olga, put an arm around her shoulders and pulled her to him. "Shhh. No more tears. You'll keep your honor."

She lowered her hands and swallowed hard. "I've never done this."

Lancer brushed back her hair. "It is a little odd."

A little odd? A little? Arthur began to wonder just how much the courtesans had taught Lancer. He straightened. "And you won't be doing it now. At least, not with me." Arthur moved toward them. "In your culture, the giving of a wife may be seen as a gift. It isn't in ours. If I were married, I would never let another man have my wife."

She cast a doubtful look at him. "Cerdic will think I displeased you."

"He will not know what takes place—or does not—unless you tell him."

Olga looked at Lancer. "Do you wish to have me?"

Lancer made a choking sound and then brushed back another strand of her hair.

"I would like nothing more than to bed you, but I think Arthur is right. We do you more honor by leaving you."

"But what if he sees you?" she asked, wringing her hands.

Arthur sighed and sank down in one of the chairs by the hearth. "He won't."

Lancer sighed, too. "Take the bed, Olga. Sleep. You'll be well-guarded this eve." He shook his head as he lowered himself into the other chair and closed his eyes. "It is going to be a long night."

* * * *

Lancer and Arthur stood in the bailey the next morning saying farewells to departing guests. All morning, they'd been getting curious looks from their men, but both had decided it would be prudent not to talk.

Uther approached with Cerdic and Olga.

Cerdic gave both of them a hard look and Arthur wondered if Olga had told him anything.

"My wife was fair tired this morning when she came to my bed." Cerdic frowned slightly. "I take it she pleased you?"

Lancer stifled his grin. "You're a lucky man, Cerdic."

The look Olga gave Lancer belied her blush. Cerdic narrowed his eyes. "She was part of the bargain and I'm glad it was well met." He nodded toward

Uther. "You'll be getting my reports." He turned and helped Olga into the carriage and climbed up after her. He glanced from Arthur to Lancer. "However, if either of you ever tries to touch my wife again, I'll kill you."

They watched as his party disappeared through the gates. "I think he means it," Lancer said. "Too bad."

Uther was about to respond when Bedwyr came up to them, leading his horse.

"My father couldn't attend because of a fall he'd taken. I'd like to ride north with Uriens and check on him," he said.

"Do so," Uther answered, "I think we can spare you a fortnight or so."

"Let me know if that hot-headed baby sister of yours is still so horse-crazy," Arthur added.

"If she's a Whisperer, horses are in her blood." Lancer smiled lopsidedly. "I'd like to meet her."

Arthur shook his head. "Lancer. Don't you have enough women to choose from around here? She's still a child."

Lancer gave him a dark-eyed look. "It would be interesting to find someone else who can talk to horses. I didn't say anything about bedding her."

This time it was Bedwyr who shook his head. "Even if she were old enough, I doubt any man is going to win her affections. Gwenhwyfar is strong-willed and determined to do things her way."

He mounted up and grinned. "But I will relay Arthur's question; she hates being called a baby. That ought to make her really mad."

* * * *

"There it is. Your new home." Cadwy stopped his horse and Arthur halted the cohort. The view was awe-inspiring. The fort was an old Roman one and sat several hundred feet high. The steep slopes had four lines of bank and ditch defense and wicked spear-like wood poked out from the first bank, forming a palisade. A thick curtain wall enclosed the summit. The cobblestone road curved to the right and left as it wound its way to the top, making it hard for any enemy troops to storm the gates. All in all, the fort was solid.

"I wonder why Uther never claimed this," Arthur said.

"It lies too far west," Cadwy answered. "Uther needs to stay on top of the eastern Saxons. But let's go in. I think you'll be pleased."

The garrison had been manned mainly by infantry, but the stone stables had been recently cleaned and the pasture fences mended to accommodate Arthur's five hundred horses and breeding stock. Barracks and officer quarters were at the far northern end of the fort wall. There was an outdoor kitchen near the main hall, as well as vegetable gardens and a walled herbal garden. An old Roman chapel-shrine stood toward the back. Best of all, Arthur discovered as he walked around, the hypocausts had been maintained and the Roman baths still worked. The central building was two-storied, with bedchambers on the top floor. It housed the Great Hall for feasting. Directly behind it, a hallway ran the length of the building, separating guestrooms, a small map room and, at the western end, the huge council room.

Arthur stepped inside, Myrddin beside him. The room contained only chairs and a long table along a wall. "This needs to be changed," Arthur said. "If I'm going to meet with all my officers, I want to be able to see everyone at the same time."

"In a circle?" Myrddin asked.

"Yes, like at a great, round table." Arthur thought for a minute. "It would also make everyone equal. No more who's sitting to the right or left or at the head of the table. That would put an end to the squabbling, especially if I were to treat with Saxons or Scotti."

Myrddin studied him. "You would treat with them?"

Arthur shrugged. "For a long time, I have thought that one day we could have peace. We already have an alliance with Aelle and another with Cerdic. I'll see about having a table built."

Myrddin started to swat at his ear, and then stopped, a look of surprise on his face. "There is such a table; one that will seat one hundred men."

Arthur had long since learned not to be amazed at Myrddin's sudden revelations, which often came after he swatted his ear. *Odd thing, that.* "I've never heard of such a thing. Where is it?"

"Would you believe me if I said in the land of Faerie?"

Arthur stopped himself from rolling his eyes. "You say the strangest things, sometimes."

"Well, then, don't you worry. I'll bring the Round Table to you."

Arthur could have sworn he heard the sound of a woman's laughter.

CHAPTER NINETEEN—RITE OF PASSAGE
497 A.D. - 498 A.D.

Glena, Gwenhwyfar's wolfhound, nudged her face gently with a cold nose. She turned over in bed and wrapped her arms around the animal.

"Brisen will have a fit to find you sleeping with me, but I don't care," she said as she stroked the soft fur. "But mayhap 'tis better we be up before she comes." She pushed aside the sheets and swung her legs over the bed.

That's when she noticed the blood. Her inner thighs were smeared with it and a small pool had collected on the bed. She looked for a wound, but found none. She jumped up. *Dear God, I'm bleeding to death. Someone, help me!* She began to shout.

Brisen bustled into the room. "What . . .?" she started to say and then stopped.

"Help me," Gwenhwyfar said. "I'm going to die!"

The nurse snorted. "You'll do nothing of the kind. 'Tis only the moontide that's started to flow. It means you've become a woman."

Gwenhwyfar stared at her. "I don't want to become a woman. I want to stay the way I am!"

Brisen shook her head. "That's not a choice you have. Wash up. I'll get some cloth for you."

Mirre came into the room as Brisen left. Gwenhwyfar ran into her open arms. "Can't I make this stop? What's making it happen?"

"There, there," her old nurse soothed her as she led Gwenhwyfar back to the bed and sat her on the edge of it. "Think of the sea, my pet. Its mighty waves rush to shore, only to flow out to sea again. The tide ebbs and flows, unceasing, never-ending. Waves build and crest, only to break and become part of the flow again. That is life. And you are a part of it. When the moontide is strong, you will bleed. It only lasts a few days and then it's gone until the next moon."

Gwenhwyfar looked at her in horror. "This will happen to me again?"

Mirre smiled. "Yes. Every moon unless you become with child."

"With child? What do babies have to do with this?"

"Once you become a woman, every moon God gives you the chance to conceive a child. It that doesn't happen, your body releases what has been prepared." Mirre went to the water basin on the chest and dipped a cloth.

Gwenhwyfar put her hands over her face and began to cry. "I don't want to become a woman; I don't want any babies. Ever!"

"Shhh! Don't say that." Mirre made the sign of the cross as she came back and handed the washcloth to Gwenhwyfar. "You're only four and ten; you have time before children are a part of your life."

Gwenhwyfar wiped the blood from her legs. "I've seen the dogs and horses mate. Why would I ever let some man do that to me?"

Mirre smiled. "When you meet the right man, my dear, he'll change your mind."

Gwenhwyfar stuck her chin out. "I doubt it."

"It is good thing to be a woman," Mirre said. "We are the Creators. All life springs from us."

"But . . . oh!" Gwenhwyfar bent over suddenly as the first cramp seared through her abdomen. "I'm hurting!"

Her nurse brushed her hair back. "Sometimes it hurts, the first day. There are herbs you can use."

Gwenhwyfar gritted her teeth and straightened. "I can't be sick. Since Da broke his leg from the fall he took, I have to be in charge. I don't have time for this." She clenched her fists to ward off another moment of pain just as Brisen returned with several strips of cloth.

"I'll take these," Mirre said softly, "and show Gwenhwyfar what to do." She turned back to her charge. "It will be all right, my child. You will see."

* * * *

"Now that you're a woman," Elaine giggled as they finished breaking their fast in the private quarters of the villa, "you'll have to start acting like a lady."

Gwenhwyfar groaned. For three days now, Elaine prattled about her taking on more household duties. *Sweet Mary! Why should I have to spend time spinning and weaving and embroidering! Cook can run the kitchen better than I!* "It's the horses that need attention while Da mends."

Elaine smoothed out a wrinkle in her fresh linen gown and patted her neatly braided hair and sniffed. "Horses! They're all you ever think about. Besides, your father hired a Master of Horse not long ago. Let him do the work." Her eyes narrowed and she contemplated. "His son is nice-looking. Is that why you spend so much time in the barn? I think he likes you, too."

Gwenhwyfar looked up at the heavens and sighed. "Ned's just friendly. You'd realize that if you ever deigned to dirty your slippers by entering the barn."

Elaine looked mildly horrified. "Not me. But someday, your husband will expect you to know those things wives are supposed to do." She dabbed at her mouth daintily with her napkin and smoothed another imaginary wrinkle.

Gwenhwyfar gave her cousin a look of disgust and then glanced at her own clothes. Her brother's old shirt was only half-tucked into her trews and she hadn't taken much time this morning to do anything but tie back her hair, part of which had already escaped. The cloth binding that collected her blood was chafing and she was irritable.

"I don't care what women are supposed to do. I'll be nobody's slave. Why do you want to get married so much?"

Elaine's eyes widened. "To be taken care of, *certes*. My husband is going to be strong and brave and good-looking. He'll pick me because I'm the perfect flower in the garden. He'll love only me." She gave herself a little hug. "And he'll wrap me in his arms and kiss me and nothing else will matter."

Gwenhwyfar rolled her eyes. "I think you've been listening to the serving girls talking about their tumbles in the hay again."

"Well, what if I have?" Elaine asked. "At least, I don't smell like hay!" Gwenhwyfar tossed down her napkin and stood. "Thank you for reminding me. I'll be in the barn if anyone needs me."

* * * *

Late November turned the morning crisp and cloudy and Gwenhwyfar thought there might be snow by afternoon. The barn held welcome warmth as she stepped inside. She greeted Prince with his favorite treat, an apple. She had outgrown him well over a year ago, but refused to let him be sold. Her father finally gave up trying. Prince would always be her friend.

Gwenhwyfar moved on to the next stall where her new mare, Cali, had taken residence. She pulled another apple out of the folds of her shirt and offered it. The mare's soft, velvety muzzle tickled her palm and she reached for a brush to give the glossy sorrel's coat more sheen.

"Can I help you with that?" Ned stood in the doorway to the stall, smiling.

Gwenhwyfar turned and regarded him. He was six and ten and tall, with brown hair and blue eyes. *Pleasant looking.* She gave herself a little shake. *Elaine has too much imagination.* "No thanks. I always take care of Cali. Prince, too." She smiled and turned back to the mare.

He stepped inside the stall anyway and reached around her. For a moment she was startled and then realized he already had a brush in his hand and was applying it to Cali's flank. Still, she could feel his closeness as he stood behind her, sandwiching her between himself and the horse, although he didn't touch her.

Glena gave a sharp bark and a second later, Gwenhwyfar heard the hoofbeats clattering into the cobblestone bailey. Ned dropped his hand and stepped back.

"I'd better see who that is."

Gwenhwyfar followed him out, relieved to have space about her again. "Bedwyr!" She raced across the yard and threw her arms around her brother's neck as he dismounted. "What are you doing here?"

He swung her around and set her down. "Uther granted me a leave and I thought I'd ride north with Uriens and check on Da. How is he?"

"Getting better," Gwenhwyfar said as they walked inside. "Cranky, though, since he has to hobble with a crutch and can't go far."

They went to the solar where Leodegrance was sitting near the large windows with his leg propped up. "Can't even get the warmth of the sun today," he grumbled.

Gwenhwyfar poured wine for Bedwyr and her father and then sank down on a stool near the lit brazier. She loved listening to Bedwyr's stories when he came home. He told them about the Scotti and Uther's decision to hire Cerdic, even though he was half-Saxon.

"The Saxons have curious customs," he told his father. "The man offered his . . ." He stopped abruptly and looked at Gwenhwyfar. "Well, never mind. Let's just say he managed to embarrass Arthur and that's not easy to do."

Gwenhwyfar remembered his last visit. She sniffed. "Probably served him right, whatever it was. He's so arrogant."

Bedwyr turned an amused smile on her. "He specifically asked me to tell him if my BABY sister is still hot-headed."

"What?" Gwenhwyfar jumped to her feet. "How dare he think. . .?"

"Sit down, Gwenhwyfar!" Bedwyr laughed. "I told him that'd make you mad."

She bristled. "I am not a baby. I'll prove it to you. Meet me in the practice field in five minutes. And bring your sword." She turned and stomped away. *I am not a baby!*

* * * *

She waited for him when he came around the corner to the area that had been roped off for swordplay. She flexed her arm, feeling for the balance of her sword.

Bedwyr stepped inside, still amused, and took his position opposite her. "You don't have to prove yourself to me."

"But I do," Gwenhwyfar answered. "And I think you'll find I've improved since your last visit." She lunged unexpectedly and thrust.

Bedwyr's reflexes were quick enough to avoid a touch, but his expression was surprised. "Mayhap you have, little sister. Now, let's see what you can really do."

He cut low to the left and she parried, trying to avoid a press for his strength was greater than hers. Her strategy was a series of quick strokes and retreats.

They continued on for some minutes. Finally, Bedwyr feinted to the right and Gwenhwyfar was committed to her lunge before she saw the ruse. With no impact, she flew past him and fell to the ground.

He knelt beside her laughing. "You're pretty good. Mayhap, you should enlist in Arthur's cohort."

Gwenhwyfar struggled to a sitting position.

Bedwyr put out his hand to help her up and stopped in mid-air, his expression strange. Gwenhwyfar followed his look and felt herself blush furiously. A trickle of blood seeped through the inner left leg of her trews.

"When did this start?" he asked as he lifted her to her feet. "Had I known, I wouldn't have made you work so hard."

She turned on him, her eyes flashing. "Don't you ever let me win because I'm a girl. This makes no difference!"

"But it does, Gwenhwyfar. It changes everything. Now I'll have to start worrying about young bucks, like that one over there." He pointed toward the barn.

She turned. Ned was standing near the ropes watching her. *Sweet Mary! How long had he been there? Did he see the blood?* She turned sideways, away from him. "That's the new Master's son. And you don't have to worry about me. I have no intention of getting involved with any man." She started toward the house.

Bedwyr followed her, carrying both swords. "You may change your mind one day. At least one thing is clear. I'll tell Arthur you're not a baby anymore."

* * * *

Two days after Bedwyr left, the snow began falling, large wet flakes softly blanketing everything in a mantle of white. Then the winds picked up, howling from the north and driving ice pellets ahead of the snow, stinging any exposed skin as the villa's servants struggled to do their chores.

On the fifth day, Gwenhwyfar woke to blue skies and brilliant sunshine. The wind had calmed and she'd been stuck inside the house too long. She broke her fast quickly, dressed warmly, and headed to the barn.

"Want to go for a run?" she asked Cali as she saddled her. "We've both been penned up too long." She led the mare out and mounted. As she rode through the gate, she inhaled the cold, sharp air gratefully. The world had been transformed into a children's wonderland. Shards of crystal ice glistened from every tree branch. For as far as her eyes could see, the land lay white and pure, untouched by humans.

She hadn't gone far when she heard the horse coming up behind her. She turned and frowned. It was Ned. *What's he doing out here?* She halted Cali and waited.

"Should you be out here by yourself?" he asked when he caught up to her. "You'd better let me ride with you."

"That won't be necessary; I ride alone often," Gwenhwyfar answered, "but thanks for your concern." She nudged Cali forward. *I'd wanted a wild ride today. By myself!*

"Still, riding in the snow can be dangerous. You never know where there's an ice patch," he persisted. "I'll come along."

Annoyed, she kicked the mare into a canter. Snow flew up from the flashing hooves, creating a cloud around her. Cali tossed her head and tugged at the bit.

"Okay," Gwenhwyfar said, leaning over her neck, "let's leave him behind!"

The mare stretched out, lengthening her stride, setting into the pace that was so flat and easy to ride. Gwenhwyfar laughed and tossed a look behind her. Ned was far in the distance.

Gwenhwyfar had forgotten about the creek. As she turned around, her eyes widened and she yanked on the reins, trying to slow Cali before she struck the icy mass. Too late. The horse skidded and slipped, falling to one knee. Gwenhwyfar half-fell, half-launched herself out of the saddle.

"Cali! What have I done! Are you okay, girl?" The mare stood favoring her right front leg. Gwenhwyfar bent over it, feeling the knee and cannon and fetlock. *Nothing broken, mayhap a strain. I'll never forgive myself if I've hurt you.*

Ned rode up. "Is she okay?"

Embarrassed, Gwenhwyfar nodded. *My foolish pride did this.* "She's limping. I'll walk her back."

He held out a hand. "Come on. Ride behind me."

Gwenhwyfar hesitated. *'Tis a long walk back and the snow's deep.* She sighed and took his hand and vaulted up.

He looked pleased with himself. "You'd better hold on to me."

"I'm fine," Gwenhwyfar said as she held on to the cantle and wished she had decided to walk. Ned had been following her around far too much since the day he'd watched her swordplay with Bedwyr.

They arrived home without further incident. Gwenhwyfar wrapped Cali's leg and gave her an extra serving of oats. "I'll bring you an apple after supper," she whispered.

She kept her word. She waited until the house was quiet and the stables dark, then she took a blanket and two apples and went out to Cali's stall. She talked to Prince as he ate his and then moved into Cali's stall. She checked the bandaged leg for swelling or heat. "I'm going to sleep right outside your door," she said as she watched the mare finish her treat.

Gwenhwyfar went into the tack room and took several saddle blankets for her mattress and rolled another for her pillow. The barn was warm enough to shed a cloak and boots and she curled up under her blanket and listened to the horses huffing softly. An occasional hoof struck the floor as one or another shifted its weight. She heard Cali finally lie down and then she was asleep.

She awoke to something heavy holding her down. Before she could open her eyes, a mouth was on hers, pressing hard, prying her lips open. She struggled, but to no avail. *Ned! Stop!* She tried to call out, but he thrust his tongue in her mouth and she thought she would gag. A hand pawed at her shirt, kneading her breast.

Gwenhwyfar stretched out her arm, trying to find anything she could hit him with. Her fingertips scrapped her boot. With an effort, she grabbed it and swung with all her might. She heard a resounding smack and Ned momentarily went limp. Then he shook himself and rolled off of her.

Gwenhwyfar assumed a crouching position, brandishing the boot in front of her. "Don't you ever touch me again!" Her breath came in great gulps, the adrenaline still pumping.

"Don't hit me again! I swear I won't hurt you." He held a hand up, looking confused. "But I thought you wanted . . ."

"Wanted?" She was outraged and swung the boot at him. He ducked. "Why would you think that I wanted . . . this . . .? It was awful!"

He cringed momentarily and then frowned. "Why are you out here then? 'Tis what the serving wenches do when they want a man. They come to the barn or the barracks."

Gwenhwyfar hadn't known. Slowly, she lowered the boot. "You thought I would come to the barn for a tumble?" she asked incredulously. "You were going to force yourself on me!"

"NO! I swear!"

She felt herself getting angry again and she began to shake uncontrollably. "I was struggling; you wouldn't stop." She grabbed her cloak and threw it over her shoulder. "I'll see your father fired for this."

"Please!" Ned pleaded. "It's not his fault. I've been watching you for weeks. You have few visitors, no man has coming calling. Your only friend seems to be Elaine. I thought you liked me. Then, tonight . . . when you came here . . . I'm sorry. I promise I'll never try anything again. Please don't dismiss my father. He needs the job."

Gwenhwyfar looked at him dubiously. *Da still can't walk. His father is good with the horses.* She straightened her shoulders. "All right. I'll not say anything. But you keep away from me." She turned and walked out the barn door, sliding it shut behind her. Then, she ran to the house through the snow, not feeling its coldness on her bare feet.

* * * *

The nightmares began not quite a week later. They were never quite the same, but they always involved someone chasing her, catching her, trying to rape her. Gwenhwyfar would wake, tearing at the sheets, soaked in sweat.

Ned kept his word, although she still found him watching her. Even so, when she saw him over the next several months, the feeling of his weight pressing her down, the taste of his mouth would resurface and she would feel like she was going to be ill.

Beltane approached and that morning, as they were breaking their fast, her father suggested the girls go A-Maying.

"Pack lunches and spend the day collecting the greens and the flowers," he said, "and then come back and decorate the Maypole."

Elaine clapped her hands. "We can make a party out of it!"

"I'll arrange an escort," Leodegrance said as he rose from the table.

Gwenhwyfar and Elaine went to change clothes and a short time later, emerged from the villa. Gwenhwyfar stopped short in her tracks, dismayed. Ned was a member of the escort. *What excuse can I make?*

"I don't think I'm feeling very well," she said.

Leodegrance looked at her sharply. "You've lost weight and been pale all winter."

The spring sunshine will do you a world of good."

Ned led Cali toward her. She nearly snatched the reins from him and mounted before he could assist her. She glared at him. *Remember, you gave your word!*

He looked at her for a long moment and then turned away. Gwenhwyfar relaxed as she watched him help Elaine mount. Getting Elaine on a horse anytime was a near miracle and even then, she insisted on riding sidesaddle with her skirts carefully arranged to be fashionable. She was flirting now, letting Ned hold her until she was settled and asking him to adjust the hem line on her skirt. Gwenhwyfar saw him grin and took a deep breath. Elaine was young to know so much about flirting, but at the moment, Gwenhwyfar fervently wished her luck.

The morning went well and by lunch, they had gathered all the greens needed for the evening's festivities. They stopped for lunch in a small glade near a creek. Elaine had grown bolder each hour and now, as Gwenhwyfar sat in the shade with her back against a tree, she could hear Elaine persuading Ned and another of their escort to walk with her. She'd eaten too much, she said. Gwenhwyfar shook her head. Elaine ate like a bird.

Gwenhwyfar watched as Elaine disappeared around a bend that followed the creek. She turned back to discover two of the young soldiers already dozing some distance away. She closed her eyes. A nap wouldn't hurt.

"Can I talk to you?"

Startled, her eyes flew open. Ned was kneeling beside her.

"Why aren't you with Elaine?"

He shrugged. "I think she wanted some time alone with John."

Gwenhwyfar frowned. "She shouldn't be alone with one of the soldiers."

Ned nodded. "I know. I sent the other two after them."

Slowly, Gwenhwyfar glanced around. Her two dozing friends were nowhere to be seen. She was alone with Ned. *Alone.* She turned back.

"What do you want?" She tried not to tremble. *How far away are they? Will anyone hear if I scream?*

"I want another chance," Ned said, moving closer. "I'm no monster."

Gwenhwyfar started to get to her feet, but his hand caught her arm. "Please," he said and pulled her to him. "Kissing can be fun."

Her hand raked his face, leaving red welts in its wake. He looked nonplused for a moment and then rage took over. He pushed her unto her back, pinioning her arms to her sides. "I told you this can be fun," he said. "Now I'll show you."

Gwenhwyfar started screaming. Distantly, she heard footsteps running and she felt herself growing lighter, as though her body were floating in the air. There was a shout and a flurry of movement and then she knew no more.

* * * *

Late that night, Gwenhwyfar lay in bed, exhausted, but she couldn't sleep. *If the escort hadn't arrived back in time, what would have happened?*

She'd been hysterical by the time they'd gotten there and all the way home, she'd shaken uncontrollably. Seeing her face and hearing the story as it came pouring out of her, Leodegrance had immediately banished Ned and his father from his property.

So why can't I sleep? I have nothing more to fear. Fretfully, she tossed and turned until near dawn when, completely drained, she fell into a trancelike sleep.

She was on a small hill, standing inside a circle of bluish menhir stones. It was so peaceful inside the circle. Then she heard two horses galloping up the road.

The men stopped by the small copse of trees just at the bottom of the hill and dismounted. She heard a whip and then her horse's scream as he thundered away.

"Gwenhwyfar!" one of them called. "Where are you?"

She froze. These men had tried to kidnap her before. She crouched behind a stone and listened to them begin to search. She waited for what seemed an eternity until they were behind the hill on the other side, and then she ran for their horses.

Too late. She was caught. She struggled, biting, scratching, kicking and managed to knee one of them in the groin, but the other wrestled her to the ground. He slapped her face while the first one grabbed her hands and held her down. Her shirt was ripped open and she felt the cool air on her bare breasts. She cried out in pain as the man squeezed one of them hard and leaned over to bite the other.

More hoof beats. A black stallion skidded to a stop and a dark-haired man was running toward her. Suddenly, the men released her and ran. She curled herself into a ball, trying to hold her shredded shirt together.

"It's over, Gwen. You're safe." The man's voice was familiar and the hands that touched her were gentle. He wrapped his arms around her and she buried her head in his shoulder, knowing that this man would always protect her. Always.

He stroked her hair until her tears subsided. "How badly have they hurt you?"

"I feel unclean," Gwenhwyfar said, "and angry."

"Shhh. I'll find them. And kill them." He put a finger under her chin and lifted it. "You have my oath."

His face was blurry and she felt dizzy, but for a moment, she had a glimpse of smoke-colored eyes. She closed her own. "Make me feel clean again. Please."

And then he was kissing her, the pressure of his lips gentle. He nuzzled her neck and Gwenhwyfar clung to him, pressing herself against him with a need she didn't know she had.

Softly, he parted her lips with his tongue and she welcomed him, loving the taste of his mouth. The kiss deepened and grew . . .

Gwenhwyfar woke, clutching her pillow. Another nightmare and this time with two men. But who had been her rescuer? He was no one she had ever seen and yet she felt so secure and completely safe with him.

And the kisses . . . her body began to tingle, a thoroughly new sensation.

Would she ever meet a man with whom she could feel like that? She blushed in the darkness, glad she was alone.

Her fear subsided. The nightmare was over, but who had that man been?

CHAPTER TWENTY—THE DUX BELLORUM
498 A.D.

Arthur watched as the red-headed tavern wench bent over, affording Lancer a glimpse of her breasts before she set the wine down. She tossed her hair back and gave him a smile. "Can I do anything else for you?"

He studied her. "No, thanks. I'm fine."

Arthur raised an eyebrow as the disappointed girl walked away. "No flirting tonight, Lancer? She was practically begging you."

"I didn't notice."

Arthur laughed. "You had to notice. You've been looking for red-haired women ever since you had that dream a few weeks ago."

Lancer turned to him. "It's just that it was so much like the one I had before I came to Britain. And again in my fever dream. I just can't get her out of my mind. If only I could have seen her face more clearly . . ."

"Well, while you're searching for your mystery lady, there's no reason to turn down what's available. Although," Arthur said, "I do miss Salome since we've moved to Cadwy's. She always had a surprise or two."

"That she did." Lancer grinned suddenly. "Did she ever convince you to try her specialty?"

Arthur gave him a wry look. "No. I draw the line at being trussed up."

Lancer nodded. "You're not the only one, but it gave me an idea of what it felt to be helpless. I'd never want a woman to feel that way with me."

Arthur nodded toward the red-headed girl watching them hopefully from the other side of the room. "I'll bet she wouldn't mind feeling helpless."

Lancer shook his head. "I'd never force a woman to do anything she didn't want to do. Anyway, having our hands free gives me a lot of other options." He looked over at the girl and gave her his lopsided smile. Her eyes widened and he stood.

"I'll see you later, Arthur."

Arthur watched him cross the room and put an arm around the girl. Ever since the odd night of guarding Olga, he found himself being more discriminating. He still had difficulty understanding how a man could share his wife. Lancer and the serving wench left the room. *Lancer is young, nearly ten years younger than I am. Ah, well.* He smiled to himself as a thought came to him. *If Lancer ever finds his mystery woman, what would he do?*

* * * *

Near mid-summer a letter came from Marc. Arthur read it with increasing incredulity. He was sitting in the council room with his lieutenants. Finally he tossed the vellum down.

"Marc wants us to invade Eire!"

"What? Why?" Bedwyr asked. "We've got enough problems keeping the Saxons in check."

"You remember Tristan saying there was to be a Trial by Combat to determine whether Marc had to keep paying truage? Apparently, Marc invited King Anguish to send his champion to Kernow and Tristan fought him. Unfortunately, Tristan gave him a blow to the head that not only cracked his skull, but a portion of his sword broke off. The man's dead."

"Trial by Combat isn't supposed to be to the death," Gwalchmai said. "What was Tristan thinking?"

"If you've ever competed with Tristan, you'd know. It's almost like when the battle frenzy comes on me," Lancer answered. "He's strong as a bull then."

"Who was the champion?" Gryflet asked.

"A man named Marhaus," Arthur replied. "King Anquish's brother-in-law. The queen is crying for him to be avenged."

"Let him come to us then," Gwalchmai said. "Uther sent word not long ago that Colgrin is amassing another army. We can't afford to be across the sea."

"True enough," Arthur answered, "and we don't need to start a war. Mayhap, if we advance to the Demetia coast with a show of force, it will make the Scottis think twice about revenge."

Bedwyr nodded. "Anquish might take on Marc alone, for Kernow's army is small. But if he sees Uther's cavalry behind him..."

Arthur frowned. "If I take all of the cavalry, I leave Uther with only infantry. If I leave part of the horsemen, the Eire king might not be persuaded to halt."

"It's a risk," Lancer agreed, "but if you allow Anquish to land and Colgrin takes advantage of that, our forces will be split and we'll be battling both sides."

Arthur was quiet for some time. Finally he nodded. "Send word to Marc. We'll meet him in Demetia."

* * * *

Their strategy worked well enough to stop the Scotti ships offshore. Arthur brokered a peace talk between Marc and Anquish, albeit under heavily armed guards from both sides. The Eire king wanted to meet Tristan and get a formal apology, but Marc told him Tristan had taken a grievous wound to his leg from Marhaus and was recuperating at home. Arthur thought Marc looked rather crafty about the statement, but he let it go.

Anquish seemed somewhat pleased to learn Tristan hadn't escaped cleanly. "And to seal the treaty, that we remain at peace, what can we offer?"

I hope the Scotti don't have a custom about sharing wives. Before Arthur could suggest anything, Marc spoke.

"I have been widowed several years," he said carefully as he looked into Anquish's face. "If you truly want peace, I will marry your daughter, if you have one. Nothing could be more binding than that."

Arthur stared at him. *Sight unseen?* His marriage to Leonora had been bad, but at least he'd had felt lust for her. The crafty look was back on Marc's face and Arthur wondered what he was up to.

The Eire king took his time before answering. "I do have a daughter, Iseult. She's only five and ten. I had thought to give her a choice."

Marc smiled magnanimously and spread his callused hands. "I can assure you that I will give her all the time she needs to know me and I will treat her well. Everything I have will be hers."

A flash of greed spread across the Scotti's face and was quickly extinguished. Again, he wondered why Marc would be so eager for this alliance. *It isn't that unusual though.*

Finally, Anquish nodded. "Done." He stood and the two men exchanged handshakes. "It may take my wife a fortnight to prepare the child and her dowry."

Marc beamed. "I shall send my ships after the full moon."

Arthur watched as the Scotti king and his escort left. Then he turned to Marc. "Do you want to tell me why you're so eager to marry a woman you've never met?"

Marc laid his hands over his portly belly and grinned. "I'm surprised you haven't heard. Iseult is supposed to be the most beautiful woman in Eire. At least, from Tristan's account and he has a good eye for women."

Arthur raised an eyebrow. "Tristan? And when did he see her?"

The crafty look came over Marc's face again. "When Tristan's wound did not heal, I sent him to an Eire healer under an assumed name."

"Why not send him to Nimue? Why did you send him to enemy territory?"

"I wanted to assess the king's strength," Marc answered. "It seems the healer turned out to be Iseult. Tristan says she has magic in her hands." He leaned back with a satisfied smirk. "Ah, to have a young, beautiful woman with firm flesh lying under me again." He winked at Arthur. "I may have to cut the wedding day short."

Arthur stared at him, thinking of the promise he had made Iseult's father. *All the time . . . Marc had never been known for patience. Poor girl.*

* * * *

Colgrin lost no time while they were treating with the Eire king. His army marched all the way to Verulamuim, just north of Londinium before Uther's infantry could stop him. The battle was fierce and Uther took a spear through the chest, collapsing a lung. His men forced a retreat back to the Anglian border, but he called them off once he was wounded.

Arthur found him ensconced in one of the first floor guest rooms at Cadwy's when he returned—Nimue and Myrddin at his side. His face was gray and his breathing shallow.

"How is he?" Arthur came to stand by Nimue. As always, when he was standing this close to her, the need to touch her was almost irresistible. Determinedly, he squelched the thought and stepped back. *Concentrate on Uther.*

Nimue looked up at him, her aquamarine eyes troubled. "He bleeds inside. The wound was jagged. The medics did the best they could. If he lives, he will not be well."

If he lives? Uther is the high king! Chaos would reign were he to die! Arthur looked down at the heavily bandaged chest. Nimue had placed holders of frankincense and myrrh incense at the foot of the bed and the heady fragrance filled Arthur's head as he watched her lift Uther's head and hold a cup to his lips.

"What's that?" he asked.

"A tincture of white willow bark," she answered, "to stop the internal bleeding."

Uther opened his eyes. The pupils were dilated and Arthur wondered what else Nimue had given him. He didn't seem to be in pain, so it must have been strong.

"Arthur," he whispered, "there is something I must say."

Myrddin frowned and stepped forward. "The time is not yet, Uther."

The two men looked at each other in silence and Arthur wondered what Myrddin meant. He thought a glimmer of light flashed past Myrddin's ear and Nimue reached out, only to have her hand stop in mid-air.

The faerie looked at Nimue reproachfully as she landed on Uther's forehead and stroked it with her magic. All Arthur saw, though, was Uther beginning to smile.

"So," he said weakly to Myrddin, "it isn't time for me to die?" He turned to Arthur. "I'm afraid I'm going to be laid up for a long time. Someone has to lead the army. All of it, not just the cavalry. I'm handing you a title, Arthur. Dux Bellorum."

Arthur was stunned. Second only to the king himself. The title was rarely issued since it gave the holder tremendous power. *What faith Uther must have in me!* He swallowed hard, aware that both Uther and Myrddin were watching him. "May God grant me the strength and wisdom to lead the men."

* * * *

"The first thing you'll have to do is convince the vassal kings that you intend to lead them," Myrddin said later as they sat in the small map room, planning strategy.

"I'll have Uther's writ," Arthur answered. "Won't that help?"

"You will still have to prove yourself. They already know you as Uther's strongest captain, but these kings are all older than you are. Some of them, particularly Nathanlaod of Venta, are likely to look askance at your authority."

"Why him?"

Myrddin sighed. "He is a distant relative of Uther's and always thought he should be second-in-command. Mayhap, if we start with the kings who are definite allies, he'll be pressured into pledging allegiance to you until Uther is healed. We'll see."

* * * *

One by one, the vassal kings came to Cadwy's fort. Leodegrance and Uriens were the first, followed by Marc and Pellinore. Cador of Kelliwic and Agricola of Glevum joined them, as well as Cato of Dumnonia. Reluctantly, Nathanlaod gave his acceptance, but only after he realized several Scotti allies had vowed to aid Arthur.

The kings were gathered in the Great Hall for the feast that was about to begin. A cot was brought in so Uther could observe the festivities. The sun was setting when Gromer Somer Joure, the one ally they had from Pictland, arrived with his sister with a big commotion. The steward threw open the door and they could hear a woman cursing in the courtyard. Arthur raised an eyebrow as she entered.

She was, singularly, the most unattractive woman he had ever seen. Her face was covered in blemishes, her mouth and nose were too big and her eyes too small.

For a moment the hall was silent. Then Gwalchmai, who could flatter a woman as easily as a bird took flight, rose to the occasion.

"The firelight turns your hair to spun gold, my lady," he said as he took her cloak and smiled at her.

She turned on him. "My hair looks like brittle straw and you know it!"

He blinked and tried again. "Your smile would dazzle me with its brilliance, I'm sure, if you would but favor me with it."

He received a snarl.

"May I present my sister, Ragnell," Gromer said disheartenedly. "She is not in the best temper."

They were subject to another battering of curses. She finished by peering up at Gwalchmai. Staunchly, he stood his ground.

"Your sweet talk," she hissed. "Do you know what a woman really wants?"

He grinned at that and began to answer, but she stomped off to a far table. Some of the men began to laugh and Arthur was hard put not to join them. It wasn't often that Gwalchmai's flattery didn't work.

"I'll wager you can't get her to smile the entire time she's here," Lancer challenged.

Gwalchmai turned red. "I'll accept that challenge."

Gromer shook his head. "You're a fool. No one knows what she wants."

* * * *

Over the next several days, Arthur had many occasions to laugh. After the fierce persuasion it had taken to get the kings allied, it felt good to laugh, albeit at Gwalchmai's expense. And Gwalchmai was determined not to let Lancer win the bet. Gwalchmai followed Ragnell around like a pup, talking to her, asking her questions about herself, telling her stories of their battles. All to no avail. If she didn't bare her teeth at him, he was met with stony silence.

One day, though, as Arthur was passing the herbal garden, he heard Gwalchmai pleading with her. This time, she answered. Arthur paused to listen unashamedly. Mayhap, Gwalchmai might win, after all!

"Why do you keep following me?" she asked. "I know about your silly wager and I know of your reputation and Lancer's. I'm surprised he isn't dogging my footsteps, too. I'm just another conquest for your male pride. Why don't you just give up?"

"Because, beneath your harshness, I think there's good and I might actually like you," Gwalchmai answered. "You're gentle with the dogs and horses."

"I'm ugly and I know it. Why don't you just take your pick of pretty and willing women and leave me alone?"

There was silence for several moments and Arthur was about to move on.

"I don't think you're ugly. You have good cheekbones and your eyes would be pretty if you weren't always squinting in anger. I don't think you're ugly," Gwalchmai repeated. "That's all I have to say. I would give you what you want, if I knew what it was you wanted."

Arthur heard a gasp. "What did you say?" she asked.

"Tell me what you want and I'll get it for you. Your will is my command."

There was more silence and then, in a voice Arthur had never heard him use, Gwalchmai said, "Your smile is beautiful."

Arthur hurried on, lest they find him.

* * * *

Ragnell stayed on at Cadwy's while her brother went south with Marc to arrange for some tin to be taken north. Arthur was amazed in the change in her. Her face cleared up and when she smiled, there was a radiance about her face that redefined it totally. Gwalchmai was always with her when he wasn't working and more and more, Arthur suspected he was falling in love.

Still, it came as a surprise when Gromer returned and Gwalchmai asked for her hand in marriage. Ragnell wanted to get married immediately and Gwalchmai, grinning like a fool, asked Arthur for leave to accompany her to her homeland to meet her people.

"You're really willing to forsake all other women?" Arthur asked. "How can you be so sure?"

Gwalchmai smiled. "I'm more sure of this than of anything I've ever done. I don't know how to explain it. Somewhere between being nice to her to win my wager and the day in the garden, something happened. I suddenly realized I did mean every word I said. Ragnell has a strength I didn't know existed in women."

Arthur gave his permission and two days later, as he stood in the bailey watching them leave, he mulled it over.

Lancer came to stand beside him. "Why so serious, Arthur?" He grinned. "Don't tell me you're thinking of getting married, too?"

Arthur gave him a level look. "No, but mayhap it's time I start thinking about it."

I doubt I'll ever meet a woman who can make me feel like Gwalchmai does about Ragnell." *Nimue might, but she's forbidden territory.*

"Well," Lancer said, "I'm not going to settle down unless I find my mystery lady." He looked off into the distance. "I wonder if she's really out there."

CHAPTER TWENTY-ONE—WHEEL OF FATE
498 A.D.

"Raiders? After we've had the first frost?" Gwenhwyfar asked her father excitedly and jumped up from the dining table. "Did we take any hostages? Where are they?"

He shook his head and reached for a warm oatcake. "Sit down. Finish breaking your fast. A small group tried to steal sheep. The regular watch drove them off."

I can't believe I slept through that! Cameliard was situated in a peaceful valley and it was rare to hear of such incidents. "Were they Saxons?" she asked.

Leodegrance frowned. "No. At least we don't think so. The captain of the guard thought they were Picts."

"Picts?" Gwenhwyfar's voice rose. "I didn't think they came south of the Wall."

"That's what our man said. It was too dark to tell for sure since the moon is new, but he saw no glint of armor."

Gwenhwyfar had never seen a Pict, but she had heard they painted their skin blue and fought with no clothes. Something about releasing the warrior spirit. She thought they might be even more dangerous than the Saxons. And they had been that close to the villa! She shuddered "What do you think, Da?"

"Well, they've started raiding along the Wall once Angus and Cabran moved their troops. It's possible. Small marauding parties taking a few cattle or sheep at a time. More of a nuisance than real danger probably."

"Do you think Brigid will be safe?" Brigid was the young wife of Mador, one of a small group of Bretons who settled on nearby farmsteads in the last year. Gwenhwyfar had met her when her father threw a feast to bid them well come. There was something delicate about her, as though she had suffered much pain and loss. Gwenhwyfar was to find out in time that indeed she had, but at that meeting she only felt as she did when she came upon a stray or lost animal. Brigid needed a friend.

Her father turned to her. "It would be best for you to stay inside the villa's grounds, I think, until we know if this is over."

A sense of uneasiness washed over her. Her da knew how much she enjoyed her freedom to ride. Now that she'd met Brigid, she took to riding over to the holding several times a week. Her new friend was gentle and practical, unlike Elaine who prattled incessantly and usually about boys or other trivial matters.

"Da, would you send soldiers to guard Brigid and Mador's holding?"

Her father patted her hand. "If I sent men there, the other homesteaders would expect the same. I don't have enough men to scatter them and still be prepared to protect the villa compound. Don't worry. Mador is a good man. He will protect her."

* * * *

The feeling of unease stayed with Gwenhwyfar. She missed her riding. She was brushing Cali one gloomy, grey day as dark clouds scudded across the autumn sky when she made up her mind.

"We won't stay long," she said to Cali as she saddled her. "I just want to make sure Brigid is all right and to let her know to be alert. Da won't even know I'm gone."

She led Cali to the postern gate and made sure it was closed behind them. There was about a quarter mile of cleared land before the forest began. If she could make that, she'd be free. She forced herself to walk Cali sedately down the hill, hoping her father hadn't given any of the guards orders to stop her.

The woods were dark and quiet as she entered the narrow trail. Cali picked her way gingerly over fallen boughs and soggy patches from recent rains. Once or twice, Gwenhwyfar thought she heard a twig snap, but since Cali didn't seem alarmed, she thought it probably only a deer.

They broke through to a meadow on the other side. She could see Brigid's small house from here. Breathing a sigh of relief, she put Cali to a canter.

Brigid came out and smiled as Gwenhwyfar dismounted. "I was wondering why you hadn't come."

"There've been raiders," Gwenhwyfar said. "I just came to warn you."

Fear flashed briefly across Brigid's face. "Saxons?"

Gwenhwyfar knew that Saxons had killed her family and nearly raped her several years ago. "No," she said gently. "Picts."

Brigid's brown eyes widened. "So far south?"

Gwenhwyfar nodded and looked around. "Where is Mador?"

Brigid looked concerned. "He's helping one of the neighbors bring in the late harvest."

"He's not here?"

She shook her head. "All five Breton families work together, moving from one place to another. He won't be back for another two days."

"Then you need to come home with me," Gwenhwyfar said. "Pack some things." Quickly, she led Cali to the small shed that served as a stable and looped the reins around her neck. "We won't be long, girl," she said as she closed the door.

They went inside and Brigid quickly gathered some items. "I hoped to put the fear of raids behind me," she said. "Mador told me this area was one of the safest in Britain."

"It is, usually," Gwenhwyfar answered, "but our Scotti allies had a dispute to settle; that's why the Picts are taking advantage. Don't worry, though. Arthur will send troops to guard the Wall if there's real danger."

Brigid's face brightened at the name of Arthur. "Then all will be well."

Gwenhwyfar stared at her. *How can she have so much faith in that man?* That Arthur was a strong military leader, Gwenhwyfar had no doubt. Her own brother had pointed that out numerous times, but the look on Brigid's face was more akin to worship.

Brigid turned to her. "Will Arthur be coming here?"

"I don't think so. Most of the raiding is taking place close to Uriens' fort. Why?"

A little smile played on her lips. "It was Arthur who rescued me from the Saxons that day. If it hadn't been for his gentle caring, I would have gone mad."

Arthur? Gentle? "Did Arthur send you to Armorica?" Gwenhwyfar asked.

"No." She smiled. "He sent for a priestess of the Lake to come for me. I was so terrorized though, that the Lady sent me to her sister in Armorica. That's where I was really healed."

"Was her sister a priestess, too?" Brigid had always been reluctant to talk about any of this before and Gwenhwyfar knew little about the priestesses.

Brigid nodded. "Her name was Niniane, but 'twas her son that did the healing."

"Her son? How?"

The older girl blushed. "He . . . he made me lose my fear of being touched by a man."

"How did he . . .?" Gwenhwyfar stopped, feeling herself become red. "Oh."

"My Mador is a good man and treats me well. I'd not be married today had it not been for Galahad. He's going to make some woman very happy one day." She finished putting some things in her sack. "Shall we go?"

Gwenhwyfar walked to the door and was about to open it when movement caught her eye outside the window. She motioned to Brigid and slipped closer, squinting against the glare of the yard. There it was again. A rustling of branches along the hedge Brigid had planted in front of the house. Gwenhwyfar glimpsed something blue among the green leaves. Then again, she saw it move.

Picts.

"Do you have any weapons in the house?" she whispered. "A sword?"

Brigid shook her head. "Mador always carries his. The extra weapons are in the stable."

Damnation. Gwenhwyfar didn't bother to make the sign of the cross this time. *I have no idea how many are out there and I'm unarmed.* She thought quickly. Do Picts rape and murder like the Saxons? She assumed they did. There wasn't any way she could get to Cali without being seen. The door was barred, but there were too many windows. Windows. They had to get out of there.

"Stay down." She crouched her way to the kitchen and reached for two dinner knives. They weren't daggers, but they were better than nothing. "Here." She gave one to Brigid, whose face had turned deathly pale. "There isn't time to be scared. Just follow me."

She crawled to the window at the back of the house and slowly lifted her head and peered out. She could detect no movement anywhere. The grove of trees protecting the house from the north wind was less than a hundred feet away. Could they make it? She studied the trees. Yes. There was one with fairly low branches. They could climb.

Quickly, she whispered her instructions. Brigid looked as though she were about to faint. Gwenhwyfar gave her a little shake. "No one is going to rescue us. We're all we've got."

Brigid looked at her and slowly nodded. She took a deep breath. "Let's go."

She gave Brigid a leg up and pushed her through the window. "Run!" She hoisted herself out and sprinted after Brigid. They reached the trees and Gwenhwyfar unceremoniously shoved Brigid up the trunk. "Climb higher," she said, "and for God's sake, lift your skirts." *The tree isn't going to be able to hide both of us.* Quickly, Gwenhwyfar looked behind her. Nothing yet. She spotted another tree that looked good, but the lowest limb was out of her reach. *Dear Lord, help me.* She stuck the knife in her boot and crouched, then jumped. Her fingers brushed the limb. *Don't panic.* She could hear noise in the house now; any moment someone would look out that back window. *Jump!* Desperately, she lunged upward. Her hands caught the branch and for a moment she hung in the air, then she swung her legs gaining momentum until she could propel one leg over the branch. She dragged herself to a sitting position.

The Pict opened the shed and led Cali out. Gwenhwyfar almost wept. *Cali. My beautiful horse.* He studied the mare for a moment and then looked around. He looped the reins around a post and started toward the back of the house.

The Pict rounded the corner, a wicked-looking seaxe in his hand. Where he'd gotten hold of a Saxon long knife, Gwenhwyfar didn't know. He was horrific-looking. The man was well over six feet, his long brown hair bushy and matted. His entire body was painted with woad in spirals and ancient symbols and he was naked. Gwenhwyfar had never seen a naked man before and she shuddered at the size of him, remembering how Mirre had finally explained what takes place between a man and a woman once the moontide started. *Hail Mary, Mother of God, pray for me in this my hour of need . . .*

He approached the trees now, peering intently through the low growth on the ground. He stopped directly below Brigid's tree. *Don't look up! Please, Brigid, don't move!*

He hesitated and looked back at the mare. *He knows someone is here!* Slowly, Gwenhwyfar reached for her knife.

The Pict started moving again, coming closer to where Gwenhwyfar sat crouched. Her blood thundered in her ears and her skin felt as though a thousand needles pricked it.

Just then, Brigid's foot slipped. The Pict whirled. "There you are!" He laughed and started to walk toward her. "Come here. Let's have some sport."

Gwenhwyfar hurdled off the limb and onto his back, one arm going around his throat, trying to cut off his air, the other slicing down with her knife into his shoulder. He dropped his seaxe at the impact and roared in anger and tried to shake her, but she had ridden too many horses to be thrown. "Run!" she screamed to Brigid. "Get Cali!"

Brigid jumped down from the tree and faced them. Her face was set and her eyes held an unnatural glow. In her hand she held her knife. "Hold on to him, Gwenhwyfar."

Deliberately, she walked toward them, as calm as though she were going to church. The Pict swung at her, but she side-stepped.

"This one's for all women who have been raped," she said calmly and plunged her knife into his groin. The glaze never left her eyes.

He grunted and fell to his knees, a surprised look on his face. Then he screamed in pain.

Gwenhwyfar grabbed Brigid's hand and ran to Cali. Quickly, she helped her mount and vaulted up behind her. She swung the mare around as the Pict lumbered toward them, the seaxe in his hand.

"Hold on," Gwenhwyfar said and gave Cali a kick in her flanks and pulled back the reins. The mare reared, her forelegs thrashing out at the Pict. She came down, ears flat and teeth bared.

The Pict instinctively stepped back and Gwenhwyfar wasted no time. "Take us home, Cali, take us home!"

* * * *

"I'm sorry, Da." Gwenhwyfar had never seen her father so angry as she watched him pace back and forth in front of the hearth in their council room. "I had to go. Brigid would have been . . ."

Her father stopped and looked at Brigid, seated beside Gwenhwyfar. He took a deep breath and then shook his head, as though trying to clear it. "Yes. It worked out for you this time. I'm glad Brigid wasn't hurt. But you disobeyed an order from me. If you were your brother, I'd have you flogged for that."

Gwenhwyfar twitched her shoulders involuntarily, for her father did that once, before Bedwyr went to Arthur. "I'm sorry, Da. I had to do it. Punish me as you will."

Her father gave an exasperated snort and began pacing again. "No riding for a month. You are not even to see your horse. Is that clear?"

Gwenhwyfar met her father's angry look. "Yes, Da."

"You'll spend your time with Elaine, learning women's skills."

Gwenhwyfar groaned inwardly. Elaine, who had insisted on being there only because she wanted to see what her uncle would do, smirked. *This is going to be hell.*

She straightened her shoulders. "Yes, Da."

"And furthermore . . ." her father began and then stopped. He walked toward her and pulled her up and into his arms. "My God, child, you could have been killed. I've already lost your mother. I love you, Gwenhwyfar. I love you."

He nearly suffocated her from his fierce hug, but Gwenhwyfar didn't mind. She began to cry and then realized from her father's shaking shoulders that he was crying also. *I love you, too, Da.*

* * * *

She was struggling in the middle of a Great Hall she didn't recognize. Two masked men held her, one around her shoulders while the other attempted to catch both legs. She kicked at him furiously, using the one foot he had grasped as leverage. Her boot smashed into his face and he yelped in pain and dropped the other leg. She sagged to the floor and her captor lost his grip momentarily. Curling herself into a ball, she rolled away from him.

A sword slid across the floor toward her. She grabbed it and sprang up. A dark-haired man had run in from the back hall. The same man she had dreamed about before. She was sure of it. He edged his way toward her, lunging and thrusting, giving her time to get to him. They fought back to back, holding off the intruders.

One of his cuts went true, slicing the sword arm of one of the masked men and by that time, help had arrived . . .

Gwenhwyfar leaned heavily against him, feeling the protective curve of his arm around her as he shouted orders to the soldiers who appeared. Then it was quiet and they were alone.

"Why would anyone want to abduct me?" she asked shakily as they both sat on one of the trestle benches.

"I don't know, but I'll find out," he said. "I swear, they won't hurt you again."

She looked up at him. As before, the dream would not allow his face to come into focus, but she was aware of his unusually-colored eyes. The color of smoke.

As if mesmerized, he bent his head closer until their lips brushed. She slipped her arms around his neck in the most natural of motions. He rained tiny kisses across her forehead, along the curve of her cheek to the corner of her mouth and then lightly nibbled his way down her neck and back up to her mouth.

His kisses were soft, the pressure increasing gently until she invited his tongue with hers. A tingling began in her stomach that quickly became a throbbing between her legs. As his kisses deepened, her breasts ached for his touch. She pressed herself against his chest . . .

Gwenhwyfar woke up, gasping for air. *Sweet Mary! The sensation had been so strong, so intense. I had no idea my body could respond like that.* She could still feel his muscular arms around her, his strong hands sliding across her back, pressing her closer. And she trusted him completely.

But who is he? Have I imagined some dream-hero to rescue me from every nightmare? Does he really exist? And if he does . . . Gwenhwyfar closed her eyes and snuggled under the covers, arms wrapped around her pillow and sighed contentedly. *If I ever meet him and he can really make me feel that way, he will have my heart and soul. There could be no other.*

* * * *

"What did you expect Da to do?" Bedwyr asked with an amused look as he sat across from Gwenhwyfar in their private living area and watched her trying to embroider.

"Damn!" she said as she stuck herself with the needle for the fourth time that day.

"You'd better not let Da hear you talk like that, or you'll be embroidering entire altar cloths for the church next."

Gwenhwyfar gave him an annoyed look. Bedwyr had arrived home yesterday on one of those perfect late September days. The sky was cloudless, the sun warm, the breeze cool. Brilliant shades of red, orange and gold sheathed the trees and provided a backdrop for the flocks of geese flying southward. She desperately wanted to go riding with him and show off some new skills she'd taught Cali, but she was confined to the house.

"I'm still glad I went." Mador came for her as soon as he got back and his undying gratitude was something that kept Gwenhwyfar sane through the tediousness of the women's work she was assigned to do.

Bedwyr sobered. "I wonder if Arthur knows she's back."

Gwenhwyfar looked up. "How did you know about that?"

"I was there. It was the day we got Octa. Personally, with the befogged shape her mind was in, I didn't think she'd ever recover."

"She told me it was some priestess's son in Armorica that healed her." Gwenhwyfar gasped as the needle stuck her again and sucked her finger. "Galahad, I think she said his name was."

Bedwyr stared at her and then began laughing. "If anybody could 'heal' her, he would be the one."

Gwenhwyfar frowned. "You know him?"

"*Certes*. He's the one who saved Arthur's life at Gurnion. The women call him—well, I don't know what they call him—but there certainly is no lack of them around wherever he is." He tilted his head and studied her. "Actually, I think you'd like him."

Gwenhwyfar gave him a wry look. "He is probably as arrogant as Arthur is if he's got that many women following him around."

"He's hard to describe, but 'arrogant' isn't a word I've heard any woman use." Bedwyr grinned. "It's his love of horses that you'd like. He's a Whisperer, too."

She laid her loop down and gazed at him. "I've never met another Whisperer."

"That's what he said when I mentioned you were one." Bedwyr stood and walked to the door. "Mayhap the two of you should meet."

Gwenhwyfar nodded, a strange feeling fluttering in her stomach. "Mayhap we should."

CHAPTER TWENTY-TWO—THE OFFER
498 A.D.

The wound Uther took punctured a lung and even by early fall, he was still not recovered fully. When the message came from Uriens, he simply turned it over to Arthur.

"He says a Scotti by the name of Fergus Mor has come ashore between Angus' lands and Cabran's. While they're dealing with him, the Picts have started raiding again, coming south of the Wall." Arthur looked around the table at his former lieutenants, now made captains, each in charge of one hundred cavalry. He had newly promoted Gaheris, giving Gaheris his former company of men. "What do you think?"

"If Uriens is asking for our help, the Picts must be raiding often," Gaheris said.

Arthur looked back at the letter. "They've been stealing cattle and sheep, but recently a whole village was destroyed."

Lancer whistled. "That sounds more like Saxons than Picts. Are you sure you cleared the Caledonian woods?"

"I thought we had," Arthur replied with a worried look. "But raiders tried to attack Cameliard recently. That's where I sent Bedwyr and his company last week."

"They're nearly twenty miles in. Picts came that far south from the Wall?" Gaheris asked in surprise. "I think Lancer may be right; that sounds more like Saxons."

"Whichever it is," Arthur said as he lay the paper down in front of him, "I think taking the full cohort would be a good idea. Five hundred horsemen can man the Wall night and day, working two shifts. At least until Angus and Cabran can work something out with Fergus. That needs to be done before the snow blocks passage and allows Fergus the winter to settle in."

The men stood. As they were making their way to the door, Arthur said, "Gaheris, one more thing. Gwalchmai and Ragnell are with Uriens, visiting your aunt. They've brought your mother and brother with them."

Gaheris looked dubious. "If Agravaine is with them, there's bound to be trouble."

Arthur raised an eyebrow. "Why?"

Gaheris shook his head. "I don't know, but my brother seems to breed it wherever he goes."

* * * *

When they reached the north, Arthur distributed the four companies, sending Gwalchmai toward Cameliard and Gaheris and Gryflet west. Lancer's company remained with him.

"I'm not looking forward to seeing Morgana again," Arthur told him as they rode up to the gates of Uriens' holding. "That woman always reminds me of a cat ready to pounce and I'm the prey."

She came out of Great Hall with Uriens to meet them. Arthur resigned himself to her embrace, feeling her deliberately press her breasts against his chest, and wishing mightily that he could wipe the smirk off Lancer's face. Then he noticed Accolon, standing not far away, clenching his fists. *He's jealous. So that's how it is. Has the woman no sense of morals at all? She must be at least two or three and ten years older than him.* None too gently, he pried himself loose and clasped Uriens's shoulder.

Another woman emerged from the house. She must be Morgana's sister, Arthur thought, but they looked nothing alike. Margawse had hair the color of a brilliant sunset and ginger-brown eyes that seemed to snap at him. She was much taller and not as curvaceous as Morgana. Lamorak accompanied her and from the way she looked up and smiled at him, Arthur wondered if they, too, were involved. *There must be at least twenty years difference in their ages! Mayhap wantonness runs in the family.*

He didn't have long to ponder on the subject, for he met Agravaine that evening at supper. The youth was surly and from the glowering looks he kept sending Lamorak, Arthur had no doubts that his mother's supposed hostage was more than that.

Arthur studied Agravaine as he sat across the table from him. He was short and lean and didn't resemble either of his tall brothers. *A different father, mayhap?* He had been rude when Gwalchmai introduced him and Gaheris cuffed him for it. Grudgingly, he'd apologized, but Arthur knew he didn't mean a word of it.

Now he eyed the pretty, blue-eyed serving wench who waited on Lancer seated next to him. Lancer held out his wine cup and smiled at her. She brushed against him as she refilled the cup and lingered just long enough to send a distinct message. Lancer broke into a grin and Agravaine's eyes narrowed.

"I'll have some more wine," he said.

The girl ignored him and gazed into Lancer's eyes.

Agravaine's swarthy face turned even darker. He reached up and jerked her around. "More wine. Now."

As Arthur watched, Agravaine squeezed the girl's arm hard and she winced. Before he could act, Lancer clamped a hand on Agravaine's shoulder and bore down.

"Let her go."

Agravaine glared at him. "She's a servant. I can handle her anyway I want to."

Lancer's chop on the crook of his arm to break his hold was swift and from the way his arm dropped, Arthur knew it was also numb.

Agravaine knocked his chair to the ground as he lunged for Lancer, shoving the girl into the table. Spilled wine swam everywhere. He brought his fist up, only to have it caught by Gwalchmai who'd been seated to his left.

"Enough, Brother. We are guests here."

"Let me go! That devil nearly broke my arm! I want to fight him."

"Shall we go outside?" Lancer asked, his eyes turning a smoky grey.

"Yes," Agravaine hissed, struggling against both of his brothers now.

"Don't be a fool," Gaheris said. "He'll do a lot more than just break an arm."

Margawse arrived at the table, her eyes blazing. The slap she gave Agravaine resounded through the now quiet hall. "You will not disgrace this family again. Do you want my sister to think us barbarians?"

Agravaine rubbed his stinging cheek. "He started it."

Lancer stepped forward. "You were hurting the girl. But I will apologize for using excessive force." He held out his hand.

Arthur inhaled sharply. He knew Lancer was doing this for the sake of Gwalchmai and Gaheris, for Agravaine got what he deserved.

Agravaine scowled.

"Take it," Gwalchmai said. "'Tis not often that Lancer will back out of a fight."

Resentfully, Agravaine shook his hand.

"Now leave," Margawze said and looked at Gwalchmai. "See to it he stays in his quarters for the rest of the night."

As they left, and the hall once more resumed its noise, Lancer walked over to the girl who was scrabbling to sop up the overturned wine.

"Leave it." Lancer touched her shoulder lightly and turned her around. "Let me look at your arm."

She looked at him apprehensively and slowly held out her arm. She sustained a cut when she hit the table. Gently, Lancer traced the bruise Agravaine had made. "You are going to be sore for a few days. Let me walk you to the infirmary for a bandage for that cut."

Her expression changed to one of wonder and Arthur knew still another female had fallen hard for Lancer. He watched as Lancer guided her away, her face still awestruck. *It isn't that he tries to enthrall them. As hard as he is on his men, Lancer really likes women. I think, mayhap, he even understands them.* Arthur sighed. *I don't think I ever will.*

* * * *

Gwalchmai approached Arthur the next morning as they were saddling the horses. "Would you consider taking Agravaine into the army?"

Arthur turned around in the stall, one hand resting on Valiant's withers. "He's too hot-headed."

Gwalchmai nodded. "That's my point. He's six and ten and my mother said he's getting out of control. And he hates Lamorak."

Arthur raised an eyebrow. "I noticed." He turned back to adjust the saddle blanket, smoothing it before he lifted the saddle.

"It's just that he's never forgiven Pellinore for killing our father, Lot. Lamorak reminds him of that daily."

Arthur thought he knew what was really causing Agravaine's hostility, but he held his tongue. *No man wants to hear his mother is bedding a man who's young enough to be her son.* He adjusted the saddle and cinched it before he turned around. Gwalchmai looked miserable.

"All right," he said. "Mayhap military discipline is what he needs. I'll put him in Bedwyr's unit when we return. Lancer would be tougher, but I don't think we need daily eruptions. For now, he'll ride with you."

Gwalchmai's face broke into sunshine. "Thank you, Arthur. You won't regret this."

I hope not, Gwalchmai. We'll see.

* * * *

Arthur rode with Lancer's company as they patrolled the Wall east of Uriens' fort. He sent Gwalchmai's company west. Better to keep Agravaine separated from Lancer until some discipline had been taught. He'd had a report from Bedwyr that one more raid had been attempted and indeed they were Picts, blue with woad and buck-naked.

"Evidently," Arthur said to Lancer as they sat their mounts at one of the stations that dotted the Wall every mile, "his sister got quite a scare. She came upon one of them unexpectedly."

"Gwenhwyfar?" Lancer asked. "Was she hurt?"

Arthur shook his head. "Bedwyr says she hiked herself into a tree and hid." He frowned. "He also said something about her stabbing the Pict with a knife, but I find that hard to believe."

A look of admiration swept Lancer's face. "She sounds resourceful."

Arthur snorted. "More like stubborn. Bedwyr said Leodegrance had strictly forbidden her to leave the villa's grounds."

Lancer grinned. "Something that's forbidden is always more tempting."

"You would know about that, considering the number of husbands out there who don't suspect a thing." Arthur laughed.

Lancer shrugged. "A lot of married women are lonely. I've only taken what's been offered willingly." A gleam came to his eye. "I've never deliberately seduced a married woman."

"Well, if I ever remarry, leave my wife alone, will you?" Arthur said jokingly.

Lancer stopped smiling and his tone was serious when he spoke. "Honor between friends, Arthur, is worth more than fulfilling a lustful need. Your wife will be off limits. Trust me."

* * * *

They had been at Uriens a little over a month when word came from the north that the boundary dispute with Fergus was settled. Angus and Cabran returned to their holdings. The Pictish raids also stopped after Arthur's men were seen lining the Wall and now they would be leaving in the morning.

Uriens provided a huge feast for that last night. Roast fowl swimming in gravy, boar, venison and mutton were carried in on steaming platters. Warm fragrant bannocks and soft oatcakes accompanied a variety of cheeses and there were rich puddings and dried currants, along with fresh apples and pears.

Morgana placed Arthur in the seat of honor to her right at the high table this evening. For the entire length of his stay, he managed to avoid her as much as possible and made sure he wedged himself in between two men at mealtimes. Even so, he felt her eyes on him much of the time and if he glanced her way, her stare would be bold and inviting. Tonight, however, he was trapped. Uriens insisted that, as *Dux Bellorum*, he sit at the high table with them.

She wore a low cut silk gown in blue so dark it looked almost black in the dim oil lamp light. The color only accented her ebony hair and ivory skin and made her eyes look like obsidian. She was a picture of black and white. The musky scent of her perfume was nearly overwhelming and the image of a badger flitted through Arthur's mind. *Cunning creatures.*

She laid a well-manicured hand on his arm and Arthur forced himself not to squirm.

"Your title," she said, "*Dux Bellorum.* It's a great honor, isn't it?"

He wondered what she was up to. "It means leader-in-war. Since Uther is not fully recovered, he wanted the men to recognize that he transferred some of his power temporarily. As soon as he's well, he'll take command again."

Morgana frowned at Uther's name. She grabbed a bannock and tore it between her two hands, letting the pieces fall on the table. "I don't care if he recovers or not. He was responsible for my father's death. Did you know that?"

Arthur had heard some of the story, but he didn't care to argue the point. "That was before my time."

Her eyes blazed at him. "He sent me to that miserable convent where I spent ten long years. If it hadn't been for . . ." She stopped and changed the subject abruptly. "Tintagel should be Margawse's and mine, not his!"

Arthur didn't think this was the right time to tell her that Marc would probably annex Tintagel and Terrabil by treaty once Ygraine was gone. He thought swiftly, wanting to bring this conversation to an end. "Didn't Gorlois leave some lands in the south to you and your half-brother, Maelgwyn?"

She brightened considerably. "Yes. Just west of the Isle of Avallach." She tilted her head and gave him a slanted look. "Not too far from Cadwy's fort. I hear that's where you reside now."

I should have kept my mouth shut. "Cadwy still owns it. It's very defensible and with our large numbers of light cavalry now, it's more centrally located for dispatch."

She smiled coyly and touched his arm again. "I don't need its military history, Arthur. I was just thinking I might inspect my land soon. I could call on you."

The last thing I want is for you to come south, even for a visit. "We don't do much entertaining." She laughed lightly, only to Arthur it sounded like glass shattering.

"You may have to, now that you're the *Dux.*" Her eyes widened suddenly. "Actually, you're the second-in-command. If something happened to Uther, would you be king?"

"Nothing is going to happen to Uther." The thought niggled at him. What would they do? Uther had no heirs, unless anyone still believed that his kidnapped son would resurface. Hardly likely, after all these years. As far as military went, he was already in charge, but if they had no high king, it wouldn't be long before the vassals would begin fighting among themselves again. If that happened, the Saxons would prey on the weak. Suddenly, he wished Myrddin were here, but once the dispute was settled, the druid headed south.

"Still," Morgana said as she leaned closer, her full breasts nearly bursting from the bodice of her gown, "if you were high king, you'd need a woman to do all that entertaining for you. A queen or a consort. Mayhap, both." Her fingers brushed his face lightly. "I can't marry you, but I could be your consort. I could give you an heir."

Inwardly, Arthur shuddered. *A child by you is the last thing I want.* He moved his chair slightly back, away from her touch. "I'm not planning to be high king. In any case, I doubt Uriens would approve."

Morgana shrugged. "It's been done before. Uther would have taken my mother, even if my father hadn't been killed, and made her his consort. The high king has that right."

Arthur ignored the remark for it was true. The high king did have that right, even though it would be foolish for one to use it and infuriate the numerous Christians. "I would think you keep yourself occupied as it is." He nodded his head toward Accolon, who had just come in the door, and was staring at them.

Morgana looked across the room and gave Accolon a big smile and then she turned to Arthur. "He is adorable, isn't he? And so anxious to please." Her face took on the look of a cat that just finished an entire pitcher of cream. She stood and then leaned down, giving Arthur a good look at her semi-exposed breasts. "I'm anxious to please, too. Remember that, should you become high king."

CHAPTER TWENTY-THREE—THE PLOT
498 A.D.

The feast was finished and the entertainment about to begin as Morgana made her way through the crowds to Accolon who waited by the door of the Great Hall. *I've planted the seed in Arthur's mind. When the time is right, I will let him know he already has an heir.* Meanwhile, Medraut would stay hidden. The possibility of being consort to a high king was like a delicious dessert. What true power she would have.

She reached Accolon and looked up at him and smiled. "Why weren't you at the feast? I missed you."

His chin jutted out and he looked away. "You seemed to be enjoying yourself with Arthur."

Morgana laughed and ran her hand up his arm to his shoulder. "Don't be jealous, Love. He's the *Dux Bellorum*. I had to be sociable. He's become a powerful man."

Accolon glanced down. "And you like power."

Morgana wasn't perturbed. "*Certes*, I do. And you like powerful women." She brushed a breast against his sleeve. "Or have you forgotten what I did to you last night?"

A corner of his mouth began to quirk. "I don't think I care to forget."

She stretched on tiptoe and whispered, "Would you like more?" She gave his ear a sharp nip.

"Ouch!" He rubbed his ear, but he grinned. "I don't think tonight will be good. By the time the last drunk has gone to bed, it will be near dawn."

"I meant now," she said.

He gave her a startled look. "Now? Where?"

Morgana slanted a look at him. "My bedchamber, *certes*."

"What? Are you mad? Uriens is awake. What if we're found?"

"You worry too much, my sweet. Why would anyone think to come to my bedchamber with all this entertainment and drink going on?" She positioned herself in front of him, her fingers playing with the laces of his trews. He hardened and she smiled. *Power. Men are so easy. One day I'll have Arthur in my power, too.* "We have time . . ."

Accolon groaned and then his eyes widened in near terror. Quickly, Morgana stepped back, flicking a pretend piece of something off his shoulder. She turned around.

"There you are!" Uriens said heartily. "I've been looking for you! The bard has composed a song about making the Picts retreat and wants to dedicate it to you." He gave Accolon a quizzical look. "Arthur wants to see you."

Accolon and Morgana both looked up to the high table where Arthur still sat. Morgana realized that he had been watching them the whole time, although he must be too far away to have seen what she did. The grim look on his face said otherwise. He was probably going to warn Accolon about the consort offer she'd made. She sighed. Not only was she not going to be able to take her lover tonight, but she'd have to persuade him into believing Arthur was a liar; that in fact, the whole consort idea had been his, not hers. *That would certainly make sense.* She glanced up at Accolon. *I know what he likes to have done in bed.* If that didn't work, the woodrowel and vervain would.

* * * *

"Are you feeling better?" Morgana walked into Medraut's bedchamber the day after Arthur left and set the cool drink down on the table beside the bed.

"A little," he answered and eyed the cup. "Do I have to drink more of that stuff?"

"This is something different," Morgana said as she handed him the cup. "It will taste better than the other drink you've been having."

He sniffed suspiciously, his grey eyes narrowed in concentration. He took a sip and looked surprised. "It is good."

She laughed. "It's mint. It should settle your stomach."

Medraut breathed a sigh of relief. "My tummy has been hurting for a moon now, ever since those soldiers came. I haven't even been able to leave my room because I need the potty."

For a fleeting second, Morgana felt remorse that she'd been giving her son ground mandrake root each morning to make him ill, but it had to be done. Although he was only six, he already looked a lot like his father. She wasn't ready for Arthur to see him. Not yet. Yet, she couldn't keep a normally active child confined to his room.

"Get dressed," she said briskly, "and come outside. I want to see if you can still wield your wooden sword."

Medraut followed her outside a short time later, licking honey from his morning oatcake off his fingers. She sat on a bench under a shade tree near the fencing area waiting for him, but now she jumped up.

"How many times have I told you to wash your hands?" Morgana gave his fingers a sharp rap with her hand.

He put the offending fingers behind him. "I'm sorry, Mother."

"Well, you should be. Making me repeat myself does not show intelligence on your part." She looked around. "Where is Accolon? He's to teach you how to parry." She smiled as Accolon came around the corner of the hall.

"Good morning, Medraut. It's good to see you up and well." He turned toward Morgana. "My lady."

She wondered how much Arthur had told him last night, but it was hard to tell. His face was closed to her, as it always was when they were around Medraut. She heaved an inward sigh. She would have to wait for tonight to find out.

"Ready to begin?" he asked and Medraut smiled, taking his position with his small wooden sword.

Accolon had him practice his footwork and then take some practice thrusts and lunges at the straw-stuffed effigy that was set up. They reviewed the points where the sword would do the most damage and where an armored warrior was most vulnerable.

"I think it's time for you to have a real opponent," Accolon said. "Me." He tapped Medraut's sword with his and it flew out of Medraut's hand. Morgana frowned and Medraut turned red as he stooped to retrieve it.

Accolon tapped his hip. "You'd be dead if you ever do that in real battle. Never leave yourself exposed."

Medraut blushed even more. "I won't forget."

"Good. Now meet my blade and try to push it away."

For some moments Morgana watched Medraut. Then she noticed a soldier's son had come to the ring to watch. He was perhaps a year older, but close to Medraut's size and he carried a wooden practice sword.

"Did you want to join us?" she asked and the youth grinned happily. "I think it would be good for Medraut to get some real practice with someone his own age."

Accolon gave her a surprised look. "Are you sure . . . ?"

"You're too easy on him. Let him try and get the feel of a real fight."

Medraut and the boy took their positions. They circled, each trying to stab at the other. The older boy cut suddenly to the right and Medraut quickly tried to parry, but received a hard hit to his arm. He nearly dropped his sword, but one look at his mother's face made him struggle on.

He managed to land a blow on the boy's shoulder and was rewarded with a yelp of pain. The other lunged and with a low cut smacked Medraut across his knees. With a scream of rage, Medraut attacked the boy, fists flailing. Soon, both of them were rolling in the dirt, raining punches.

Accolon pulled them apart by their collars. "Enough. You're to be practicing swordplay."

"He didn't fight fair," Medraut wailed.

Morgana came up to them. "Accolon, take the child to his father and explain what happened." She gave him a moment's long look. "I'll talk to you later."

Accolon's blue eyes flickered with a hint of interest, but he kept his face passive. "As you wish, my lady."

When he had gone, Morgana walked with Medraut back to the bench and sat down. "I'm disappointed in you."

"Why?" The child stifled his tears. "He wasn't supposed to do that."

"Let me tell you something, Medraut. When you're old enough to fight real battles, rules aren't always followed. Winning is what matters, at whatever cost. Do you understand? When you win, you have power. And power is what counts most in this world. With it, you can do whatever you want."

He nodded. "I'll remember."

Morgana leaned closer to him. "What I really want you to remember is this. You can never—ever—afford to lose your temper. When you do, you lose control. And being in control is what makes you win. As you grow up, I'm going to teach you how to learn where your opponent is weak and to use that weakness for your own gain. But you must not lose your temper; you must be able to think."

He nodded again. "I'll try."

She looked straight into his eyes. "I have great plans for you. I want you to be the next *Dux Bellorum*."

Medraut's eyes widened. "Like that Arthur who was just here?"

"Yes. Just like him."

He sighed a little and looked disappointed. "I wish I could have met him."

Morgana laughed and patted his head. "Oh, have no doubt. You will, Medraut. One day you will."

* * * *

Morgana turned on her side in the soft straw and leaned over Accolon. She licked the thin line of blood one of her nails had drawn as she'd raked his shoulder at the height of passion a few minutes ago. He was still panting slightly and in the shaft of moonlight that cut through the dusty window of the stable's granary, she could see the sweat glistening on his body.

"Are you still angry?" she murmured.

He grinned and squeezed the breast that was lying on his chest. "I can't stay mad at you."

Morgana gave a self-satisfied purr. "I'm the one that should be mad at you for believing anything like what Arthur told you. Why would I possibly want him when you satisfy me so well?" In truth, she was a little angry. It had taken her nearly thirty minutes to coax the clothes off of Accolon and then he'd made her do all the work. Not that she minded exactly, but now it was her turn.

Her fingers trailed a path down his belly and played with the silky hair at his base until he began to groan and stiffened again. "You know what I like."

Accolon growled and like a crouching tiger, he sprang, slamming her against the floor, pinioning her arms above her head. He took a nipple between his teeth and pulled just hard enough to make her moan. He bit down and she gasped in pain, but arched her back and pushed herself against him asking for more. He took the other breast in his mouth, suckling fast and hard and drove himself home, pummeling her the way she liked.

"More!" she cried and felt the tip of him pounding against her womb. The pain of being bitten had subsided into a throbbing heat that enhanced the frantic ramming he was doing. Already she felt the sting of the raw flesh being pelted, but she drove him on.

The moment was coming. The pain and the pleasure would blend as one feeling, greater than either of the parts. The whole . . . "Oh! Yes . . ." And the world exploded.

As she curled in Accolon's arms still catching her breath, she wondered what it would be like again with Arthur. More and more, she liked the idea of being his consort.

* * * *

The idea of being a king's consort stayed with her for several days. The thought of Uther dying was a welcome one. She'd even help it along if she could. *Mayhap I should visit my lands and pay a visit . . .*

Britain would need a high king if it were to stay united. As power-hungry as she was, she was aware that Uther, much as she hated him, had been able to hold the petty, arguing vassal kings together. But it was Arthur who had the major battles over the past eight years. She shuddered to think where the Saxons would be now, if Arthur hadn't.

There might be some squabbling among the kings once Uther was gone, but Arthur would be the natural choice to hold the Saxons in check. And the druid was always with him. *Some say 'tis Myrddin's magic that wins battles, but I know power where I see it. Arthur has the power.*

High king. Yes. That's what she wanted Arthur to achieve. Even if he took a wife, queens merely served as pretty centerpieces. It was the King's Consort who sat at his side and helped him make decisions. *And, certes, there is the evening sport!* Most of the petty queens she had met would be only too happy to relinquish that duty, glad to retire to their 'lady chambers' at night.

Most of all, though, if Arthur were high king, Medraut would be his heir, even if some future queen bore him children. That meant that, one day, Medraut would be high king. *Sooner, mayhap, than later?* Morgana smiled to herself. *That means I will be the Queen Mother.*

Ah, power. It was a good thing.

* * * *

Morgana gazed into the flames, her eyes glassy from the agaric mushroom she had ingested some time ago. She giggled, not sure how much time had passed. The priestesses on the Isle call this mushroom sacred, she thought and laughed again. But it works for anyone! Sometimes, she achieved the Sight this way. It was what she was hoping for tonight.

The flame faeries in the hearth of her bedchamber danced in front of her eyes, wearing skirts of blue and red and orange. The male fire drakes gyrated behind them. Morgana felt her mind slipping into the whirling dance of flame. One of the fire drakes became more dominant, growing larger, overshadowing the others. The glowing red dragon turned its head and looked out of the fire.

The Pendragon.

Suddenly, Morgana found herself peering out of the hearth into a room that held a great round table. Uther Pendragon sat in one of the chairs; beside him was the druid, Myrddin. A powerful faerie—the queen herself—hovered by his ear. Interesting.

"I'm not healing the way I should," Uther said. "I think it's time."

Myrddin took a deep breath. "Mayhap. I had hoped he could win one big decisive battle. That would go a long way toward acceptance."

"The men accept him now. Once I acknowledge him as my son, there will be no doubt who the next high king should be."

"Still, I feel uneasy," Myrddin answered. "There's something out there—or mayhap someone—that may foil our plans."

Uther laughed and then bent into coughing spasms. "Something always tries to foil our plans. He's ready. After all, Arthur's a grown man."

Morgana blinked, back in her own bedchamber and a tingle flowed through her. *Arthur is Uther's son? The child that was kidnapped and that I wished were dead?* She'd always sworn to hate her half-brother should they ever meet.

Her brother. A chill washed over her, even though the room was warm. Her brother . . . and she bore his son. She hadn't known who he was on that Beltane night. Incest. How would Arthur handle that when he knew? Then she shook her head. The hag in the forest had known her pagan history. From the times of Isis and Osiris, the ancient Egyptians revered the marriage of brother and sister, such as Cleopatra and Ptolemy. From Babylon came the brother-sister bride of Dumuzi and Inanna: Baal and Astarte yet another example.

Arthur was a professed Christian though . . . and then she laughed. If there was ever more proof than she needed, it was right there in his Christian Bible. Mayhap her years in the convent were going to land something of value, after all. They had studied a poem King Solomon had written called the *Song of Songs:* "... *Thou hast ravished my heart, my sister, my spouse* . . ." She frowned a little, remembering the nuns never wanted to take the phrase, or in fact the entire poem, literally. They alluded to the Christos being a bridegroom and his bride was the Church. Still, it had been the only thing she had studied in those ten years that made any sense. The entire poem was too full of intimate details to have been written for some mystical ideal.

Somehow, she would have to convince Arthur of that.

Consort. Eventually Queen Mother. Ah, Power. It was a good thing.

CHAPTER TWENTY-FOUR—THE FUTURE KING
498 A.D. – 499 A.D.

"You're saying your SISTER really did fight a Pict?" Arthur stared at Bedwyr incredulously. They had all returned to Cadwy's and he and Lancer were having a cup of wine after supper in the Great Hall when Bedwyr joined them. "Why didn't she just stay in the tree where she was safe?"

"She would have, but her friend gave herself away. According to Gwenhwyfar, she had no choice but to attack."

"And with only a table knife?" Lancer asked admiringly. "By Mithras, Arthur, we should ask her to join us. I wouldn't mind fighting beside another Boudicca!"

Bedwyr gave him a strange look before he turned back to Arthur. "Her friend's name was Brigid. I think you know her."

Arthur looked puzzled. "Not the girl I sent to the Lake?"

Bedwyr nodded. "She married a Breton and a group of them moved to Britain about a year ago to settle some holdings my father has."

"So she married?" Lancer asked softly. "I'm glad to hear it."

Bedwyr grinned. "Gwenhwyfar says you 'healed' her."

Arthur was surprised. "You, Lancer? I thought your mother healed her. You only told me that Brigid was alive and well. What did you do?"

Lancer looked uncomfortable. "Let's just say there was a reason my mother decided to hire eight courtesans."

Bedwyr choked and Arthur raised an eyebrow. "Eight? We knew about Salome, but . . ."

"Eight," Lancer replied, "and Brigid was number nine. It is a mystical number. If you do your sums in multiples of three, the end number is always nine. My mother told me there was great healing power in that."

"So it's true then," Bedwyr said, "you do have fey blood. Is that why women find you so irresistible?"

Lancer shrugged. "Do they?"

Both Arthur and Bedwyr stared at him and then they burst out laughing. "Sometimes I think you really don't know," Bedwyr said.

* * * *

It was shortly after Yule that Uther received word from Catwallaun of Gwynedd that there was Scotti unrest in the West.

"Apparently Catwallaun is trying to wrest the isle of Mona away from the Scotti king." Wearily, he laid the letter down on his desk and looked at Arthur. "With the reports that are coming in that Colgrin plans another raid this spring from the eastern borders, I dare not send your men west."

Arthur nodded. "Too bad Cunneda didn't wipe all of them when he was relocated years ago. That settlement has always been a hotbed of unrest."

Uther looked thoughtful. "Cunneda was relocated there after his tribe turned disloyal on Vortigern. Didn't Angus tell us there's a northern king that periodically causes troubles for him and Cabran and even Margawse?"

Arthur tried to remember. Something about constantly wanting to challenge boundaries, Angus had said, and that the man was more of a nuisance than anything else. "His name was Caw."

"Ah, yes." Uther smiled. "Mayhap, after we clash with Colgrin again, you could take a diplomatic party north and persuade Caw to relocate as Cunneda did before him. He can work on wiping out the Scotti while Catwallaun concentrates on Mona."

Arthur sighed. "Colgrin has more lives than a cat. How many times have we been to war? He always escapes."

"I'm getting too old to chase him much longer," Uther said with finality. "I'm not going to wait for him to come to us. We'll advance the march in late February, before they would expect us. This time it will be to the death."

A shadow seemed to pass in front of Arthur and he wondered if the sun had suddenly gone behind a cloud and left the tent so dark.

* * * *

The day the army began its march was dismally cold. The rain threatened to turn to sleet and the wind howled from the north like a banshee. The infantry marched double time to keep warm and the three companies of cavalrymen huddled inside their woolen cloaks, thrown over their light armor. Even the horses were miserable, hanging their heads low to avoid the stinging hard rain.

"We could have waited another day," Gwalchmai grumbled as he rode up to Arthur and Lancer. "I wish I had drawn the long straws like Gaheris and Gryflet and been able to man the fort. They're all warm and dry."

"King Uther seems possessed over this war," Lancer answered.

Arthur remained quiet. Since his discussion with Uther the month before, he'd noticed a change in the king. He seemed more resigned and less agitated than usual. Ygraine also came to the fort and stayed the entire month. Even now, as they left, she remained there. The uneasiness settled over Arthur again.

They camped the night before the expected battle on the borders of Anglia. Tomorrow, they would find out if scouts had alerted the Saxons. If not, their march in as far as Camulodunum should be fairly easy.

Arthur stretched out beside the small fire he'd built and idly thought about seeking out one of the camp followers. Mayhap physical release would calm the restiveness within him tonight. Lancer was probably already enjoying the soft, naked body of some girl lying beneath him. Arthur sighed and sat up. *I'm near thirty and tired of wenching.*

"Can't sleep?" Uther was making the rounds with Myrddin.

Arthur shook his head and the two men sat down beside him. "I hope this battle will be short and sweet," he said. "Colgrin has been a pain in the ass for a long time."

Uther nodded. "Whatever it takes, this time we finish him."

A flash of light suddenly illuminated the northern sky. Streaks of green and pink danced across the horizon. Myrddin inhaled sharply.

"Cerdic once told me," Uther said softly, "that those lights reflected off the armor of the Valkyries as they searched for the souls of their dead warriors."

Arthur shivered in spite of the fire. "Well, let's hope he's right. The Saxons will die and ours will be the victory."

"Yes," Uther replied, but his voice was flat. "Let us hope."

Myrddin looked from one to the other and said nothing.

* * * *

They were met with the full force of Colgrin's army not far inside the Saxon borders. The barbarians stood silhouetted against the ridge of Mount Agned. As the infantry charged down the hill, Uther's men formed the shield wall and moved forward to clash with them. The three companies of cavalry moved forward, too, to serve as right, left and rear flanks.

"Where are their horsemen?" Arthur asked Uther. Most of the Saxons fought on foot, but Colgrin had adopted some of the Roman habits and had a small unit of mounted men, hardly more than a good-sized bodyguard.

"I don't know." Uther scanned the countryside. "Too many hills here, they might come out from anywhere."

He had hardly spoken when from behind them came the sound of thundering hooves. Arthur shouted at the backs of the cavalry and whirled Valiant, sword drawn. They were outnumbered ten-to-one. Arthur hoped someone heard him, but he didn't have time to look back. He slashed the first warrior to meet him and unseated a second. He recognized Colgrin and tried to make his way toward him. *This time! This time it will be over!* Uther had knocked another from the saddle. Arthur swung again, this time gashing a leg.

Then Lancer was beside him, hewing men down like stalks of grain. One look told Arthur the battle frenzy was on him. He would remember little when this was over.

Others joined them then, and the battle turned. Colgrin sounded his retreat and the Saxons scattered over the hills. Arthur started to give the order to pursue, but he looked to Uther first.

Uther slumped in his saddle, hanging onto his horse's neck, a dazed look on his face. From his side, a sword protruded.

"The king is wounded!" Arthur shouted as he leapt off his horse. "Form a line here!" Fifty of the horsemen immediately formed a circle and the retreat was sounded. They would be fighting now to protect the king and get him back across the border.

Lancer reached Uther at the same time Arthur did. Together, they lifted him from his horse and laid him on the ground. He groaned in pain as the medic prodded the wound as gently as he could.

"I can't remove the sword until he can lie still. He'll lose too much blood with the jarring," the medic said.

Arthur nodded. "Quickly," he said to one of the men, "make a travois. Hitch it to his horse."

Myrddin appeared through the crowd. "I'll walk beside him. Mayhap, I can staunch the flow of blood a little." He looked up at Arthur. "Send your fastest scout to ride to the Lake. Nimue must be waiting when we get to Ambresbyrig. This wound will be infected by then and she'll know what to do."

Arthur gave the order and assessed the battle. Colgrin's soldiers weren't pursuing them, seemingly content to stand and watch them leave. *Probably because Colgrin can't be found.* Whatever the reason, he was grateful. Uther's showdown was going to have to wait.

He bent down over Uther. "Hang on. We're going home."

Uther managed a feeble smile. "Yes, my son. Take me home." His eyes closed as he drifted into unconsciousness.

Startled, Arthur looked at Myrddin. "Why did he call me that?"

Myrddin's hawk-like gaze softened. "Now you know who your father is."

* * * *

"Why was I not told before?" Arthur looked across the table in the map room at Myrddin and Ygraine. Uther was in the infirmary, being tended to by a worried Nimue and this was the first time Arthur dared to ask the question. He was still in shock from the revelation.

"And I," Ygraine said, "was led to believe you had been kidnapped. I didn't find out you were alive until you joined the army." She turned an angry face to Myrddin. "Why was I not told either?"

Myrddin waved away her wrath. "For Arthur's protection. An heir to the high king is always at risk for assassination. Ector didn't know who Arthur was either. Even Uther didn't know where I had taken him."

"You fool," Ygraine answered. "What if you had died before Arthur came of age? His inheritance would have been lost forever."

The arch-druid raised an eyebrow. "A fool? I had to protect the dynasty."

"What dynasty?" Arthur was puzzled. "Britain?"

Myrddin shook his head. "Not just Britain. Your lineage on Uther's side includes Macsen Wledig and Bran the Blessed who was married to Joseph of Arimathea's daughter, Anna."

Arthur stared at him. "Are you saying that Joseph was an ancestor?"

"That's not all," Myrddin said with a slightly smug smile. "Your mother is of the Blood Royal, also."

"My mother was Vivian the First of Avallach. You know how I feel about following the pagan ways; she was no queen," Ygraine said snappishly.

Arthur felt like his mouth was hanging open with all the surprises he was hearing. "You're the *sister* of the Lady of the Lake?" He could have sworn he heard a soft giggle from somewhere near Myrddin's ear, but that was ridiculous.

"Yes. And I'm not proud of it. I long ago was born again as a Christian."

"Well," Myrddin continued, ignoring the furious chatter of the faerie in his ear, "I'll not argue with you."

He shrugged. "Anyway, Arthur has a destiny to fulfill and now he's alive to do it."

Arthur felt a twinge of guilt. Considering that he'd never fully quelled his lust for Nimue, he certainly wasn't fit to be king! Neither was Uther then, given his reputation. He decided to put a stop to the argument.

"Mother." He said the word slowly and carefully and it had its desired effect. Ygraine's countenance changed. Her face softened and her voice was gentle.

"Son." Tears crept into her eyes. "I've wanted to say that for so long."

Arthur took her hand. "It doesn't matter which path you choose, I think, as long as you believe in something. Tolerance is a Christian virtue, is it not?"

"I suppose so," she began doubtfully when they were interrupted by Nimue's appearance in the doorway.

"I think you had better come," she said.

Ygraine's face turned ashen and she rushed past Nimue. Arthur followed her quickly.

Even as they entered the room in the infirmary, Arthur could hear the labored breathing beginning to rattle in Uther's throat. *My father. He's dying and we haven't had a chance to talk.*

Ygraine had grasped Uther's hand and was sitting on the edge of the bed, tears streaming down her face. "Don't leave me," she cried.

Uther opened his eyes and attempted a weak smile. "I've loved only you, my wife. Only you." He turned his head toward Arthur. "Son."

Arthur approached the bed and took his other hand. "I wish I'd known earlier."

Uther slipped a glance at Myrddin and then back to Arthur. "It was better this way. I didn't want the men to think you favored. You had to earn your way." He coughed horribly, a pinkish froth forming at his mouth. "I wish we'd had more time, though."

Arthur watched as his father closed his eyes for the last time, knowing there was nothing more anyone could do.

* * * *

Messengers were dispatched to the ends of the kingdom. While they waited for the kings to arrive for the funeral, Uther's body lay in state, wrapped in herbed shrouds, and kept fresh on layers of ice brought up from Myrddin's cave below the Tor.

Nimue stayed on to freshen the herbs daily and Arthur appreciated her quiet strength. She seemed to know when he needed to talk and when he needed privacy and she kept everyone away at those times. Ygraine, though, seemed hostile to her and wanted nothing to do with her. Ygraine sat by her husband's side most of each day and would stare sullenly at Nimue as she changed the herbs. Almost like a jealous lover, Arthur thought. When he asked his mother about it, though, all she would say is that the priestess was pagan and she wanted nothing to do with those from Avallach. Then she'd informed Arthur that she would take vows at the abbey near Ambresbyrig as soon as Uther had been laid to rest.

For Arthur, the future was overwhelming. As the kings began to arrive, they paid homage to him, but he thought some looked askance of him. *Am I fit to be the high king? What if some vassal wants to challenge me? We can't afford to fight among ourselves with Colgrin preparing to attack. Will the men follow me, now that my father is gone?*

The funeral, itself, proceeded with all the dignity and respect accorded a high king. Four black horses pulled the caisson on which Uther's casket was draped. Lancer lent Pryderi to Arthur to ride at the head of escort to the Giant's Dance.

The sun slowly set, casting its ember rays through the slants in the sarsen stones and washing over the lintels as Uther was lowered into the ground inside the horseshoe of bluestones. The priest, who did not approve of the burial site, recited the Requiem at the fort and now stood frowning outside the circle as Myrddin completed the ritual.

The crowd eventually dispensed, leaving Arthur and Myrddin alone in the gathering twilight. Neither of them spoke for some time. Finally, Arthur looked up at the great trilithons, dipped in silver moonlight and silhouetted against the night sky. He took a ragged breath.

"Do you think I can do it, Myrddin? Lead the people?"

Myrddin appeared to study the full moon as it rose above the circle, flooding them suddenly in white light. "Long ago, the Grail Maiden came to me and said the child of Uther and Ygraine was destined to be a great king."

Arthur breathed deeply again. "More than anything else in life, I want to see Britain united and the need for bloodshed gone."

Myrddin placed a hand on his shoulder. "'Tis the reason you were born, my son."

* * * *

The day after their return to Cadwy's, Myrddin called a council. He looked each vassal king in the eye with his sharp golden gaze. "The purpose of this meeting, before you leave, is for each of you to declare yourself for Arthur. To pledge your loyalty to him as high king."

Nathanlaod grunted. "How do we know what kind of a king he'll make?"

Arthur stood and silence suddenly fell. "I will tell you what I envision, my lords. If the vassal kings unite, we can stay the Saxons. I see a land of peace where fighting men can protect the poor instead of preying on them. A land where rich and poor, young and old, men and women are accorded dignity and respect. A land of prosperity with war and bloodshed behind us."

The council room buzzed with dozens of conversations. Arthur saw some of the men give him furtive looks. Finally, Pellinore banged the table for silence.

"You have my fealty, Arthur."

"Hear, hear," said Leodegrance, "and mine."

"Mine, also," Uriens added.

Marc looked askance for a minute and then he nodded. "I, also, pledge."

Nathanlaod hesitated and looked around the room. "I say Arthur must prove himself first."

"He's done well as *Dux Bellorum*," Myrddin said, somewhat testily.

Nathanlaod turned to him. "Aye. But Uther has been in command. You know our battle at Mount Agned was foiled. Colgrin still waits. Let's see what Arthur can do before we declare him king."

Another furor commenced. This time it was Arthur who held up his hand. "I agree with Nathanlaod. There can be no doubts in anyone's mind. I need each one of you to support me without hesitation. I've told you my goal is to bring unity and peace to Britain. I cannot unite this land if any of you doubt." He glanced at Myrddin, but the druid was scanning the faces of the kings. "I don't think Colgrin will wait for us to come to him a second time. He will lead his men over his borders and soon. I'm surprised he didn't take advantage of my father's death to do so." Arthur looked around the room, trying to discern how many men were still doubtful. "I want to avenge my father's death before I become high king. It's the only way I know to prove I'm worthy."

"Hear, hear!" The kings pounded the table in unison with the wine cups. Arthur gave them one curt nod, turned and left the room.

He paused in the outside hall and closed his eyes. *Give me strength, Lord, and give me the wisdom to lead these people. For unity and for peace. Amen.*

CHAPTER TWENTY-FIVE—DESTINY
500 A.D.

Arthur felt edgy. An uneasy peace had been kept in the months following Uther's death, but how long Arthur could hold Colgrin to his lands, he didn't know.

He pushed aside the maps he'd studied and poured a cup of wine, then passed the skin to Bedwyr. "Now Myrddin tells me I need to think about taking a wife. He's made a list of several women, all of whom would ensure allegiance from some of the vassal kings who aren't thoroughly committed to me."

Bedwyr raised an eyebrow. "An arranged marriage? Didn't you already have one of those?"

"I know, but if I am to be king, I must think of Britain first. Emotionally, I'm ready to settle down. I'm thirty; I've sowed enough wild oats. Myrddin also raised the issue of heirs, in case I die young." He sighed. "An arranged marriage seems to be working for Marc. I hear Iseult is beautiful and he's madly in love. Mayhap I'll get lucky."

"Leonora was beautiful too, Arthur, and you know how that went."

He felt a flicker of pain at the memory. "Who then? Someone I've already seen and know?" He grinned suddenly. "How about your sister? How old is Gwenhwyfar?"

"Six and ten," Bedwyr answered slowly, "but she thinks you're . . . 'arrogant' is the word she used."

"Really? Why?"

Bedwyr shrugged. "She's always trying to prove herself as capable as a man. She doesn't like being treated like a mere girl."

Arthur raised an eyebrow. "Then she is most unusual." He thought a minute and then grinned again. "She was fun to tease though, the last time I saw her."

"Well, she's as hot-headed as ever." Bedwyr shook his head. "I think all you'd do is fight. She cares more about horses than anything. If she were to marry, Lancer would be a better choice for her."

Arthur studied him. "Lancer? What makes you think he'll ever settle down? He even told me as much, once. The only person he'll give his heart and soul to, he said, was his 'dream' lady. And we all know those kinds of dreams don't come true."

Bedwyr grinned. "I usually dream of women I've already had. I guess in Lancer's case, though, those dreams would be pretty crowded." He looked thoughtful. "Was Gwenhwyfar one of the names on Myrddin's list?"

"No. Myrddin never mentioned her."

"How about Elaine, Arthur? From what Gwenhwyfar says, she's always talking about wanting to be married. She's pretty and she's learned all the household skills Gwenhwyfar doesn't have a clue about. She's always neat and clean. Gwenhwyfar can't even keep her hair combed. Elaine likes to be a hostess and has a calm temperament. You certainly know what Gwenhwyfar would do if she didn't like someone's opinion. Elaine would serve well as a queen."

"She sounds about as interesting as yesterday's bread," Arthur said wryly. "I'd at least like someone with a little fire in her soul." He picked up the maps again. "At any rate, I don't have to worry about becoming king until I'm finished with Colgrin."

* * * *

Arthur made his final plans a week later to march into Anglia when Cerdic sent a messenger.

"He said it's urgent," the man said as he handed the note to Arthur in the hall.

Arthur furrowed his brow in consternation as he read the message. *Damnation! Why now?*

"What is it?" Lancer asked.

"Sea raiders," Arthur answered, "sailing west."

"Past Clausentum?"

"Yes. They were barely visible on the horizon."

Lancer looked puzzled. "The next port is Isca near Kernow. We've never known Saxons to sail that far. They usually land near Aesc in friendly waters. Do you think they could be striking at Eire?"

"I doubt it," Arthur answered uneasily. "Fifteen keelboats. That sounds like a war party to me."

Lancer whistled. "That's nearly six hundred men!"

"I know. And they may already have landed. The winds would have been behind them and this note says they were spotted yesterday."

"Is Cerdic going to pursue them?"

Arthur shook his head. "His orders are to protect Clausentum. Who knows if this is a decoy meant to lure him away? I'll send Gwalchmai with a scouting party and have our men prepared to march west first." He sighed as he crushed the note. "We'll have to wait on Colgrin. Again."

* * * *

His scouts returned within three days, riding horses that were lathered in sweat and nearly spent. Gwalchmai slid out of his saddle as Arthur met them in the bailey.

"They've surrounded Aquae Sulis!"

"What?" Arthur stared at him. "That means they marched up the Ermine Way and no one tried to stop them? What about the fort at Lindinus?"

Gwalchmai shook his head. "We didn't go that far. We saw what had been pillaged and burned far before that. We just followed the trail."

By Mithras! How could this happen? Arthur gave orders for his cohort to be ready within hours, then he sent men to raise the armies of Cador, Cato, Agricola, and Marc. "We'll meet at Lindinus and march north together," he said. All these kings had a vested interested in protecting the west. He just hoped Hoel and the men left in Cadwy's charge at Ambresbyrig could hold the east, lest anything should arise there.

Arthur fretted as he waited for the other kings to arrive at Lindinus. They would be there within a day, but every minute seemed to extend itself into timelessness. Any delay allowed the walls of Aquae Sulis to be broached. It was well-defended, but it was no fort. Still, his own numbers wouldn't easily squash six hundred men. It was the only reason Arthur hadn't attacked with only his own cavalry.

But the sight that greeted Arthur's eyes the next morning as they approached Aquae Sulis wasn't what he had anticipated.

What looked like a wheat field was really blond Saxon heads as far as he could see. Lancer rode up to him and cursed.

"Bel's fires! There must be ten thousand men out there."

"Yes." Arthur looked around and spotted Colgrin's banner as well as Aesc's and a minor warlord whose lands bordered the Thames. He looked for the sea raiders' banner and found it. He'd seen it before. The man was a German mercenary named Chelric. Briefly, he wondered how much he had been paid to lure the army west while Colgrin marched down the Icknield Way and Aesc along Harrow Way to converge here. As fast as they must have moved, there would have been little time for burning the villages along the way. He prayed Cadwy and Hoel were advancing behind them.

Arthur studied the shield wall the Saxons presented. They seemed to have learned a lot of strategy from their battles with Arthur. They stood solidly locked, shield to shield, allowing only enough space for the second row of men to have their spears pointed out. Row upon row of them. Arthur sighed. This was going to be the bloodiest battle he'd ever forced his men into.

He gave the signal for the infantry to advance. They, too, formed a shield wall. The Saxons moved forward to meet them. The clash of metal on metal sounded like rolling kettle drums and the earth vibrated.

The fighting continued throughout the day. Sometimes, the Britons managed to break the wall and several cavalry would rush in, but for the most part, the Saxons held the ground. Near sunset, they retreated under the protection of their shield wall to the top of a nearby hill.

"I want a body count," Arthur told Lancer as both men leaned heavily on the swords, exhausted from the continual advance and retreat that had been the cat and mouse game all day.

Lancer nodded and gave the order. The man came back an hour later as they finished washing their cuts and scratches in the River Avon.

"What's the news?" Arthur asked as he took a towel and wiped his chest.

"We've well over a thousand wounded. Three hundred dead." The man hesitated. "Captain Gaheris took a bad shoulder wound."

Arthur looked up. "Will he make it?"

The man nodded. "The medic thinks so."

"Good then. Ask Gwalchmai to form a party to escort the wounded who need more tending back to Cadwy's fort. There's no need for them to stay here."

After the man left, he turned to Lancer. "What's your gut feeling about tomorrow?"

Lancer pulled a tunic over his head and pushed his damp hair back. "I don't think we should wait for them to form that shield wall again. We can't break it without killing our horses."

Arthur nodded. "My thoughts, too." He looked up at the campfires atop the knoll. "Charging uphill isn't my idea of good strategy, but Mount Badon isn't that high. Mayhap, before the break of dawn, they'll not be roused enough and can be taken by surprise."

Arthur let Gryflet lead the charge the next morning, holding back Lancer's men. "We'll let the Saxons wear themselves out," he said, "and then we'll see what our best cavalry can do."

But they were met with resistance. The Saxons apparently kept a night watch, fully prepared to meet them. Throughout the day as Arthur watched, more and more of his men were wounded and more horses were killed than he wanted to count.

Then suddenly in late afternoon Cadwy's army appeared on the horizon of the hill called Banner Down and further, to the north, Hoel's army poured over Holt's Down. They would attack coming up the back slope, Arthur knew. He waited until the Saxons turned to meet this new enemy.

"Now!" he cried as he dropped his arm for the charge and one hundred fresh horsemen streamed up the slope.

He had no more time then for observation. Their heavy horses crashed through the ranks, the shield walls broken now in the confusion of fighting in two different directions. He cut and slashed, his sword moving as an extension of his arm. Blood flowed from a Saxon's throat and entrails fell out of another as he made his way to Colgrin's banner.

He heard Lancer's familiar battle scream, but had no time to look. More Saxons surrounded him, trying to protect Colgrin. Bedwyr appeared on his left, the vambraces on his arms bloody. Lancer drew up to his right, his sword tip still covered with some man's intestines. Blood ran down his thigh unto his greaves.

Together, the three of them broke the circle protecting Colgrin. Lancer and Bedwyr spun their horses, creating mighty second weapons of steel hooves and bared teeth.

Arthur only saw the ax start to spin as Colgrin threw it. He brought his shield up to deflect it and struck down with his sword in a blow that cleaved Colgrin's head in two. His brother, Baldulf, lifted his ax, but Lancer touched Pryderi's flanks and the horse gave a mighty leap, trampling the Saxon beneath him. Arthur reached down and pulled the standard from its holder and threw it to the ground.

"This war is over!" he roared. "Your leaders are dead!"

Slowly, Hoel and Cadwy worked their way through the Saxons and even more slowly, the Saxons began to retreat. A steady stream of them headed down the hill, despite the battle horn of Aesc sounding them to hold the line.

"Let them go," Arthur panted as they sat their horses atop Badon hill. "We'll pursue them tomorrow, all the way to the coast, if necessary." He turned to Lancer. "How badly are you hurt?"

Lancer grimaced and Arthur noticed how white his face was beneath the dirt and grime and dust.

"Not bad," Lancer said and then he slumped unto Pryderi's neck.

* * * *

"He'll be all right, won't he?" Arthur asked Nimue as he watched her stuffing the wound on Lancer's thigh with moldy bread. When the medics had brought Lancer home he was already delirious with high fever. Even now, two days later, he was still only semi-conscious.

Nimue wrapped his leg, taking care not to disturb the sheet that covered his loins. Arthur smiled a little at her modesty, knowing Lancer wasn't the least bit inhibited.

She looked up at Arthur now, her aquamarine eyes bright and clear and Arthur felt like he was swimming in the warm waters off Lyonesse. *Not all priestesses took vows of chastity; why did Nimue have to?*

"I think the fever is breaking," she said as she applied a cool cloth and wiped the sweat from Lancer's chest. "I'll make a poultice of echinacea and marigold once the infection is drawn out." She laid a hand on his forehead and her brow furrowed. "He keeps dreaming of this woman with copper hair."

Arthur was startled, and then he remembered that Nimue had the Sight. "His dream lady. She really exists?" he asked.

"Oh, yes." Her frown went deeper. "But she will bring much sorrow."

Arthur laughed then. "Are you telling me there's a woman who will refuse Lancer?" Nimue looked at him with troubled eyes and he sobered. "What is it?"

"She will not be able to refuse him. Somehow, though, I think the sorrow will come to you."

Arthur stared at her and then shrugged. "I doubt a woman could come between us. We wouldn't let her."

* * * *

A delicate shimmer hung in the air just above the foot of his bed and the night air had taken on a balmy texture of sea salt and apple blossoms. From somewhere, and yet Arthur knew it was inside his head, he heard the deep fullness of a harp chord, drawn out slowly, spreading through time, never breaking its rhythm even though the melody changed. Softly it rose and fell, bringing the essence of the light softly emanating from the shimmer that was elongating, forming itself into the shape of a woman.

She stood before him in a simple gown of white with gold girdle, her pale moon-colored hair flowing around her. Her presence radiated warmth and love. Arthur rubbed his eyes, sure that he was dreaming.

"Who are you?" he asked hesitatingly.

She didn't answer the question directly. "Always believe in your dreams, Arthur. For I have a great gift to bestow on your kingdom. One that will one day bring peace to your land." Her hands made a symbol and a translucent object began to take shape. It looked like a cup and then it was gone.

"What was that?" Arthur asked.

"It is the Holy Grail. When enemies drink from it, they will no longer fight."

"Please, I must have it then," Arthur exclaimed. "I can stop war!"

She smiled a little sadly. "You will be a great king, Arthur, but you are not the one who will receive the gift. The warrior who will achieve this will not shed blood."

Arthur hung his head. "I know of no such warrior."

Her voice floated to him, even as her form started to dissolve. "He is not yet born, but he will be the son of your greatest friend. Have no fear."

The room grew still and the air from the window was cool. Arthur drew the covers closer, wondering if what he had seen was real or a reaction to the bloody mess of Badon Hill. He wanted so much to believe.

* * * *

While Lancer and Gaheris were recovering, Arthur made plans to ride north to persuade Caw to accept lands in the west that would be greater than those he now held.

"It was Uther's wish and it will give me a chance to visit my sister, Margawse, and see if all is running smoothly," he told his captains one morning as they broke their fast. He turned to Myrddin. "I could use your help with negotiations. Will you come?"

Myrddin shook his head. "I have too much to do here, now that we've set the day of your crowning for Lugnasad. We'll need the support of both Christians and pagans." An annoyed look crossed his face and ne swatted at his ear. "I know," he muttered.

"You know what?" Arthur asked

Myrddin started, a bit guiltily. "Oh, nothing. Take Bedwyr with you. He's diplomatic. I need to spend some time on the Isle, speaking to the Lady. There is a sacred rite that must be performed at your kingmaking."

Arthur had no idea of how truly meaningful those words were going to be for his own destiny.

* * * *

"I sent a messenger that we'd be stopping at Cameliard on the way north," Bedwyr told Arthur as their group approached the hill that led to the villa. "They should be prepared for us. Da may even have convinced Gwenhwyfar to wear a dress."

They slowed to a trot as they rode through the gate and Arthur stared at the girl who emerged from the barn. He brought Valiant to a sudden halt, settling the horse from an attempted half-rear. *This is Gwenhwyfar?* He remembered seeing a rather gawky, tall stick figure of a girl who trailed after Bedwyr everywhere. This—woman—was still slender, but her hips curved from a small waist and the trews she was wearing showed long legs. Even under the over-sized linen shirt she wore—half-tucked in and half out—he could see her breasts were well developed. But Bedwyr was right about the hair. There was some straw in it and most of it had escaped the braid and swung wildly about her face like copper-colored fire. There was even a smudge of dirt on her nose.

Gwenhwyfar walked forward, hand extended to him. "You beauty!"

Arthur started and then realized she wasn't looking at him. Her eyes were on Valiant. *She notices my horse first?*

"Careful!" Bedwyr dismounted and pulled her hand away from the sidling horse. "That isn't some lady's palfrey!"

"I think I can recognize a palfrey when I see one!" she said.

"Still as sassy as ever," Bedwyr said and leaned forward, sniffing. "You don't exactly smell like a lady either."

Arthur watched as she swung at her brother. Bedwyr laughed and ducked.

Arthur cleared his throat and she seemed to suddenly remember he was there.

"I bid you a belated well come," she said with a tint of pink to her cheeks.

Arthur dismounted. "You've certainly made it an interesting well come, my lady." He couldn't help emphasizing the last word as he looked over her attire. He almost grinned at the flash of ire in those green eyes. *By the gods, I like spirited women!*

They were interrupted by her father and her cousin coming to meet them. Arthur assumed the girl was Elaine. She was much as Bedwyr described her. Her hair, nearly the same color as Gwenhwyfar's, was neatly coiled about her head, her light blue dress was clean and matched her eyes and she smelled of roses. Arthur's nose twitched. Gwenhwyfar must have been grooming one of the horses.

"Why hasn't anyone seen to your horses?" Leodegrance asked after greetings had been done. He waved at two of the stableboys who reluctantly came forward. As one of them reached for Valiant's reins, the stallion tossed his head and jogged sideways. Before Arthur could move, Gwenhwyfar stepped forward.

"Allow me, my lord." She took the reins and put a hand on the horse's neck. They looked at each a moment and then, unexpectedly, Valiant nudged her gently. She laughed and rubbed his forelock and led him away. "You just needed to know I'm a friend," Arthur heard her say. He stared after her in amazement. He'd seen Lancer quiet horses that way, but never a woman before. She really was a Whisperer.

* * * *

A storm loomed on the horizon as they sat down to the evening meal in the villa's large dining room. No Great Hall here, Arthur thought as he listened to the sound of the fountain in the atrium across the hall.

He studied the two young women. Elaine tried to flirt all evening with him, coyly looking sideways at him, or swinging her head so her loose hair flowed around her face. She was pretty enough, he supposed, and she had no end of things to talk about, but most of it was idle chitchat. Still, she played the role of hostess well.

Gwenhwyfar, on the other hand, discussed horses with Palomides throughout dinner. Most of Arthur's remarks she either ignored or argued the point before turning back to her discussion with the Saracen. He was slightly annoyed since women rarely—ever?—refused him. Gwenhwyfar presented a challenge though and he found himself fascinated with her.

She wore a dress of pale gold, which accented the highlights of her hair and from across the table, Arthur detected a hint of lavender wafting from her. She twisted a strand of hair around her finger as she talked to his Master of Horse.

"Tell me more about these horses you brought from Mecca. Valiant is beautiful. Can they really outdistance the wind?"

"They can," Arthur answered now, determined to get her attention. "I'd like to have all my light cavalry ride them one day."

Gwenhwyfar turned to him, her face serious. "That would stop the Saxons. You have no need for heavy armor since they fight on foot. Think what distances you could make in a day!"

Arthur looked at Bedwyr in amusement. "Mayhap I should enlist your sister for my war council!"

She bristled. "You don't think a woman's opinion important?"

"I do." He tried to hide a smile. "It's just that most women don't care to discuss horses and warfare." Several of his escort laughed and again, he caught that momentary spark of anger in her eyes. He liked it.

"The horses," Palomides said, "are more valuable to the sheiks than some of their many wives."

That remark shocked Elaine and set off a minor discussion on morality and choice versus arranged marriage. Interesting topic, Arthur thought. Gwenhwyfar brought the argument to an end by saying, "Christians don't force their women to marry at all. The choice is theirs."

Arthur couldn't resist. "Have you chosen such a—brave—man, Gwenhwyfar?" *He'd have to be brave to control you.* Then he thought again. *But who would want to? She's glorious, wild as she is.* A familiar throbbing began in his loins. *What would she be like in bed, bucking under me? I want to find out.*

She looked nonplussed at his blunt question. Then she lifted her chin, green fire in her eyes. "I have no intentions of getting married. I will run Cameliard one day."

Arthur grinned insolently.

Gwenhwyfar inhaled sharply. "Do you not think a woman capable?"

He knew he shouldn't goad her, but he loved to see her temper flare. She was unlike any other woman he'd ever met. "I would think you capable of anything, my lady," he said baldly.

Gwenhwyfar frowned.

Bedwyr leaned forward. "What is wrong with you, Gwenhwyfar? *Certes*, you'll marry someday. Da and I won't always be here to protect you."

"I don't need a man to protect me! I've been taught how to fight!"

"That," Arthur said dryly, "I can believe." Laughter from his men followed that remark and from the furious look she gave him, he felt he might have pushed her too far. He started to apologize, but she stood and interrupted him.

"Should I ever decide to marry, Arthur Pendragon, YOU would be the last person I'd consider!"

Total silence fell. Arthur leveled a penetrating gaze at her. *Oh, yes, I want you.* A small smile played upon his lips. "We'll see," he said.

A bolt of lightening flashed through the room, as thunder crashed and the storm that had been brewing all day unleashed its fury.

Gwenhwyfar turned and fled from the room.

* * * *

Lancer looked up from his noon day meal as Gryflet burst through the doors of the Great Hall at Cadwy's. He stood quickly. "Is there trouble? Why have you returned? Where's Arthur?"

Gryflet motioned him to sit. "Arthur's on his way to Caw," he said as he sat down on a bench opposite Lancer and Gaheris. "Trouble? I'm not sure. Arthur's decided to get married."

"To whom?" Lancer asked as he bit into a meat pastie.

"Bedwyr's sister, Gwenhwyfar."

"What?" Lancer nearly choked on his food. "The one he says is so hot-headed?"

"She is that," Gryflet said. "They did nothing but argue through supper."

"Then why does he want to marry her?" Gaheris asked. "A man can find a nagging woman anywhere."

Gryflet shook his head. "Not nagging. More defiant. He'd goad her and rile her temper. He seemed to be enjoying it immensely. She finally told him he'd be the last man on earth she'd marry."

Lancer grinned. "Ah, a challenge. Arthur never can turn those down."

"Then how is he going to marry her?" Gaheris asked in a practical tone.

Gryflet shrugged. "I don't know. After supper, Arthur and Bedwyr met with Leodegrance behind closed doors. The next morning, Leodegrance announced Arthur would be marrying Gwenhwyfar. Arthur told me to come back and alert Myrddin that the wedding will take place the day before the crowning. I'm to ride next and fetch Ygraine so she can begin making the wedding arrangements."

"He won't be pleased. I don't think Gwenhwyfar was on Myrddin's list of considerations," Lancer said.

An anxious look crossed Gryflet's face. "I hope he doesn't kill the messenger."

Lancer raised an eyebrow. "Arthur's the one who's going to have to live with her, not Myrddin. I don't believe in arranged marriages."

"Yes, well." Gryflet sighed. "If I live after Myrddin's wrath, I'm to organize an escort to go fetch her. Arthur wants her at Cadwy's when he returns."

"I'll go get her," Lancer said.

Gryflet looked at him dubiously. "You're not a good choice, Lancer. You know how you and Arthur like to compete. You'll seduce her and there'll be hell to pay."

Lancer's smoky eyes turned dark and Gryflet sat back. "I'll say this once. Long ago, Arthur and I agreed that a future wife would be off limits. This is one woman I will leave alone."

"*Certes*, Lancer." Gryflet's voice held a slight tremble. "I didn't mean to imply you would . . ."

"Yes, you did," Lancer answered, "but I don't go back on my word. I'll gather a group of men and leave in the morning. Gaheris, do you want to join me?"

Gaheris smiled. "I wouldn't miss this for the world."

Lancer gave him an annoyed look. "You, too? You don't think I can leave a man's woman alone?"

He grinned openly. "You don't have a good track record for doing so. Admit it."

"Then I'll have to prove it." He turned back to Gryflet. "I'll leave in the morning."

Gryflet sighed and stood. "There's just one more thing."

Lancer looked at him warily. "What?"

"She may not want to come."

"Why?"

"Well, we left in the morning while she was still sleeping."

"You mean she didn't *know*?" Lancer was incredulous.

"The pact was between Arthur and her father," Gryflet answered. "You know betrothals are often arranged that way."

"But Gwenhwyfar should have a choice," Lancer said. "What if she says no?"

Gryflet shrugged. "It's her father's job to convince her. And yours, I suppose, if she's still argumentative when you get there."

Bel's fires! What has Arthur gotten himself into? "For *certes*, I can extol Arthur's virtues and strengths until my breath runs out, but she should have the right to choose."

Gryflet rolled his eyes. "The trouble with you, Lancer, is you *like* women too much. Arthur wants her here when he returns. One way or another. Let me send someone else."

"No." Lancer set his jaw. "I ride in the morning."

* * * *

The sun was warm that early June morning as Lancer's party set out for Cameliard. Puffy balls of cotton in the sky held the promise of rain by afternoon, but this morning the birds were singing and the breeze was light. Everything would be all right.

He had no idea he was riding toward his own destiny.

About the Author

An avid reader of anything medieval, Cynthia Breeding has taught the traditional Arthurian legends to high school sophomores for fifteen years. She owns more than three hundred books, fictional and non-fictional, on the subject. More information on Arthur, Gwenhwyfar and Lancelot is available on her website, listed below.

She lives on the bay in Corpus Christi, Texas, with her Bichon Frise, Nicki, and enjoys sailing and horseback riding on the beach.

Readers can reach her snail-mail at: 3636 S. Alameda, B-116, Corpus Christi, Texas 78411 or on her website: www.cynthiabreeding.com.

Praise for Highland Press Books!

In **Fate of Camelot**, Cynthia Breeding develops the Arthur-Lancelot-Gwenhwyfar relationship. In many Arthurian tales, Guinevere is a rather flat character. Cynthia Breeding gives her a depth of character as the reader sees both her love for Lancelot and her devotion to the realm as its queen. The reader feels the pull she experiences between both men. In addition, the reader feels more of the deep friendship between Arthur and Lancelot seen in Malory's Arthurian tales. In this area, Cynthia Breeding is more faithful to the medieval Arthurian tradition than a glamorized Hollywood version. She does not gloss over the difficulties of Gwenhwyfar's role as queen and as woman, but rather develops them to give the reader a vision of a woman who lives her role as queen and lover with all that she is.

~ *Merri, Merrimon Books*

* * * *

Rape of the Soul - Ms. Thompson's characters are unforgettable. Deep, promising and suspenseful this story was. I did have a little trouble getting into the book at first, but as I pushed on, I found that I couldn't put it down. Around every corner was something that you didn't know was going to happen. If you love a sense of history in a book, then I suggest reading this book!

~ *Ruth Schaller, Paranormal Romance Reviews*

* * * *

Southern Fried Trouble - Katherine Deauxville is at the top of her form with mayhem, sizzle and murder.

~ *Nan Ryan, NY Times bestselling author*

* * * *

Madrigal: A Novel of Gaston Leroux's Phantom of the Opera takes place four years after the events of the original novel. Although I have not read Leroux's novel, I can see how Madrigal captures the feel of the story very well. The classic novel aside, this book is a wonderful historical tale of life, love, and choices. However, the most impressive aspect that stands out to me is the writing. Ms. Linforth's prose is phenomenally beautiful and hauntingly breathtaking.

~ *Bonnie-Lass, Coffee Time Romance*

* * * *

Cave of Terror - Highly entertaining and fun, *Cave of Terror* was impossible to put down. Though at times dark and evil, Ms. Bell never failed to inject some light-hearted humor into the story. Delightfully funny with a true sense of teenagers, Cheyenne's character will appeal to many girls of that age. She is believable and her emotional struggles are on par with most teens. I found this to be an easy read; the author gave just enough background to understand the workings of her vampires without boring the reader. I truly enjoyed the male characters, Ryan and Constantine. Ryan was adorable and a teenager's dream. Constantine was deliciously dark. I look forward to reading more by this talented author. Ms. Bell has done an admirable job of telling a story suitable for young adults.

~ *Dawnie, Fallen Angel Reviews*

* * * *

The Sense of Honor - Ashley Kath-Bilsky has written an historical romance of the highest caliber. This reviewer was fesseled to the pages, fell in love with the hero and was cheering for the heroine all the way through. The plot is exciting and moves along at a good pace. The characters are multi-dimensional and the secondary characters bring life to the story. Sexual tension rages through this story and Ms. Kath-Bilsky gives her readers a breath-taking romance. The love scenes are sensual and very romantic. This reviewer was very pleased with how the author handled all the secrets. Sometimes it can be very frustrating for the reader when secrets keep tearing the main characters apart, but in this case, those secrets seem to bring them more together and both characters reacted very maturely when the secrets finally came to light. This reviewer is hoping that this very talented author will have another book out very soon.

~ *Valerie, Love Romances and More*

* * * *

Highland Wishes by Leanne Burroughs. This reviewer found that this book was a wonderful story set in a time when tension was high between England and Scotland. The storyline is a fast-paced tale with much detail to specific areas of history. The reader can feel this author's love for Scotland and its many wonderful heroes.
This reviewer was easily captivated by the story and was enthralled by it until the end. The reader will laugh and cry as you read this wonderful story. The reader feels all the pain, torment and disillusionment felt by both main characters, but also the joy and love they felt. Ms. Burroughs has crafted a well-researched story that gives a glimpse into Scotland during a time when there was upheaval and war for independence. This reviewer is anxiously awaiting her next novel in this series and commends her for a wonderful job done.

~*Dawn Roberto, Love Romances*

* * * *

I adore this Scottish historical romance! **Blood on the Tartan** by Chris Holmes has more history than some historical romances—but never dry history in this book! Readers will find themselves completely immersed in the scene, the history and the characters. Chris Holmes creates a multi-dimensional theme of justice in his depiction of all the nuances and forces at work from the laird down to the land tenants. This intricate historical detail emanates from the story itself, heightening the suspense and the reader's understanding of the history in a vivid manner as if it were current and present. The extra historical detail just makes their life stories more memorable and lasting because the emotions were grounded in events. The ending is quite special and bridges links with Catherine's mother's story as well as opening up this romance to an expansive view of Scottish history and ancestry. ***Blood On The Tartan*** is a must read for romance and historical fiction lovers of Scottish heritage.

~*Merri, Merrimon Reviews*

* * * *

The Crystal Heart by Katherine Deauxville brims with ribald humor and authentic historical detail. Enjoy!

~ *Virginia Henley, NY Times bestselling author*

* * * *

I can't say enough good things about Ms. Zenk's writing. ***Chasing Byron*** by Molly Zenk is a page turner of a book not only because of the engaging characters but also by the lovely prose. In fact, I read the entire thing in one day. Reading this book was a jolly fun time all through the eyes of Miss Woodhouse, yet also one that touches the heart. It was an experience I would definitely repeat. I'm almost jealous of Ms. Zenk. She must have had a glorious time penning this story. As this is her debut novel, I hope we will be delighted with more stories from this talented author in the future.

~*Orange Blossom, Long and Short Reviews*

* * * *

Moon of the Falling Leaves is an incredible read. The characters are not only believable but the blending in of how Swift Eagle shows Jessica and her children the acts of survival is remarkably done. The months of travel indeed shows hardships each much endure. Diane Davis White pens a poignant tale that really grabbed this reader. She tells a descriptive story of discipline, trust and love in a time where hatred and prejudice abounded among many. This rich tale offers vivid imagery of the beautiful scenery and landscape, and brings in the tribal customs of each person, as Jessica and Swift Eagle search their heart.

~*Cherokee, Coffee Time Romance*

* * * *

Jean Harrington's ***The Barefoot Queen*** is a superb historical with a lushly painted setting. I adored Grace for her courage and the cleverness with which she sets out to make Owen see her love for him. The bond between Grace and Owen is tenderly portrayed and their love had me rooting for them right up until the last page. Ms. Harrington's ***The Barefoot Queen*** is a treasure in the historical romance genre you'll want to read for yourself! Five Star Pick of the Week!!!

~ *Crave More Romance*

* * * *

Almost Taken by Isabel Mere is a very passionate historical romance that takes the reader on an exciting adventure. The compelling characters of

Deran Morissey, the Earl of Atherton, and Ava Fychon, a young woman from Wales, find themselves drawn together as they search for her missing siblings. Readers will watch in interest as they fall in love and overcome obstacles. They will thrill in the passion and hope that they find happiness together. This is a very sensual romance that wins the heart of the readers.

This is a creative and fast moving storyline that will enthrall readers. The character's personalities will fascinate readers and win their concern. Ava, who is highly spirited and stubborn, will win the respect of the readers for her courage and determination. Deran, who is rumored in the beginning to be an ice king, not caring about anyone, will prove how wrong people's perceptions can be. ***Almost Taken*** by Isabel Mere is an emotionally moving historical romance that I highly recommend to the readers.

~ *Anita, The Romance Studio*

* * * *

Leanne Burroughs easily will captivate the reader with intricate details, a mystery that ensnares the reader and characters that will touch their hearts. By the end of the first chapter, this reviewer was enthralled with ***Her Highland Rogue*** and was rooting for Duncan and Catherine to admit their love. Laughter, tears and love shine through this wonderful novel. This reviewer was amazed at Ms. Burroughs' depth and perception in this storyline. Her wonderful way with words plays itself through each page like a lyrical note and will captivate the reader till the very end. The only drawback was this reviewer wanted to know more of the secondary characters and the back story of other characters. All in all, read ***Her Highland Rogue*** and be transported to a time that is full of mystery and promise of a future. This reviewer is highly recommending this book for those who enjoy an engrossing Scottish tale full of humor, love and laughter.

~*Dawn Roberto, Love Romances*

* * * *

Bride of Blackbeard is a compelling tale of sorrow, pain, love, and hate. With a cast of characters, each with their own trait, the story is hard to put down. From the moment I started reading about Constanza and her upbringing, I was torn. Each of the people she encounters on her journey has an experience to share, drawing in the reader more. Ms. Chapman sketches a story that tugs at the heartstrings. Her well-researched tale brings many things into light that this reader was not aware of. I believe many will be touched in some way by this extraordinary book that leaves much thought.

~ *Cherokee, Coffee Time Romance*

* * * *

Almost Guilty - Isabel Mere's skill with words and the turn of a phrase makes ***Almost Guilty*** a joy to read. Her characters reach out and pull the reader into the trials, tribulations, simple pleasures, and sensual joy that they enjoy.

Ms. Mere's unravels the tangled web of murder, smuggling, kidnapping, hatred and faithless friends, while weaving a web of caring, sensual love that leaves a special joy and hope in the reader's heart.

~ *Camellia, Long and Short Reviews*

* * * *

Beats A Wild Heart - In the ancient, Celtic land of Cornwall, Emma Hayward searched for a myth and found truth. The legend of the black cat of Bodmin Moor is a well known Cornish legend. Ms Adams has merged the essence of myth and romance into a fascinating story which catches the imagination. I enjoyed the way the story unfolded at a smooth and steady pace with Emma and Seth appearing as real people who feel an instant attraction for one another. At first the story appears to be a straightforward, but as it evolves mystery, love and intrigue intervene to make a vibrant story with hidden depths. Beats a Wild Heart is well written and a pleasure to read, but you should only start reading if you have time to indulge yourself. Once you start reading you won't be able to put this book down.
~ *Orchid, Long and Short Reviews*

* * * *

Down Home Ever Lovin' Mule Blues - How can true love fail when everyone and their mule, cat, and skunk know that Brody and Rita belong together, even if Rita is engaged to another man..
Needless to say, this is a fabulous roll on the floor while laughing out loud story. I am so thrilled to discover this book, and the author who wrote it. I adore romantic comedy. Rarely do I locate a story with as much humor, joy, and downright lust spread so thickly on the pages that I am surprised that I could turn the pages. Down Home Ever Lovin' Mule Blues is a treasure not to be missed. Thank you, Ms. Rogers, for all of the laughter, and joy that you bring to the reader of your fabulous book. Major Kudos to you! Now, when is your next book published? I am ready for more . . .
~*Suziq2, Single Titles.com*

* * * *

Saving Tampa - What if you knew something horrible was going to happen but you could prevent it, would you tell someone? Sure, we all would. What if you saw it in a vision and had no proof? Would you risk your credibility to come forward? These are the questions at the heart of Saving Tampa, an on-the-edge-of-your-seat thriller from Jo Webnar, who has written a wonderful suspense that is as timely as it is entertaining.
~ *Mairead Walpole, Reviews by Crystal*

* * * *

When the Vow Breaks - This book is about a woman who fights breast cancer. I assumed the book would be extremely emotional and hard to read, but it was not. The storyline dealt more with the commitment between a man and a woman, with a true belief of God. There was some sentiment which became even more passionate when this scared man disappeared without a word just as Jill needed him most.
The intrigue of the storyline was that of finding a rock to lean upon through faith in God. Not only did she learn to lean on her relationship with Him but she also learned how to forgive her husband even before he returned to the

States. This is a great look at not only a breast cancer survivor but also a couple whose commitment to each other through their faith grew stronger. It is an easy read and one I highly recommend.

~ *Brenda Talley, The Romance Studio*

* * * *

A Heated Romance - A fascinating romantic suspense, A Heated Romance tells the story of Marcie O'Dwyer, a female firefighter who has had to struggle to prove herself.

While the first part of the book seems to focus on the romance and Marcie's daily life, the second part seems to transition into a suspense novel as Marcie witnesses something suspicious at one of the fires. Her life is endangered by what she possibly knows and I found myself anticipating the outcome almost as much as Marcie.

~ *Lilac, Long and Short Reviews*

* * * *

Into the Woods by R.R. Smythe - This Young Adult Fantasy will send chills down your spine. I, as the reader, followed Callum and witnessed everything he and his friends went through as they attempted to decipher the messages. At the same time, I watched Callum's mother, Ellsbeth, as she walked through the Netherwood. Each time Callum deciphered one of the four messages, some villagers awakened. Through the eyes of Ellsbeth, I saw the other sleepers wander, make mistakes, and be released from the Netherwood, leaving Ellsbeth alone. There is one thread left dangling, but do not fret. This IS a stand alone book. But that thread gives me hope that another book about the Netherwoods may someday come to pass. Excellent reading for any age of fantasy fans!

~ *Detra Fitch, Huntress Reviews*

* * * *

Dark Well of Decision - Like the Lion, the Witch, and the Wardrobe, ***Dark Well of Decision*** is a grand adventure with a likable girl who is a little like all of us. Zoe's insecurities are realistically drawn and her struggle with both her faith and the new direction her life will take is poignant. The secondary characters are engaging and add extra 'spice' to this story. The references to the Bible and the teachings presented are appropriately captured. Author, Anne Kimberly is an author to watch; her gift for penning a grand childhood adventure is a great one. This one is well worth the time and money spent; I will buy several copies for friends and family.

~*Lettetia, Coffee Time Romance*

* * * *

In Sunshine or In Shadow by Cynthia Owens - If you adore the stormy heroes of 'Wuthering Heights' and 'Jane Eyre' (and who doesn't?) you'll be entranced by Owens' passionate story of Ireland after the Great Famine, and David Burke - a man from America with a hidden past and a secret name. Only one woman, the fiery, luscious Siobhan, can unlock the bonds that

imprison him. Highly recommended for those who love classic romance and an action-packed story.
~ Best Selling Author, Maggie Davis, AKA Katherine Deauxville

* * * *

Rebel Heart by Jannine Corti Petska - Ms. Petska does an excellent job of all aspects of sharing this book with us. Ms. Petska used a myriad of emotions to tell this story and the reader (me) quickly becomes entranced in the ways Courtney's stubborn attitude works to her advantage in surviving this disastrous beginning to her new life. Ms. Petska's writings demand attention; she draws the reader to quickly become involved in this passionate story. This is a wonderful rendition of a different type which is a welcome addition to the historical romance genre. I believe that you will enjoy this story; I know I did!
~ Brenda Talley, The Romance Studio

* * * *

Pretend I'm Yours by Phyllis Campbell is an exceptional masterpiece. This lovely story is so rich in detail and personalities that it just leaps out and grabs hold of the reader. From the moment I started reading about Mercedes and Katherine, I was spellbound. Ms. Campbell carries the reader into a mirage of mystery with deceit, betrayal of the worst kind, and a passionate love revolving around the sisters, that makes this a whirlwind page-turner. Mercedes and William are astonishing characters that ignite the pages and allows the reader to experience all their deepening sensations. There were moments I could share in with their breathtaking romance, almost feeling the butterflies of love they emitted. This extraordinary read had me mesmerized with its ambiance, its characters and its remarkable twists and turns, making it one recommended read in my book.
~ Linda L., Fallen Angel Reviews

* * * *

Cat O' Nine Tales by Deborah MacGillivray. Enchanting tales from the most wicked, award-winning author today. Spellbinding! A treat for all.
~ Detra Fitch, The Huntress Reviews

* * * *

Brides of the West by Michèle Ann Young, Kimberly Ivey, and Billie Warren Chai - All three of the stories in this wonderful anthology are based on women who gambled their future in blindly accepting complete strangers for husbands. It was a different era when a woman must have a husband to survive and all three of these phenomenal authors wrote exceptional stories featuring fascinating and gutsy heroines and the men who loved them. For an engrossing read with splendid original stories I highly encourage reader's to pick up a copy of this marvelous anthology.
~ Marilyn Rondeau, Reviewers International Organization

* * * *

Faery Special Romances - **Brilliantly magical!** Ms. Rogers' special brand of humor and imagination will have you believing in faeries from page one. Absolutely enchanting!

~ *Dawn Thompson, Award Winning Author*

* * * *

Flames of Gold - Within every heart lies a flame of hope, a dream of true love, a glimmering thought that the goodness of life is far, far larger than the challenges and adversities arriving in every life. In **Flames of Gold** lie five short stories wrapping credible characters into that mysterious, poignant mixture of pain and pleasure, sorrow and joy, stony apathy and resurrected hope.

Deftly plotted, paced precisely to hold interest and delightfully unfolding, Flames of Gold deserves to be enjoyed in any season, guaranteeing that real holiday spirit endures within the gifts of faith, hope and love personified in these engaging, spirited stories by these obviously terrific writers!

~ *Viviane Crystal, Reviews by Crystal*

* * * *

Romance Upon A Midnight Clear - Each of these stories is well-written and will stand-alone and when grouped together, they pack a powerful punch. Each author shares exceptional characters and a multitude of emotions ranging from grief to elation in their stories. You cannot help being able to relate to these stories that touch your heart and will entertain you at any time of year, not just the holidays. I feel honored to have been able to sample the works of such talented authors.

~*Matilda, Coffee Time Romance*

* * * *

Christmas is a magical time and twelve talented authors answer the question of what happens when **Christmas Wishes** come true in this incredible anthology.

Christmas Wishes shows just how phenomenal a themed anthology can be. Each of these highly skilled authors brings a slightly different perspective to the Christmas theme to create a book that is sure to leave readers satisfied. What a joy to read such splendid stories! This reviewer looks forward to more anthologies by Highland Press as the quality is simply astonishing.

~ *Debbie, CK2S Kwips and Kritiques*

* * * *

Recipe for Love - I don't think the reader will find a better compilation of mouth watering short romantic love stories than in **Recipe for Love**! This is a highly recommended volume–perfect for beaches, doctor's offices, or anywhere you've a few minutes to read.

~ *Marilyn Rondeau, Reviewers International Organization*

* * * *

Holiday in the Heart - Twelve stories that would put even Scrooge into the Christmas spirit. It does not matter what *type* of romance genre you prefer. This book has a little bit of everything. The stories are set in the U.S.A. and Europe. Some take place in the past, some in the present, and one story takes place in both! I strongly suggest that you put on something comfortable, brew

up something hot (tea, coffee or cocoa will do), light up a fire, settle down somewhere quiet and begin reading this anthology.
~ Detra Fitch, Huntress Reviews

* * * *

Blue Moon Magic is an enchanting collection of short stories. Each author wrote with the same theme in mind, but each story has its own uniqueness. You should have no problem finding a tale to suit your mood. **Blue Moon Magic** offers historicals, contemporaries, time travel, paranormal, and futuristic narratives to tempt your heart.

Legend says that if you wish with all your heart upon the rare blue moon, your wishes were sure to come true. Each of the heroines discovers this magical fact. True love is out there if you just believe in it. In some of the stories, love happens in the most unusual ways. Angels may help, ancient spells may be broken, anything can happen. Even vampires will find their perfect mate with the power of the blue moon. Not every heroine believes they are wishing for love, some are just looking for answers to their problems or nagging questions. Fate seems to think the solution is finding the one who makes their heart sing.

Blue Moon Magic is a perfect read for late at night or even during your commute to work. The short yet sweet stories are a wonderful way to spend a few minutes. If you do not have the time to finish a full-length novel, but hate stopping in the middle of a loving tale, I highly recommend grabbing this book.
~ Kim Swiderski, Writers Unlimited Reviewer

* * * *

Legend has it that a blue moon is enchanted. What happens when fifteen talented authors utilize this theme to create enthralling stories of love? **Blue Moon Enchantment** is a wonderful, themed anthology filled with phenomenal stories by fifteen extraordinarily talented authors. Readers will find a wide variety of time periods and styles showcased in this superb anthology. **Blue Moon Enchantment** is sure to offer a little bit of something for everyone!
~ Debbie, CK²S Kwips and Kritiques

* * * *

Love Under the Mistletoe is a fun anthology that infuses the beauty of the season with fun characters and unforgettable situations. This is one of those books that you can read year round and still derive great pleasure from each of the charming stories. A wonderful compilation of holiday stories. Perfect year round!
~ Chrissy Dionne, Romance Junkies

* * * *

Love and Silver Bells - I really enjoyed this heart-warming anthology. The four stories are different enough to keep you interested but all have their happy endings. The characters are heart wrenchingly human and hurting and simply looking for a little bit of peace on earth. Luckily they all eventually find it, although not without some strife. But we always appreciate the gifts we receive when we have to work a little harder to keep them. I recommend these warm holiday tales be read by the light of a well-lit tree, with a lovely fire in the fireplace and a nice cup of hot cocoa. All will warm your through and through.

~ Angi, Night Owl Romance

* * * *

Love on a Harley, is an amazing romantic anthology featuring six amazing stories by six very talented ladies. Each story was heart-warming, tear jerking, and so perfect. I got tied to each one wanting them to continue on forever. Lost love, rekindling love, and learning to love are all expressed within these pages beautifully. I couldn't ask for a better romance anthology, each author brings that sensual, longing sort of love that every woman dreams of. Great job ladies!

~ Crystal, Crystal Book Reviews

* * * *

No Law Against Love - If you have ever found yourself rolling your eyes at some of the more stupid laws, then you are going to adore this novel. Over twenty-five stories fill up this anthology, each one dealing with at least one stupid or outdated law. Let me give you an example: In Florida, USA, there is a law that states 'If an elephant is left tied to a parking meter, the parking fee has to be paid just as it would for a vehicle.' In Great Britain, 'A license is required to keep a lunatic.' Yes, you read those correctly. No matter how many times you go back and reread them, the words will remain the same. Those two laws are still legal. The tales vary in time and place. Some take place in the present, in the past, in the USA, in England . . . in other words, there is something for everyone! Best yet, profits from the sales of this novel will go to breast cancer prevention.

A stellar anthology that had me laughing, sighing in pleasure, believing in magic, and left me begging for more! Will there be a second anthology someday? I sure hope so! This is one novel that will go directly to my 'Keeper' shelf, to be read over and over again. Very highly recommended!

~ Detra Fitch, Huntress Reviews

* * * *

No Law Against Love 2 - I'm sure you've heard about some of those silly laws, right? Well, this anthology shows us that sometimes those silly laws can bring just the right people together.

I can highly recommend this anthology. Each story is a gem and each author has certainly given their readers value for money.

~ Valerie, Love Romances and More

Now Available:

Historicals*:*
Cynthia Breeding
Prelude to Camelot
Cindy Breeding
Fate of Camelot
Dawn Thompson
Rape of the Soul
Ashley Kath-Bilsky
The Sense of Honor
Isabel Mere
Almost Taken
Isabel Mere
Almost Guilty
Leanne Burroughs
Highland Wishes
Leanne Burroughs
Her Highland Rogue
Chris Holmes
Blood on the Tartan
Jean Harrington
The Barefoot Queen
Linda Bilodeau
The Wine Seekers
Judith Leigh
When the Vow Breaks
Jennifer Linforth
Madrigal
Brynn Chapman
Bride of Blackbeard
Diane Davis White
Moon of the Falling Leaves
Molly Zenk
Chasing Byron
Katherine Deauxville
The Crystal Heart

Cynthia Owens
In Sunshine or In Shadow
Jannine Corti Petska
Rebel Heart
Phyllis Campbell
Pretend I'm Yours
Jeanmarie Hamilton
Seduction
Non-Fiction/
Writer's Resource:
Rebecca Andrews
The Millennium Phrase Book
Mystery/Comedic:
Katherine Deauxville
Southern Fried Trouble
Action/Suspense:
Eric Fullilove
The Zero Day Event
Romantic Suspense:
Candace Gold
A Heated Romance
Jo Webnar
Saving Tampa
Contemporary:
Jean Adams
Beats a Wild Heart
Jacquie Rogers
Down Home Ever Lovin' Mule Blues
Young Adult:
Amber Dawn Bell
Cave of Terror
R.R. Smythe
Into the Woods
Anne Kimberly
Dark Well of Decision
Anthologies:
Deborah MacGillivray

Cat O'Nine Tales
Deborah MacGillivray/Rebecca Andrews/Billie Warren-Chai/Debi Farr/Patricia Frank/ Diane Davis-White
Love on a Harley
Zoe Archer/Amber Dawn Bell/Gerri Bowen/ Candace Gold/Patty Howell/Kimberly Ivey/ Lee Roland
No Law Against Love 2
Michèle Ann Young/Kimberly Ivey/ Billie Warren Chai
Brides of the West
Jacquie Rogers
Faery Special Romances
Holiday Romance Anthology
Christmas Wishes
Holiday Romance Anthology
Holiday in the Heart
Romance Anthology
No Law Against Love
Romance Anthology
Blue Moon Magic
Romance Anthology
Blue Moon Enchantment
Romance Anthology
Recipe for Love
Deborah MacGillivray/Leanne Burroughs/ Amy Blizzard/Gerri Bowen/Judith Leigh
Love Under the Mistletoe
Deborah MacGillivray/Leanne Burroughs/Rebecca Andrews/Amber Dawn Bell/Erin E.M. Hatton/Patty Howell/Isabel Mere
Romance Upon A Midnight Clear
Leanne Burroughs/Amber Dawn Bell/Amy Blizzard/Patty Howell/Judith Leigh
Flames of Gold

Polly McCrillis/Rebecca Andrews/Billie Warren Chai/Diane Davis White
Love and Silver Bells
Children's Illustrated:
Lance Martin
The Little Hermit

Upcoming

Children's Illustrated:
John Nieman & Karen Laurence
The Amazing Rabbitini
Shanna Covington
The Wood Thing
Young Adult Paranormal
Amber Dawn Bell
A Ghostly Affair
Contemporary:
Teryl Oswald
Luck of the Draw
Rebecca Andrews
Daddy By Choice
Gail MacMillan
Passion and Prejudice
Mary Wourms
The Price
Lisa Fish
The List
Madison Pryce
Charades
Action/Suspense:
Chris Holmes
The Mosquito Tapes
Brynn Chapman
Project Mendel
Romantic Suspense:
Ann Merritt

A Cry From the Cold
Lee Roland
Static Resistance and Rose
Historicals:
Isabel Mere
Almost Silenced
Jean Harrington
In the Lion's Mouth
Cynthia Breeding
Magic of Camelot
Freddie Currie
The Changing Wind
Sandra Cox
The Sundial
Anne Holman
The Master of Strathgian
Jean Adams
Eternal Hearts
Candace Gold
A Twist of Fate
Jennifer Linforth
Abendlied
Judith Leigh
Joshua's Faith
Gail MacMillan
The Caledonian Privateer
Martha Farabee
The Jewels of Orchard Hill
Dawn Thompson
Counterfeit Lady
Judith Leigh
A Father's Hope
Dawn Thompson
Renegade Rider
Dawn Thompson
Odin's Daughter
Kemberlee Shortland

A Piece of My Heart
Dawn Thompson
Children of the Wind
Katherine Deauxville
Enraptured
Dawn Thompson
Drake's Lair
Eyes of Love
Anthologies:
Breeding/Ahlers/Bowen/Flanders/Hatton
A Dance of Manners
Elizabeth/Admirand/DeVane/Downs/Nina
Operation: L.O.V.E.
Judith Leigh/Cheryl Norman
Romance on Route 66
*Breeding/Bowen/Hatton/Howell/
Ivey/Nutt/Scott*
Second Time Around
Romance Anthology
The Way to a Man's Heart
*Burroughs/Barclay/Blizzard/Howell/
Van Arsdall*
The Miracle of Love
Inspirational Romance Anthology
Faith, Hope and Love
Burroughs/Andrews/Bell
A Pirate's Treasure
*MacGillivray/Breeding/
Wildes/Young/Burroughs*
Castle of Dreams
*MacGillivray/Breeding/
Burroughs/Bowen/Houseman*
Dance en L'Aire
WW II Romance Anthology
Love and Glory
Young/Ivey/Chai
Grooms of the West

MacGillivray/Breeding/Rogers
Love On A Dead Man's Chest
Romantic Suspense Anthology
Masquerade
Romance Anthology
Love Divided
Romance Anthology
Mardi Gras Fever
Romantic Suspense Anthology
Foreboding Senses
Paranormal Romance Anthology
After the Sun Goes Down
Flynn/MacGillivray/Breeding/Rogers
Romancing the Dragon

Cleora Comer
Just DeEtta
Don Brookes
With Silence and Tears
Katherine Shaw
Love Thy Neighbor

Check our website frequently for future releases.

www.highlandpress.org

Highland Press

Historical Line

☐ 978-0981557380	Fate of Camelot	$12.49
☐ 978-0980035698	Almost Guilty	$12.95
☐ 9780980035605	Moon of the Falling Leaves	$12.49

Highland Press Publishing

PO Box 2292, High Springs, FL 32655

www.highlandpress.org

Please send me the books I have checked above. I am enclosing $_____ (Please add $2.50 per book to cover shipping and handling). Send check or money order—no C.O.D.s please. Or, PayPal – Leanne@leanneburroughs.com and indicate names of book(s) ordered.

Name_____

Address_____

City_____State/Zip_____

CPSIA information can be obtained at www.ICGtesting.com
Printed in the USA
LVOW11s1641110914

403636LV00001B/80/P